THE HOLLYWOOD HIGH CHRONICLES

book 6

Retribution Clause

by **Melissa Velasco**

ISBN 978-1-960378-31-6   (paperback)
ISBN 978-1-960378-32-3   (eBook)

1ˢᵗ Edition

Models contracted through DMe Talent Agency:
Deidre Michelle (Agent) @dmetalentagency11

Front Cover Models: Maddie Dawn Cordero, Julian Gopal, Winslow Trullinger, Chance McCord, Michael Lemert

Back Cover Models: Maddie Dawn Cordero, Fred Padilla

Makeup and Hair: Nathaniel Garcia
Costume Concept: Melissa Velasco
Cover Concept: Melissa Velasco
Photography: Tino Duvick @brokenchainphotography
Front Cover Design: Tino Duvick and Anna Hall
Editor: Kyle Fager
Typeset: Anna Hall
Proofreader: Doris Nehrbass

Retribution Clause *is dedicated to every reader who faces
that moment where you know your life is about to change,
it'll be painful and heartbreaking, and you have to gut up to
face it. We don't lie down on the battlefield. We're Misfits.*

*So lace up your ass-kicking boots and forge ahead.
One foot in front of the other. Grit your teeth, look the
unimaginable in the eye, and fearlessly push ahead. You
can do anything. You know no other way.*

RETRIBUTION CLAUSE

Incredible discontent slides through me, making my head spin. *I have no idea how to get through this screening in a professional way.*

"Melanie, I'm so glad to see you," the director, Jack Griffin, gushes. He looks a bit overzealous about seeing me as I step into the studio lobby.

I smile, albeit unsure. "Thank you for the invitation."

"Of course!"

"I'm impressed," I say sheepishly. "Two months is really quick."

The director laughs. "It didn't feel quick from my end of things. I'm really hoping you like it so we can get it to the marketing stage. I need some help with the end, but the rest is looking good."

"I'm sure I'll like it." I'm not really all that interested, if I'm being honest with myself, but I don't want to tell the director that. Mostly, I just want to move on with my life.

"Are your parents coming in?" the director asks hopefully.

"No, sir. They're at a work party." I clear my throat. I'm relieved they aren't here to watch me do unspeakable things on a big screen, but I'm also nervous to be alone. My boyfriend, Trey Valdez, refused to come with me. His fury about the movie has made him very difficult to deal with. It seems that when I left for filming, his proclamation of being okay with the whole thing didn't hold long-term validity.

"Everyone's already seated. I'll escort you."

"Um . . ." I wince a little. "Could I watch from the projection booth?"

The director's brow furrows. "I don't want to ostracize you to that cramped booth, Melanie. You deserve a seat of honor with the cast and crew."

"I'd rather not, but I'm here."

"Okay," the director relents as he escorts me down a hall. He opens a door, and we step into a stuffy little room. The projector takes up a lot of the space, but there's a metal chair situated where I can watch through a window. The director closes the sliding window before turning a knob on the wall. The more he turns it, the louder the sound coming from the fancy private screening theater on the other side of the window. "You sure?" he asks with a raised eyebrow. "The screening room is really nice."

"Thank you. I'll be fine. I can see and hear the movie." I give a small smile. "That's why we're here, right?"

"That's why we're here," he replies. With that, he departs, pulling the door closed after him.

"Think she's coming?" The voice piping through the speakers belongs to Zane Drell, A-list movie star, heartthrob, and traitor who I've been avoiding as much as possible lately.

Through the window, I watch as Ms. Alice, my and Zane's agent, sits next to Zane. "She's supposed to be here," she says, the speaker picking it up. "You nervous?"

Zane nods. "I haven't seen her since the big blowup."

"You made it two months," Ms. Alice says encouragingly.

"It hasn't gotten easier."

"How are things with Brian?" The Brian in question is Zane's brother.

Zane shakes his head. "He won't even look at me."

Ms. Alice sighs. "You know I generally support your decisions, but an affair with your brother's fiancée is . . ."

"I'm already aware," Zane murmurs. "It gets worse though." He looks to Ms. Alice. "The memory Melanie picked up was actually Rachelle's. It came complete with Rachelle's tacky glee about my gossip, and everything that went on after I spilled Melanie's dirt."

"What do you mean by, 'memory Melanie picked up?'"

Zane leans closer into Ms. Alice so the other people in the room don't hear, but the damn audience microphone is right above them in the rafter, so I can clearly hear him. "Melanie has the same memory-seeking ability that Pierre did. But for her, it's new enough that she doesn't have a handle on it. Sometimes she picks up memories unintentionally."

"What exactly was this memory of?" Ms. Alice asks suspiciously.

Even from the other side of the window, it's clear in profile that Zane goes pale. "Melanie's stepfather took over for a night at the hospital. I landed at Rachelle's, and she prodded into why I'd been MIA. I needed a breather, and I spilled Mel's business. Unfortunately, I was far more candid and graphic than I should have been. Things were horrible in the hospital. I was in an exhausted place. All through my tacky description, Rachelle was an immature gossipy mess. She took the whole thing as a win because she knew I was interested in Melanie. I further reinforced that win with a roll in Rachelle's bed right after my shit-talking session."

Ms. Alice's head drops. "Damn it, Zane. Sacrificing a sixteen-year-old to the mean-girl firing squad?"

Zane's shoulders bunch tighter. "I love her."

"Rachelle?"

"Hell no," Zane spits.

Ms. Alice exhales fitfully. "You already know how I feel about your age difference with Melanie. It's a PR nightmare that I'm hoping like hell you avoid for at least the next two years."

"Nothing's really going on physically between Melanie and me," Zane assures her.

"You know for a damn fact that she's in love with you," Ms. Alice scolds.

"She *was* in love with me," Zane corrects. "Now she hates me. I'm most certainly in love with her, though."

My heart clenches. I know all this, of course, but I've never heard him say it like that.

"How did Melanie react to the memory?"

Zane scoffs. "Well, she sent it to me, Rocco, and Brian. Once the affair was revealed to my brother and best friend, Brian stormed off while Rocco gave me hell. Then Melanie completely dissolved into the single saddest display of dejection I've ever witnessed. It destroyed me, because I didn't mean ANY of what I blathered to Rachelle. I would help Melanie in that hospital for the rest of her life." He looks to Ms. Alice. "You know that. You visited the hospital twice and had to help with the magazine that spilled the dirty details."

"You need to see this from Melanie's perspective, Zane," Ms. Alice clips back. "You're a millionaire A-list actor. Rachelle is older, gorgeous, and has a long acting career under her belt. I guarantee Melanie feels like a pathetically worthless no one. She spent how many weeks crapping a hospital bed, partially paralyzed, while Zane Drell wiped her ass?" In profile, I see how Ms. Alice's face scrunches. "I get that it was rough, but I can't believe you'd tell Rachelle any of that. You should have trauma dumped with me, or Rocco, or ANYONE with more tact than *Rachelle*."

"I can't believe I told Rachelle either," Zane says, dejected. "It was all so personal." He gives doe eyes to Ms. Alice. "You know those super private relationship moments where two people trust each other and get through the worst together?"

Ms. Alice nods.

"I had that with Melanie," Zane whimpers. "And I gossiped about it like it was nothing. It wasn't nothing, though. It was *everything*. I got to live with my girl, help her through things so horrible that it bonded us, and I got to be the man I always want to be with Melanie."

"Sounds more like a husband than a best friend," Ms. Alice commiserates.

Zane slowly nods. "I had that same thought a thousand times in that hospital room. I'd watch Melanie sleep, determined to marry her one day. She wasn't some no one who deserved to be gossiped about. I'll never understand how I could sink to that level the moment I had a break from the hospital."

"Sounds like you learned from it," Ms. Alice says softly.

"I learned that Melanie deserves a lot better than me," Zane replies. "I'd kill anyone who did that to her, yet here I sit."

Ms. Alice pats his arm before making her way to her seat on a little couch in the back row. I scan the room's occupants. All the cast and crew appear to be in attendance. Rachelle is on the opposite side of the room from Zane. She keeps looking his way, but he's staring off into space, oblivious to her.

The projection room door opens, and a man comes in, smiling at me. He flips a switch, and the projector comes to life. After he pushes a few more buttons on the wall, the screening room darkens, and then he leaves. I sit back in my metal folding chair and watch the opening credits. A flyover of New York at night reveals the beauty of the bustling city as the word *Glamour* graces the screen in a glittery, scrolled font. The screen goes dark for a moment before my image fades in. I raise my head, looking directly into the camera. A smile crosses my lips as Zane comes into view, and we dance. There's applause from the on-screen audience as the piece closes.

The dialogue starts, and I get lost in the story. The characters Zane and I play are famous, and the relationship's not all it's cracked up to be. The story is gritty—full of intrigue, rejection, isolation, and betrayal.

There's chatter in the screening room, but I choose not to dwell on their take. It's better if I just accept it for what it is.

Some scenes hurt to witness, like our characters' wedding scene. Others I can just shrug through. I feel dead inside in an unstable way, but lately, that's nothing new.

The projectionist comes back in halfway through the movie and turns the lights up slightly in the projection room. "I need to change to the second reel," he explains while he fiddles with a film canister. "Fifteen-minute intermission."

I nod.

"You're remarkable in this movie."

"Yeah?" I ask with a hopeful lilt.

"Unreal."

"Thank you. It's my first movie."

His bushy eyebrows rise. "You did THAT in your first movie?"

"Lucky me."

As the projectionist leaves, I hear the director say through the wall-mounted speaker, "I'm going to go check on Melanie."

"Wait, she's here?" Zane asks in a rush.

"I've got her in the projection booth."

Zane looks my way, but I'm sitting in the dim light, and I'm not sure if he can see me.

"I'll sit in there," Zane says dejectedly. "She should be out here."

The director's head shakes. "I'm not about to put you and Rachelle in that little room together. Melanie suggested she watch from there, and I agreed."

"This is her first screening," Zane insists. "She should be a part of things."

"I agree," Ms. Alice says with a clipped tone. "I don't blame her for sitting in there, though. I'm just glad she showed."

The director and Ms. Alice make their way up the aisle, and the door opens a moment later.

"Hi, honey," Ms. Alice gushes while she hugs me. She surveys the cramped space. "That movie is unreal. You're fantastic in it."

"You think?"

"Yes, Melanie, I think." Ms. Alice sighs. "But I don't want my lead in this movie hiding in a closet. I'm asking you to get in there, show your face, and be proud of your work."

"Does everyone in there know what happened?"

"Does it matter?" Ms. Alice asks. "I'm considering your career here."

I cringe. "All right. I'll try."

The director beams at me.

"Good girl." Ms. Alice guides me down the hall to the door at the end. We enter, and the room falls into a hush.

"Good times," I mutter to Ms. Alice as every pair of eyes in the crowded room locks on us. Apparently, the cast and crew are privy.

The silence is broken by a boisterous, "Melanie!"

Charlie Winter strides over. He's the only other teenager in the cast, but we didn't get to know each other well during filming.

He plays my younger brother, even though he's actually a year older than me. He's a striking brunette, with soft brown eyes that are currently lancing in my direction.

Only Ms. Alice and I can see his eyes narrow as he smirks sardonically. "Wanna sit with me and avoid all this drama?" He fires a harsh look over his shoulder at Zane.

Ms. Alice spurts laughter while Zane instantly blushes.

"Wow," I say. "Subtle."

Charlie grins. "Better to just say it. Now, come sit with me and watch the rest of this porno."

Surprised by Charlie's candor, I giggle. "Okay," I agree, and he grins wider.

"Wanna go bowling after this?"

My eyebrows rise. "Unfortunately, I'm due home to my live-in ball and chain after this, but I'm flattered."

Charlie gives me a baffled look. "You're married?"

"No. I live part time with a guy who treats me like crap."

He appears confused. "Why?"

"Because I'm an idiot."

Charlie chuckles. "Bowl with me."

Though I'm worried on the inside, I laugh a little. There's no way I can bowl; I've been so sick.

I exhale hard. "Where are we shacking up?"

Charlie leads me past Zane, who's staring desperate daggers at me. I stop and close my eyes. The room is still painfully silent.

"I'll be right there," I say with forced brightness.

Charlie looks unsure.

I turn with my heart pounding and face Zane. He stands, and I quietly say, "It's good to see you again. Excellent work on the movie so far."

Zane doesn't seem to know what to say.

I force a stiff smile. "Okay, there's that."

I start to walk away, and Zane grabs my arm. "It's good to see you, too."

My expression slides to the floor, and I can't wrestle it back into neutrality, but at least I don't cry.

"Movie's about to start." Charlie is clearly attempting to rescue me.

"One more to go," I say to Charlie, who looks at me like I'm insane. I turn to Rachelle and add, with aloof politeness, "It's nice to see you again."

"Wow," the costumer mutters. "Class in spades."

"If that bitch had me kicked off set when I was there to work, I wouldn't be that nice," Gary Drew, who played my character's father, says.

I wince as Rachelle turns a forlorn red. Judging by the glares collectively aimed at her, the rest of the cast agrees with him.

"For those who don't know," the director says, "Rachelle asked me to close the set to Melanie when it was time for Rachelle to film amorous scenes, but it's my fault I didn't remember Melanie still had filming."

"Why did you want Melanie to leave?" the costumer asks Rachelle.

"Because," Charlie butts in, "my brother, AJ, who's a Surfrider kid, told me that Zane and Rachelle wanted to ditch Brian and Melanie so they could hook up. Hence Rachelle demanding Melanie be removed from set."

Zane's eyes nearly bug out of his head. "AJ is your brother?"

Charlie grins at Zane. "Oh, but wait, there's more," he oozes. "You see, my father runs the Methodist church in West Hollywood. Guess who the teen group leader is?" Charlie swings an elated look toward Rachelle. "Franky Orick, but you'd know him as Franky Fabulous."

Rachelle inhales fitfully and whimpers, "Not Franky."

Franky Fabulous runs a gossip show on *Splash TV* that celebrities detest because his stories are salacious yet well-researched.

Charlie nods happily. "Indeed. We're a very open-minded church." He casts a grin Zane's way. "Naturally, because my father is the pastor, and Franky's boss at church, he told Franky all about how I was in a movie with Zane Drell. THEN my brother, who teaches some of the kids' classes, filled Franky in on how Rachelle's a backstabbing Zane humper."

Zane may be going for a world record in humiliation.

Charlie inhales dramatically. "Now, you must understand that my mother, who was my chaperone on set, adores Melanie." Charlie fires a dazzling smile my way. "That's because I swear I fell in love with you the first time you walked onto set in that gold satin dress."

I wince. "I suppose that naughty scene could be interest-inducing."

Charlie crinkles his nose. "Nope. It was your eyes that did it. Love the eyes," he says, pinning me with that gaze. "You do realize I'm seventeen, not a player, and I think Rachelle is repulsive, right?"

I giggle, despite the tension.

"Anyway," Charlie continues, "Franky is running a story." He flashes another winning smile. "I gave him every granule of dirt. He and I are tight."

"Oh boy," I mutter, though I'm partly amused. Rachelle and Zane deserve it.

Zane plunks onto his screening couch, covering his face. "Please call Franky off."

"If it helps," Charlie tells Zane, "the exposé Franky plans to run is more about destroying Rachelle than you." He slides evil eyes Rachelle's way. "She treated me like a four-year-old on set. Demeaning, belittling . . . She even baby-talked at me. I'm a seventeen-year-old human, not a newborn gerbil." Charlie's eyes narrow. "I've also had the lead in three TV shows and two movies, not to mention twelve other supporting roles. Last I checked, I have a trophy case full of awards that are staggering, and she's a two-bit B-list 'actress' who screws movie executives for roles."

Rachelle's hands cup her mouth as she burns with humiliation. "I'm sorry."

Riveted shock reverberates from the onlookers.

Charlie shrugs. "Franky Fabulous hates you, Rachelle. You used a slur I won't repeat about him in an interview—something alluding to his sexual preferences. That's really why he's doing this."

"She did *not* say that," I gasp, horrified.

Charlie nods. "The TV show was *Putting on the Ritz*. Franky showed us the footage."

I give Rachelle a nasty look, along with everyone else in the room. Tears brim in her eyes.

Zane looks gut-punched. "Is that slur footage going to be in Franky's exposé?"

"Of course," Charlie replies.

"I do NOT want to be associated with that," Zane barks at Rachelle. "Homophobia is a death sentence in this industry. I've never felt that way!"

"Well, Zane," Charlie interjects, "the exposé focuses on Rachelle being your brother's fiancée and you having no infidelity morals." He smiles. "There's nothing about you hating homosexuals."

"I'm going to die of shame," Zane mutters, while Chelsea Alice, his agent, appears on the verge of fainting.

"This is a media nightmare." Ms. Alice boils over at Zane and Rachelle. She points a rigid finger at Rachelle. "You're off my roster. Find a new agent."

"Please, no," Rachelle whimpers.

Ms. Alice smirks. "Don't put me down as a reference."

"You're the only agent I've ever had," Rachelle pleads.

Ms. Alice chuffs. "Your list of indiscretions was already mind-boggling before this tidbit."

Rachelle lowers into her seat and quietly sobs while her professional and personal life spiral.

Ms. Alice looks to Zane. "I'm not cleaning this media mess up for you. Start doing damage control."

Zane closes his eyes, pained.

"There's ooonnne little caveat I forgot to mention," Charlie says, drawing the word out as Zane looks at him pleadingly. "Franky's willing to scrap the exposé for an exclusive interview with Melanie."

"About?" I ask, uncertain.

"You being the newest darling of Tinseltown," Charlie says, fixing me with adoring eyes.

"Uh huh," I reply, deadpan.

Charlie chuckles. "Franky promised it'll be purely positive—unless you'd rather see them go up in flames."

"Tempting," I admit.

Charlie looks to Zane. "Anyway, I plan to sit with Melanie for the rest of this movie while she finds humor in it."

"It's *so* amusing thus far," I say to Charlie with exaggerated sarcasm. "A regular romp through ha-ha-ville!" I shoot a dramatic expression at Ms. Alice. "Thank you so much for inviting me in here."

Ms. Alice looks aggrieved on multiple levels. "I didn't anticipate

Charlie having a stash of social grenades up his sleeve."

Charlie laughs. "I've been waiting to detonate my news for a while." He guides me through the crowd to a couch. Once I sit, he settles beside me and regally chortles, "Let the games begin!"

I snicker while the others return to their seats. Several people glance my way, and Charlie waves, making comical faces at each one who stares. I lean toward him and whisper, "Thank you for having my back." He nods, and I add, "I'm not sure that I want Zane destroyed, though."

Charlie stares into my eyes. "He messed with you the entire filming—flirting, acting like you were his girl. There's no way you knew about Rachelle through all that."

"I found out after I'd made a flirtatious fool of myself," I admit.

"Forget Zane," Charlie encourages, shuddering with disapproval. "Rachelle is repulsive. If Zane couldn't sense that . . ."

"You think she's gross?"

Charlie scoffs. "Be glad you weren't there while she filmed. She was horrible to everyone. We all hate Rachelle."

Unfortunately, he says that loudly. Zane and Rachelle both look like they'd rather drop off the face of the earth than face this scrutiny.

The lights fade, ending any further discussion. The second half of the movie starts, and I sink lower into the couch. A scene where Zane's character is about to hump Rachelle's is ironically next. The room erupts in disgusted noises as Rachelle and Zane flirt on-screen, clothes whipping off in a flurry. My character walks into the shot mid-humping, and people in the screening room gasp at my dramatic reaction. Apparently, it's convincing.

Emotions surge in me, and I get dizzy. A desperate urge to get back to Trey overwhelms me. My hands shake, and my stomach flip-flops.

Through a cold sweat, I lean toward Charlie. "I can't do this, but thanks for being amazing."

I slip from my seat and head out the back door. Free from the watchful eyes in the screening room, I rush down the hall to a restroom. I barely make it to a stall before I throw up, then slump on the tile floor. My head spins. I groan, resting my forehead in the crook of my elbow on the toilet seat.

There's a creak behind me, and the stall door nudges my shoulder. I look up to see Ms. Alice, who asks compassionately, "You okay?"

I nod, uninterested in explaining how out of control I feel. As my stomach settles, I stand, smoothing my fitted white suit. My red satin cami top and red heels felt like the best choice for faking it until I make it today.

Ms. Alice watches as I wash my hands and rinse my mouth. "Ready to head back?" she asks.

"No."

"The director needs music help for the end credits," Ms. Alice says, raising her eyebrows. "No one does that better than you."

I gather my curly hair into a messy bun and internally grumble while maintaining a professional expression. We return to the viewing room just in time to see me pause in the hallway on-screen as Madonna's "Erotica" blares. I hang back by the door, unwilling to walk across the screening room while this particular scene plays.

Halfway through the steamy moment, I realize I'm next to Zane's couch. He's intently watching what was my first scene on a movie set—so many spectators, monitors everywhere, the set overrun with people. It was a lot, but not nearly as difficult as I'd wanted it to be. Welcome to life with Melanie Slate.

The debauchery ends with my head tipped back on the final note, straddling Zane. The next shot is Zane running into Rachelle at a bar, where their affair continues, despite his character's promise that it's over.

I roll my eyes.

Zane murmurs, "Melanie." I glance down, and he pats the couch, inviting me to join him. I shake my head and scurry back to my seat.

Charlie leans over. "I'm so sorry you had to do that scene."

I shrug dejectedly. "Whatever. I got the part because of it."

Charlie reaches for something on the little end table on his other side. "These were offered," he whispers, "but the stuffed shirts turned them down. I snagged one for you."

He hands me a caramel apple, and I light up. No clue why I can manage food now, but it sounds perfect. My mouth drops open comically. "Yes, you did, Charlie Winter! Turkeys and tacos, you're magic."

Several people glance back to see what's causing my excitement. I smile congenially. "Just enjoying a post-porn-scene caramel apple gift." I waggle it by the stick while Charlie quietly laughs.

Most of the cast offer endearing looks my way, while Rachelle gazes at me with sad eyes.

I gesture at the screen. "Dreamboat's about to plow you again. Don't miss it." I take a huge, crunchy bite. Laughter ripples through the room as I eye Rachelle while chewing. "Nom, nom, nom," I say to Charlie.

Zane presses a fist to his mouth, attempting to curb his amusement.

Rachelle dramatically moans on-screen, and my eyes fly wide. It's so over the top, and I'm already on emotional overload. She makes horrid, fake faces, and Charlie and I lose it. With each new wounded-animal yowl she emits, we laugh louder.

A wave of giggles spreads through the audience, and the

director finally hollers, "Hold." The film freezes on Rachelle's absurd sex-face. Everyone dissolves into uncontrollable laughter.

Mr. Griffin asks, "Is it really that funny?"

I double over, thoroughly disrupting the hush as the rest try to regain composure. "Oh, Mylanta, YES. I needed that laugh so bad." I waggle the caramel apple at the screen. "That's comedic gold." I groan out a happy, "Uggggghhhhh," as I settle. "So good."

Charlie arches an eyebrow at the director. "Anyone else think it's funny?"

Hands go up all around, except Rachelle's.

"It's horrid," Zane admits. "Nothing about that scene is believable."

"You should mute the sound and play 'Pour Some Sugar on Me' over it," I suggest, to much amusement.

"What makes it funny?" the director asks.

"Her breathing and vocalizations are off," I inform.

"How so?" he presses.

"Sex and excruciating pain share a particular breathiness. The breathing shudders. The sound climbs strained octaves when it's real. She sounds like she's faking it—and that's hilarious." I lean back, chomping my caramel apple while the rest of them gape at me.

"Is that why your scenes seem so real?" the director asks.

"Indeed. I'm no stranger to earth-shattering sensation."

"Ohhhhh," Charlie drawls. "I'm so out of my league sitting next to Melanie, and I'm loving it."

The director groans, while others send Charlie amused looks. "We can't afford to reshoot that," Jack admits.

"I won't reshoot it," Zane says, giving him a hard look.

"Any suggestions?" the director asks. "We can't have theater-goers howling with laughter."

Rachelle puts her face in her hands, mortified.

"Don't worry, Rachelle," I say. "Your amateur humping isn't a lost cause. I'm telling you, Def Leppard is your solution."

The director sighs dejectedly. "Roll film."

"Hooray, more hilarity," I murmur to Charlie, who laughs.

After a bit more tawdry lying from Zane's character (that my character clearly doesn't believe), I notice the director stiffen at the front of the room. "Here we go," I whisper to myself, and Charlie side-eyes me. I watch with bated breath as my character on-screen stares at her reflection in a dressing-room mirror. The hum of dead noise slowly builds. Her breathing swells through the speakers, and her eyes harden with the look of someone who's done.

The atmosphere in the screening room shifts, turning dreadfully serious.

Inhale . . . exhale . . .

Her gaze drops, and the camera pans down her shoulder, revealing track marks as it travels lower.

Inhale . . . exhale . . .

We see her hand, then the bruised hip, knee, and foot. She's wearing only black panties and a red tank top.

Inhale . . . exhale . . .

The camera shoots back up the leg that's trembling from rapid movement on the counter, The image stops on a close-up of her hand frantically crushing a mound of blow. She forms two neat lines. A rolled hundred-dollar bill is scooped up in her left hand as she bends. The camera zooms in on the white powder as one line vanishes. Then she reverses the bill, and the second line disappears. Her hands slam onto the sink, and the camera tilts to show her eyes in the mirror . . .

Inhale . . . exhale . . .

Powder dusts both nostrils.

Inhale . . . the swelling of white noise . . . deep exhale . . .

Her eyes widen on-screen, disturbingly vacant, as she shows a shift to a high I've never actually experienced but did a good job of portraying in this scene. Slack-faced, wholly dejected, she looks empty. My character isn't seeking an energetic buzz from the cocaine; that isn't the point.

Inhale . . . exhale . . .

She turns, and the camera follows into the dressing room, cluttered with cards, flowers, costume accessories, and photos on a bulb-lined vanity. In the mirror's reflection, we catch a wedding picture of her and Zane's character in happier times.

Inhale . . . exhale . . .

She opens a black case, revealing a drug kit. She grabs a bottle and syringe.

Inhale . . . exhale . . .

The needle punctures the rubber cap, pulling a dose.

Inhale . . . exhale . . .

She taps out the bubbles with a glossy red fingernail. We watch the needle pierce the crook of her arm.

Inhale . . . exhale . . .

The plunger is pressed, and then there's a huge, swirling rush of white noise before one giant inhale.

. . . Silence . . .

The camera pans to the ceiling as her head falls back.

Then we see from above as she tips her head upward, mouth slack, eyes wide, nostrils still dusted with coke.

She exhales one heavy, "Finallyyyyyy."

We watch, from that ceiling vantage, her body dropping in slow motion. She bounces slightly upon hitting the floor, going limp.

. . . Inhale . . .

A heartbeat rattles through the speakers, rising in speed. Then it abruptly slows, and as quiet descends, the faintest smile graces her lips just before vomit spurts out in a graphic spray.

Her eyes roll dead. Silence lingers for an uncomfortably long moment . . .

. . . Exhale . . .

Everyone in the theater exhales collectively. One person murmurs, "God, no."

Gradually, the backstage bustle seeps into the audio—people calling, items clanking, an orchestra tuning. The camera soars up to show the entire backstage area alive with preshow excitement. Her body remains prone, eyes blank, on that dressing-room floor.

Zane's character saunters into his own dressing room, where Rachelle waits. She rises from the couch as he closes the door. They meet in the middle, latch onto each other, and she lands on the vanity while they go at it. She tips her head back, eyes shut, drawing a sharp inhale. All other sounds die except that inhale as the camera zooms toward her eyes opening.

The screen goes black, and we hear a knock followed by a scream. Zane's character appears on the screen, zipping up and racing for the door. Chaos unfolds in the hall.

"HELP MEEEEE!" someone shrieks from my character's dressing room, and the surrounding commotion muffles as the sound of blood rushes through Zane's character's ears. His heartbeat—guh-gum—pounds. It quickens when his breath picks up, and the camera perspective staggers down the hallway in slow motion. All external sound is absent, replaced by that heartbeat, as he turns into my dressing room.

Inside, we silently see my character's father and brother screaming and crying while my father's character cradles my limp body.

Sniffling and choked sobs fill the screening room. I glance around to see tears trickling down faces. Then I look back just in time to see Zane's on-screen expression—he slides down the wall, mouth open in raw horror. The emotion is so potent you can practically feel it in the room.

The shot lingers on his shaking hand, still wearing his wedding ring, then cuts to my dead eyes.

"No," someone whispers in the screening room, just as Zane's gaze shifts to the door, where Rachelle is screaming. We don't hear her, though; we only hear a muffled rush of shock. He looks back at me, and the screen blinks out.

My eyebrows lift as the lights come on.

"That's it?" someone asks.

"What the hell?" another person blurts.

"You can't end the movie like that," the costumer protests. "We were hooked, and then it just stopped."

I bite my lip, deciding to speak up. "You want a suggestion?"

The director looks at me. "I'll take any help I can get, because something vital is missing."

I swallow hard. "All right, here goes."

CHAPTER 2

A little baffled, I exhale hard. It seems the director took every one of my suggestions. My intuition—which I rarely get during benign moments—guided me. After several impromptu filming sessions in the screening room and hall, we landed at an editing bay about an hour ago.

"How sure are you?" the director asks me.

"Positive. The scene is legit."

"All right, get those film clips spliced," he orders the editor. Then he looks my way and says, "Now for the tough one."

My eyebrows rise, because I thought we were done.

Apparently not, because he adds, "We need to fix that love scene that made you laugh."

I sigh, my head falling. The last thing I want is to fix anything for Rachelle. It always seems like the other woman wins at my expense.

"Do you think you can fix it?" Rachelle pleads bashfully.

I ignore her. "All right," I reply to the director. I might not want to do this, but I need to be professional. "You've got two options, in my estimation." I glance Zane's way. "Babe, will you grab my 'deep thoughts' CD folder?" I wince inwardly at my casual address for him. Old habits die hard.

Zane smiles a bit to himself as he unzips my backpack and pulls out the correct CD folder. I have three in there, but he knows my stuff as well as he knows his own. After handing it over, he watches me take a deep breath and pull a CD free. This could get messy, but I have no choice. Luckily, the room has mostly cleared out. After we spent so long working, a lot of people got bored and wandered off, promising to return in a few hours to see the revised sections. We're left with the costumer, the director, Charlie, Zane, Rachelle, and the main editing team.

I hand the CD to the sound engineer, explaining, "We can either work this from Zane's character's perspective or my character's."

"Explain," the director requests, looking confused. "It's a scene that has nothing to do with your character."

"Agreed," I reply, "but there's a weak element in the movie that we can fix with a five-minute song. Rex and Lynette's marriage really isn't fleshed out. My character hops into the mix in the sequel, yet there's not enough buildup to make the audience feel anything about his cheating. If you want empathy, we need to show all the happy stuff proving why he's hers." I wobble my head. "The other route is for Rex"—I gesture to Zane—"to truly not give a damn. We have unused footage for either direction. Song choice is key."

"Okay," the director says. "We're going the empathy direction for your character, then. Villainizing Rachelle's character has a better bent."

"We need the slow-motion walk-in at the wedding, and anything else you have of Lynette and Rex that got scrapped."

"We've got a lot of unused behind-the-scenes stuff of you and

Zane too," the director informs me. "You two were so cute most of the time, we thought we'd use those little montages for credits. But it was so personal, we nixed the idea."

I sigh. "We may need it. Let's review."

"Track?" the sound engineer asks, waggling the CD.

My expression cages as I tell him the track number. Moments later, Ani DiFranco's "Falling Is Like This" streams through the speakers.

"We're not using this song for this scene," Zane insists, while Rachelle simultaneously chimes, "I love this album."

I scoff, incredulous. "Unreal."

"Before you flip out," Zane says, "yes, I played it for Rachelle. No, it wasn't like what this album means to you and me." He meets my eyes and adds, "I saw Rachelle the night I got the demo reel. I played it in the background while we talked."

"How is that different from you playing it for Melanie?" Rachelle asks. There's no cattiness. Instead, she sounds compassionately curious.

"In the hospital, she went from relearning to walk, to relearning to dance, to this CD," Zane reveals. "I slow-danced to most of these songs with Melanie until we wore the finish off the tile floor in her hospital room."

Rachelle ducks her head. "That's really sweet."

"Yeah, well, I don't want any of these songs in a scene where my character cheats on hers—especially with you," Zane replies to Rachelle with clipped hostility. He looks at me imploringly. "This is our song, and you know it."

Everyone listens as Ani DiFranco sings about falling in love, with all its messy simplicity. I swallow hard at the sight of Zane looking destroyed.

When the song ends, the director says, "I love it."

"The answer is no," Zane insists. He gives me hard eyes. "I know how you operate. If that song goes in this scene, it belongs to Rachelle. It means everything to me, and I'm not losing it to her."

"The song can still be yours and Melanie's, even if it's in the movie," Rachelle says.

I clamp down on my churning emotions. "Zane, that was a really sweet time, but you and I both know it's negated."

Zane's eyes close, and everyone holds still, giving us space. I trust Charlie, the costumer, and the director with this. Rachelle needs to hear this too. She flippantly gossiped about my hospital nightmare with Zane. By girl code, she deserves to see the damage.

"Please skip two tracks," I request, adding, "This song is perfect." I watch Zane's face as "You Had Time" plunks into its haunting, sporadic pulse. He swallows hard, staring into my eyes as the lyrics begin. It's a raw exploration of two people growing apart, with no idea how to move forward except to keep going. We vowed never to let ourselves relate to this song personally.

I glare at Zane, but my expression is exhausted. "She didn't earn my personal details," I mumble.

"I know," Zane replies quietly.

As Ani gently croons about him carrying the heavy stuff and me making jokes, we lock eyes again. From the edge of my vision, I see Rachelle tearing up; the collapse of my situation with Zane seems to bother her. I still can't stand her, but maybe she isn't as monstrous as I assumed.

"I heard you have a boyfriend," Rachelle says softly.

I scoff. "That disaster is already imploding."

Zane's jaw clenches. "We need to talk."

Raising my eyebrows, I flick a hand in Rachelle's direction. "Need more of my dirt to impress her?"

He swallows hard.

When the song ends, Rachelle says, "I had zero clue what you two were until now." She looks up at Zane. "If I'd known, I wouldn't have pushed like I did."

"Nothing from this album," Zane pleads, ignoring Rachelle. "Please. It might not mean anything to you anymore, but I can't give up these songs. And for the record, I didn't give them to Rachelle by playing this at her condo. It was before the hospital stuff. I had no idea Ani DiFranco was one of your favorites. Once I found out, I had to share it with you."

"You gave her the CD?" Rachelle asks.

Zane nods. "She loves it. Ani's witty, brutal honesty speaks to Melanie on a cellular level."

I pull a different CD and take back the unreleased one from the sound engineer. "All right, none of those songs." Zane looks relieved, while Rachelle exhales hard.

Their solace is cut short as I say, "I'm sacrificing my favorite Ani song to fix Rachelle's inability to handle a love scene."

Ani DiFranco's "Grey" comes through the speakers, and Zane and Rachelle's faces go slack. Apparently, they know the song.

Ignoring them, I request, "Start showing the behind-the-scenes footage. I know the vibe we need."

Film rolls, showing Zane and me laughing and hugging between takes. I select clips here and there; it all hurts to watch. A shot appears of me, breezing out of the wardrobe room in the wedding dress. That's when it gets unbearable. The behind-the-scenes footage isn't usable for the direct storyline because cameras and tech people are behind me, but Zane's expression is telling. He's completely mesmerized while the costumer pins the dress tighter, and I tip my head back, laughing at something she says. Zane's expression shifts softly in the clip, and several spectators gasp quietly.

Rachelle says, "Zane, I've never been sorrier. I just wouldn't let it go because you made me feel wanted."

"My brother always wanted you," Zane murmurs, not taking his eyes off the monitor.

"I know," Rachelle replies quietly. "But that was different. You're Zane Drell."

He shakes his head and points at the screen. "You got the public image of me. The man looking at Melanie in that dress is Zane Drell."

Almost to herself, Rachelle breathes out, "I get it now."

The next clip is of me watching Zane work through a scene. I'm smiling softly, with twinkling eyes. He finishes and, mid-conversation with an assistant, heads my way. Wrapping me in his arms, he doesn't skip a beat in the chat. It's all so natural that we look like a couple. He sits on a couch, pulling me into his lap after the assistant leaves, and while he reads the revised scene pages, I curl up and doze off. He rubs my back absently, eventually resting his cheek on my head.

"Now you see why we couldn't use any of this," the director says softly. "It's too personal."

"Well, you're out of luck, because that's going into this scene," I murmur. "From the point where Zane sits until he rests his cheek on my head."

"Please don't put that in a scene between Rachelle and me," Zane pleads.

"No choice. There's very little leftover footage showing your character caring about mine, so we need to use some of this strategically." I push my sadness aside and lean over the table, ready to finalize the changes.

CHAPTER 3

"Here we go," the director says, sounding confident. "Let's see if we have a movie!"

After long hours, we're all gathered in the screening room again. So many people wandered off and gathered their spouses while we were altering the scenes, and the room is now filled to popping. I absently take the seat next to Zane as the lights dim and the film starts. Zane and Rachelle appear, mid-humping, as Ani DiFranco's "Grey" plays in the background. The scene alternates shots between their boisterous hookup and my character doing some lonely pacing and waiting for Zane's character to get home. On-screen, my character glances at the wedding photo, and then cuts back to Zane and Rachelle's affair, followed by the behind-the-scenes clips I chose. Together, they illustrate everything our characters lost to his meaningless fling.

The lights come on, and everyone exhales.

"That does the job," the costumer says, tears in her eyes.

I look at Zane. He's got his head in his hands. Even if it's just fiction, it doesn't feel that way to us.

"Do you think it'll play, Zane?" the director asks.

Speechless, Zane nods.

"Thank you, Melanie," Rachelle says quietly. "That scene works way better than the tacky moaning."

Hating that I sacrificed that song to something like this, I nod. "Grey" is the anthem of my loneliness.

Someone resets the film, and the lights dim again.

"I'm sorry," Zane whispers.

"I know you are," I whisper back. It's not what he wants to hear, but it's the truth.

The final clip shows my character gasping, "Finally," and collapsing to the floor. After the scream, a stunning montage unfolds. We hear me singing "White Rabbit" by Jefferson Airplane, while the footage switches between my performance projected on my white suit that we shot earlier today when my ideas started coming together.

I'm content in offering this song because I'm like dark Alice.

On the screen, Zane's character looks at his wedding ring as EMTs lift my body bag onto a gurney. The image splits between my body being wheeled away and me strutting alone in a red-lit hallway in my white suit and red cami that we filmed today. When the stretcher with my body bag finally exits through the door, the image shifts to me pushing open a door into a blazing white light, leaving my red hell behind. I disappear into that brightness.

Zane gapes wide-eyed beside me on the couch.

The screen blacks out. *Glamour* flashes in glowing gold script. I grin as Sophie B. Hawkins's "Damn I Wish I Was Your Lover" drifts in for the credits.

The lights come up when the song ends, and Zane stares at me with tearful eyes. "It's magic," he breathes.

I can't help my slight smile. "I'm glad it worked."

"That's what was missing," the director says. "Thank you, Melanie."

"You're welcome."

"We've got a blockbuster," the director belts, bursting with excitement. "That's a wrap!"

Cheers erupt and a celebration flares. People start mingling and uncorking champagne. I step aside as Zane meets a mob of coworkers' spouses, curious about the biggest star in the room. Internally, I'm destroyed. Zane greets everyone politely while I wait, needing to talk with him. My nerves feel raw from what we lost. It's not like we were ever truly official. My age and soulmate connection with Trey made that too complicated, but still . . .

Rachelle catches Zane just as the final well-wishers peel away. "Can I talk to you?" she asks.

He sighs and follows her up the aisle toward the back corner. He doesn't even acknowledge that I've been waiting.

Well, there it is. I'm done. I grab my purse from the couch, slip from the screening room, and head up the hall, still lit in red. When I reach my car outside, the night air encases me with cool finality.

The moment I fixed the movie, I became obsolete. It's always like this. Glancing over my shoulder at the building, I realize I poured everything I've got into that film canister. That's all I can do. I start the car, my energy pulsing erratically.

CHAPTER 4

"**P**resley, can we talk?"

Presley Verelle stumbles toward me, already tipsy. *Great timing, Mel.* She seems to be deeply engaged in the raging party I've just come home to. My head spins and my stomach churns.

"Are you seriously dragging me away from the best party we've had all year?" Presley snaps. "I just want to have fun. Get in a better mood. Then we'll talk." She shoos me off in typical Presley fashion.

We've been at odds lately. The sicker I feel, the more she seems to avoid dealing with me. She's always been blunt, but I'm not usually on the receiving end of it.

She dodges away and says sarcastically to our friends, "Who invited the mood killer?"

"I live here," I call out. "Nobody had to invite me."

Everyone's been insane this past month. The advanced choir team made it to Nationals, so most of our group are tied up in choir rehearsals, on top of daily musical rehearsals. Add that the seniors are interviewing with colleges, and the sophomores and juniors are slammed with PSAT and SAT prep, and everyone's patience is wearing thin. Unfortunately, I'm left in the dust, even as my general health seems to be getting progressively worse every day.

Another wave of cold sweats hit, and my hands shake. From across the room, Mama Mabel meets my eyes. Her brow creases with concern.

I can't deal with this party.

I head for the bedroom I share with Trey at Mama Mabel's brothel. Yes, I said *brothel*. I know it's weird, but we live here part time. We're regularly asked why we live at a brothel, being that we're teens and all. The answer is complicated. Our lives are insane, and Mama Mabel gets us. She's our godmother. Our parents trust her.

As I pass him in the hall, Tanner Devick offers me a joint. The smell makes my stomach threaten to revolt again. I sidestep him, continuing my rushed trek.

"Uh oh, here comes another wobbler," Trey drunkenly taunts me.

That's all it takes. I bolt into my room. Unfortunately, Trey's spent the past month and a half acting like a jerk. He's always working, and when he's not, he splits time between school, baseball, and being rude and condescending to me. The reminder of how mean he's become makes my stomach lurch. I barely reach the toilet in time. My drive-through dinner from earlier comes back up, tasting even worse the second time. Groaning, I flush the toilet and squeeze my eyes shut.

I grab a washcloth from the linen cabinet, wet it, and drape it on the back of my neck. My brown eyes seem dead in the mirror reflection, and my complexion is so off I hardly recognize myself. With each flare of illness, I wonder how anyone can miss my obvious desperation. It's literally written on my face.

I brush my teeth, head into the bedroom, and change into sweats and an oversized Nirvana T-shirt. I collapse onto the bed, letting my head hang over the edge, as I try to calm my spiraling thoughts.

The door flies open, and Trey rushes in with Adam Stone, Marcus Vinsky, and Tanner. They're rowdy, shoving each other.

"Trey, Melanie looks bad," Tanner says when he notices me on the bed.

Trey rolls his eyes. "Tuesday night sounds great," he says to Adam. "I've wanted to meet your work friends."

"Trey, we already have plans," I start to say. I'm cut off by Adam's glare.

"Seriously, Mel, can it," Adam says. "Trey needs to cut loose or he'll lose it."

Adam is my ex. We share a soulmate connection that our Zen-master friends, Darren Whipple and Bear, walled off in support of Adam's marriage to Valerie Merser. We hoped that shutting down that connection would end all the heartbreak and grief hanging between us, but I'm starting to wish we hadn't. My bond with Adam far surpassed the one I have with Trey, and I miss it.

To add to the confusion, I was married for a few hours to a surfer named Pierre "Riptide" Strader, who died at an international surfing competition. I'm only sixteen, I know. Don't get caught up on my physical age. I'm on my 203rd lifetime, and my life moves fast.

"Are you really going to let Adam talk to me like that, Trey?" My voice sounds hollow.

Trey gives me an annoyed side-eye.

What I'd give for him to treat me like Riptide did. I can't keep going like this. I look down, feeling heartbroken all over again. This side of Trey is jarringly out of character for the guy I fell in love with. Being overworked clearly doesn't suit him.

When the boys exit, a severe wave of hopelessness crashes

through me. The foreign sensation feels like it's not coming from me at all. Terror seizes me when my own psyche lands in a tiny mental corner, and I'm forced to watch helplessly while this other presence takes the driver's seat. I'm no stranger to sadness, but this is different. It's monstrous.

Almost without control, I leap off the bed, snatch a photo of Trey and me dancing at Adam's wedding, and crack the frame against the nightstand, shattering the glass. As my right hand grips a shard of the glass, my mind shifts eerily calm. I'm screaming mentally, but no sound escapes my hijacked mouth. With the fragment of psyche I have left, I call for Trey, but our mind-to-mind link has gone dead again.

I watch my hand lift the shard. The *me* that's *not* me experiences a twisted sort of peace, like it wants to end this misery. I'm still screaming in silence. The shard presses to my wrist and . . . something heavy slams into my side. As I careen onto the mattress, the invading presence explodes out of my body. Tanner flips me over. My eyes flutter open. Shock reverberates like a gong in my head. Tanner pries my hand open and carefully takes the glass away. We both stare in shock as blood wells up from a long cut across my palm.

"Melanie, what were you thinking?" Tanner gasps. "Talk to me!"

I'm in serious trouble. That wasn't me. Unable to process what happened, I collapse into Tanner's arms, sobbing hysterically.

"Damn, Mel." Tanner eases back against the pillows. He takes a tissue from the nightstand and folds my hand around it to stop the blood as he pulls me to his chest. My body trembles, and a panicked keening sound rips out of me.

The door opens. Finley Ferrell and Presley enter. Presley's eyes widen at the sight of me on top of Tanner.

"HOLY AFFAIR!" Presley slurs drunkenly. "Seriously, you're screwing around with Tanner?"

Finley eyes me lying against her fiancé, and her gaze narrows in confusion. "Presley, give us . . . ," she starts, but Presley storms out before she can finish her statement. "What's going on?" Finley asks.

"I'm not having an affair with Mel," Tanner says quietly.

Finley gives him a look. "Obviously, Tanner. She's upset."

When she notices the bloody shard of glass on the nightstand, Finley gasps and rushes to the bathroom. She returns with a first aid kit and starts cleaning and bandaging my wound.

The door slams open. Trey barges in with Victoria, Adam, and Marcus behind him.

"If Tanner and Melanie are having sex, I want front-row seats while Trey kills everyone," Victoria exclaims. "This is gonna be epic!"

I roll my eyes. Victoria Garcia, Trey's ex, is vampy, loud, and never subtle.

Trey surveys the situation. I'm in bed with Tanner and Finley, but we're all clothed. Unsurprisingly, he overlooks the fact that I'm in full meltdown.

Marcus glances through the open door. "Bow chicka BORING," he grumbles. "I thought we were going to get to watch Trey kill Tanner! Let down *much*?"

Mama Mabel enters and flicks her gaze at me. "What happened, Melanie?"

Trey squints like a confused idiot. "Why's Melanie in my bed with Tanner and Finley, and everyone's dressed?"

Mama Mabel scowls at him. "Because, you drunk jackass, she's clearly hurt. She's not having an affair."

"Huh." Trey frowns.

"That sucks," Adam says as he sips his beer. "I was hoping to see Mel have another wobbler while Trey chokes her out."

The room dissolves in laughter as Mama Mabel herds the onlookers away.

Tears roll down my cheeks. "Why doesn't Trey care about me anymore?" I ask Tanner.

Tanner glances over me at Finley. "I'll talk to him tomorrow when he's sober," he says as Finley finishes the bandage. "Melanie, if you EVER try something like that again, I'm calling the cops and having you admitted for a psych eval."

I sit up.

"I'm crazy busy this week, and a little hammered," Tanner goes on, "but I promise I'll find time to help you figure this out."

Finley squeezes my uninjured hand, and they leave before I can thank them. Now that I'm calmer, I realize I should get out of here in case whatever took me over is still lingering in Mama Mabel's place.

I grab my backpack, shove a few essentials into a duffel, and hurry out. Nobody notices me slip through the raging party in the parlor. I exit through the dining room, enter the garage, hop into my car, and hit the visor's remote. The door rolls up, and I pull away in a rush.

CHAPTER 5

My cell phone rings, startling me awake. It takes me a moment to realize I fell asleep on the beach. I blink to clear my head as I sit up. Hastily, I unzip my bag, pull out my phone, and raise the antennae. "Hello?" I say groggily.

Mama Mabel's frantic voice comes over the line. "Melanie Katherine Slate-Strader-Valdez, where are you?"

Uh-oh. My godmother just used every name I've ever had and one I've yet to officially gain. Not good.

Sheepishly, I answer, "Surfrider."

"YOU'RE WHERE?" Mama Mabel squawks, apparently spiraling into mom mode. "Are you telling me you slept the entire night on the BEACH like a surf bum?"

I wince. "Maybe."

"The very idea!" she bellows. "Trey, you get your hungover ass up this instant! Melanie just slept all night on the beach!"

"What?" From Trey's tone, I gather he was sleeping when she sprung the news on him.

"I don't know what your dysfunction is lately, but you need to pull it together," Mabel says, apparently scolding Trey.

"Mabel!" I exclaim through the line.

"Yes, Melanie?" she huffs.

"See if you can get through to him, because I've CERTAINLY had zero luck."

I hang up and watch the waves, contemplating all the things that have been going wrong with my metaphysical abilities. While I thought that whatever was screwing with me might have been confined to Mabel's, I discovered last night that it's still with me. I feel weird, and my control over myself keeps slipping. Now that I'm aware of it, I've realized it has happened a lot lately. Mostly, I've been getting distracted in odd ways. I need to talk to someone before I lose control and unintentionally hurt people. Considering I have the ability to black out half of Hollywood when I'm mad, I've got a hell of a loose cannon living unchecked in my psyche.

My phone rings again, and I sigh. I don't want to deal with Trey, but I answer.

"HELP!" screeches Ms. Alice.

My heart races as I jump to my feet. "What's wrong?"

"Get to Pierre's store," Ms. Alice yells. "PLEASE hurry!"

"Tell her to bring Demitri," someone screams from the background.

"He's out of town," I say, grabbing my stuff before sprinting up the cliffside path. "Tell me what's going on."

"Oh my God, someone *do* something," Ms. Alice screams.

I hear a crash.

"Chelsea!" I shout into the phone.

No response. I try calling her name two more times, but all I hear is screaming, chaos, and crying.

I hang up and call Demitri Cantrell, the dance pro extraordinaire of our Misfit group. He's also an ethereally stunning heartthrob, and one of my best friends. While that should be enough to place him in the top-shelf echelon of social status, his secret claim to fame is that he's an incredible metaphysical healer. He saved me from certain paralysis after I plunged from a cliff in a stolen car. And he healed me after I was crushed to a pulp by a collapsed building. The fact that Ms. Alice requested him, given that only she, and a handful of others, know what he can do, is a very bad sign.

The moment he answers the phone, I bark, "Did you already leave town?"

"Yes. We left early this morning," Demitri replies. "What's wrong?"

"I don't know, but Ms. Alice called," I gasp out. "She was screaming and begged both of us to go get to her."

"Find out what's happening and call me back," Demitri says.

I hang up, jump in my car, and hit the gas. The usual ten-minute drive takes five, and I screech into the parking lot of the surf shop once owned by my deceased husband, Pierre "Riptide" Strader.

Rocco Rutelle runs over and yanks open my car door. "Run!" he barks, tears streaking his cheeks.

My eyes widen. I take off into the surf shop, which I've never stepped foot in before.

"Go!" Luis bellows as I enter, pointing deeper into the store.

I sprint past rack after rack of swimsuits, shirts, and wet suits. Ms. Alice is leaning against the back wall, struggling to breathe. She points to a door, and I dart through.

My mouth falls open when I see Zane on the floor. I rush to him while hitting redial on my phone.

"Talk to me," Demitri barks.

"Zane," I gasp. "Dead."

"WHAT?"

"Help me," I beg, trying to process the earth-shattering shock.

"We can't get his heart to start," Ms. Alice wheezes, still barely able to breathe.

Rocco runs in. "Can you fix him?"

My hands land on Zane, and I scan his vibe. "No pulse, Demitri."

"Okay, Meley," he calmly coaches through the phone. "See if you can shock him with an energy load."

"Is an ambulance on the way?" I whimper, feeling ill equipped to handle this.

"We called," Rocco replies.

I put my hands back on Zane's chest, forcing myself not to look at his purple face or bruised neck. "Ready."

"Three, two, one," Demitri counts.

I send a massive energy load, and Zane's body arches before slamming back to the floor. *No response.* "Demitri," I say, panicked.

"Do it again, Meley," he instructs.

I direct another energy surge to his heart, trying to mimic a rhythm. Zane's body arches and slams down again. He inhales slightly. I scramble to feel his pulse.

"Breath and pulse," I announce through tears. "What do I do now?"

"Okay, try scanning him for injuries," Demitri instructs. When I try, I get nothing.

"Nothing, D."

"Can anyone else hear me?" Demitri asks.

"We're here," Rocco says. "Rocco, Pepe, Luis, and Ms. Alice."

"All right, what happened?" Demitri demands. "I need details."

"We opened the shop," Rocco says. "I came to the back storage room and found Zane hanging from the rafter."

"Warm or cold?"

"Cold," Rocco replies grimly.

"When's the last time anyone saw or heard from him?" Demitri asks.

"He left the screening after-party at eleven," Ms. Alice informs.

"He called me when he left the party," Rocco continues, voice shaking. "He tried Melanie several times, but no one answered. He panicked when he realized she had left the party, and he came to my condo. We talked for a long time about what happened at the screening. I fell asleep, and when I woke up, he was gone. He must have gone downstairs while I was asleep."

"What time did you fall asleep and then find him?" Demitri presses.

"Asleep at two in the morning. Found him at nine."

"Melanie?" Demitri says.

"Yes?"

"Put your hands around his head and scan."

I do, and my breath ratchets up. "He has no soul hum," I whisper.

"Damn it!" Demitri bellows.

I hear distant pounding through the phone. It sounds like he must be running.

"I need everyone to listen," Demitri says, winded. "Melanie must keep his heart going. I need the ambulance gone. I can't heal an international movie star if paparazzi or the media get involved. Almost nobody knows about my abilities, and it must stay that way. Too many people suspect Melanie's abilities already, which is dangerous."

Ms. Alice goes to look out the front window. "Ambulance just arrived," she calls and rushes back in.

"Get rid of it!" Demitri demands. "Act clueless. This was a prank call. Tell them everything is normal."

"Go, go," Rocco yelps at Pepe. They race out with Luis and Ms. Alice and close the door behind them.

I glance up at the rafter overhead, where a cut rope hangs. I whimper, "I can't go through this again!" The old pain and fear from losing Pierre comes roaring back.

"I've got my stuff," Demitri says. "We just got here. I haven't unpacked yet. I'm running, Melanie."

"Demitri, where are you going?" Victoria yells in the background.

"There's an emergency at home!" he calls. I hear his Jeep door slam.

"I'll call you back," I bark as an idea sparks. I hang up and dial another number. Brian Drell, Zane's brother, answers. "Has anyone called you?" I ask.

"About?"

"Zane."

"Conversation over," Brian snorts.

"No, no, no. Wait!" Tears slip down my cheeks. "He hung himself."

"WHAT?" Brian screams.

"I've restarted his heart, but Demitri's in Las Vegas. We think we can save him, but we can't take Zane to a hospital. He's been gone too long for normal intervention, so we need to hide him here."

"Las Vegas?" Brian yelps. "How's he getting to you?"

"Car."

"I just landed at the Reno airport and dropped off my customers," Brian tells me, voice cracking. "I'll pick him up in the helicopter. How bad is this?"

"He's brain-dead, Brian," I confess. "But if anyone can help him, Demitri can."

Sobs punctuate Brian's words. "I've screamed, berated, and destroyed Zane over Rachelle. You wouldn't talk to him. Rachelle wouldn't leave him alone."

"Brian, just get Demitri. I'll do everything I can to bring Zane back."

"What if you can't?" Brian panics.

"We're not going to worry about that." I take a huge breath.

"Promise me you won't leave Zane alone," Brian begs.

"I'm not leaving."

We hang up, and I look down at Zane's pale, slack face and severely bruised neck. Panic surges in my chest.

The door reopens, and Rocco, Ms. Alice, Pepe, and Luis hurry in.

"The shop is locked," Rocco says. "We got rid of the paramedics." He swallows hard as my phone rings again.

I answer, and Demitri says, "I'm headed to the private airport in Vegas. Brian's coming to pick me up. We'll have to get my Jeep later."

"I'll keep Zane going until you arrive," I gasp. Trepidation leaks into my tone as I ask, "What if we can't fix him?"

"I'll handle it, love," Demitri says softly. "Zane was already gone when you found him. If that's nature's order, I'll rebalance the scales."

Suddenly, Zane's heart stops again.

CHAPTER 6

My universe has boiled down to a hypnotic rhythm. I had to get into a zone to counter the debilitating sickness triggered by my panic. Now I'm a shell of myself as I send energy pulses into Zane's failing heart. His dead body recognizes natural order, and his heart isn't meant to beat. Fighting Mother Nature is exactly the task I can handle right now, though. I'm at my best when pressed to my core. My core is a determined beast.

Pulse . . . guh-gum . . . stillness . . .

Pulse . . . guh-gum . . . stillness . . .

Pulse . . . guh-gum . . . stillness . . .

Someone yanks me, and my eyes snap open. The sounds of crying and panic invade my foggy mind as chaotic energy floods my senses and destroys the trance I'd gotten myself into. The room is an emotional disaster. I blink dazedly as Bear and Darren reach for Zane. Tanner, who pulled me back, stares in shock.

"You're here?" I ask them blankly. The trance hasn't fully faded yet.

"Demitri called us," Bear says. "He's about an hour out." Bear looks down at Zane. "We'll take over while you get a break."

"How long have you been doing this?" Darren asks.

I can't answer.

The question is still drifting through my mind when Rocco steps in. "Two hours," he says.

Darren's eyes widen. He picks my cell phone up from the floor next to Zane and dials. "Melanie kept Zane's heart going for two hours with energy pulses," Darren says. "He's dead, D." People scream and sob in the background, but Darren ignores it, adding, "His body isn't cold because of Melanie's efforts."

"Scan her!" Demitri demands through the phone.

Darren rests his hand on my back. "No hum," he says grimly. Moving his hand toward my stomach, he adds, "Hum in her gut is still there."

"Is Trey there?" Demitri asks.

"No. I need to boost her, D. She doesn't have another hour left in her."

"NO!" Demitri barks. "It'll unsettle her remaining energy. Only Trey, Adam, or I can safely boost her."

"Trey didn't answer my call," Darren says. "I'll try Adam."

"Don't bother. He won't show. He's busy with Valerie's pregnancy issues," Demitri snarls. "Melanie, are you listening?"

I don't respond.

Darren tells him, "She hears you."

"Lie down, don't move, and keep your heart rate calm," Demitri coaches.

I manage to lie down. I notice Rachelle across the room, sobbing alongside Zane's hysterical mother. I've never met his mom, but I recognize her from a memory Zane gave me during that ugly affair reveal.

"Demitri," I manage to say.

"Talk to me, Meley."

"Is there a reason Rachelle is here?"

"What?" Brian asks. Apparently, the phone is on speaker.

"She snuck in while I was keeping Zane alive."

"Mom?" Brian shouts.

"I'm here," Brian and Zane's mother answers. "I called Rachelle."

Brian snarls, "Zane and I don't speak anymore because he had an affair with Rachelle."

Zane's mom whips her head toward Rachelle in shock. "What?"

"I didn't tell you," Brian says, "because you're hung up on Rachelle being part of our family. Rachelle also screwed Melanie over. They don't get along. Demitri and Melanie don't trust her, and she has no business being there."

"She already knows too much, Demitri," I inform him.

"I swear I won't tell anyone what I've seen," Rachelle sobs. "Just please help Zane."

"This is crazy," Demitri mutters. "If you people can't respect the effort going into saving him, I can't help."

"Demitri, please," Brian begs. "Mom, you have to get Rachelle out of there."

"Too late," Rocco says. "There's paparazzi outside. They got here two hours ago, thanks to me mentioning Zane's name on the 911 call."

"I had no idea about Rachelle and Zane," Zane's mom screeches.

"Rachelle knew," Demitri reminds. "She had no business showing up. Melanie isn't going to be disrespected like this. None of you appreciate how crucial secrecy is for our abilities."

"I had ZERO clue my mother would call Rachelle," Brian insists.

"You have to help my boy," Zane's mom pleads.

"Umm, guys?" Darren looks at Rocco. "This is a moot point.

Bear and I can't keep Zane going. This appears to be a Melanie-specific ability, and she's tapped out."

"Noooooo!" Zane's mother drops to her knees and scrambles to her son's side, her grief crashing through the room.

My head sags, and Ms. Alice, Pepe, Luis, and Rachelle lose it, tears flowing.

"Melanie!" Brian's voice trembles with fear through the phone.

I dig deep and manage to sit up. *Points for me.* I glare at Rachelle, who's sobbing. "You're here for a reason," I growl as my dark-water side rises from my exhausted core. "You have no idea what this will do to us both." Narrowing my eyes, I connect an energy line to Rachelle and invisibly yank. Her eyes widen, and she begins trembling uncontrollably. I feel a spark of revival as she collapses to the floor and breathes raggedly.

"That was quick," Bear snarks.

"Rachelle has proven to be a pretty shallow well," Darren groans.

"She's already drained?" Demitri asks, baffled.

"She's a sagging heap, and I only restored half an energy reserve." I snort. "Your ex is useless, Brian."

"What do we do?" Bear asks.

"She'll refill. Until then, I push through," I reply, crawling back to Zane. I straddle him, pressing my hands to his chest. I glare at his mother. "If we get screwed over by Rachelle's blabbing, I'll kill her and you."

"Melanie, please don't hurt my mom," Brian pleads.

"That's the deal," I snarl. "Take it or leave it."

Rachelle looks at Zane's mom in panic. "I won't say anything! I swear!"

"Just get my boy back," his mom begs.

My head drops as I force myself to find resolve. "I'm about to be in deep shit. Somebody put on music with a steady rhythm. I need all the help I can get. Sending pulses is easier to a beat."

Tanner rummages in his satchel. Moments later, J. J. Fad's "Supersonic" explodes from a boombox.

"Seriously?" Bear asks.

"Sorry. I've only got my sassy mix on me," Tanner replies.

"Leave it," I grumble. "It's got the right beat cadence." I steel myself. "Here we go, Zaney. You and me." My eyes close, and I start sending pulses into Zane again. Sinking back into my trance quells my growing backlash state from energy overuse.

"She's doing it, Demitri," Darren warns.

"Melanie, don't," Demitri insists. "Even if I get there and do my part, there's no guarantee we can help him."

"Too late," I whisper, giving it everything I've got.

CHAPTER 7

"How much longer?" I ask via an incorporeally sent mental whisper, barely audible in the stockroom. Sending energy pulses has become truly torturous. I'm hardly functioning.

"We're landing at lifeguard headquarters, Meley," Demitri says through the phone. "A Jeep is waiting to drive us to you."

"She's in trouble," Darren says.

"I'm sure," Demitri replies, sounding calm, though I hear the hint of panic in his tone.

Salt-N-Pepa's "None of Your Business" pounds out of the boombox. Tanner starts rapping along, right in Rachelle's face. I manage a feeble laugh. Tanner flashes a grin my way. As the second verse kicks in, I mumble the lyrics.

Tanner drops to his knees in front of me, spitting out his lines. Something about his antics boosts my core, giving me a shred of extra energy. I look at Rachelle and rap along with more bite.

"What's happening?" Demitri asks through the phone.

"Melanie's handing Rachelle a Salt-N-Pepa smackdown while pumping pulses into Zane," Darren replies, amused. He and Bear laugh while Tanner sashays around, getting more over the top.

Rocco, Pepe, Luis, and Ms. Alice look baffled. My ability to send pulses improves as Tanner's showy rap grows more exuberant.

"Keep it up, Tanner," Bear urges, watching me with hope.

Tanner bobs his head side to side, rapping inches from Rachelle's face.

I grin, pulling energy from what Tanner is exuding.

He kneels right in front of me, pumping me up. "Yes, giiirrrl," Tanner crows, and I throw myself into the next stanza.

When the song ends, Tanner glares at Rachelle with pursed lips and a cocked hip.

"I'll take any amount of rap sass if it helps," Rachelle says. She looks at me. "I'm so sorry, Melanie." Her gaze shifts to Zane's still body. "He's been destroyed this whole time. He lost you and Brian, and Ms. Alice got distant. He couldn't face his parents. The Surfrider guys backed off. So, he was left with me and Rocco."

"I wasn't exactly available to him either," Rocco admits.

Rachelle stares at her trembling hands. "The irony isn't lost on me that I was all he had in the end."

I keep sending pulses. "Zane is predisposed to severe depression," I remind her. "Toying with him was cruel."

"He is?" Rachelle asks.

My eyes widen. "Are you serious?"

"I didn't know."

"He gets a little sad," Zane's mother says, trying to downplay the situation.

I throw an angry glare her way. "He's on prescription depression meds!"

She looks stunned.

"I get that you see Rachelle as family, but she broke one son's heart and used the other. Maybe reconsider your loyalties."

"Aren't you sixteen?" Zane's mother asks condescendingly.

My eyes flash. "You're kidding me, right? After all the hours I've been at this?"

Demitri's voice comes over the phone, angry. "We're almost there, but there's a huge crowd outside."

"I'm coming to the door," Rocco says. "Big smiles, act normal. You're here to help with a restock."

"Got it," Demitri says.

Rocco leaves just as En Vogue's "My Lovin' (You're Never Gonna Get It)" starts playing. Tanner's mix CD has the perfect beat each time a new song comes on. I continue my relentless efforts.

The stockroom door opens and Demitri steps in. He tightens his jaw when he sees me. I must look rough. Brian breezes past Rachelle to hug his sobbing mom. Demitri kneels by Zane, placing hands on his massive chest, and bows his head.

"What's the verdict?" Bear asks.

"I think Zane was dead for hours before being found." Demitri looks to me. "What happens if you stop pulsing?"

"He's dead," I reply.

Demitri sighs. "Everyone here needs to understand that Zane is gone."

More crying and exclamations fill the air. In my exhaustion, their reactions seem ridiculous. They've seen the reality of what's happening. I sit back and take my hands off Zane's chest.

"Don't you dare! Don't you dare give up on my boy," his mother screams. She unleashes rage that drains the last of my will. "You did this to him, and now you're giving up?"

Demitri stands in a flash, but Brian beats him to the punch. "How dare you! You threw Zane headfirst into fame with a big grin on your face!"

"How dare YOU," she snarls back. "I gave him a career path. You have no idea how much we all sacrificed."

"You've benefited plenty," Brian accuses. "He got you out of a crappy apartment, and now you live on the ocean."

"I didn't use my son!"

"You never got him help when he needed it," Brian rails. "Just because he became a successful actor didn't mean his depression vanished. For years, you pretended everything was fine."

"Enough," Demitri barks. "Have your family fight later." He looks at me. "Your life force has kept him going. How long did his heart beat on its own before you had to pump him again?"

"A few minutes," I say, wiping sweat from my brow.

"That shouldn't have been possible," Demitri mutters, studying Zane's body.

"We saw it," Ms. Alice confirms.

"I don't doubt Melanie," Demitri defends. "I just don't get how a dead man was revived after that long."

"Maybe he tied the noose wrong," Rocco suggests.

Demitri looks up at the cut rope. "He did it right." He shakes his head. "Bear, thoughts?"

"Why ask HIM?" Zane's mom demands. "The people that *matter* want Zane back!"

Demitri shoots her a furious look, but I interject. "He's her baby, D. She doesn't get it. I can't blame her."

"I asked Bear because he understands the spirit journey," Demitri says coolly.

Bear nods. "Zane has the right to die," he explains. "It's a natural process in a soul's journey. But sometimes we reorder the process. It's a privilege with extreme responsibility."

"Why aren't you still pulsing?" Zane's mom snaps at me.

"Because he's gone, and a few minutes won't change that," Demitri answers on my behalf. "You have no idea what Melanie's done to herself trying to save him." He looks at Bear. "If I fix his body, then what?"

Bear shrugs. "If you manage to repair it, we still face whether Zane's spirit would return."

"Pierre," Demitri says, then waits. Nothing happens. "He's MIA," he mutters. "Perfect."

"These people are INSANE!" Zane's mother exclaims.

"Stop, Mom," Brian scolds. "You don't understand them."

"They're calling a dead boy to help with this?" She sounds beyond confused.

Demitri closes his eyes. "Melanie, this isn't . . ."

"I already know." I scoot away from Zane, tears filling my eyes at how futile it all feels. "I can ask this of me, but not of you. I'm sorry I dragged you here."

"I'm sorry I called my mother," Brian says. "If she and Rachelle weren't here, would you do this differently?"

"Yes," Demitri admits.

Brian covers his face. Guilt rolls off him in waves we can all feel.

"You didn't do this," I assure him. "Zane did it to himself."

"You're just going to give up and murder my son?" Zane's mother cries.

That does it. "How dare you," I say, standing to face her. "You took no responsibility for his mental decline, you called Rachelle, and you haven't appreciated a single thing we've done."

"Don't YOU have a responsibility?" she squawks. "You claim you can save him!"

"I never claimed that." I tip my head back, taking a massive breath. "The privilege and trap of having abilities is never-ending hope that I can help, even when I shouldn't." I look down at Zane and tears fall. "He sought peace, and I spent hours disturbing that because I'm selfish. I can't deal with the death of another man I love. It was wrong of me, though."

Tanner wraps his arms around me. "I'm sorry, Melanie."

"You're sorry she's giving up on my son?" Zane's mom blisters.

The look Tanner gives her is scary. Tanner has two sides. The first is flamboyantly boisterous, whether he's mad or happy. Only the level of snark changes in that dichotomy. The second side, though . . . That side is deadly serious, and that's when you know you're about to really get it. "I'm sorry because Melanie lost another man she loves," Tanner growls. "She doesn't let many people in, but Zane was special. Honestly, before he messed up with Rachelle, she might've loved him best of all her guys."

Zane's mom gives me a scathing once-over. "Let me guess: He bought you a car?"

My eyebrows rise, but Brian defends me. "She never asked him for anything. He got her a teddy bear and a silly hoodie. Meanwhile, Rachelle got a Mercedes last Christmas."

"Maybe that's why Melanie wanted to save him," Zane's mom snips. "She hasn't gotten what she wants yet."

"These people are insane," I say, exasperated.

"No, we're not," Rachelle counters. She steers a pointed glare toward Zane's mom. "I get you're desperate to blame someone, but I'm defending Melanie. She spent HOURS giving everything, and you were cheering her on, until Demitri and Melanie concluded it was impossible. Now you turn on them?"

"That's my son," passionately peels from Zane's mom as she collapses to her knees, truly absorbing the fact he's gone.

Brian kneels, hugging her as they both break down.

I gesture Bear, Tanner, Demitri, and Darren over. Rocco, Ms. Alice, Rachelle, Luis, and Pepe gather with us.

"Where do spirits go when they commit suicide?" I ask Bear.

"I'm not sure, but I have an educated guess," Bear says. "There are consequences. Part of life is living through pain and negativity. It teaches and helps souls grow. I suspect there are layers of compassion to suicide in the afterlife. Some people really do have it bad and must get out. Others though?"

Our collective gaze pans to Zane's corpse.

"He's a multimillionaire with success," Bear continues. "Does that warrant suicide?"

"So, you think his soul faces punishment?" Darren asks.

"How could it not?" Bear replies.

I turn to Demitri. "Can you do it?"

He eyes Rachelle warily.

"I've felt what Melanie can do," Rachelle admits fearfully. "I won't betray you."

"Bimbo has survival instincts," Tanner quips.

"I'm willing to try," Demitri says.

"What about me?" I ask. "Once his body's fixed?"

"If," Demitri cautions.

I give him a wry look. "You're so magical people notice it immediately. The rest of us are incognito, but you're like a wonder-angel."

Bear nods. "You can do this, Demitri. We saw the miracle you worked when Melanie was crushed."

"That was different. Melanie was alive," Demitri points out.

"True, but Melanie can spark life in him," Bear insists. "His body warmed back up the whole time she worked on him."

"What if Zane doesn't want to come back?" Darren asks.

"That's a whole different set of ramifications," Bear replies. "It's Zane's soul journey. We're toying with his destiny without permission."

"That's why I wanted Pierre," Demitri explains.

"How often does he answer?" Darren asks.

"Half the time," Demitri admits.

"Pierre isn't Zane's spirit guide." I sigh. "He may not even know what's happening to Zane."

"Also true." Bear ponders. "There are a lot of souls, and spirit guides stay busy."

"Do we chance it?" I ask Demitri.

He hesitates and stares at Zane. "I—I'm struggling."

"If it helps, I'm not giving Zane another shot," I inform D.

"You're not?" Rocco looks baffled.

"No," I say sadly. "He betrayed my confidence. But that doesn't mean I want him dead."

"You'll bring him back and let him figure out who he wants to be, but ditch him because of who he was?" Demitri asks.

"Sometimes you can't have it all," I say. "But another chance at life is still a nice gift."

"What if he still wants you?" Demitri asks.

"He won't. I'll bet you a Tower Records run, ice cream, and a Hawaiian pizza that if he comes back, he celebrates with everyone but me."

Demitri arches an eyebrow. "You've got a deal. I'll even eat the pizza without picking off that damn pineapple."

"You and me?"

"This is insane," he mutters, crossing the room to kneel on one side of Zane while I kneel on the other. "Here we go, Meley," Demitri says. "Pump him up."

I straddle Zane.

Tanner blurts, "Bow chicka bow wow."

I shoot him a look. "So sexy. Nothing like humping a dead guy to rev up my Sunday."

"Focus, please," Bear nervously pleads. "Epic mission in progress."

I press my hands to Zane's chest and shut my eyes. Tapping into my depleted reserves, I begin to send energy pulses. His heart stutters as I build a steady beat.

"Good, Meley," Demetri guides. "I'm going in. Keep it up. This'll be complicated."

Time falls away. All I feel is the ritual thump of energy.

CHAPTER 8

"Melanie," someone breathes from a distance. I don't respond at first. I can't speak yet.

A hand runs down my spine, sending tingles up my back. I gasp and open my eyes lethargically to see Demitri's soft smile. "You did good, babe." He gestures to Zane, and my jaw drops.

Zane's breathing on his own. His color is back, and his bruised, swollen neck looks healed.

"Oh my God." I turn stunned eyes to Demitri. "You did it?"

He nods with soft wonder in his eyes. "Your life force curled around each organ as I started repairing it. It's like you infused him with your spark. All I had to do was heal the organs instead of reversing death damage."

I glance at Zane and let out a raw, "FUCK!"

Demitri laughs. "Not the response I expected."

I shake Zane, still straddling him. "Babe?" No reaction. My head drops. "Fuck."

"Talk to us, Melanie," Bear urges.

"That means I have to drag his soul back," I whisper, swallowing hard.

"Here we go," Tanner says, kneeling by Zane's head so I can see him.

"What do you suggest?" I ask, blinking fluttery sarcasm Tanner's way.

"You dive into that hot hunk, find the part of him you love," Tanner says with an eyebrow waggle at my straddling pose, "and drag his womanizing soul back to face the music."

"What the hell is my life?" I mutter. "This is insane. I need a massive energy source."

"Wanna drain Rachelle again?" Rocco asks.

I give him a patronizing look. "I said massive, Roc."

Everyone laughs, even Rachelle.

An idea sparks. "Screw the paparazzi," I say with a smirk.

"Zane hates them," Demitri chuckles.

"Exactly. And I'm about to flip them off on his behalf." I close my eyes and send a searching line outside, finding a big crowd of idiots. I bubble invisibly around them to attach the line and yank. Energy floods me so fully that my head tips back. *"Yesssss,"* I breathe out the audible thought.

"Holy shit," Zane's mother whispers.

"Yeah," Tanner snarks, gesturing at me. "That's who you were rude to."

I look down, realizing I'm softly glowing. "Huh. That's new."

I sever the line, leaving the paparazzi groggy but alive. "I'm going in," I gravel at full dark-water power.

"We'll anchor you," Bear offers. He and Darren flank me.

I close my eyes and place my hands on Zane's chest. I smile, recalling Zane in his Skeletor hoodie, laughing so hard while I rested on his lap. That moment of happy Zane is pure gold.

Latched onto that memory, I send a seeking line into Zane's body. I find a distant spark of his soul, attach, and start pulling. A unique resistance meets my effort. My intuition pulses, and I barely have time to send the audible mental thought, *"Oh shit, tether me,"* before my soul is ripped out of my body.

I rocket through space, leaving time behind, and plunge downward into my own personal rabbit hole.

"Ride the waves, Alice," a voice chuckles.

"Pierre?"

"Yup. Now I can reach you."

"Where are we?" I can't see anything.

"You're in a vortex," Pierre sends cryptically. *"I'm with a very unhappy jury."*

"Marvelous."

My torpedo journey through a dark spiraling void comes to a halt so abruptly that I lose every ounce of spirit equilibrium. It takes me a moment to regroup and survey the space I've landed in. Everything around me is a dull, lifeless gray. Pierre strides across the void, stopping beside me. We're facing five indistinct forms that look like a softer shade of gray than the rest of the space.

Pierre takes my hand and introduces me. "This is Melanie."

"You're not welcome here," hums from one of the gray blobs.

"Nice to meet you too," I reply.

"You've broken every rule with this act," comes another blobby hum.

"Oh, come now," I cat back. "I'm sure there are a few rules left unbroken."

Pierre squeezes my hand. *"Tread carefully,"* he sends cautiously.

"She doesn't respect natural order," one blob accuses.

"How could she?" Pierre retorts. "Look inside her past lives."

We wait in silence for a long time. I glance at Pierre. He makes a lackadaisical "wait" gesture.

Time drags. Finally, Pierre and I sit, taking a spiritual load off.

"*They're not big on brevity,*" I send to him.

"*No,*" Pierre sends with a smile. "*I'm going nuts. Spirit-guide life suuucks.*"

"*No fun?*"

"*Not much,*" Pierre sighs. "*I feel like a ghost here.*"

"*You are a ghost.*"

He chuckles. "*I mean it's lonely. I miss living.*"

My expression softens. "*I miss you.*"

"*Me too, Seashell.*" Pierre smiles gently. "*I'm glad you didn't give up on Zaney. He made a monumental mistake.*"

"*Does he want saving?*" I send.

"*Oh, yeah. He's a wreck. I can't reach him to clarify much, though.*"

"*Why?*"

"*These jerkoffs locked him in Suicide Solitary. They kicked me out.*" Pierre glares at the gray blobs. They remain busy snooping through my past lives.

"*Think we can free him?*"

"*We'll try,*" Pierre sends.

"*You sure you want to fight them?*" I ask. "*I'm just lowly Melanie, but you're a spirit guide now.*"

Pierre gives me a look. "*You aren't lowly, Melanie. That's precisely what they're learning right now. Regarding me, I need to push back against something just to break up the tedium.*"

"*Should we negotiate or blow up this gray void?*"

Pierre shrugs. "*No clue, but I hope for an epic battle.*" He cracks his ghostly knuckles, and I snicker.

"*What's happening back home?*" I ask.

"*Who knows,*" Pierre sends. "*I'm sorry I couldn't answer Demitri. These guys contained me. I can't survey home while I'm in here.*"

"*Zane's mom is a bitch.*"

"I love her," Pierre sends laughing. *"She tries. She just doesn't grasp energy workers. She's a Normal who barely processes three dimensions, let alone four."*

"Is this the fourth dimension?" I ask, peering around the dull void.

"No, it's five."

"Boring," I remark.

"Exactly," Pierre snorts. *"This is a place for souls who commit infractions. Think of it like solitary. Usually for suicides, but it varies by circumstance."*

I nod. *"So Bear was right."*

"He usually is," Pierre says. *"The bigwigs weren't thrilled your crew figured out so many puzzle pieces."*

"We've had so many lifetimes," I remind him. *"Bear subconsciously remembers a lot."*

"We're ready for you," a blob announces.

I look to Pierre. *"I love you."*

Pierre squeezes my spirit hand. *"I love you too, Seashell."*

We stand before the five gray shapes.

"You're impressive, Melanie Slate," one intones.

"Thanks."

"There are trades you can make, but remember . . ." The blob's voice darkens. "Consequences."

"Fill me in," I request.

"I've said all I can."

I raise an eyebrow. "So how am I supposed to understand?"

"You must know there are consequences," it repeats.

I nod sarcastically. "Consequences. Got it."

"Are you willing to accept them?"

"It's like playing Where's Waldo? *in the damn dark,"* I send to Pierre. Then to the blob, "What are they?"

"We can't tell you," it says.

I roll my eyes, becoming exasperated. "You're talking in annoyingly vague circles about what sounds monumental."

"I'm being very clear," the blob insists.

I give Pierre a look. *"Welcome to my nightmare. Everything with the higher-ups is like this,"* he sends.

"Fine," I say, defeated. "If I agree, Zane returns?"

"Yes," another blob rumbles, "but you'll bear his consequences."

At this point I'm flat done. "Either be clear or get on with it."

"We've told you enough," the blob insists with finality.

I sense them intensely focusing on me.

"She doesn't have to face twelve altered lifetimes," one says, earning the speculative attention of the other blobs. "She could lose everything in another trade. Zane for . . ."

I feel them energetically probing me. *"Any clue?"* I send to Pierre.

"None," he replies. *"I'm not one of them."*

A chattering sound, like happy hyenas, creepily peels for a moment, before the energy settles. "One for one," a blob announces, sounding pleased.

"One for one," the others repeat.

"Kick ass. One for one," I echo.

"You agree to the terms?" one blob asks.

"Babe?" I prompt Pierre.

"Yes, Seashell?"

"Her name is Melanie," a different blob corrects.

"I call her Seashell," Pierre replies.

"A seashell is a dead ocean creature's remains," the blob states matter-of-factly.

"I call her Seashell because she's beautiful and a treasure you delight in finding," Pierre bristles.

"Awww," I say, touched. "I didn't know that's why you call me seashell."

Pierre kisses me quickly, ignoring the blobs' disapproval.

"ENOUGH, Ocean Corpse," a blob scolds me.

I glare at Pierre. "You want me to get through my remaining lifetimes just to dwell in this nonsense?"

"This is a special corner of the afterlife," he says. "Our part is more vibrant, but just as oddly disconnected as these gatekeepers are."

"Gatekeepers?"

Pierre nods. "Zane must go through a type of rehab for his suicide indiscretion. Think of it as a very long stretch where lessons about the gift of life are taught through gray monotony."

"Like purgatory?"

"No," Pierre replies. "This isn't purgatory. It's simply a space where all color, feeling, and connection is neutrally dull, but there's promise of release."

"What a waste of time." I shake my head. "I don't know, Pierre. If this is what's waiting for me, I'm going to start misbehaving to extend my lifetimes."

"You won't have time to misbehave," I'm informed by a blob.

"What does that mean?"

"It means, Ocean Corpse, that you're about to face the trade. It will reorder your life, and teach you humility," the gray blob informs.

"Humility?" I snort. "I'm treated like dirt. Humility, and subsequent humiliation, aren't new to me."

"Do you accept?" the blob demands.

"Yes," I growl, losing patience.

After a long silence, the center blob rumbles deeply, "It's done."

"Interesting," another blob replies, with no intonation.

"Feel any different?" Pierre murmurs.

"Nope."

He shrugs. *"They're an odd bunch."*

"Melanie Slate, you made the trade." The calm voice shifts without warning, screaming, "And, so it *iiisssssss!*"

I'm hit by something dank and powerful. Defenseless, I rocket into nothingness. I try to scream, but sound is ripped away. Without promise of anything solid or tangible, I become a part of the energy around me until I slam into something. My eyes fly wide open, and my body blasts back into the surf shop's stockroom shelving, projected by the force of my soul's return to my body. I crash into storage shelves and land with a smash onto the tile floor. My head ricochets off the floor, and I see stars.

Everyone gasps, but they barely have time to react to my dramatic return before Zane's eyes open. A cascade of screams and tears fill the air as his mother, Rachelle, Rocco, Pepe, Brian, Ms. Alice, and Luis swarm him. They hug him frantically, exclaiming and chattering. It appears that Zane came back to the land of the living with all of his facilities intact.

From where I'm sprawled, I watch Rachelle nearly tackle him. "I can't believe you're alive!" she exclaims.

Zane rubs his face and shakes his head. "I don't know what I was thinking."

Demitri bypasses the celebratory circle and rushes to me. Bear, Darren, and Tanner join him as he places his hands on me. "Broken ribs," he murmurs. His hands heat against my side, and I feel the pain receding.

I sit up. Bear, Darren, Demitri, and Tanner all stare at the cheering group.

"They haven't even said thank you," Tanner marvels. His words have no flamboyance or sass, just disbelief.

"This is what it's like for you?" Demitri says softly to me.

"What?"

"Being drained to the point of sickness and then tossed aside as soon as you're not needed." He looks stunned. The people he helped were usually grateful.

"Every time," I whisper. "I'm just a means to an end in this lifetime. The gray blobs wanted me to learn 'humility.'"

"Humility?" Tanner echoes, aghast. "After what you did?"

"How'd you bring his soul back?" Darren asks with an edge of awe.

I hold out my arm, and my circle of friends grips onto me. They close their eyes. I replay everything that happened, fast-forwarding through the dull bits. When they open their eyes again, I see terror on their faces.

"What did you DO?" Demitri grabs my cheeks, panicked. "How could you accept that trade?"

"We don't even know the trade," I say.

"'One for one,' Melanie?" Bear's roars. "A life for a life? For someone who can't even say thanks?"

I shrug. "I couldn't leave him there."

"Didn't you feel how happy those gatekeepers were?" Bear says. His eyes bulge. "The powers that be were JUBILANT! They didn't give a shit about some Normal who checked out because he was sad!" Bear looks to Darren. "Did you feel it?"

Darren nods stoically, but there's fear under the surface. "Pierre outed you as special. Mistake number one. Then you gave them all the time they needed to figure out exactly how special you are. Mistake number two. They're KEEPERS. They keep prizes, and you were willing to trade yourself for a far lesser prize."

"Those keepers don't care about ZANE!" Bear bellows, taking up the thread. "He's special HERE, but it's shallow-human-special. No one gives a damn about fame and money in the spirit realm. What they care about is POWER!"

Demitri stands while wiping tears from his eyes. "We need to stabilize you, Meley," he says. "Will you come home with me?"

I nod. He helps me up, but my legs wobble. He scoops me into his arms.

"D, you're not in much better shape than me," I say. He looks exhausted.

"I don't care," he replies. He looks at Zane. "Melanie took your consequences. She has a death sentence now, and you didn't even thank her."

Zane's eyes widen. "I thought I just somehow woke up."

"SOMEHOW WOKE UP?" Demitri rages. "Screw you, Zane Drell!"

"Show him, Melanie," Tanner suggests.

"Don't show the rest of these jerks," Demitri snaps. "Just show Zane everything from Ms. Alice's call to now."

Zane crosses the room. "Can I hold her?" he asks Demitri.

"Not a chance," Demitri growls. "You have no idea what she did for you. You proved it the second you woke up, hugged Rachelle, and ignored Melanie."

I touch Zane's arm, sending him the entire memory.

"Can we all see the spirit realm part?" Rocco asks.

"No," Demitri barks. "If you cared, you'd have checked on Melanie once you knew Zane was okay."

"Melanie, I'm sorry," Ms. Alice rushes to say. "We just got swept away."

"I understand," I say sadly, looking at Zane. "I'm glad you're alive. I don't know how we managed it, but . . ."

"Melanie, I'm so sorry," Zane insists. "I promise I'll watch the memories."

"Pierre says hi," I offer.

"Pierre?" Zane and the others look shocked.

"Any trade was worth seeing Pierre," I say. "I got to spend time with him while the creepy gray forms spied on my past lives."

"Like aliens?" Pepe asks.

"No," Darren snaps, "like a spirit mafia. Melanie sold her soul to beings that have no sense of time or compassion." He glares at Zane. "All so you could have back this worthless cause."

"What do you mean, sold her soul?" Zane asks nervously.

"It's just a phrase, honey," his mom cuts in.

"No, it's not." Rachelle's eyes widen. "Did you miss Melanie lying still on the floor for ages while Darren, Demitri, and Bear panicked? Demitri sobbed. Then Melanie screamed and flew across the room!" She looks at me. "That crash into the shelves was ratchet! Are you okay?"

"Ew," I whimper. "Don't be a thoughtful ally, Rachelle." I wince. "Be a worthless hoebag, please."

Rachelle offers a soft smile. Sisterly energy radiates from her as she says, "You can still hate me even though I'm not all bad."

"Ohhh, eeewww," groans from me.

"I'm sorry we didn't check on you," Ms. Alice murmurs, getting back on topic.

"It's okay," I reply. "I had my people."

"How bad is it?" Zane asks warily.

Demitri sets me down before turning with a ferocious rush. He roars and punches Zane so hard that Zane topples into stacked boxes.

Zane staggers to his feet, but he doesn't attack Demitri. "I'm sorry," he quietly says.

Demitri lifts me again. "Zane, you're dead to me. Don't ever attempt suicide again, because I won't save you. Melanie took on your karmic fallout for your selfish act."

Zane's face drains of color, and his mouth falls open.

"Watch the memories." Demitri sneers. "Then use your fancy acting ability to explain to your mother, girlfriend, and clueless friends how Melanie gave up everything for you."

Still cradling me, Demitri walks us out of the stockroom.

CHAPTER 9

I exhale hard as Demitri rubs my back. Mr. Cantrell sits on the edge of Demitri's bed, patting my ankle under the covers.

"Better?" Mr. Cantrell asks.

"Kind of," I quietly reply. "Are you okay that I'm here?"

"We're not about to send you back to Mabel's or your parents' house like this," Mr. Cantrell says. "I'm very concerned about this trade you made."

"So far, so good," I say with a shrug of my free shoulder. "No death yet."

My cell phone rings, and I groan.

I start to reach for it, but Demitri grabs it first. "I'm handling this," he snarls.

"Might not be them, D," Mr. Cantrell says. "Be nice when you answer."

"Hello," Demitri says, pressing the speaker button and setting the phone on his chest next to my head.

"Demitri? Please don't hang up," Zane pleads.

"What do you want, Zane?" Demitri asks, nowhere near polite.

"I watched all of it," Zane quietly informs.

"And?" Demitri says.

"I'm horrified." Zane clears his throat. "I'm so sorry for my choices that led to this. Is Melanie okay?"

"Melanie's curled up with me in bed," Demitri scoffs. "Her energy has stabilized, and the vomiting stopped. I'll get her back to where she needs to be. Melanie isn't your concern anymore."

"Please," Zane begs.

"Please what?" Demitri growls back.

"Please understand how much I care," Zane pleads pathetically.

"You greeted Rachelle, while Melanie was a broken heap on the floor," Demitri reminds. "Zane, how do you explain that?"

"I . . . ," Zane falters. "I woke up, and it took me a minute to figure out what was happening. I remember nothing from the spirit realm. Rachelle was right there and hugged me first. I was in a daze and just relieved to be alive. People kept talking to me, and Rocco and Brian blocked my view. I didn't realize you and Melanie had saved me until everyone got quiet while your group was talking. Then I put it all together."

"You don't deserve this second chance, Zane," Demitri coldly says, and I wince.

"That's not nice, Demitri." I mutter with a slight frown.

"Melanie, I'm so sorry," Zane says. "I'm scared of this trade you made."

"That trade isn't your concern," I reply. "Enjoy being alive, and don't take it for granted. That's all I ask."

"Can we please come to you?" a female voice asks.

"Who is this?" Demitri asks.

"Cindy, Zane's mom," the woman says.

"Definitely not!" Demitri barks. "Are you having this conversation in front of those people?"

"Yes. We're all at Rocco's," Zane informs.

"Word of advice," Demitri schools, "don't have private conversations in front of people who don't care about Melanie."

"We do care," Rocco insists.

"Oh, don't even get me started on YOU, Rocco," Demitri boils back. "YOU should have been with us while we helped Melanie. You've obviously spent too much time with Normals."

"I'm aware," Rocco softly replies. "I was so relieved to have Zane back, but that's no excuse for ignoring the energy workers who gave their all."

"You never once stepped in to tether Melanie's soul," Demitri accuses.

"I . . ." Rocco pauses. "I had no clue what to do."

"You grab on, channel in, and hold her spirit with everything you've got," Demitri informs him. "I'm not sure why you were granted metaphysical abilities. You're not worthy of them. You're pathetic, Rocco."

"I'm sorry," Rocco says as he lets out a long exhale.

"You'll never back us," Demitri replies coldly. "I don't trust you."

"I'll back you with everything in me when this comes to a head with Melanie," Rocco promises. "We aren't letting them take her."

"Don't get in our way," Demitri warns, while he and his dad exchange fierce looks.

"Is there a plan?" Rocco asks bashfully, ignoring the brush-off.

"I have no idea what we're up against," Demitri says, "but YOU are all irrelevant."

"Please let me help," Zane begs. "I . . . I need to be there."

"How would you be helpful?" Demitri says condescendingly.

"I'm good at keeping a hawkeye on Melanie," Zane says. "When she was in the hospital, we were one unit. She couldn't even go to the bathroom alone, and I was right there. Please, PLEASE, let me help watch while we wait to see what's going to happen. I won't fail any of you."

"Sit up, baby girl," Demitri softly says.

I do as he asks, and he sits up with me.

I look at the phone, unsure of what to say.

"I don't give a damn that they're listening, Meley," Demitri says, tipping my chin so I face him. "I'm asking you to understand that I'm terrified, heartbroken, and lonely, because you're my other half."

That's quite a revelation. Demitri and I share a tangled history. He once gave up our future together as potential spirit guides so he could have a soulmate bond with Victoria. It was messy.

Demitri swallows and his eyes grow misty. "Grant me the grace of not letting Zane weasel in," he says. "He can't help you. I can, and I will."

"Done," I whisper. I'm taken aback by Demitri's admission.

He leans in and kisses my cheek. He squeezes his eyes shut with distress as he pulls away. "Hang up," he tells me, voice flat.

"Wait, ple—" Zane pleads, but I end the call before he can finish.

I scoot higher on the bed and guide Demitri's head to my chest. Cataclysmic sobs wrack his body while I hold him. My shirt is quickly soaked in his tears. Mr. Cantrell shifts closer on the bed and puts a hand on his son's back. We wait silently.

"I can't lose you," Demitri whispers. "We have to find a way to reverse your agreement. Let Zane face his consequences himself."

"It's done, Demitri," I say.

Demitri props himself on one elbow, and my gorgeous best friend looks more human than ever. He's so beautiful that only extreme upset makes him appear like a normal person.

I manage a small smile. "And you're supposed to live your remaining lifetimes with Victoria."

"I know I'm different with you when Victoria's around," he admits.

Surprise zings through me. We definitely need to discuss this. "You change when she's here, but how you're being with me right now means so much," I say through pursed lips. *I hate how distant and dismissive he is when Victoria's around.*

"I won't change," he says. "I need to work on that."

"Yes, you will, Demitri. You always change when she's around. It's okay, though. You should live your life with your soulmate."

Demitri slumps to rest his head on his father's lap and sobs. Mr. Cantrell rubs his back. "You have no idea how many times he cries like this," Mr. Cantrell says, addressing me. "When it's just us, Demitri is very clear about his feelings. He feels stuck with Victoria."

"Do you see how different he is with her than when he's not?" I ask.

"I hate it," Me Cantrell says. "I feel like I lose my son. He gets distant and cold. It's bizarre."

"I'm so sorry," Demitri gasps.

"It's all right, son." Mr. Cantrell looks at me. "I scanned Demitri and Victoria last time she was here, suspecting something amiss, but it's just how they are together."

Demitri wraps his arms around me and pulls me to him. With our heads on his father's lap, we hold on to each other and endure the exhaustion.

CHAPTER 10

Demitri left this morning with his dad to pick up his Jeep in Las Vegas. While it would have been nice to have Victoria just drive his Jeep back, Demitri had the keys, and Victoria is a horrible driver. Her parents brought her back from the wedding, in a snit. Since Brian wasn't around to fly them back to Vegas, they had to do it the hard way in Mr. Cantrell's car. I took a while to leave Mr. Cantrell's house after they set off, because going back to Mama Mabel's was not exactly an appealing idea. I didn't know what to expect from Trey.

Resigned to my fate, I walk through Mama Mabel's front door and overhear her in the parlor.

"You and Valerie need to stay right here with us," Mama Mabel coos. "We can help take care of her."

I freeze and my mouth falls open. I catch Trey's gaze across the room. I'm finally stable enough to send mind-to-mind to Trey, *"Is Mama Mabel serious?"*

"Holy crap, this can't be real," Trey sends back.

Valerie squeals and claps her hands. She's only six weeks from her due date with twins. These last weeks have been a nightmare, because Valerie is unbelievably needy. Trey and I can't stand how she and Adam have basically invaded the place on our days here.

I give Mabel a flabbergasted look. Bringing Adam and Valerie in as permanent residents is guaranteed to destroy the sanctity of my home away from home. I scoff to myself. *It hasn't been a sanctuary, but whatever. Things getting worse is going to be a nightmare.*

"This is perfect!" Adam beams and hugs Mabel. "Thank you, Mabel. We'll go home, grab our stuff, and be right back!" He and Valerie practically skip out of the parlor.

Mama Mabel appears pleased that she's found a solution to Valerie's late-term pregnancy issues. She's a midwife, not practicing anymore, but she has been helping Valerie. Unfortunately, she's oblivious to what Adam and Valerie have been putting us through.

"I'm out," I tell her and rush to my room to grab my book and the stack of homework I need to turn in tomorrow.

Mama Mabel follows me. "Melanie, wait," she says. "What's going on? I thought you and Trey were close friends with Valerie and Adam."

Exasperated, I turn to face her. "We were," I say, "until Valerie started taking COMPLETE advantage of her pregnancy. All she does is whine and find excuses to con everyone into doing everything for her. Adam's been a total thoughtless monster. They're a real piece of work."

"It's true," Trey says as he leans against the doorjamb. "I meant to schedule a talk with you about how Melanie and I can't stand it anymore, but everything's been crazy. Valerie orders Melanie around constantly. They hang out here like it's their personal clubhouse."

"Now they'll be living here FULL TIME," I bark, fed up.

"I'm out too," Trey states as he folds his arms.

"It can't be that bad," Mama Mabel says as she glances from me to Trey.

"Just wait," I scoff. "You might need a personal assistant for Valerie, or she'll hog your staff."

"Melanie, you're obviously exaggerating," Mama Mabel says with a disdainful look.

I open the dresser and start packing outfits for Trey and me.

Trey ducks into our bathroom to collect his toiletries into a tote bag. When he reappears, he shoots Mama Mabel a serious look. "It really is that bad," he says. "I know you've been busy and missed most of it, but I give it a week, *tops*, before your staff starts quitting."

As I sling the duffel bag over my shoulder, Trey grabs our backpacks. We hug Mama Mabel and bolt through the door. We pass Valerie and Adam in the foyer, dragging suitcases. They're in yet another heated argument.

"Whoa, what's wrong, you two?" Mabel asks them.

Trey gives me a look that says, "You've got to be kidding." We ignore whatever's going on with those two and head through the parking lot.

"To your parents' house?" Trey asks.

"Yup."

CHAPTER 11

"**M**elanie, please solve the equation," Mr. Metzler requests from the front of the classroom. He holds out a piece of chalk, and I close my eyes to steady my spinning head. I feel worse than usual.

I get up from my desk, move to the board, and take the chalk from Mr. Metzler. The numbers swim before me.

"Melanie, are you sure you're okay?" Mr. Metzler asks.

"Yes, sir," I say, staring at the problem on the board. My eyes refocus. I exhale, relieved, and solve it quickly.

The bell rings, and I move through the crush of students, eager for lunch. I pack up my stuff and head out of the room. Trey waits across the hall with one foot propped against the lockers as he scans the messages on his pager. His raven-black hair and tan complexion look extra handsome with those golden-brown eyes, but he's not smiling.

"Trey, we need to talk," I say. "You slept the whole time we were at my parents' house, so we never handled what's going on with me."

"I'm sorry, but there's a security issue at work," he offers. "I have to deal with it and get back to class before the bell. Are you staying at Mama's or your parents' tonight?"

"Parents'."

"I'm working all night, so I'll be at Mabel's." He kisses my forehead and turns to go.

I grab his arm. "Can this wait? I really need to talk to you, and you promised we'd slip away for lunch at Smokers' Corner."

"Destiny's room was broken into," Trey informs. "Some of her stuff is missing, and I need to check the security tapes. Mabel's panicking."

Trey is Mama Mabel's head of security, which some might consider insane since he's only seventeen. But no one else she's hired has ever done better. He's methodical and calculating. He anticipates everything—except, of course, when it comes to me. His position with Mabel includes room, board, and salary. He wasn't supposed to start until he graduated next year, but the universe has pushed us to this point. He's been staying more and more at Mabel's. His parents aren't thrilled with the amount of time he's away from home now, but the head of security job is incredibly involved. The only reason they've held their tempers is that the job comes with a full ride to Cal State Northridge. They can't afford college tuition, and that future perk has curbed their displeasure. Still, Trey and his parents struggle, putting strain on the relationship. It doesn't help that they also hate me. It's a mess.

I watch him take the stairs two at a time and vanish around a corner.

I sigh. *I guess we'll add "no time for me" to the list of his sacrifices lately.*

Tanner comes up behind me so suddenly, it makes me jump. "Wow," he says. "Trey left in a hurry. What's up?"

Despite my mood, I turn and smile at him.

Tanner sports one of his trademark outrageous outfits, tight leather pants, a black ruffled-neck shirt, and a purple-and-black paisley jacket. His heeled motorcycle boots make him even taller.

"Any chance you've got time to talk?" I ask hesitantly.

Tanner's fiancée, Finley, races past. "Tanner, we gotta dash!" she says as she passes.

Tanner gives me a quick hug. "We've got advanced choir rehearsal at lunch. Sorry, Mel, I have to jet. I promise I'll make time soon."

As he hurries after Finley, I close my eyes. My head starts spinning again.

CHAPTER 12

Irritation blooms as I glance at the clock. It's 10:38, and still no word from Trey.

I can't stand it. I pick up the phone in my room at my parents' house, dialing the private line that Trey and I share at Mama Mabel's. After four rings, the answering machine picks up. I hear Trey's recorded voice: "You've reached Trey and Melanie. Leave a message . . . or don't. Whatever."

I really need him to change that.

My mom opens my door and pokes her head in. "Bedtime, Melanie. School tomorrow," she says authoritatively. "You're here tonight, so it's our house, our rules. Remember what we agreed on."

When she disappears again, I sigh, exasperated. Living half the week at my parents' house, with all these teenage rules, is so frustrating. Two days a week, I live with Trey at Mabel's and am free to come and go with no one dictating anything. You'd think my parents would relax given that I've never been late to school or gotten bad grades, but nope.

Knowing Mom's probably watching the crack under the door, I flip off the overhead light. I hear her footsteps fade. Rolling my eyes, I lift the receiver again and dial the staff line at Mabel's. Relief washes over me when I hear the voice of Constance, one of my favorite employees there.

"Constance, it's Melanie. Is Trey all right?"

"Depends on your definition of 'all right,'" Constance replies. "Things are crazy. Physically, he's fine."

"Explain," I say tensely.

"There was an incident with Valerie. You weren't here to warn Trey not to be himself, and he blew up. Then, he and Mabel went at it. After that, there was a brawl in the parlor, and he had to handle that chaos. It's been hectic."

"Well, that explains why he never called." I sigh.

"Honestly, we could use you tonight. The crowd's rough, and your rep with the bikers might calm them down. I've heard several speak in hushed tones about 'La Diabla.' I think if you were here, they'd be afraid you'd blast them into next week and behave. Any chance you could come?"

My high school friends and I ended up tight with the Hellhounds, a biker club that runs the Hollywood Underground with Mabel. They dubbed us the Hellcats. The Hellhounds have a serious reputation, but these days, I'm the one who's built a reputation. The Hellhounds call me Firebird—others call me La Diabla—ever since I energetically attacked a dozen bikers known as the Reapers after an earthquake. They tried to steal our supplies. I took them out.

"Hang on," I say. "I'll see."

I dash down the hall and find my parents in the den, watching TV. "Constance just called. There's trouble at Mabel's. The bikers are out of control, and they need 'La Diabla' to keep them in line."

"Ummm . . . no, you can't drive to Hollywood at eleven p.m.," Mom says with a scrunched face. "They'll manage. Go to bed, Melanie."

Grinding my teeth, I return to my room and pick up my phone receiver. "Constance, that's a no-go. Apparently, I'm stuck being a normal teen tonight."

Constance snorts. "I don't know how you keep up this half-and-half existence. I'd lose my mind."

"I AM losing my mind," I admit. "Please have Trey call me."

She promises, and we hang up.

I sit cross-legged on my bed, shutting my eyes. I focus on my mind-to-mind soulmate link with Trey. *"Trey, I need to hear from you,"* I send.

My eyes fly open. Something felt horribly wrong. When I tried reaching him, my message veered off halfway and just evaporated. I try again, with the same bizarre result. Not being able to contact Trey telepathically panics me. I close my eyes and try to sense Trey's energy. He's alive, which calms a fraction of my worry. But what's going on?

Is this how normal teenagers live, just waiting by the phone? It's unsettling. My heart races, my nerves fraying.

After I've read the same book page three times and tidied my room to avoid another scolding, the phone finally rings.

I snatch it up. "Trey?"

"Hey, Mel," he says. "Why aren't you answering me mind-to-mind? You have me blocked."

My eyebrows knit. I check. "I absolutely don't have you blocked, Trey."

"Hang on," he says. "I'm sending something now."

I wait, but get nothing.

Trey sighs. "See? I can't get through," he says.

"This is one more item for the list," I say, resigned.

"What list?"

"The list I've been trying to talk to you about. I'm having weird issues, and we need to handle it together."

"Can this wait until tomorrow?" Trey asks. He sounds exhausted. "I've had a brutal night."

"What happened?"

"Everything," he says with a loud exhale. "Turned out it was Valerie who broke into Destiny's room. Took her shampoo, towels, and a blanket. I pitched a bigger fit with Mabel than I should have, but I'm fed up with Valerie and Adam. We have rules about personal space that I'm supposed to enforce, but Mabel sided with Valerie, claiming she didn't realize her boundary mistake. I got labeled 'mean.' Adam jumped my ass. Valerie cried. Mabel yelled at me."

"So I missed lunch with you because of Valerie?" My voice is tight.

"Yes."

"What about that brawl Constance mentioned?"

"It was no big deal," Trey grumbles. "Two drunks started swinging, and I de-escalated it. Now I need to do interviews for new bouncers. I'm short-staffed."

"I'm not okay with Valerie taking the only time I had with you today. I needed to talk, but you took off for an emergency. Valerie being a brat isn't an emergency, Trey. It's her normal M.O."

"Melanie, I'm done for the night. I'm exhausted. I agree Valerie's out of line, but I had to check. We didn't need an actual break-in."

"Don't snap at me, Trey."

"Goodnight, Melanie."

He hangs up, leaving me holding the phone in frustration.

CHAPTER 13

"**M**elanie," Mr. Isley, our dance director and choreographer, bellows over a microphone. "Get your crap together. What is wrong with you?" He's an intimidating mountain of a man, with a formidable dance career, and I know disappointing him leads to a torturous rehearsal. I try to avoid that, but today I'm off my game.

Demitri leaps off the stage and heads toward Mr. Isley, who's standing at the back of the auditorium. I see him gesture for Trey to join them.

My ability to see and hear through Trey kicks on again, and I'm baffled. *Why does it only work sometimes?*

I hover quietly at the back of Trey's mind and eavesdrop.

"I don't want to alarm anyone," Demitri says, "but I think something's seriously wrong with Mel. If I'm right, she needs to stop these dance rehearsals immediately."

Mr. Isley looks frustrated. "Okay, what is it?"

Demitri hesitates. "I think she's pregnant," he finally says.

"I assure you she's not," Trey snorts. "She assumed that too, but she's taken so many pregnancy tests, it's practically a new budget item at Mabel's. All negative."

"Then that can't be it," Mr. Isley says.

"I'm telling you," Demitri insists. "She should try a different brand. I'm positive."

"Why do you think she's pregnant?" Trey asks, annoyed.

"Her energy's off," Demitri says. "She can't hold her weight properly. The shoulder lift felt odd. Plus, she's gained weight."

Trey and Mr. Isley glance my way.

Trey shrugs. "She barely eats. Half the time, it comes right back up."

"That sounds like pregnancy to me," Mr. Isley says.

"She's anxious," Trey says as he shakes his head. "She's been jittery and sick for a while now."

"I already ordered a skintight unitard for her," Mr. Isley says with a grimace. "She'll have to slim down. She'll bust the zipper."

I let out a tiny snarl in Trey's mind, and I sense his surprise as he realizes I'm there.

"Hello, dear," he says out loud.

"Shit," Demitri mutters. "Is she listening?"

"Apparently," Trey says.

"The last thing I need is La Diabla having an eating disorder, freaking out, and blowing up the school," Mr. Isley says and rubs his head.

Sighing, I grab my water bottle and hop off the stage. I gather my things and walk up the aisle.

"Melanie, come here a moment," Mr. Isley calls, appearing contrite.

I stop, winded. "Look, I don't know what's up, but something's been off for a while, and it's getting worse," I say. "I'm positive I'm not pregnant though. I appreciate the concern, Demitri."

Worry etches Demitri's face.

"Sir, I want your show about singing cats to be a hit," I tell Mr.

Isley. "Frankly, the show has no real storyline. It's purely spectacle, and dance is all that's gonna limp this shitty production into the audience's hearts. But I don't have it in me anymore, and apparently my butt's not shrinking. I suggest you replace me with Justine. She's the only other person my size." I roll my eyes and correct myself. "Well, the size I used to be." I pan a sardonic glare to Trey. "Are you planning to spend time with me at Mabel's tonight?"

"I can do dinner, but it'll be late." Trey exhales, frustrated. "I've got three bouncer interviews."

"At least someone's getting bounced," I snark, shooting a fierce glare at him.

"Maybe we just found the real issue," Demitri murmurs under his breath. He and Mr. Isley drift a few steps away, pretending to give us space.

Trey rubs his forehead. "I'm dead on my feet, Mel," he says. "It's not personal."

I lean to see Demitri and Mr. Isley. They're the ones who gossiped about me. They can hear this, too. "Apparently, I'm fat. So, it sure FEELS personal."

"Damn it, Melanie," Trey fumes. "I'm not the one who said you were fat. Frankly, I've found the little bit of extra weight to be jaw-dropping. You've been a hell of a distraction while I try to work late, and you wander around our room."

"Obviously," I retort sarcastically. "Actions speak louder than words." I whirl and head for the exit, adding harshly, "No action!"

Mr. Isley calls after me, "We still have an hour left, Melanie."

"Justine has an hour left. Replace my fat ass with her! I'm going home to eat snacks, just to piss you off."

CHAPTER 14

I get to Mama Mabel's and enter through the kitchen door from the garage. Passing into the parlor, I spot Adam holding court with a few of his friends who work at his custom motorcycle shop. The parlor looks like a frat house. Beer bottles and pizza boxes litter every surface, and the guys appear thoroughly settled in their seats.

I glance at my pager for the time. "Mama Mabel has a private bachelor party tonight. Guests arrive at six."

"It's only five," Adam says.

"Very good, Adam," I say while gesturing around the room. "Don't you figure it'll take time for you to clean up this disaster and clear out the smell of mechanic funk and pepperoni?"

"Mabel's staff is quick," Adam says. "The guys plan to leave at five-thirty."

I make eye contact with Constance, who's glaring in from the dining room door. Mama Mabel peeks around Constance and rolls her eyes.

I turn back to Adam and decide to be blunt. "I don't know what's gotten into you, but you've turned into a selfish piece of work. Get up, pull your head out of your ass, and clean up this disaster. The staff aren't here to wait on your pig-fest, Prince Charming."

I start to walk away.

"Your ex-girlfriend is a bitch," blurts one of Adam's friends.

I whip around and pull back my fist to clock him. His eyes widen, and Mama Mabel rushes across the room to grab my arm before I can swing.

"Ease down, Firebird," Mama Mabel says.

My dark-water side crackles to the surface, and I feel a giant energy bubble swelling in my chest.

Adam jumps up and throws a tight shield around me that his friends can't detect. He spins me to face him. "What is WRONG with you?" he demands. "He's an ass, but you can't kill him."

"What does that mean?" the jackass friend asks.

Adam turns to his friend. "Ever heard of La Diabla?" he asks.

"The Amazon who took down twelve guys?" his friend replies.

"Yeah, except she's tiny, and you just called her a bitch."

"This spinner is La Diabla?" His friend looks me over in disbelief.

Adam doesn't get the chance to reply, because Trey springs from where he's been leaning on the parlor doorjamb. "Did you just call my girl a spinner?" he snarls.

"What's a spinner?" Constance asks Mama Mabel.

"It's a rude term for a tiny female some moron deems a good time in bed," Mama Mabel informs, glaring at Adam's friend.

"What's your handle?" Trey demands as he storms toward Adam's friend.

Adam's friend looks confused.

"He's not in a club," Adam says. "His name's Jeff."

"I'm Shivers," Trey growls before he punches Jeff squarely in the jaw.

Jeff staggers left and topples an antique coffee table in the process.

"Damn, Trey, was that necessary?" Adam yells as he jumps between them.

"He called me a bitch too," I goad Trey.

I feel Trey's rage radiate unchecked through our connection. My stomach churns violently.

Constance sees me about to hurl and races ahead of me down the hall to my room. She pulls out her key ring and uses the master key to unlock the door. I dash in behind her, making it into the bathroom too late, losing it all over the tile floor.

I slam the door before Constance can see the gross mess. My cheeks burn with embarrassment. I grab a roll of paper towels from the cabinet and start wiping up. Halfway through this revolting process, I hear a knock at the bathroom door. "Now's really not the best time," I say.

The door opens, and Mama Mabel surveys the mess. "So I see," she says.

A blush creeps over my grayish complexion. I feel clammy with cold sweat. "I'm sorry, Mabel. I didn't mean to trash your bathroom."

"I'd never blame you for being sick, Melanie. It's an easy fix. Please stand up."

"I'll die if the staff has to clean this for me." I'm overcome with humiliation. "I'd rather do it myself."

Constance peers into the doorway behind Mabel and sprinkles some sawdust-like stuff on the mess. "You can either smear the goo around, or I can do it the quick way," Constance says. "This is a bar, Melanie. We see a staggering amount of vomit."

"Someone want to fill me in?" Trey asks from the bedroom.

Mama Mabel steps aside, and Trey comes into the bathroom.

I duck my head. Normally, I'm more polished than this. Here I am, standing in puke-splattered shoes.

Trey studies my face. I hear his thoughts through our connection. *'She looks awful. Her skin's waxy, and now that Demitri mentioned her weight gain, I see it's not in my head. She's a nervous wreck lately. I can't believe she ever burned bright enough to earn the nickname Firebird. She's pathetic. I'm sick of her "girl drama." Valerie's already driving me insane. I can't handle drama from Melanie too.'*

"Seriously, Trey?" I say as my heart clenches. "Why would you send that to me?"

Trey looks stunned and angry. "I didn't send you anything," he defends. "God, Melanie, I can't even have a private thought?"

"I wasn't digging in your mind." Tears start to spill down my cheeks. "I swear. That came down our connection line."

"Uh-huh," Trey mutters icily, turning to walk away. I know he's likely headed back to his office yet again.

I slip past Mama Mabel to grab my backpack. Deciding to skip my night at Mabel's, I leave through the parlor to go back to my parents' house.

CHAPTER 15

I'm nearly bowled over by a rush of mental chatter from the passing students when I step into the hallway. Random thoughts swirl intrusively through my head.

'Damn, she's hot,' a boy thinks about a cheerleader ahead of him.

'I hate this miserable job,' thinks a teacher walking by.

'I can't be late! I can't believe I forgot my paper in my locker,' scream the thoughts of a worried girl as she scurries by.

My back against the lockers, I desperately try to process this roaring flood of other people's thoughts. Another one of my meta-physical abilities has gone out of control. *Why is it happening?* I've never experienced random, irrelevant mind reading like this.

Scanning the throng, I spot Tanner. He's watching me with narrowed eyes. "Melanie, what's going on with you?" he asks as he approaches.

I inadvertently hear his thought *'I should've helped her long before this. Something's wrong. I'm gonna force Trey to talk to me. I can't believe he blew me off this morning.'*

"I need to get out of this crowd," I plead. "Please, can you talk to me?"

Tanner takes me by the arm and guides me through the double doors into the Commons. We cut left and move across Quad Two toward Smokers' Corner. We slip behind the tall hedges that hide us from the school buildings and sit down. The fourth-period tardy bell rings.

"I know you, Mel. Something's seriously wrong," Tanner says calmly.

"My abilities are totally wacked," I say, panicked. "Sometimes it's just me, but sometimes it's like something else takes over my mind. That day you found me with the glass shard? I got shoved to the back of my psyche and that—whatever it was—had control. If you hadn't come in, I might've died."

"You think it's a haunting?" Tanner asks.

"No idea. I need Trey to check, but he's avoiding me."

"What else? Let's list everything so we can tackle it," Tanner encourages.

Finally! Someone who'll help. "Thank you, Tanner." The floodgates open. "I have zero control over my link with Trey, plus I can't even connect half the time. My stomach's a heaving nightmare, and now I'm hearing random thoughts from people for no reason. I can't spot or hold my weight in dance rehearsals. I'm always dizzy. *And* Mr. Isley called me fat!"

"That's a lot!" Tanner lets loose an overwhelmed exhale. "Wait, he literally said you're fat?"

I nod, scowling. "He, Demitri, and Trey had a delightful discussion about how I suck, and I'll bust the zipper on my hideous costume. Naturally, that's the conversation my malfunctioning intuition chose to broadcast through Trey."

"I'll personally talk to them." Tanner sighs. "Even if Mr. Isley needed a new costume, there was a better way."

"Thank you for actually listening," I say, relieved and finally able to breathe. "Trey's been impossible. Last night, I picked up a savage thought from him, that he swears he didn't send. Everything about my metaphysical side is going haywire."

"We definitely don't want you going nuclear," Tanner says with concern. "You could level the city."

"Mr. Isley essentially said the same." I laugh shakily.

My phone rings. I fish it from my backpack and extend the antenna. "Hello?" I say quizzically. My phone never rings during school.

"Melanie, we just got a call from your stepfather's aunt," my mom's anxious voice sounds out. "Uncle Vincent isn't doing well. We need to head to Montana for a week. I spoke with Mabel, and she's fine with you staying there. Can you see if Trey can stay too, then call me back?"

I sigh. I'd wanted more time with Trey, but talk about bad timing. He's stayed at his parents' house so rarely lately that it'll cause a fight if I ask him to stay more at Mabel's this week.

"I'm sorry, Mom. How's Rich handling it?"

"He's really upset. His aunt and uncle practically raised him. This is scary, but hopefully Vincent pulls through."

"I'll talk to Trey and call you right back," I say, wanting to be supportive.

We hang up, and I fill Tanner in.

"We can test your link," he says. "Try reaching Trey mind-to-mind."

I close my eyes and focus. Typically, it's easy, but now I feel like I'm pushing through thick mud. The message fizzles before reaching Trey. I open my eyes. "No-go, Tanner. Something's very wrong."

"We'll figure it out. Let's track down Trey the old-fashioned way. You can pass on your mom's message, and I'll insist he hear you out."

He stands, offering a hand to help me up. As I stand, my head swirls with bright spots.

Tanner steadies me. "You've been doing dance rehearsals like this?"

I nod with my eyes shut, waiting for equilibrium. "It's all I can do not to faint every time," I say once everything stops spinning.

We cross the football field and walk toward the main buildings. The closer I get to the school, the louder the voices are in my head. By the time we reach the bungalows, I'm completely overwhelmed.

I shake my head. "I can't do this," I whisper. "It's like half the school is blathering in my mind."

"Hang tight, Mel," Tanner says. "We'll figure it out."

He puts an arm around me, and we head through the doors into the two-story building. We reach the Magnet office, and I'm visibly sweating. Tanner pulls me through the door and plunks me in a chair by Ms. Austin's desk. Ms. Austin isn't here, but that doesn't faze Tanner. He strides to Ms. G's office and leans against her doorjamb.

"Hey, Tanner," Ms. G says. "What's going on?"

"Ms. G," he says, flashing his charming grin. "I need a student request slip."

She emerges from her little office and knits her eyebrows when she sees me. Ms. G is our Magnet counselor. She's a short, ample woman with a no-nonsense jovial disposition. She's also incredibly intuitive. "Tanner, what's this about?" she asks. "And why does Melanie look gray?"

The mental jabber from the entire school suddenly clicks off in my head. I'm left sweaty and sick, but so relieved to have silence in my mind that I could cry.

Tanner turns on the charm. "You ask excellent questions, but that's no surprise."

"Cut the smooth talk, Tanner," Ms. G snips. "Out with it."

"All right." He sighs. "First, and least pressing, Melanie needs to discuss her unexpected living arrangements for the next week with Trey. Family emergency, standard stuff. Second, Trey's being a world-class douche-knocker, and he seems totally oblivious, dismissive even, about Melanie's need for support while we solve a topsy-turvy mystery. Third, we've got no clue what's wrong with Melanie. All I can surmise is that she knows something's wrong, Trey's doing backflips trying to ignore it, Mr. Isley thinks the problem is that she's fat, Demitri thinks she's pregnant, and I seem to be the only one who's noticed that there's an energy-leveling Firebird disaster on the horizon. Does that clear it up?"

"Thank you, Willy Wonka, for that riddled delight," she says dryly. "Go get a slip from Ms. Austin's top drawer. She's out with the stomach flu. Fill it out so you can get Trey. Do you know what class he's in?"

"Chem lab B," I interject.

"Don't snag more passes than the one for Trey," Ms. G calls after Tanner as he goes to Ms. Austin's desk. "I've met you, sneaky devil."

"You might want to make more copies," Tanner says. "I love collecting freebies."

"You ditch all the time without passes, so I don't know why you'd need one now," Ms. G replies as she helps me to her office.

"Because I delight in irritating you," he chirps back.

She laughs, motioning for me to take a seat behind the desk. "I just love that boy."

Tanner hooks an arm around the jamb and playfully swings on the doorjamb. Ms. G and I watch Tanner being Tanner and laugh.

"You're such an odd duck," Ms. G tells him. "Now scoot and fetch Trey."

"Fix Melanie, would ya?" he cheerfully requests as he leaves with a wave.

Ms. G turns to me. "All right, lay it out fast, so I have ammo if Trey resists."

I open up about my growing list of issues.

Ms. G is used to my weirdness by now. She listens intently. "First, I don't like Mr. Isley's weight comment. You're perfect as you are. Second, you're sure the pregnancy tests are negative?"

I nod and look down. This is the second time I've had a super personal pregnancy conversation at school in as many days. It's awkward.

"Okay, then that's not it." Ms. G sighs. "Frankly, it sounds like a nervous breakdown. You've had one before with dizzy spells and a racing heart. You ended up in the hospital."

"This feels totally different," I say.

"As a counselor, I know breakdowns well. They can vary."

Tanner returns with Trey, who looks annoyed.

Ms. G gestures to a chair. "Sit, Trey. Tanner, grab another seat."

Trey huffs as they settle into the small office.

"Why are you irritated already, Trey?" Ms. G asks. "We haven't begun."

Trey slumps. "I was reviewing for a chem test when Tanner yanked me out. I have no time to study, thanks to my work schedule. This better be good, Melanie."

I'm disappointed by Trey's less than receptive attitude.

Tanner snaps surprised eyes at Trey. "And that right there is part of the problem. Let me tell you a few things. I love Melanie, and I can see something's big-time wrong."

Trey glares at Tanner. "Did you people drag me here to tell me that you and Melanie are having an affair?"

"Yes, exactly," Tanner mocks. His expression morphs radiantly.

"Melanie's dark side has apparently melted your brain." He stands and swivels his right hip into an exaggerated stance. "We didn't come to Ms. G because Melanie's body is whirling off into dizzy panic, or because her metaphysical side might blow up half the city. No, no!" He waggles his finger at Trey, and I grin.

"Nor did we come here to discuss the fact that her abilities, energy, and metaphysical side are a complete topsy turvy disaster," Tanner continues. "Pay no mind to the fact that Melanie's abilities are ever-developing. What happens if she loses her energetic shit, you ask? If she farts in third period, she might level all of Hollywood."

Ms. G and I crack up, and even pissy Trey can't keep a straight face.

"Nope! We came here to let Melanie's soulmate," Tanner glances Ms. G's way, "who, I might add is one evil mother-freaker, know that I've decided to give up the sweetest fiancée a guy could ask for." He dramatically pauses, switching hips and hitting a different supermodel-esq pose. "Why would I do that, you curiously demand? Well, I'll tell you! I got sick of my gorgeous fiancée who smells like cotton candy and showers me with romance and poems. Threw that heaven right straight out the window because I want something reeeaaal edgy, now. Yup! My prime desire in life is to crawl into Melanie's backseat while her dark side revs and see what it's like to get tantrically murdered by the Queen of the Underworld while I pop like warm champagne."

Trey cracks up, rubbing his tired eyes. Ms. G's expression comically morphs into a bizarre mixture of shock and amusement.

I double over laughing from the look on her face, and the action makes my head spin. A new round of cold sweats hits, and my skin goes ashen and waxy. My forehead beads wet, and my eyes glaze a touch as I sit up and will my stomach to settle.

Tanner aims a disapproving glare at Trey. "Really, Trey? First, we're best friends, and I wouldn't do you like that. Second, I'm not insane enough to even THINK about locking myself in an amorous situation with Melanie. I don't like to spontaneously combust, and I've heard enough details from you and Adam that I ain't going there."

"I apologize," Trey says. "I'm an idiot."

"I just learned more about you than I'd expected," Ms. G says to me.

I blush crimson. "For the record, I can do the calm, sweet thing like Finley does," I tell Tanner.

Trey snorts. "When? I still have a Texas-sized bruise from two weeks ago!"

I throw him an exasperated look. "You hush. You're just as bad." I huff. "We're singlehandedly keeping the drywall guy busy at Mabel's."

Trey looks amused. "Now you hush."

Ms. G rolls her eyes. "Every new detail I learn about you two leaves me wondering if I should call the police or a priest."

Trey closes his eyes, taking a deep, grounding breath. "What is it, Melanie?"

Now that I have his attention, I rush to explain myself. "As unfortunate as the circumstances are that led to it, I'm going to be staying at Mabel's for the next week. Can you be there?"

Trey tips his head back. "You have to be kidding! I specifically scheduled work every night that you weren't supposed to be there. No offense, Melanie, but I've got so much to do that I'm not thrilled with the added pressure of having you there every night, needing to talk. I'm drowning in responsibilities."

My phone rings. I answer, knowing it's my mom. "Sorry, Mom. Took a bit to pull Trey from class."

"Why not just send him a mental message?" she asks.

I don't want to get into all that. "I'll stay at Mabel's. You two be safe going to Montana."

We say our goodbyes.

"Look, can you set aside your annoyance and exhaustion?" Tanner gently asks Trey after I hang up.

Trey glares at him, but Tanner stands firm. Trey shuts his eyes and takes a deep breath to calm himself. He opens his eyes.

Tanner guides him. "Now truly look at Melanie."

Trey turns to face me. His brow furrows as he really studies me.

"Try tapping my energy," I whisper.

He tries. "I can't," he says. "You're blocking me again."

I shake my head. "I swear I'm not. Push through it."

"We agreed never to force our way in," Trey reminds me.

"I'm *telling* you to."

When Trey shuts his eyes, I feel pressure in my psyche. An invisible barrier pops like a bubble, and a strange swirl of energy whips through me before star-bursting in my gut.

"Trey, my stomach."

He sets his hands on my body. His eyes go blank as he "looks" internally. A moment later, he grabs my phone from me and dials. Then he rests his hand on my stomach again, re-scanning. He shakes his head, clearly puzzled.

Someone on the other end picks up.

"Mabel, it's Trey," he says. "Can you schedule Melanie with Dr. Fontaine ASAP?" He listens, then continues, "When does he finish with Destiny? . . . Right. We'll leave soon. I need Bear to check one thing first." He listens again. "No, she's not okay, and I've been oblivious. Yeah. Love you too. Bye." He hangs up.

"What's going on, Trey?" Ms. G asks.

"No offense, Ms. G, but it'll sound crazy," Trey says. "We've shared enough weirdness for one day."

"I suspect a nervous breakdown," Ms. G offers.

"I suspect possession," Trey replies.

My jaw drops as Trey meets my eyes.

CHAPTER 16

Trey pulls into Mama Mabel's garage right behind me, quickly getting out of the car. Mama Mabel comes through the door from the kitchen to meet us.

"Dr. Fontaine's just about done with Destiny," she announces. "She has that stomach bug that's going around, and I'm starting to wonder if Melanie might have it too. You spend a lot of time together."

"This is bigger than the stomach flu," Trey says firmly.

"Your color's been getting worse lately," she says as she studies me. She ushers us inside.

"Thank goodness," Adam says to Mabel as he pops out into the hallway from his room. "Valerie needs to see Dr. Fontaine right after Destiny."

"Valerie can wait," Trey snaps. "Melanie's next."

"Valerie's having contractions again," Adam retorts. "That takes priority."

"Is Melanie with Trey?" Valerie calls out from the room

"Yes," I say, already annoyed.

"Oh good!" Valerie chirps happily. "Melanie, can you get me

one of those little snack cakes you like from the kitchen? They're my new favorite."

"You have *got* to be kidding," I mutter. I roll my eyes and head down the hall toward the kitchen.

"Mabel, we need to talk," Trey says as I walk away.

I reach the pantry and inspect my assigned shelf. Each resident here has their own space. It appears that Valerie's cleared out nearly all of my snack cakes. Only one remains. I check my case of fizzy water, discovering that it's empty.

"Melanie, you don't look so good," Constance says as she walks into the kitchen.

"I feel terrible, but I'm seeing Dr. Fontaine in a few minutes," I inform her. "Also, Valerie took all my snacks and the fizzy water that keeps my stomach from flip-flopping. Can you please add those to the grocery list?"

"Valerie's about to push me over the edge," Constance huffs. "She won't follow protocols and keeps sending whoever walks by to fetch something for her. The staff have taken to using the back hallways just to avoid passing her room. She leaves the door open to call them in."

"She's impossible," I say, commiserating.

"Go lie down. I'll send someone for your fizzy water now, so you'll have it soon," Constance says.

"Don't worry about me. I appreciate it, though." I head back through the dining room with the lone snack cake. I toss it at Adam. "Your princess cleaned me out. Put her stuff on your request list, please."

"Rude much?" Adam remarks.

I throw Trey a frustrated look.

Apparently, he's also had a gut full. "You people are incredibly inconsiderate," he snarls. "Stay out of our pantry shelf, and tell your buddies they aren't welcome here anymore. Also, from now on, fetch your wife's junk food yourself."

"Speaking of my friends," Adam barks, gearing up for a fight. "You kicked them out after you slugged Jeff. Don't ever say 'I'm taking out the trash' about my friends again."

"Won't be a problem anymore, because they aren't coming back," Trey growls.

"All right, simmer down," Mama Mabel says stepping between them.

"Hey, Melanie?" Valerie calls out from her room. "Can you grab my blanket from the parlor? I forgot it there."

Exasperated, I head to the parlor. I find Valerie's blanket on my and Trey's favorite love seat surrounded by empty snack wrappers, an empty water bottle, a coffee mug, and a stack of fashion magazines. I pick up the blanket and notice a hot cocoa stain on the antique velvet cushion.

Mama Mabel arrives by my side. She surveys the mess and takes the blanket from my hand. "Don't touch a thing. I'll handle this." She marches back toward the hallway, and I hear her say, "Adam, come here. Now."

I watch through the doorway as Dr. Fontaine steps out of Destiny's room. "Who's next, Mabel?" the doctor asks.

"Valerie. She's having contractions again," Mabel says. "But please don't leave till you see Melanie. She was supposed to be next."

The doctor steers Adam into their room and shuts the door behind them.

Mama Mabel dumps Valerie's blanket by the door, but I realize she didn't get a chance to make Adam clean up the parlor. I return to the room and bend to pick up Valerie's trash. Dizziness strikes hard. I grab the love seat's carved wooden arm when my knees buckle. Mabel and Trey followed me to the parlor, and Trey gathers me against his chest to steady me.

"You have *got* to be kidding," Trey says as he surveys Valerie's catastrophe. He reaches, pushing the intercom button. "Constance, can we get you in the parlor, please?"

"Babe, I've got it," I say quietly. "Valerie's been running Constance ragged."

Another wave of dizziness hits, and Trey keeps me from collapsing. I hear him think, *'I really messed up. She's in worse shape than I ever realized.'*

Hope stirs that he finally understands.

"Constance took off to restock the entire pantry. Sapphire found all her protein bars missing and lost it a few minutes ago," Randall, our chef, announces as he pokes his head into the room.

"This isn't working," Mama Mabel mutters. She looks at me. "I'll clean up. Go lie down."

"Yet again, we can't talk to you because of Valerie's mess. Literally, this time," Trey points out.

"I'll be in soon. I promise." Mabel glances up from collecting the wrappers from the floor to give Trey an apologetic look.

Trey scoops me up and carries me to our room. He leaves the door open for Dr. Fontaine and sets me gently on the bed. I curl up, feeling clammy.

Trey closes his eyes, and I feel him probing our connection.

"The blockage is back," he mutters.

I groan hopelessly.

Mama Mabel enters, starting to close the door.

"Don't shut it," Trey says. "I don't want to risk missing the doctor. With Melanie's luck lately, I'm not taking chances."

"How long has this been happening?" Mabel asks, surveying my weakened state.

"Two months," Trey answers, "but it's gotten way worse."

"Damn, Melanie!" Mabel exclaims. "Why didn't you tell me sooner?"

I sense waves of guilt from Trey and Mabel.

"First, I want you to know how grateful I am for this job, room and board, and everything you do for us, Mabel," Trey says. "You're unbelievably generous."

"But?" she prompts.

"But I'm working myself to death," Trey says, nodding at me. "Between school, baseball, and this job, I have zero time left. I haven't touched Melanie in two weeks."

"With your connection, that's surprising," Mabel says.

"And I haven't had time to see how sick she is," Trey laments. "She kept trying to talk to me, but I had no downtime. I knew it would be an all-night discussion, and I was ducking it because I couldn't spare the hours or handle an argument."

"This can be fixed," Mabel assures him. "You're not supposed to be the bouncer on our open nights. How's hiring going?"

"All my applicants have felony convictions or can't be trusted," Trey mutters.

"Doctor says Valerie just has indigestion," Adam says as he busts into the room uninvited.

Shocking. When you devour everyone's snacks, you pay the price. I can't help but let out a loud laugh, and Adam glares at me.

"She's chatting with the doctor," he says. "As often as she sees him lately, they've become friends. He'll be in eventually."

I stare at Trey, annoyed that Valerie's still monopolizing the doctor when I need him.

"Adam, I need a favor," Mabel says.

"Sure, what?"

"Melanie's sick, and Trey needs the night off to help her. I need you to act as bouncer tonight," Mabel says.

"No can do," Adam responds. "I'm taking Valerie to Jeff's birthday bash in Manhattan Beach. She finally feels up to going out."

"If she's feeling so marvelous, why did she need to jump ahead of me on the doctor list?" I snap from the bed.

"We were worried it was contractions." Adam shrugs. "Sorry, Mel."

Adam scoots past as Dr. Fontaine enters and looks worried when he sees me on the bed. "List your symptoms," he orders.

I give him the entire rundown, including my metaphysical concerns. He's dealt with me enough that the weird stuff barely fazes him now.

"Ms. G, the school counselor, thinks Mel's having a breakdown. Demitri thinks she's pregnant. I think it might be possession," Trey says.

"What?" Mabel exclaims.

I startle, unintentionally sending a swirl of frantic energy shooting around the room like invisible fireflies.

"What was that?" Trey asks.

I shake my head, baffled but glad he felt it too.

"Lie flat," Dr. Fontaine instructs.

I roll onto my back. He palpates my abdomen, which is uncomfortable but bearable.

"Cancer is unlikely," he says. Noticing Trey and Mabel's alarm, he hastens to add, "She's only sixteen. Rare, but possible. Pregnancy is a solid guess, though."

I mention the pile of negative pregnancy tests.

"Huh," the doctor says. "In that case, let's confirm you aren't pregnant or anemic. I'll test your blood cell counts, which will eliminate a bunch of issues if it's normal." He takes supplies from his bag and draws a vial of blood. "I'll phone shortly with results.

I'm running the labs myself," he says as he packs up his things.

After the doctor leaves, Trey checks his watch, picks up the phone on the nightstand, and dials Arch Terani, who the Misfits have always thought of as our unofficial leader. Trey waits impatiently for an answer. "Arch, it's Trey," I hear him say. "I need a favor. Paid, of course." He listens, then asks, "You free tonight? Perfect. I need a bouncer at Mabel's. Thursdays are usually light, but we pay thirty-five dollars an hour, plus hazard pay if there's trouble." He pauses, listening, then chuckles. "Yes, I'm serious. Mabel pays well. Really? That's great. If you can do Thursday and Saturday nights, even better. I'll get the paperwork ready, and you can sign when you get here at six. Awesome, you're hired. Thanks, Arch." He hangs up.

Mabel nods approval. "Excellent solution, Trey. Talk to Marcus and Tanner too. I'll waive the twenty-one-plus rule for them. Your friends are all level-headed and can handle trouble."

Constance appears with a fresh can of fizzy water. She hands it to me and turns to Mabel. "Candice just quit. Valerie snapped her fingers at her—twice, wanting hot cocoa. Candice was one of our best."

"That's the second person this week," Mabel moans, clearly upset. "I'll personally call Candice and apologize. This is unacceptable." She looks to me. "You were right about Valerie."

"Told you so," I halfheartedly whisper, but it lacks gusto.

Constance and Mabel leave, quietly closing the door.

"What do we do?" Trey asks.

"I was hoping you might have a clue," I say.

"I got nothing."

I close my eyes, defeated. "Then go get Arch's paperwork ready and see if you can get some work done. I need a shower."

"I'll be quick." He exits, closing the door behind him.

In the bathroom, I strip down and step into the lukewarm shower stream. I sink to the tiled floor, letting the water flow down my back until it runs cold. Somehow, that temperature helps me. When I finally stand up, I'm not dizzy. I realize that the calmer I stay, the fewer symptoms I have. It may help me get through whatever this is.

I dry off with a red towel and hang it up, trying not to get overheated. I close my eyes and send, *"Trey, I figured out something."*

He starts in surprise, obviously hearing me mind-to-mind. Through his eyes, I see he's labeling some folders for Arch, Tanner, and Marcus.

"All three?" I send hopefully.

"Yes, they're thrilled. They'll make more here in a night or two a week than at their current part-time jobs," he sends. *"You got through to me telepathically."*

"Yep. I don't know what's going on, but I learned a few tricks. If I stay calm and my body doesn't heat up, I can do this."

Trey's relief floods the link. *"I missed you. It's been so quiet in my head,"* he sends.

"I haven't been able to talk to you that way more than a few times in a month. You're just noticing?"

Guilt rolls through our connection. *"I've been buried under work. I'm sorry."* His emotional vibe shifts flirtatiously. *"Just out of the shower, huh?"*

I giggle in our shared thoughts and feel him smile.

"So . . . if you feel better, mind looking in the mirror for me?" he sends.

I send a seductive vibe back. Maybe I'm finally getting the old Trey back again.

I step out of the bathroom and into the bedroom. My mouth

falls open and my heart rate soars, severing my link to Trey, when I see two people on my bed. "What are you doing in my room, Adam?" I shriek. I scramble to cover up with both arms, but there's only so much I can hide. I'm small, yet curvy, and the two intruders are already ogling me. Fear and adrenaline merge, making my legs so weak that I can't even retreat to the bathroom.

A friend of Adam's, someone I've never met, lounges on my pillow and wipes neon orange cheesy poof dust onto my black velvet bedspread. "Man, I love it here," he boasts with a grin. "Hot naked chicks all over. How much to rent this one for the night?"

Trey bursts into the room, quickly sizes up the situation, and turns deadly eyes on Adam. "What the hell are you doing here with my naked girl?"

Mama Mabel, Tanner, and Arch rush in, drawn by Trey's shouting. My head drops as my audience multiplies, embarrassment washing over me in a fresh wave of cold sweat. My knees start trembling again.

"Whoa," Tanner says, wincing. "Didn't see that coming. Sorry, Mel. Somehow I always see more of you than intended."

Arch stares at the floor and snaps his fingers at the intruder. "Up and out. Now," he barks.

Adam's friend ignores Arch, still eyeing me like a sleazeball.

Tanner hustles to my closet, grabs my red satin robe, and blocks me from the guy's view while tactfully averting his own eyes. He helps me into the robe when he realizes how badly I'm shaking.

Mama Mabel scans the room with ice in her gaze. "Adam, why are you in here, and who the hell is he?" She jabs a finger at the friend.

He licks the orange gunk off his fingers, then wipes them on his dirty jeans, extending his hand to Mabel. "Dave. Pleased to meet you."

"Sorry," Adam says, sheepishly. "I needed to borrow a dress shirt. I didn't know Melanie was showering."

"Trey's shirt looks insane on you," Tanner says, eying Adam up and down. "He's two sizes smaller."

"Valerie likes me in tight shirts," Adam gossips with a smirk. "This is our first date night in months, and I wanted to surprise her."

"Can we focus on the bigger problem here?" I say, exasperated. My heart pounds. My energy surges in a swirling chaos, and I test my link with Trey. Gone again. I realize this humiliating intrusion has undone any progress I'd just made.

"Oh, by the way," Adam says, while checking his hair in the dresser mirror, "Dr. Fontaine called. Your white blood cell count is fine."

I try to wrap my mind around layer after layer of intrusions that Adam's managed within mere minutes. "You talked to my doctor and announced my results in front of a crowd?" I ask, aghast.

Mama Mabel's face twists with a rage I've never seen from her. "GET THE HELL OUT OF MY HOME AND NEVER COME BACK," she bellows at Dave. She lunges forward, and Dave scrambles.

Arch and Tanner grab him by the armpits and haul him out.

"How did you get in here?" Mabel demands as she whirls to challenge Adam.

"Some new staff chick let me in."

"Did you get permission from Melanie or Trey?" Mabel barks. "Obviously not, since Melanie was naked and had no clue you were here. SHE SHOULD BE SAFE AND COMFORTABLE DOING THAT IN HER OWN ROOM!"

"The staff lady didn't say no," Adam mumbles, clearly put off.

"First, her name is Monica. She started two hours ago and isn't acquainted with the rules yet. Second, you *do* know them."

Tanner and Arch return.

"This job is awesome!" Arch crows happily. "Been here five minutes and already got to punch a guy."

"Right? I'm stoked," Tanner agrees. He goes to retrieve some toilet paper from my bathroom. He kneels by me, tipping my head back to help with my bloody nose.

"Sorry, Melanie," Trey says. "I didn't know this was happening or I'd have helped you." He turns to Mabel. "Before she walked in on Adam and his buddy soiling our sanctuary, she'd stabilized enough to talk to me telepathically, which hasn't happened more than a few times this month."

"How did you intercept a call from Melanie's doctor?" Mabel asks Adam.

"It rang," he says gesturing to the phone on Trey's nightstand.

The fury that flares from Trey doubles me over as my energy tornadoes. My nose bleeds harder, and I feel a surge of panic that's weirdly disconnected from me, like something else is fueling it.

"Chill, bud," Tanner warns, looking up at Trey from where he kneels in front of me. "When Mabel got mad, Melanie got sicker, and now your anger's making it worse. The more chaos she senses, the worse her symptoms seem to get."

"I realized in the shower that if I stay completely calm, I can mentally communicate with Trey again. I also don't get dizzy," I explain.

Trey tamps down his rage. "That's our personal phone line," Trey says quietly to Adam. "I'm not happy the doctor gave her private medical results to anyone else. I believe this warrants a discussion with him."

"Sorry." Adam seems worried, likely because Dr. Fontaine deals with Valerie constantly these days. "I answered the phone, and he never asked who I was. Probably assumed it was you."

"Rightfully so, considering that no one should answer that phone but Trey and Melanie. Don't you get that?" Mabel says. She keeps her voice calm for my sake.

I stand unsteadily. "I'm leaving. I have to go home." I pivot to Trey. "Not even our room is safe now."

"No," Trey says firmly. "Adam, get out. Don't ever come back. We're done."

Adam tries to argue, but Mabel cuts him off. "Take off Trey's dress shirt—NOW."

Adam grudgingly does.

She points at the closet. "Hang it back where you found it," she orders.

Adam complies.

Mabel gestures to the bed. "You owe them a new bedspread. This one is covered in greasy orange prints from your filthy friend. Take it off and get a clean, spare bedspread from the linen closet."

Adam rolls his eyes, which makes Mabel's rage spike again. I whimper as another round of dizziness strikes.

"DO IT," Mabel roars.

Adam mutters curses under his breath as he pulls the dirty bedspread off the bed, marches into the bathroom, and returns with the silver bedspread. He fluffs it over the bed.

"Get out. Leave Trey and Melanie alone," Mabel orders with finality.

He leaves, clearly sour, and Arch and Tanner share a look.

"What a douche-nugget," Tanner flamboyantly says.

We all laugh as Tanner's humor lifts the tension. I catch a glimpse of my disastrous condition in the mirror. "I need to clean up again," I mutter.

CHAPTER 17

Eventually, I fall asleep with Trey snuggled against my back. We agreed to tackle everything in the morning with clearer heads. I drift off on a wave of strange dreams. Colors in a lighter hue—pink, orange, lavender, blue—all swirl around me in watery silence as I float. It's peaceful.

A fist pounding on our door wakes me.

"Damn it, what now?" Trey mumbles, rubbing the back of my head as I sit up. "Go back to sleep. That warm rainbow water was nice."

He shoves the covers off and gets up.

"You saw my dream?" I ask.

He nods while crossing to the monitor. "I busted through that weird barrier again to see if I could find clues. Are you mad?"

"Relieved. I need your help, so do that whenever you can. You have my permission."

Trey checks the monitor. "Incoming. It's Arch."

He opens the door, and Arch walks in.

"Massive brawl," Arch informs, clipped. "Two biker clubs showed up, and they apparently hate each other."

Trey snatches up a shirt and follows Arch out, closing the door behind him.

I push back the covers and move to the monitor just in time to see a huge guy slam into our door. The wall shakes. Trey appears in the camera's view, and the giant nails him with a right hook to the eye.

Suddenly, my dark-water side flares, unhindered. I roll my neck, feeling the fierce energy that I've missed so badly. Newly revived, I go to the closet and grab tight black leggings that lace up the sides. I slide them on and yank on my black leather Hellcats vest over the tank I slept in. I pull on my heeled motorcycle boots and add bright-red lipstick from the dresser. I check my reflection. I look closer to the old me than I have in months.

I stride out to fix this. Arriving in the parlor, I see bikers punching each other as furniture and glasses crash to the floor with shatters and thumps.

Gathering my renewed energy, I sense some strange shield snap over me that I didn't conjure. I roll with it, projecting a mental directive that booms like a struck tuning fork. *"STOP!"* My non-corporeal voice bounces against the walls.

Everyone freezes mid-fight. A couple of men pause mid-punch, others stop mid-roll on the floor. All eyes turn to me.

"Enough!" I growl.

"Who does this chick think she is?" a big guy demands.

"She's La Diabla," Arch says. "And you idiots just woke her up."

Surprise ripples through the crowd.

"I thought you'd be bigger," another biker says.

"That's what your bimbo said last night," I retort with a scornful look.

Bikers all around the room crack up, and Trey tips his head back, roaring with laughter.

I sweep my gaze over them. "Next idiot who wakes me faces a fiery death in the parking lot," I warn.

Brows shoot up, and some of the bikers actually cower.

I cock my hip. "So if I let you stay, can you be good boys and behave?"

They nod.

I wave to the bartender. "A round on me . . . if these toddlers keep it civil."

"Thanks, Ms. Diabla," one pipes.

Tension leaves the room in a whoosh. "Sorry, Ms. Diabla," the crowd says in a chorus.

Trey bursts out laughing.

I shoot everyone a glare over my shoulder and march back to our room. As soon as I sink onto the bed, I start shaking uncontrollably again, and my nose bleeds.

Trey enters. "Tell me why your dark-water side suddenly rose," he says, baffled. "You haven't felt it in a month."

He sees my face and grabs tissues from the box. He kneels to tip my head back and press the tissues to my nose. "Did the fight cause it to emerge again?"

"Yes," I say in an unsteady voice. "I saw you get punched on the monitor. Instantly, my dark-water energy came roaring back. Then it vanished again. And Trey, when I shouted at them, a shield that wasn't mine engulfed me."

Trey's eyes widen.

CHAPTER 18

I pull up to the open garage. Adam has a pile of motorcycle parts scattered all over my parking spot. I glare past my sweeping windshield wipers, but Adam does little more than glance up at me. I pull the gearshift into reverse. My tires screech as I yank the steering wheel to the side and circle to face the parking lot.

I park in a spot, put my head on the steering wheel, and scream my frustration. It's already been a horrible day. Mr. Isley insisted that I not only attend rehearsal, but that I also stay an extra hour after everyone else left to guide Justine through my part. So, there I stood trying to coach her through the duet with Demitri. She was a gangly mess, an impressive feat given how tiny and un-gangly she is. I close my eyes, and the memory bubbles up, the one of her flopping and flailing about while Demitri fought not to drop her.

I grab my backpack and open my car door. Pelted by the deluge of pouring rain, I run for the open garage. I'm winded and soaked through to my soul by the time I cross the threshold. My head spins, and my knees shake from the physical exertion and my overwhelming frustration.

Crouched near the rear wheel of the motorcycle, Adam looks up from his work. "Sorry, Mel. A client's pushing for his completed motorcycle, and I'm on a time crunch. I planned to work on it in the parking lot, but the rain started."

My knees give out and I collapse onto a slick brown liquid that I'm guessing is motorcycle oil on the floor.

"Very dramatic, Melanie," Adam condescends.

A new wave of anger expands in my chest. It's too much so quickly after my frustration when I pulled up. My stomach heaves, and I throw up on the floor.

Adam stands quickly and crosses to the intercom speaker on the wall. He pushes a button. "Trey, come get Melanie from the garage." He gives me an irritable side-eye. "Bring a cleanup crew. I don't have time for this."

I slump on my side and grip my aching stomach. Trey rushes through the door and sees me, soaking wet and curled around a vomit puddle. He looks over the motorcycle parts in my parking spot and grits his teeth.

"So help me GOD," he snarls at Adam, "if I find out Melanie just parked in the parking lot and ran through the rain, I'll beat you into next Sunday."

Mama Mabel rushes through the door with Constance quick on her heels as Trey levels Adam with his threat. She surveys the situation but doesn't get a chance to say anything.

"It's them or us," Trey bellows at Mama Mabel.

Mama Mabel radiates shock at Trey's harsh tone. When it comes to her, he's usually polite to a fault.

"Baby, wait here," Trey instructs me. He pulls his keys from his pocket and dashes through the garage door into the parking lot.

We hear the rumble of his muscle car.

He pulls up with the passenger side door as close to the open garage door as possible. He rushes back in, soaking wet. He glares at Adam one more time before slinging my backpack on his shoulder and kneeling next to me. He brushes my wet hair from my face. "We're going to your parents' house," he says. "They're still out of town, and I'm going to take care of you there. We can't deal with this insanity anymore."

"Please get me out of here." I sob so hard that I can't breathe. I've felt sick longer than I can handle.

Trey scoops me up. "If this is how it's going to be here, then I need to put in my resignation," he says to Mabel.

Before Trey can tuck me into the car, Darren and Bear run through the open garage door. They're sopping wet, and Bear shakes the water off his head like a dog.

"Perfect," Bear says as he focuses on me. "I need to speak with Melanie."

"Why?" Trey asks.

"After a lengthy discussion with Adam and Valerie, Darren and I would like to discuss the negativity that Melanie's displayed toward them," Bear says. "Valerie's going through a lot, and we think we can help."

Trey's mouth drops open while I try to wrap my mind around what I just heard.

"I think we might only have half the story, Bear," Darren says placing a hand on Bear's arm, after glancing at the vomit puddle.

Bear takes stock of everything and everyone in the garage with more attention to the details. He turns to Adam. "Is Melanie still sick?"

Adam rolls his eyes. "Melanie's always having issues. She's got it out for Valerie, and being sick is no excuse."

"I'm moving Melanie and me out," Trey barks. Then he looks to me and softens his tone. "You're going to get wet for a minute."

Darren bolts ahead of us and opens the passenger door.

When Trey rushes out, we're pelted by the pounding rain. He places me in my seat. "Thank you, Darren," he says as he closes the door.

I watch through the rain-covered window as Darren and Trey exchange words. Darren rushes back into the garage, and Trey runs around the back of the car, hops in the driver's side, and slams the door. He reaches into the back seat to grab a flannel.

I rest my head on the headrest and breathe in the scent of diesel fumes, leather seats, and Trey's cologne. This helps clear my head. From the first time he took me on a date, it always smelled like home in Trey's car. Now that he's so busy, and I have my own car, I'm rarely in here.

I exhale as Trey tries to dry me off with the flannel. It does no good because my clothes are soaked. His caring enough to try means a lot, though. I ground and center my insanely erratic energy before sending it down and out like an internal exhale. My frustration and upset dissolve on a strange wave of clarity. I send my thoughts through our mind-to-mind connection, *"I love you so much, Trey. I need you back. I need to be a priority. I can't handle the distance."*

Trey's mouth drops open, and he's bowled over by the emotion behind my mental words. "My priorities got screwed up," he admits.

Bear chooses that moment to knock on my passenger window.

Trey shakes his head at Bear as he pulls away from Mabel's. "Tonight, it's just me and you," he says. "I promise."

― ―

We pull up to my parents' dark house, and with a twinge of guilt, I realize how much I miss them. They're still in Montana with Rich's uncle.

Trey grabs my backpack and puts it over his shoulder. The rain has slowed to a gentle sprinkle. "Sit tight," he says. "I'm going to get you."

I watch him round the back of the car and take my house keys from the front pouch of my backpack. He opens my car door and picks me up, closing the door with his foot. He carries me up the brick front walkway and unlocks the front door. The familiarity of my house makes my entire body relax. I curl up against Trey and feel him glance down at me. He radiates calm through our connection.

He closes and locks the door but doesn't turn on any lights. He heads through the hall and sets me on my feet in the bathroom that's lit softly by moonlight coming through the window. He turns on the water and plugs the bathtub. I start to undress but he takes my hands and puts them at my sides. He undresses me and gets my toothbrush prepped. He hands it to me and leaves briefly, coming back with two candles that my mom keeps in a kitchen cabinet. He lights them and sets them on the counter of the little brown-and-peach bathroom.

I finish brushing my teeth and turn to find Trey undressed. Silently, he takes a hair tie off my wrist and turns me around to face the mirror. He digs in a drawer and pulls out a hairbrush that he runs slowly through my knotted wet hair. I close my eyes, completely content for the first time in a month.

Trey carefully twists my hair into a bun and drapes his arms over my shoulders, staring into my eyes in the mirror over the sink. He continues to say nothing, but his expression speaks volumes. He rests his forehead on the base of my neck and runs his hands down my sides and around my front. I gasp. His hands stop on my stomach, and I feel him energetically searching. After a long moment, he reaches up, putting his hand on my forehead and guides my head back to rest on his shoulder. He runs his fingertips from my forehead to my chin with a featherlight touch. My entire body relaxes, and my head lolls to the side. This is hands down the most romantic interaction we've ever had. The silence should be odd, but we work well in silence together.

With zero tension, I'm able to send through our connection, *"I love when you run your fingers down my face."*

"I know you do," he replies. His mental voice is grave with concern. He steps into the bathtub and pulls me gently toward him. He settles into the water. I step in and sit down, resting my back against his chest. The water is the exact right temperature.

Trey places his hand on my forehead and slowly shifts my head to fall to the side. His hands slide down my front and settle over my stomach again. He sends a steady calm hum through his hands into my abdomen, and the barrier that isn't mine gently slips away. With that same buzzy firefly feeling from before, a star bursts in my gut.

Trey deeply inhales slowly, and I inhale with him. We exhale together.

"Baby, I'm positive you're pregnant," Trey whispers.

I inhale sharply with panic gripping my chest.

"Shhhh. Don't panic," Trey whispers. "Listen to me. We'll be okay. I don't know why the tests are coming up negative, but we need to get you to a gynecologist who can check for us."

"How sure are you?" I whisper.

"One hundred percent," he calmly responds.

"Mabel's a midwife. Can we ask her?"

"It's worth a shot. You should also ask Adam if he'll drop the soulmate connection blockage and check you. I need to know what he thinks. I think having his side of our trio will balance you enough to find energetic equilibrium. When he's not being a jackass, he's damn good at knowing what's wrong with you."

"What do we do? We can't raise a baby," I fluster out.

"Why?"

"We're young."

"In most ways, we're the oldest people I know, Melanie."

"How could I be pregnant?" I panic. "I never miss my pills."

Trey radiates calm. "With what we have? Honestly, I'm surprised it took this long. There's only so much that pills can do. Now that I have some hindsight, I realize I should have been more careful on my end of that responsibility."

Suddenly, oddly, the worried tension slips away, taken by something I don't understand. Completely content, I rest limply against Trey. We lie there for a long while.

Trey's cheek rests against my temple, and I feel him smile. "I know that during the hostage takeover so long ago, you saw our kids for the first time."

I softly gasp. "The oldest . . ."

"We get to meet her," Trey murmurs as his hand lays to rest on my stomach.

I bring up that premonition of our three kids and study her walking onto a movie set in a red dress. She's holding a script. I freeze the memory on the teenage girl and tap-tap on the soulmate connection line with Trey. With me this calm, he's able to channel in. Together, we study her stoic expression and pretty face. She's a brunette with a tiny frame, but there's old soul wisdom that shines through her contemplative brown eyes.

"How old do you think she is in that premonition?" Trey asks.

"Probably about my age," I reply as I open my eyes. "Sixteen."

I ponder my feelings on the matter. "I wish we had more time before we dive into this, but seeing that memory again helps."

"She's perfect," Trey marvels. "We can do this."

He sounds so certain, it makes me more comfortable with the idea. "What do we do now?" I ask.

"We dry off and go to bed."

I stand, and he hauls himself up from the water. He pulls the drain plug and grabs a towel to dry me off carefully. He dries himself off and drops the towel on the floor. He picks me up, and I wrap my legs around his waist, before blowing out the candles. Trey carries me into my bedroom and closes the door.

"We're the only ones here," I remind him, chuckling.

"Force of habit." He laughs.

Trey sets me down on the bed. He climbs under the covers after I scoot over to make room for him. My bed is a lot smaller than we're used to. He lies on his side, facing me.

"I don't want you to worry about anything tonight. We're going to figure this out." He leans over and kisses me delicately instead of with his usual anticipation-building madness.

"This is different," I send to him.

"Intense emotions cause problems for you," he sends back, *"and you've got control of your energy right now. Calm is a good thing."*

CHAPTER 19

My phone rings, and Trey and I wake. I sit up and push off the covers, but Trey puts a hand on my back as he slides past me.

"I've got it," he says. He picks up the receiver. "Hello." His voice is gravelly from sleep. He listens for a long stretch and finally says, "Mabel, slow down . . . Mabel, stop. We love you. That's never been the issue. Being brutally honest with you, though, you've allowed Valerie and Adam to run wild. I respect that Valerie's having a tough time, but Mel and I need to fill you in on some things. Once you understand what we're going to tell you, I think it'll be clear how bad this whole 'put up with Valerie because she's struggling' request has been." He pauses to listen. "Yes. I think we know what's wrong."

I look at him across the room as he listens to Mabel talk.

He closes his eyes and slumps. "Shit. I forgot about that. Yes, I'll be there." He looks at the clock on my dresser. "We'll get ready and head that way so we can talk to you before I meet with the hand-to-hand combat trainer." He listens again. "My one condition. If Adam and Valerie continue to pull their bullshit, then Melanie and I are out. I can't allow this chaos. Melanie's finally calm enough to speak mind-to-mind with me again, but our situation is deeply terrifying. We're going to need your support, and I'm asking you to quit putting Melanie on the back burner in honor of Valerie. I'm telling you, godson to godmother, you're making a mistake that's going to haunt you when you understand the details."

He nods at whatever Mama Mabel is saying on her end of the line. "I love you, too, Mama. We'll see you in a bit." Trey hangs up. "I forgot that a weapons trainer is meeting with me at three-thirty," he explains as he glances at the clock. "It's noon. I think we need to get showered and head to Mama Mabel's. She plans to speak with Adam and then meet with us. Are you okay with this?"

"I feel better knowing that Mabel's going to know," I say. "We need to tell Finley and Tanner after Mama confirms our suspicions."

"Do you think she'll confirm it, or are we insane?"

I open my connection to Trey and send, *"Review with me."* He nods, and I send, *"I started wondering why my gifts only work part of the time."*

For a few seconds, I gather memories of the moments that my abilities worked and send images of those moments Trey's way. The first memory is me listening in as Demitri said he thought I was pregnant. I ponder how I could hear that conversation when I hadn't been able to hear any other conversations for a while. I think I could hear it because it was useful in solving this mystery. Maybe the baby was picking and choosing moments to give me a hint.

I send the image of Trey's rage coming through our connection on the night Jeff called me a spinner and I threw up.

"Why do you think that happened?" he sends.

"I was furious when Jeff said that. I think the baby is protecting me from losing the pregnancy. Huge energy surges make me sick every time. My abilities, psyche, and body go haywire, and I shut down, but it isn't me

doing it." I level him with a serious look. *"We can count on me being completely helpless, energetically, until I give birth."*

Trey sends back a wave of fear before he can stop it. I catch the wave and grind it out before it has a chance to upset me and fizzle our mind-to-mind connection.

"I'm sorry. I'm trying over here. This is a lot," he sends.

"I know. I'm struggling also. Maybe this will help you." I send the sensation of the starburst energy in my stomach when we were in Ms. G's office.

As the sensation runs through him, Trey closes his eyes and smiles.

I send the need to be calm and not physically warm, and Trey nods. Next, I send a collection of all the moments over the past three months when I instinctively turned down a drink at parties with my friends. Without even realizing it, I quit smoking too.

Next, I send a memory of seeing Trey get punched while I watched the monitor in our room, and the feeling of my dark-water energy rising because of something out of my control.

Trey sends back curiosity and confusion.

"I think the baby got pissed because someone hit its daddy," I send in answer.

Trey's eyebrows rise, and he whistles. "We're going to have our hands full with this child. If it can already do that, then it's going to be a hell-raiser."

CHAPTER 20

We walk right into a mess in Mama Mabel's parlor. Adam yells, while Constance hollers at him over Mama Mabel's shoulder. Mama Mabel is holding back Constance. The chaos brings my soulmate connection line crashing down. Trey feels me disappear from his psyche. My stomach flip-flops, and he sees me turn gray and waxy.

"ENOUGH! What the HELL is wrong with you people?" Trey barks. "I spent all last night working with Melanie to keep her calm. We're here thirty seconds, and she's back to being sick."

"That's because she's a drama queen who's just jealous that Valerie's getting all the attention," Adam snaps back.

Trey turns in a rush and punches Adam so hard that Adam slams into the wall. The wave of rage that rolls off Trey nearly drops me to my knees. Constance rushes over and helps me settle in a chair.

Trey turns to Mabel. "Why is Adam's car in my garage spot and Valerie's car in Melanie's spot?"

"Valerie's having trouble walking to the parking lot," Mabel informs. "We need to switch you guys out until she delivers."

Trey's eyes narrow. "You can switch me out, but Melanie needs to keep her spot."

Mama Mabel sighs.

"You're such a selfish shit, Trey," Adam snarls.

"What the hell is this argument about?" Trey asks Constance.

"His mean, selfish, stuck-up wife ran off our events coordinator," Constance says, pointing at Adam. "Vanessa just quit. We've got four events this month!"

"Take that back, bitch," Adam shouts.

"Shut up, Adam," Trey says. He looks to Mama Mabel. "Why did Vanessa quit?"

Mabel glances my way and closes her eyes. Suddenly, the tension in the room drops dramatically. "I want it clear to everyone that I'm not losing Melanie and Trey," Mabel says. "I just dropped the tension level in the room because it makes Melanie sick." She turns to Adam and quietly but pointedly says, "I'm one more snide statement from launching you and Princess Peach out on your asses. I've had enough." Next, she turns to Trey. "Vanessa quit because Valerie drove her bananas. She was rude, demanding, and changed her mind a million times over this baby shower tomorrow night." Mama Mabel switches her gaze to me. "Melanie, is there any way you can start as events coordinator? Vanessa planned to retire after you graduate and take over for her, but losing her now puts me in a real position. We can keep it part time and work around your school and rehearsal schedule."

"You have to be kidding," Trey says under his breath. He shakes his head at Mabel as I slump over and put my head on my knees.

I'm completely overwhelmed. "Constance, please unlock my door. I'm going to throw up."

As Constance scuttles toward my room, I jump up to cross the parlor and follow her.

Just before I walk out, I hear Trey say to Mabel, "While I know that Melanie appreciates the trust you have in her, your timing couldn't be worse. We need to talk."

— —

After getting sick, I head back out to the hallway to continue the conversation with Trey and Mabel. I pause to lean on the doorjamb. I just lost my lunch, and my stomach's threatening to heave again.

"You and me, talk. NOW," Mabel orders Adam.

"Mabel, Melanie and I need to speak with you first," Trey implores her.

"I know you do," Mabel responds. "But I'm furious, and I need to deal with Adam so I can be calm for Melanie."

The weapons trainer chooses that moment to walk through the door. "Trey! What's up bud? You ready?" he jovially asks.

Trey glances my way. "I'll go lie down and wait for Mama," I offer. "You go ahead."

CHAPTER 21

After the longest hour of my life, I can't take it anymore. I get up and leave my room, head down the hall, and tap on Mama Mabel's office door.

The door opens, and I look past Mama Mabel. Adam is still in her office, and Destiny stands across from him with her hands on her hips.

"I'm so damn sick of this, Mabel," Destiny complains. "Harry Trenell had an appointment, and VALERIE walked in, in a nightgown, nine months pregnant!"

"He's Destiny's highest paying regular, Adam," Mabel scolds.

"I'm sorry," Adam says. "Valerie wanted to borrow a hair tie."

"This is a place of business," Mabel reminds, as she gestures me in. "Melanie, I'm sorry it's taken so long."

I step in, and Mama Mabel closes the door.

"The three of you are a good group for what I need to discuss," I say. "Can you put the Harry argument on ice for a second?"

Destiny nods in agreement. Adam looks sour.

"You guys know how I've had a hard time controlling my energy?" I press on before I lose my nerve. "Can't ground, can't attack, can't keep things straight most of the time?"

Mabel and Destiny nod, but Adam seems alarmed because he hadn't noticed. I take a shuddering breath.

"What's wrong?" Adam asks as he approaches and tips my chin up to look me in the eye.

I swallow hard. "I need your help. I know how to take down our soulmate blockage, and I need to tell Mabel so she can do that for us. I need you to check something for me and help me with something else so I can get it together."

"We've been doing really well with the blockage up. When that connection is open, our lives get unbearably complicated," Adam says, baffled.

"YOU'VE been doing really well, Adam, and YOUR life is uncomplicated. Meanwhile, I'm cratering."

"Can you understand why I don't want to change that?" Adam asks.

"Can you understand that I need help, and you're the only one who has the ability to help me?"

"That's a little dramatic," Adam says in a condescending tone.

Frustrated by his dismissive brush-off, I close my eyes. My head spins, and I turn ashen again.

"It's that important to you?" Adam asks.

I nod, and my face crumples. Tears fall down my cheeks as Mama Mabel gingerly guides me to sit on the couch. I'm exhausted and desperate for cooperation.

"I have two conditions," Adam says. "My first condition is that you allow Mabel to put the barrier back up after whatever you need me for is finished."

"That I can do," I say.

"My second condition," Adam continues, "is that we tell Valerie that we're taking it down before we do."

"That, I can't agree too," I say, shaking my head.

"Why?"

"I don't want Valerie in my personal business right now." I stand to leave.

Mama Mabel stops me. "Obviously, your Adam route won't work, but you haven't tried the Mama route," she says.

Terrified, I turn her way. "How intuitive are you?" I ask. "I mean the real deal? It's obvious you have abilities, but I don't know their extent."

"I'm magic, baby girl," Mama Mabel says.

"Adam, can I please speak with Mabel alone?" I request. "She can only help me with one of the two problems, but I'll take what I can get at this point."

Adam's brow furrows, and he drops his pissed-asshole persona. Suddenly the Adam I love is standing in front of me.

My heart tightens.

"Now I wish I'd just agreed to your request," Adam says. "I've only walked out on your requests a few times, and it's ended in disaster every time."

"It can't get worse for me, and your help will only make it better," I say. "Unfortunately, things will get more complicated for you, and that's a sacrifice I can't make you step up to. I understand your desire to keep your life uncomplicated, given the looming birth of twins. I respect it."

"You make it sound like I'm being selfish," Adam says, clearly offended.

Destiny snorts.

Mama Mabel clears her throat. "I'm going to level with you, Adam. You *are* being selfish, and it's unbecoming. I agreed to let you and Valerie stay here because you're family, and I'm a midwife. With the issues Valerie's had, and how close her due date is, it makes sense. With that said . . ." She trails off.

I suspect she wants to choose her words carefully.

"Being brutally honest," Mabel continues after a pause. "You two sashayed in here with zero regard for everyone else. You take what you want, do whatever the hell you please, and have no sense of decorum in front of my customers during business hours. I'd also like to add that while I know Valerie's a wonderful person, the strain she's under has brought out the worst in her. She's selfish, demanding, and this entire house has revolved around her. She keeps my staff running and fetching from the moment she wakes up until the moment she goes to sleep, and God forbid she have a sleepless night! Then none of the night staff's preparation and restock duties get done."

"You can't be serious!" Adam says, looking baffled. "Do you really feel that way?"

"Valerie demanded that Florence from my night crew leave at two in the morning to get her a candy bar," Mama Mabel says with exasperation.

My memory-watching ability flares. I sense Adam picking and choosing memories in his head. Valerie throwing a fit because she can't find something that the staff put away when they cleaned. Valerie stopping the kitchen staff's dinner preparation while she demanded a smoothie. Adam taking up my parking space in the already packed garage so he could work on his client's motorcycle.

"We came in here and went about our normal routine. Neither of us considered the impact it would have on the other residents. Looking back, I realize how selfish that was. I apologize," Adam says, sounding disappointed in himself.

Destiny sits next to me and holds my hand. Her gaze slowly slides slack as she looks at me. Her hand drifts to my stomach.

"Good. You *should* apologize. You were informed of my rather reasonable rules when you moved in, and there's zero excuse."

Mama Mabel juts a manicured finger Adam's way. "You and Valerie have a lot to learn, Adam. I'm disappointed." She glances at me and adds, "I'm not the least bit surprised that you aren't willing to sacrifice a little comfort so Melanie can gain some sanity. I'm not surprised one bit."

"Mabel," Destiny says with a warning tone, "we've got a bigger problem than that caveman."

"Melanie, I'll drop the barrier. I should have never said no," Adam concedes.

"No need. I've got this. Leave," Destiny orders with a clipped tone.

Adam backs into the hallway, and Destiny slams the door in his face.

"Where's Trey?" Destiny asks.

"With a weapons trainer in the banquet hall," I say.

"We need him," Destiny insists.

Mama Mabel pushes the intercom button for the banquet hall and calls for Trey to come to her office.

After a few moments, Trey's voice comes through the intercom, saying he'll be right there.

Destiny gestures with her thumb toward the closed door. "Thank goodness Adam said no to Melanie's request because he and Valerie can't keep their damn yap-traps shut where Melanie's concerned."

"Okay. What is it?" Mama Mabel asks Destiny.

Trey enters and closes the door behind him. He settles at the end of the love seat, before guiding my head to rest on his lap.

"I have a less accurate version of your abilities, and I want you to check my suspicion that she's pregnant," Destiny tells Mabel.

Mabel's eyes shift to me, and awareness dawns on her face. I see jagged half snippets of her remembering all the things that have been wrong with me for the past few months.

"The erratic energy shift and all the issues," she breathes as she settles into this epiphany. "I put Valerie first and now I know Mel's in worse shape." Mabel pulls herself together. "Just relax and give me a second. Woman magic's my specialty. That's why I became a licensed midwife ten years ago."

Mama Mabel delicately places her hand on my lower abdomen and closes her eyes. I feel a warm focus center under her hand. As her energy probes, I wait, but I already know because something softly glows in my abdomen when I close my eyes to watch what's happening internally.

After an extended moment, Mama Mabel puts her hand back in her lap. "Bingo. I don't know why the tests say you aren't, but you are." She contemplates this for a moment. "Pregnancy tests detect a certain hormone in the body. Dr. Fontaine has mentioned before that your body doesn't always operate how he expects it should. It might be that your energy and abilities make things unique."

I sit up, as every ounce of fear and worry tornado through my psyche all at once.

"Shit. I hate being right." Trey sharply exhales.

"That's what we thought," I say, looking at Mabel with nearly dead eyes.

"I'm going to help you with this," she compassionately promises.

A squabble between Adam and Valerie starts in the hall, and my emotions spiral. The usual reactions hit.

"Why do you let them do this?" I dejectedly ask.

"We can go back to your parents' house," Trey says.

"You aren't leaving," Mabel insists.

"Thank you for checking for me," I whimper, feeling trapped at Mabel's because of the discord.

"You're welcome."

Adam and Valerie's fight persists, escalating like it usually does.

Destiny gets up. "I'll deal with the toddlers," she informs Mabel. "This is the last nonsense I'm dealing with. This was the most peaceful home I've ever had before they invaded. If this doesn't stop, I'm moving out."

Mama Mabel looks exhausted. Destiny is the most frequently booked girl on her roster. If she loses Destiny, she loses quite a few customers.

"YOU'RE BOTH IN TIME OUT! SHUT UP!" Destiny shouts as she goes out the door.

"I'd rather not go to the baby shower tomorrow," I say as I stand and rub my face. I look to Trey, who shakes his head.

"I have to be here as head of security," Trey informs. He leaks emotion that my empathy picks up on.

Apparently, Mabel can also feel his hatred for the job. "We can discuss your workload," she says gently to Trey. "I'm sorry that Adam and Valerie have added to it."

Trey's head drops. He shakes it, saying nothing. He looks his age, which is a rarity for him. He draws me in, wrapping his arms around me.

"It's going to be okay," Mama Mabel says, but her compassionate tone is hollow.

"I'm not going to the party," I say with finality as Adam and Valerie's squabble revs back up at full bore on the other side of the door. "I'm going to head to my parents' house after rehearsal tomorrow evening. Can you come to my house after the party ends?"

Trey agrees and escorts me out of Mama Mabel's office.

CHAPTER 22

At school, surrounded by the "normal teenager" half of my reality, I'm terrified about being pregnant. I can't focus on classwork, and my head spins all day. I fail a test in third period, am late to every class, and barely make it to the bathroom to throw up in fourth period because my teacher refuses to give me a pass.

When the last bell of the day rings, I make my way through Quad One. I stop to survey the expansive field, and my eyes meet Trey's. Even from all the way across the field, I can see that he's under a great deal of pressure. Our mind-to-mind connection is out of whack on my side due to the extreme emotional stress I'm feeling, and I can't get through to him. He tips his head back, and I see him inhale sharply. I want to go to him, but I'm late for rehearsal and he has baseball practice.

I hastily decide to change my plans for the evening. If I stay at Mabel's, Trey can cut loose with the guys at the party without worrying about driving to my parents' house. I pull my phone out of my backpack's front pocket.

I dial the main staff line at Mama Mabel's, knowing that it's pointless to leave a message on the answering machine in our room.

Trey never checks it. After four rings, the answering machine for the staff line picks up. I roll my eyes. They're probably all being run ragged by Valerie as they prepare for her baby shower.

The machine beeps after the greeting ends. "It's Melanie," I say. "Please let Trey know that I'll head to Mama Mabel's tonight, instead of our original plan. Thank you."

I hang up and traverse the four-story staircase to the auditorium.

Mr. Isley gives the cast a ten-minute break, and I lie down right where I'm at on the stage while everyone else wanders off. Justine's out, yet again, and I'm back in my original role.

Demitri sits next to me. "You can't keep doing this, Meley," he says. "I'm scared to death every time you run one of these dance pieces. You look like you're going to pass out cold."

"This stays between us," I say as I put his hand low on my stomach.

His eyes close and he winces a moment after I feel an energetic search. "You're at least four months, Melanie," he says.

My face crumples, and tears run into my ears.

"Oh, Meley. Come here," Demitri says and gathers me in his lap.

I curl up in a ball with my head on his shoulder. "What am I going to do?" I warble through my tears.

Mr. Isley chooses that moment to use the cordless microphone that he's taken to bellowing through during every rehearsal. "On your feet. We're running that disaster again," he announces.

"Hold," Demitri hollers.

Demitri stands with me still cradled in his arms. He makes his way carefully down the stairs on the side of the stage and up the audience aisle to Mr. Isley. Mr. Isley looks at us quizzically.

"Turn off the mic, please," Demitri requests.

Mr. Isley shuts the microphone off. "We don't have time for a meltdown," he gruffly insists, gesturing to me.

I close my eyes and turn my face into Demitri's shoulder. Demitri shifts me, and I wrap my arms and legs around him like a needy koala bear, so I don't have to face Mr. Isley's disapproval.

"We've confirmed that Melanie's pregnant. She needs to be released from the cast," Demitri quietly informs.

"ARE YOU SERIOUS?" Mr. Isley bellows.

My shoulders shake as his anger dissolves me into a fresh round of tears. I break out in a cold, clammy sweat and turn a waxy ashen again.

"Shhhh. I've got you," Demitri quietly says with his lips against my ear.

"Are you the father?" Mr. Isley asks.

"No. Obviously not," Demitri says. "I am, however, Melanie's best friend. She's comfortable hanging on me."

"I apologize for my reaction," Mr. Isley says with a shift in his tone. "I wasn't expecting this, and the production has taken hit after hit."

"I know losing Melanie is bad, but her abilities have gone completely haywire," Demitri says, commiserating. "She gets sick as a dog when the pressure is extreme. It's not safe for me to do some of the lifts that put strain on her stomach."

"Demitri, turn around so I can see Melanie's face," Mr. Isley requests.

When Demitri turns, I peek over his shoulder at Mr. Isley.

Mr. Isley's expression softens. "I'm so used to seeing you be vicious, but when you're really happy or really scared, you look so young," he says.

"Those eyes she's giving you scare the crap out of me," Demitri says. "That's when I always know things are bad."

"I can cut you from the two biggest group numbers," Mr. Isely offers. "Unfortunately, Justine can't handle the role. Even sick, you're leagues better in this part than her. If you can get through the duet, your solo, and the smaller group piece that you specifically have lines in, then we can make it work."

I close my eyes. I want to be done with the production, but I nod and agree to the three pieces he needs me for.

"I'll keep you two after, and we can adjust the partnering in your duet."

"She shouldn't do the show at all," Demitri implores, but his plea reaches deaf ears.

Mr. Isley clicks the microphone switch on. "PLACES. NOW," he orders.

CHAPTER 23

I'm so tired that my hands shake on my steering wheel. The kicker that catapulted me over the edge was Mr. Isley holding me an extra hour and a half after rehearsal to maniacally drill me on the duet adjustments over and over. Demitri was furious by the end, and his anger radiated unchecked. The stress nearly dropped me. Our show opens in three weeks, and at this point, I'm doomed. Justine dropped out of her understudy position at the rehearsal, saying it was too much pressure. I'm forced to wear a unitard and be a vampy cat while I try not to throw up on stage. I dread changing into a sundress and playing nicey-nice at Valerie's baby shower I'm an hour late for.

Make a brief appearance and bow out as quickly as possible.

My self-coaching is halfhearted at best as I pull into the parking lot at Mama Mabel's and turn off the engine. I regret my choice not to go to my parents' house. I still don't have a parking spot in the garage because Mama Mabel forgot to add that to her discussion with Adam.

I tip my head back against the headrest. It's obvious that I'm further along than I thought. Last night, I rolled on my stomach to sleep and felt like I was lying on a baseball. The baby is big enough that I can feel it now. I close my eyes as panic bubbles up. I have to tell my parents when they get back from their trip on Tuesday. They aren't going to be happy about this.

The difference between what I'm experiencing and how everyone's treated Valerie is incredibly difficult for me to accept. I know I'm jealous, but it's hard not to be. We literally took care of her from the first day we knew her condition. In their defense, most people don't know about my pregnancy yet, and the few that know, only found out in the past twenty-four hours.

I shake my head to clear my melancholy. There's no use in worrying about this now. I'll deal with it when Valerie's baby shower is behind us.

I open my car door, step out, and decide I'm so exhausted I'm not even going to bother with the backpack in my trunk. My hand shakes as I tuck my phone into the waistband of my leggings. I slog across the crowded parking lot. I had to park at the farthest edge because of all the baby shower guests.

Halfway to the main door, I realize that something's weird. I look again, squinting in the gloomy parking lot that only has two overhead lights, and my mouth drops open when I see the house. *I just can't.*

I pull the phone, yank out the antennae, and try Trey. He doesn't answer, and his voicemail is full. His habit of never checking messages didn't used to annoy me, but I can't send him telepathic info now and my frustration makes my head spin. I dial Marcus's number. It goes straight to voicemail.

"Marcus, it's Melanie," I say after the beep. "The Vault system's enabled, and I'm stuck in the parking lot. All the security gates are down over the doors and windows."

I try the house number, and none of the staff answer, likely because they're busy hosting the baby shower. I leave a message.

I dial Adam's cell number next. It also goes straight to voicemail, which isn't surprising given that he's enjoying his baby shower.

"Adam, I'm stuck outside. Treys got the Vault system enabled," I say, leaving a message.

I hang up and turn to leave. That's when I realize with a start that I've definitely missed something. Partially masked by the night's shadows, at least fifty bikers are lined up and down the alley. I don't know if they were there when I drove into the parking lot. Either way, it doesn't matter, because I'm severely off my game. I study them in the dark and see Mack in the middle.

I instantly know that this is revenge come to call and that I'm in serious trouble. They all fire up their motorcycles in unison. Even if I get back to my car and manage to get out of the parking lot, they'll run me down, and my gas tank is sitting at empty.

I will my dark-water side to rise, but nothing happens.

Switching gears, I try to tap into my connection with Trey, but it fails. My energy spirals in wisps every which way.

Panic rises in my throat, and I try my connection with Adam, knowing it's pointless, and of course, it's still walled off.

As I stand in a stare-down with the Reapers, my wonky intuition chooses a memory from Mack. I study the images of initiation after initiation as Mack added people to the Reapers' roster. I see in Mack's memory, as he tells a new guy, *'We're gonna get the little bitch now! She doesn't stand a chance against this many of us.'*

I laugh ironically, and suddenly know that this is it. *I've been a hell of a warrior. I've saved many and loved my friends and family tirelessly. I've tried to be honorable and to make up for my mistakes where I could.*

I come to terms with what's about to happen, but don't have the gift of my usual intuition to clue me in about how bad this is going to be. I've got no abilities that supercharge me right when I need them. I have no scrappy pack of friends and family surrounding me. And, I've got no Trey, ready to tear my enemies limb from limb. I'm an ordinary, unremarkable, pregnant sixteen-year-old, standing in a dark Hollywood parking lot surrounded by thugs, and there's nowhere to run. I should be terrified by the thought, but instead I think, *'I don't even have a witty one-liner to toss their way.'* I scoff to myself.

"What's funny, La Diabla?" Mack hollers.

I don't respond, making the split-second decision that I'm not going down begging and pleading. They're going to take me out in retribution for the night I roughed them up, humiliated them, and earned the nickname Mack just used. That night Big Joe and Mama Mabel informed us that these guys fight dirty and have a lethal reputation.

So, there it is. With none of my abilities to rely on, I'm going to lean on my dignity.

Engines rev all at once, and the smell of exhaust fills the air. My heart rate rises, and the beating is painful. I stand up straight. Panic swells in my throat, but I refuse to scream.

I put a hand over my stomach, realizing with a start that I'm not the only one that's about to die if I don't do something.

I try desperately to reach Trey again, but the attempt fizzles and spirals off like invisible fireworks. All I get back is a memory of Trey's from an hour ago. He was in the banquet hall decorated in yellow and green because Valerie and Adam don't want to know if they're having boys or girls. Long ago, my intuition showed me that they're having two girls, but I've made it a priority not to fill them in.

Trey turns in the memory, surveying the room. I hear him think, *'Everyone's here and I want to enjoy this with the guys. I'm locking down the Vault perimeter system, so I don't have to check the security footage constantly.'* He heads to his security office.

He had no idea I was coming home. The staff must not have told him.

Twelve Reapers pull out from the alley one after the other and race toward the parking lot entrance. Mack leads the way, and the bikers start circling round and round, with me trapped in the middle. The sound is deafening. These are the twelve guys that I dealt with the night when they decided to take a shot at robbing our supplies after the earthquake.

I glance at the other Reapers, still revving their engines, parked next to each other in the shadow of the alley.

My connection with Trey opens just enough that I can hear his thoughts and see through his eyes, but can't get a message to him. He stops, mid dart game against Tanner, and thinks, *'What's up with the sudden motorcycle noise?'*

I watch as Adam's mouth drops open. "Holy crap! Trey, I forgot to tell you! The new staff girl told me that Melanie left a message. She's coming here after rehearsal instead of going to her parents' house. Her shift was ending, and you weren't back from baseball practice yet."

Tanner, Adam, and Trey all look at the wall to the outside, listening to the engine revving. "The Vault system's enabled," Trey barks as our connection blinks out and I'm back in my unfortunate reality.

Mack and his revenge-seeking Reapers stop in a line to my left, putting down their kickstands, but leaving their motorcycles rumbling. They get off their bikes and stalk my way, forming a straight line like schoolkids.

I glance to the side as the spectator Reapers in the alley begin methodically hitting their throttles in a synchronized hum that revs and dies down, revs and dies down. The ritualistic pattern is ominous.

The intrusive shield snaps over me, like it has every time fear rises. I now know it's the baby trying to protect itself so the pregnancy holds. Knowing what's caused the mysterious shield brings the reality of how little and helpless it feels. It's no longer scary and ominous, but the fact that the baby is trying is horrific. Faced with the Reapers, neither her nor I stand a chance.

It's suddenly impossible to breathe, and terror envelopes me in a cold sweat. Frozen in place, I watch as Mack announces for my benefit, "I'm invoking Retribution Clause by club edict. If you run, you die. Stand your ground." He circles around to the end of the line.

The first guy comes forward. When he makes it to me, he draws back his fist and punches my right cheek. My head snaps to the side. I stumble, but I don't fall through sheer force of will.

I shake my head, trying to clear my ringing ears when the next guy gets hold of my shoulder. He makes eye contact with me as he lowers his fist and hits me with an uppercut that rattles my teeth.

My vision goes spotty, but I refuse to run. I'm certain that the waiting Reapers in the alley will chase me down and kill me. I hear the metal scrape of the Vault gates going up, ending in the clang I've become familiar with. I don't have time to be relieved that I'm about to be rescued.

"MOVE," Mack screams to the guys standing in front of him in their sick-ritual line. The guys scatter, and the motorcycles in the alley rev their engines louder as people pour out of Mama Mabel's place. Mack rushes at me with a pulled-back fist. I make eye contact with Trey just as Mack gut-punches me so hard that he lifts me off the ground. He drops me, and I gasp around the pain that explodes through my abdomen as I fall to my knees.

"NOOOOOOOO!" I hear Mama Mabel and Destiny scream.

On all fours and seeing stars, I lift my head. Everyone's frozen in place, staring at me. I make eye contact with the Revenge Twelve as I struggle to stand, doubled over from the pain. I stare at my lavender leggings and can feel the blood pouring down my legs. I close my eyes, realizing what's happening.

I take a breath through the pain and gather every ounce of resolve I have. With monumental effort, I stand up straight. I slowly hit Mack with the weight of this new reality in my expression. "Fuck youuuuuu," gravels from me as my quaking hand drifts to my stomach. I tip my head, losing my hold on sanity as my dark-water side starts slowly roiling from its captivity deep in my psyche. The insanity is welcome. "Killing La Diabla's baby is a bold move for a worthless shit stain," rumbles, full-bodied and vicious, from my throat.

Mack starts backing away, suddenly losing his bravado. "I didn't know," warily slips from his lips.

"You're about to find out," I maniacally snarl as I feel my dark-water side expand, oozing back into place.

"Whoa, whoa, whoa!" the next guy in line protests. "This goes against the code, Mack. I'm out." He runs to his motorcycle and takes off down the alley.

Everyone of the Hellcats and Hellhounds who didn't know I'm pregnant looks to Mama Mabel, who's on her knees, hysterically crying while Destiny holds her. I watch realization wash across the faces of everyone in our group, along with the faces of the Reapers close enough to see what's happening.

Adam's mouth drops open. He stumbles a bit, his knees buckling as the shock reverberates through him.

Tanner reaches to steady him.

"Oh my God!" Adam rumbles with deep emotion. "That's what she needed to talk to me about."

I scan the crowd until my gaze reaches Trey, who's frozen in shock. As my blood rushes out, my abilities rush back in. Our connection blazes back to life and feels rock steady on my side. Trey's gaze shifts from my face to my legs. The crimson stain spreads rapidly, and Trey drops to his knees as tears roll down his cheeks.

All our friends take in Trey's reaction.

Suddenly, the Hellhounds and Hellcats roar their challenge. The Reapers in the alley rush at my friends. All hell breaks loose. Fists swing. People are thrown. Chaos abounds. The worst part is the damn baby shower guests who aren't a part of our metaphysical world are here watching this.

"Leave!" Constance orders them. They start dodging through the chaos, running for their cars.

Engines start all over the parking lot. Having all the vehicles backing up during all this madness is ridiculous, but Constance was right to get rid of them.

Fury washes over Trey and flows to me through our connection as he stands. He starts fighting his way through the crush of enemies, trying to get to me. He knocks unconscious or tosses aside everyone who comes in his path.

Mack and his remaining revenge-mates rush toward me, my distraction while I watch Trey giving them a window to attack. I drop under the sea of furious bikers and unexpectedly go limp. *Just give up, Melanie.* I'm lying on the ground taking hit after hit, but my willingness to give up on a wave of grief is a welcome relief. *This lifetime is horrific. I can't do this anymore.*

"Looks like Rich was wrong," I send to Trey. *"I do lie down on the battlefield,"*

"Melanie! Get up!" Trey screams in my mind. He sends a bubble laced with his knowledge that I just got back my abilities when Mack hit me.

I study the bubble, and the reality of exactly who and what I am roars in. *No one, and I mean NO ONE, fucks with a child of mine. I've done a lot of things wrong in my lifetimes, but protecting my children is the one thing I'm steadfast in.* My dark-water side rages at full force.

I put my hands on the closest Reapers that are piled on me and start drawing energy from them, recklessly filling my reserves. When my reserves are full, I keep pulling energy from every source I can seek a tendril to. My spine screams, burning and twitching, but I don't stop until I'm quaking. I growl demonically.

Homed on an attack, I shove as hard as I can with an invisible force. The woozy, energy drained, Reapers are launched off me, and I rise to my feet.

My face contorts with animalistic battle rage. *"IF YOU RUN, YOU DIE! STAND YOUR GROUND!"* I send out on a booming mental blast. The words echo and reverberate off the walls as my noncorporeal voice invades the parking lot.

The Reapers' terror is captivating as my empathic gift is overloaded with what they're projecting. I snap energy lines to each of them. They strain against me, getting nowhere.

"Hounds and Cats, CLEAR OUT!" I bellow.

I send to Trey a bubble filled with everything I'm about to do.

"RUNNNNNN!" Trey yells through uncontrollable tears.

Our friends scatter, but Trey heads my way.

"Get behind me and shield HARD," I snarl.

He does, and I put my arms out wide, pulling power from every available source. The already moonless night becomes darker as the lights within a half-mile radius go out.

I take the quaking energy and hold it tight while it thrums and buckles in my already broken body. The effort of keeping this much power in check is soul-shattering. I wait as Adam helps

Valerie through the door, the last of our group to find shelter. The door closes, and I smile sadistically.

I feel Trey radiating rage behind me.

"Here we go," I growl in our minds and release the straining energy just as Trey clamps a shield over us to avoid any backlash from the rogue, nuclear-energy bomb I unleash.

We watch as Reapers drop to the ground the moment my blast wave barrels through them. All the motorcycles in the parking lot fall over, and cars rock to one side before settling back on their tires with heavy thuds. Car alarms go off all over the neighborhood.

I turn to Trey when I'm satisfied that all my enemies are unconscious. He shakes his head to clear the boom from his ears. His expression is a mask of trauma and earth-shattering heartbreak. He starts to speak, and I feel my eyes roll into the back of my head as I collapse. He catches me.

My world goes black.

CHAPTER 24

I wake to sounds of panic that I struggle to decipher through my pain and shock.

"You aren't coming in here," Destiny says. "Mama Mabel has to check her!"

"You don't understand!" Bear pleads. "She can check her while I deal with the energy damage. The amount of energy she just took in and subsequently blasted out could kill her."

"*You* don't understand," Destiny snarls back. "The miscarriage could kill her. She needs a damn doctor. Mama Mabel's a midwife. We don't have time to wait, and we sure as HELL don't have time to waste arguing with *you*."

"Someone call Demitri and tell him to warp speed here!!!" Darren screams.

I manage to open my eyes, and my room is busting with all the Hellcat girls and Mama Mabel's girls. I'm lying on the bed. Trey is across the room with his hands on the dresser, struggling to breathe through the emotional trauma that he reverberates unchecked down our connection.

"All Hellcat girls out." I send to Trey. *"Someone in this group needs to come through this still a teenager. This is about to be bad."*

Trey turns to me, and understanding fills his eyes as I give him a route to do something productive to help me.

"Hellcats out, NOW," he orders.

Clearly distraught, the girls look at me.

"It's best that you go. Melanie's going to need privacy for this," Mama Mabel advises as she pulls on medical gloves.

They leave, as Adam shoves his way in.

"Out, Adam! Now," I gasp. I put a hand on Sapphire's arm and stop her as she tries to pull my leggings down. I look at Adam pleadingly. "I'm not doing this with you in here."

Adam starts to argue, and I scream, "LEEEAVE!"

Blood gushes faster, soaking the bed under me.

Trey storms Adam, turns him around, and shoves him out the door.

"Trey, I need you to get Tanner," I request.

Trey leans out the door and yells for Tanner.

Tanner comes in quickly, closing the door behind him. He takes a shaky breath when he sees me lying on the blood-soaked bed.

"Will you sit next to me, face away from what Mama's going to do, and hold my hand please?"

Tanner's expression melts. "Girl, I've got you," he says, before informing Mabel, "Demitri is hauling ass here."

He climbs on the bed and sits with his back to Mama Mabel and the four girls who are acting as her medical assistants. From their efficient manner, they've done this before.

"Pants off. Hurry," Mama Mabel orders.

Her girls lift me to ease my blood-soaked pants off. I scream as the slight movement sends shock waves of agonizing pain through my stomach.

"That's not a good sign," Sapphire says warily to Mama Mabel.

Mama's eyes crease in the corners as she watches my reaction.

"Having a miscarriage is painful under normal circumstances," she suggests. "Melanie took a gut punch and then was beaten by twelve men. Add to it all her abilities coming back, and the energy attack she just unleashed. I expected this. Hang tight. She might still be okay."

Trey leans against the wall behind Mama Mabel. His eyes fill with tears, and he turns a sick shade of gray.

Someone starts pounding on the door again, and Tanner gets up. "I'm not leaving," he assures me. "I promise I'll be right back."

I watch Tanner walk to the door. He cracks it open. "Darren, get away from the door," he snarls.

Darren faintly says something, and Tanner warns, "The next person that knocks on this door is going to get the brunt end of my rage. You just pulled me away from holding Melanie's hand. Every time her heart rate rises, she gushes blood."

Darren says something I can't decipher, and Tanner slams the door closed.

"Tanner, hold her hand," Mama Mabel orders.

Tanner sits back down, facing away from Mama Mabel's examination to give me some privacy. He takes both of my hands. "I've got you."

"This is going to hurt, Melanie, but I have no choice," Mabel warns.

She does something and mind-bending fire shoots through my abdomen. My back arches, and I scream out loud and down my connection line to Trey simultaneously.

"Hold her down, Tanner," Mama Mabel calmly instructs. "Destiny, hold her legs."

Tanner leans over to prevent me from moving. Mabel does something new, and I hear Trey moan across the room, while tears stream down my face. I scream again and writhe, trapped under Tanner.

My psyche blasts into the ether, riding a wave of agony. I feel everything rattle, and then the connection with Zane—the one I've never been able to explain or control—rages open. He hears me screaming in his mind, and I watch through his eyes as his gaze snaps to Rocco.

"Go, go, go!" I hear through Zane's ears as he orders Rocco.

"Where is she?" Rocco asks.

"Open your eyes, Melanie," Zane orders.

My eyes snap open because I'm not thinking even close to clearly. Following orders just kind of happens.

"Mabel's!" Zane bellows.

I see through his eyes as they run down a hall, but the connection explodes as another massive wave of pain hits.

"She's insane strong," Destiny says. "I can't hold her legs still."

"Let's give her a moment," Mabel instructs. "Let up." When Tanner and Destiny let me go, Mabel gives me a look filled with conviction. "I need you to gut up. This is going to be rough, but we can do it."

Destiny and Tanner get a solid grip on me again, per Mabel's order.

"Here we go, Melanie," Mabel says. "Deep breath."

My abdomen blazes, and fire shoots through me. I scream. The building rumbles around us as I lose control of my metaphysical side.

"You can let up," Mabel says, and I'm no longer trapped as Tanner and Destiny let me go. Destiny shakes out her arms, having given holding me down everything she's got.

The pain lessens, and I roll on my side, shaking. I watch as the door opens and Demitri slips in. He sees me, and doubles over. He closes his eyes, and his face turns pale. His expression morphs through every horrible emotion possible before he rallies.

"Are you doing this or am I?" Mabel asks.

Demitri crosses to the bed, and I close my eyes as petrifying fear and shame war for dominance in my chest. I feel Demitri's hand on my lower back, and he sends a calming wave through me.

"Her uterus is destroyed," he quietly says to Mabel. "See if you can get the baby out the old-fashioned way."

"Is the baby . . . ?" Mabel's question drifts off.

Demitri minutely shakes his head no.

"It'll take everything I have to fix her, and I'm drained," Demitri stoically informs Mabel. "You're going to need me to handle the aftermath. I need you to tap in and give this a shot."

Mabel nods. Her eyes close, and she works hard to pull herself together. When she opens her eyes, her battle-hardened side is at the helm.

We're deep in the shit.

Tanner makes the mistake of looking Mabel's way. He turns pale. "This is horrific," he mutters.

There's a fresh round of pounding at the door.

"STOP!" I yell, squeezing my eyes closed in panic.

I feel Tanner shift off the bed. He yanks the door open just enough to say something to someone that's hard to make out through the searing pain. I'm covered in sweat, and my stomach heaves. I vomit all over the side of the bed, coating Demitri's designer jeans. Blood starts pouring from my nose.

Demitri puts a hand on my shoulder, and I feel an energy scan. "She just used what was left of her reserves when the pain hit from Mabel's examination," Demitri announces. "If she goes into a backlash state, she'll die. I can't boost her, or I won't be able to heal her later. Trey, you have to fix this."

Trey turns from the dresser to face us, and I see no rational sense in his expression. I've battered him with soul-crushing pain through our connection that I can't block right now. He's traumatized. Demitri sees it too.

Demitri cups my cheek. "I'll get Bear and Darren to drop the connection barrier between you and Adam."

"After the way Adam's treated me?" I screech, in a confused panic. "I don't trust HIM!"

"Melanie, the gravity of this situation runs deeper than the social nonsense right now," Demitri coaches. "We have no choice. I'll be right back."

I watch Demitri exit and close the door behind him. He's gone for only a moment when the wall separating my soulmate connection with Adam crashes down.

I hear through Adam's ears as Arch asks in the hall, "How bad, Demitri?"

"It's bad," I hear D say.

"We're going in," Darren insists.

"Bear and Darren, I know you want to help, but I need Arch in there," Demitri sternly informs. "Someone has to have a clear head, someone whose presence won't freak out Melanie."

"Why would we freak her out?" Bear squalls.

"She's naked, screaming, and that's not for you," Demitri pointedly says.

Relief floods me. Being in this vulnerable state in front of Bear and Darren is a horrifying prospect.

"Can you handle this?" Demitri asks.

"I've got it," I hear Arch say.

"Gut up," Demitri warns just before the door opens.

Adam rushes through the door with Arch and Demitri. Arch closes and locks the door before surveying the room. "Oh my God," he mutters.

Adam sees me, and he bends at the waist like he's been punched.

"I'm so sorry I forgot to tell Trey you were coming here. I'm so sorry," he whimpers.

"Pull it together!" Demitri roars at Adam. "You don't get to break down right now, you selfish shit! You're a real piece of work!"

Adam shakes off his panic, and I'm relieved to see his competent side take over as he looks from Trey to me, before turning to Arch. "Drop anyone that knocks on that door," he tells him. "We absolutely can't be disturbed if we have any chance of this working. It looks like she's already lost more blood than she should be able to survive. That raging nosebleed might kill her."

"He's not wrong," Mabel confirms. "I'm considering setting up a blood transfusion if anyone else has Melanie's type AB negative."

Adam rounds the bed carefully to avoid disturbing Mama Mabel and her girls. He lies down on his side next to me, puts a hand on my cheek, and turns my face so our eyes meet. He gasps as my pain batters him in excruciating waves. *"Easy. Breathe Melanie,"* he sends to me as he starts syphoning off pain. He takes enough of the edge off that I manage even breaths. "Good, Melanie." Adam slides one hand under me and places it flat on my spine. He starts filling my energy reserves slowly, but it feels like white-hot fire and lightning sear through every broken part of me.

"Stop!" I send in a mind-to-mind scream.

He pulls his hand back. "My energy's too much for her," he tells Demitri. "She needs Trey. You can't refill her because you need to conserve energy to heal her, and Trey's the only other choice who won't make her sick."

Tanner lets go of my hand and slides off the bed through the vomit slick and blood. "Trey, I need you to snap out of it. Melanie needs you," he insists.

Trey doesn't respond, still trapped in his emotionally buckling shock.

"TREY!" Demitri yells.

Trey still doesn't have the gumption to respond. "If you don't fix her, I'm going to," Demitri growls. Since there's been tension for a long time about Demitri finally deciding he wants a relationship with me, his statement holds far more weight than just fixing my energy backlash. The idea hangs heavy in the air.

Adam stiffens and lets go of my hands as, "She's mine," rumbles from him.

My eyes snap wide.

Adam rises from the bed and swells to his full, mammoth size. His energy pounds the room, and something primal in me connects to it. He points aggressively my way. "THAT is my original soulmate."

"Oh, for fuck sake," I mutter as Adam's sudden bravado distracts me from my life-and-death predicament.

"Fuck you," Demitri growls as his energy flares. The room suffocatingly pounds with energy that almost hurts as Demitri and Adam prove to be something far deeper than teenage boys.

Arch pulls up his trench coat sleeve and raises a quizzical eyebrow at his goose-bumped arm. "Yo, you think you guys can focus on what matters instead of having a dick-measuring contest?"

Demitri whips his animalistic gaze toward Arch, who cranks back his neck with an almost comical expression. "Don't you give me that look, Demitri. You brought me in here to maintain order." He taps his temple. "Clearheaded guy, remember?"

Demitri's eyes narrow, and I marvel at how inhumanely ethereal he looks. He rarely drops his energetic shields, but apparently, when he does so in a full-blown rage, his metaphysical nature is a trip. "Shut the fuck up, Normal," rumbles from Demitri. All semblance of his "good guy" persona is eviscerated. I've never seen him pull arrogant rank on a Normal, particularly not with Arch.

Adam steps up to Trey and Demitri, and the three metaphysical powerhouses face off. Well, Adam and Demitri are currently powerhouses. Trey's a little lackluster pathetic, but he gets a pass what with the whole miscarriage mess and all.

"I'm dead serious," Demitri snarls at Trey. "If you fail her right now, she's mine."

Every mouth in the room drops open. Arch steps up, ready to deal with the looming deathmatch even though a Normal doesn't stand a chance against what these guys are energetically exuding.

"Can you three have a battle royale over her hand later?" Tanner screeches. "Someone needs to fix her."

Clarity comes into Trey's clouded senses. "Don't even think about it!" he snarls at Demitri.

Demitri glares at Trey furiously. "This is bullshit! Condoms aren't a mystery, Trey. Melanie is the second girl you've knocked up in a year." Demitri blasts out a challenging energy wave, and my head spins.

"This isn't his fault, Demitri," I gasp.

He looks at me with eyes full of a rage I've never experienced from him. He turns to Trey. "Every ounce of this is your fault."

"I'm already aware," Trey says, his energy deflating, bringing the level in the room down a little. "Melanie and I discussed that the night I figured out she was pregnant."

As Demitri's energy drops, I inhale a shaky breath.

"I'm SICK of standing around watching you destroy her with one selfish load of bullshit after another," Demitri says, resorting to logic instead of metaphysical badassery. "You need to leave her, Trey, because she doesn't have it in her to leave a soulmate." Demitri gestures harshly toward Adam. "Hence why Adam is still wandering around!" Demitri's eyes narrow with finality. "Get the fuck out of the way, Trey. She'll eventually end up with me either way."

Trey looks shellshocked.

Adam turns his back, stunned. I can feel through our open soulmate connection as humiliation of not even being relevant with his lifetimes-long soulmate almost takes out his knees.

"Can we focus, PLEASE?!" roars from me.

Demitri looks at me and gets a full-frontal view of what Mama Mabel's doing. She presses on my stomach, releasing a fresh wave of blood. I scream.

"I need to get this baby out," Mama Mabel insists, adding her panic into the mix. "You boys quit dicking around or you'll be arguing over who gets to order her tombstone."

"I'm a fire sign," I rasp. "I want to be cremated."

Demitri turns gray and squeezes his eyes closed. Trey fights to breathe around his panic. I feel it rolling down his open connection with me.

Demitri takes two steps my way, and Trey finally snaps out of it. He moves past Demitri and scoots through the vomit sludge to sit next to me. Demitri lets loose a screaming exhale. He's radiating waves of frustration.

"I'm going to siphon off pain while you refill her," Adam tells Trey. Adam sits on my other side. His arm and tank top are covered in blood that gushed uncontrolled from my nose when he was lying next to me earlier.

Trey takes both of my hands and drops what's left of his shields. Trey's chest caves in as he fights to breathe around the pain and terror that I'm sending in wild, blistering waves through our connection.

"Gut up, Trey," Arch sternly orders as we witness Trey's inability to overcome his fear. Trey hasn't taken a breath in so long that

I'm scared he's going to pass out.

Mabel does something particularly painful, and I scream while my lower abdomen contracts hard.

"Help meee," I keen.

Trey inhales sharply.

"We're on the edge of a critical point," Mabel informs everyone. "We can't call an ambulance because we've got fifty unconscious thugs in our parking lot. I need to induce contractions."

"Pull more pain," Trey says to Adam in a carefully controlled tone. "She's quaking on my side, and refilling her requires meditation when I do it."

Demitri leans, putting his hands on either side of my face, and sends calm in massive waves.

"Don't leave. Okay?" I whimper.

"I'm not going anywhere. Focus on me while Trey refills you. Even breaths." I lock eyes with Demitri and focus on the calm vibe he's filling me with. My heart rate slows, and he says, "Good, baby girl."

Adam lessens my pain, his hands shaking with effort. I exhale.

"Whatever you're doing, Adam and Demitri, keep doing it. She's relaxing, and that's exactly what I need," Mabel says. She turns to Destiny. "Make her drink the black cohosh tincture, now!"

Destiny tips my head up and holds a little cup to my lips. "Drink it, Mel. It's gross but it works fast, and it'll make this end."

I open my mouth, and Destiny pours in the warm, earthy liquid. I sputter. She clamps her hand over my mouth and pinches my nose closed, forcing me to swallow it like a mom with a toddler.

I gag, but don't throw it up. My abdomen suddenly feels like it's going to explode. I scream. Demitri scoots behind me and rests my head on his lap, blanching from his front row view of what's happening.

"I'm going to need Melanie to push soon," Mama Mabel tells Trey. "This hurts like hell under normal circumstances, and she's working with a swollen uterus from Mack's gut punch."

"Look at me, Melanie," Demitri guides. "Breathe with me."

I look up at him while he radiates calm. Demitri inhales and exhales methodically, and I mimic him. He nods, and I get control of my fear.

Trey exhales and slips into a meditative state. Sliding his hands under me and placing them on my spine, he starts refilling my energy stores. It doesn't hurt this time. My head eventually clears enough that I'm able to allow my dark-water side to sink under the liquid surface that lives in my mind. My calm rational side takes the driver's seat.

"Better?" Tey asks, squeezing my arm.

I nod as the nosebleed slows to a stop.

Through our connection, I feel Adam's resolve beginning to crumble. I sense him thinking, '*I can't handle this. I need to get my head together.*'

"I need to check on Valerie," Adam says. "She's in bed, not feeling well again."

"Of course you do," Trey snarls.

"NOW?" Tanner squawks. "Crap on a cracker! How can one lounging lady be so goddamn needy?"

Adam gets up.

"Valerie doesn't need him right now," Trey informs with gravity. "Adam's doing what he does. He bails every time the pressure mounts."

Trey's brash honesty does nothing to sway Adam's intention to leave that I can feel through our open soulmate connection.

"If you leave right now . . . ," Arch threatens, but he's cut off as Adam rushes past him out the door.

Trey lies down on the bed next to me, and Tanner scoots around to take the spot Adam just abandoned.

"What's your plan, Trey?" Demitri asks.

"I need you to send calm as hard as you can. I'm going to trance her out, so she doesn't feel it when she has to push."

"Let's do this," Demitiri says, determined.

Trey puts his fingertips on my forehead, closes his eyes, and struggles to trance me out. Every time I almost slip away, another contraction hits and pulls me back to reality. After several grueling minutes, my eyes roll into the back of my head. Suddenly I'm completely calm, and all the pain slides away.

"Yes," Mama Mabel says as I go limp.

An argument between Valerie and Adam blasts through Adam's side of his shared connection with me and Trey. We hear everything in our minds because neither Trey nor I can block Adam out right now.

"What took you so long?" Valerie lobs at him.

"We've got a nightmare in Melanie's room," Adam says. "They need my help, but I need a second to get it together."

"Trey can deal with it, I'm sure," Valerie snaps back. "Melanie's a selfish bitch who ruined my baby shower. I'm gonna tear her ass up for it."

I gasp, and pain starts quaking through me as their argument pulls me out of my trance state. My eyes snap open.

"Damn it!" Demitri snarls.

I writhe when a massive contraction starts, and the pain comes crashing in at full force. I snake an arm around Demitri's side and scream.

"Fuck," Mama Mabel says with frustration.

Demitri sends bigger calming waves through his hands on my cheeks. "It's okay, Melanie." He looks to Trey. "You need to focus, Trey!"

"Block off your petty squabble with the House Princess, asshole," Trey snarls out loud to Adam, who hears Trey through the open connection. "I had Melanie in a trance state when Valerie's selfish bullshit interrupted. Melanie's having contractions, and she's about to have to push."

Adam sends back horror as he realizes he's disturbed our hellacious process.

"Let that bitch know that Melanie and I accept her challenge," Trey snarls back. "As soon as Melanie's on her feet, she's going to end your fucking wife. I'll bury her dead, pregnant body under endangered plants in the desert myself."

"Holy shit!" Tanner squeaks. "We're at the pregnant-endangered-plant-murder phase of chaos?"

Adam radiates terror before his side of our trio connection fuzzes out.

Trey syphons off pain again, but his efforts barely take the edge off.

"MOVE," Zane bellows at the door and bulldozes in.

"Oh good," Tanner sasses. "Another animal just joined the menagerie!"

Arch snorts. "Welcome, Zane. Now's your cue to wade in, threaten to take Melanie, and fistfight with Trey."

Zane's eyes widen as he surveys the room, ignoring Arch. "Oh my God! What's—"

I cut him off. "Mabel, what's happening?" I ask as I feel a deep, new pain.

"It's about to be over, Melanie." Mabel says to Trey, "There's no time to trance her out."

Demitri rattles Trey's shoulder to refocus him. "We're going to need you to pull pain as hard as you can."

"I'm tapped," Trey groans.

"No time," Tanner panics. "Be tapped later!"

"This is it, guys," Arch guides from his spot at the door. "Superhero time."

Demitri wraps his hand around my cheek and focuses down and in as he works to send waves of calm, using energy he can't afford to waste. Apparently, we're all gutting up.

Sweat covers Trey's ashen face, but he steels his resolve, his hand tightening around mine.

"When you feel your next contraction coming, give me one solid push, Melanie," Mabel coaches.

I take a gasping breath as my stomach tightens, and Tanner grips the back of my head, helping me draw my chin to my chest. I engage all my muscles that rage their protest. Pain seers through me, and I start to scream.

Mama Mabel calmly says, "If you're screaming, you aren't pushing. Push through the pain, and it'll be over."

I feel Trey pull pain harder, his psyche contorting with the effort, yet I still hurt so badly I see stars.

Mabel gasps as the contraction ends and everyone looks at her. She stands, and her chest and arms are dripping with sticky crimson. "Demitri, get over here," she demands, her tone frantic.

Demitri scoots out from behind me, and Zane rushes to take Demitri's place.

Demitri runs to the bathroom. "I'm covered in vomit. I have to wash my hands before I do this."

Trey sobs, and shock reverberates down our connection. "She can't die, Mabel!" he exclaims.

"I don't think she's going to," Zane says while he ponders deeply.

"Explain," Mabel orders.

"The memory of her with the gatekeepers. They said everything was going to change and she had to learn humility." Zane's tragic gaze scans down my body. "Her 'one-for-one' trade is me for the baby."

"Thank God," Trey explodes.

I look at him.

"Melanie, I'm sorry, but . . ."

I blink rapidly, trying to clear my foggy mind. "I'm going to throw up again."

Destiny brings a waste basket my way. I lean over it, but my need to throw up evaporates as another contraction hits. Pain blisters through me, and I make a keening sound.

"Look at me, Melanie," Mabel orders. "Breathe! You can't push."

I fight every instinct that's raging through me and somehow manage not to push. When the contraction ends, I throw up in the trash can that Destiny lifts just in time.

"Do you want gloves?" Mabel hollers.

"No, her blood has no disease in it," Demitri responds from the bathroom, over the sound of flowing water. "She's already going to need antibiotics. My ability works better with no barriers."

"Apparently Trey's does also," Tanner snarks, earning a tense laughter spurt from Arch.

Demitri reenters the bedroom. "My reserves are severely bottomed out. I need someone to boost me. The choice is between Bear, Darren, or . . ." He looks to Zane. "Is Rocco here?"

Zane nods.

Tears roll down my cheeks as I squeeze my eyes close, blocking out my mortification. "No, no, no. I don't want you to do this."

"We don't have time to get you to a hospital," Demitri insists. "I need you to trust me."

"It's not that I don't trust you," I whimper.

"Look at me, Melanie," Arch says.

I open my eyes.

"I understand that there's nothing more humiliating than your male friends witnessing this, but we need to get you through it. Demitri's not about to see anything he didn't already witness in the past thirty minutes."

"This is no different from what you had to do with me while you were in the hospital," Zane encourages, placing a hand on my cheek.

Life and death be damned, the teen part of me is cratering under the weight of humiliation. I give Mabel an imploring look, and her expression softens.

"I know, sweetheart," she commiserates. "This is a lot, but it's okay."

"I need Rocco," Demitri decides. "I think Melanie will handle him in here better than the other two."

Arch leans through the door. We hear him murmuring before he comes back in, followed by Rocco. Arch shuts and locks the door while Rocco studies the situation.

Rocco takes a deep breath. "Where do you need me?"

"Refill me as I crater, and don't make it weird," Demitri requests.

"I would never," Rocco says, but he's scanning the nightmare with huge eyes.

"Yo, asshat," Tanner barks, earning Rocco's attention. "Melanie feels weird about this! Act normal."

"What the fuck?" Rocco mutters as he crosses to Demitri, stepping behind him and staring only at my face with comically huge eyes.

"Not convincing, but we'll take it," Tanner mutters.

"You can do this, Meley. I need you to trust me," Demitri says, getting down to business now that everyone is in place.

I nod, and Demitri leans over my legs. "Pull pain, Trey. I'm about to be wrist deep."

Before I can argue, my abdomen tightens. "Contraction coming," I warble out around the growing pressure.

"Don't push, Melanie!" Demitri orders. "Hold on."

There's a blisteringly painful explosion as Demitri leans farther over me. I start to scream.

Mabel grabs my knee. "Breathe in and hold it, Melanie," she instructs. "Wait for Demitri to tell you what to do."

Demitri closes his eyes and turns his head, concentrating as his forehead instantly beads with sweat. I feel an energetic searching as his hand grips something in my gut.

"Owwwww! *Stop*!"

"I know, Melanie," Demitri murmurs through deep concentration.

The need to push is overwhelming, and Trey grunts out around his pain sharing, "She has to push, Demitri."

I scream desperately.

Zane grabs my hand. "Squeeze hard, Melanie."

I get a death grip on his hand, yanking him down. He bunches around me.

"Her uterus is torn, and her cervix has swollen shut," Demitri says. "When she pushed with the contraction Mabel dealt with, the tear in her uterus worsened. The closed cervix is forcing the baby out the uterine wall, and Meley's internally hemorrhaging."

The contraction ends.

"So many lady part problems," peels from Tanner, who starts rocking back and forth, petrified.

"Act normal!" Rocco barks at him.

Tanner rattles his head, coming out of his shock.

"What a fucking circus," Arch mumbles.

I sob and let go of Zane. "Do something," I beg Demitri.

"You have two options," Demitri informs with feigned calm. "I can force open your cervix. It's going to hurt, but you'll be able to push through the next contraction, and this will be over. The other option is I can dilate it slowly, but you'll have to handle five or six contractions without pushing."

"Do it, now. I can't handle any more."

"Deep breath, baby girl. You're going to feel my hand shift." Demitri looks at Tanner and Zane. "Don't let her move." He starts to glance over his shoulder at Rocco.

"I've got you," Rocco says. "Do it."

Demitri closes his eyes and concentrates as Tanner and Zane clamp down on me. I feel his hand move in my gut, and then an energy burst rocks through me that makes me see stars as pain explodes. I scream silently this time, the pain so intense that no sound escapes. The building rumbles as I lose my mind. My head drops back as tears rush down my cheeks. Trey moans as he pulls pain. I feel through our connection as his psyche starbursts, and he nearly passes out.

"That's the first time I've seen Melanie hurt so bad she can't make sound," Arch marvels in horror.

Another contraction hits.

"Push now," Demitri says. "I'm going to help you."

I take another gasping breath as Zane puts his hand under my neck, helping curl me around my midsection. I push as hard as I can.

"Zane," Demitri snarls through gritted teeth, "press hard on the right side of her stomach."

I feel Zane blast panic before a hard jolting pain. I scream.

"Push HARDER, Zane," orders Demitri.

My eyes roll into the back of my head as my body starts seizing. I hear Zane sob, just as Demitri exhales hard.

"Good work, Zane," Demitri says with a harsh exhale.

The pain dies down some.

"Good girl," Mama Mabel says. "Lie back. It's over."

"Real over, or 'normal' over?" Rocco gasps.

"Real over," Mabel says. "You did good, Rocco."

"Trey, don't look over there," Arch warns. His voice sounds faint and far away in my shocked state.

I look at Trey, and his eyes are closed. Zane slumps, panting from emotional trauma. His hand, still on my stomach, trembles.

"What the hell did Zane just have to do?" Tanner whispers in shock.

"He pushed the baby's head back through the torn uterine wall," Demitri stoically explains.

Zane's hands shakily drift to cover his face. When he drops them, blood prints are left behind.

Demitri's hand and arm are coated in blood all the way to his elbow. He wipes his sweaty forehead on his other sleeve and looks like he's going to pass out.

"You did good, Demitri," Mabel compassionately says. "You saved her."

Demitri's head sags, and he exhales hard, muttering, "That was fucking brutal."

Tanner makes a heaving sound. Sapphire puts a trash can in his arms just as he throws up.

"Are you okay, Melanie?" Demitri asks.

I try to clear my foggy head but can't. "I don't know." My teeth start chattering. I whimper, "I'm sorry, Demitri."

I try to roll over on my side, and Mabel stops me.

Trey looks at Demitri's arm and closes his eyes tight.

"That was horrific," Arch says. "You're a fucking beast, Demitri."

Destiny steps up to Demitri and wipes his arm and hand down with a wet towel.

Mama Mabel kneels back in her unfortunate spot and does something new that hurts. I gasp, and Trey pain shares again.

I try to tip my head up. Zane puts his hand over my eyes and gently pulls my head back down.

Mama Mabel stops whatever she's doing, and the pain lessens. Trey and I both sag, but he keeps syphoning off pain, bringing the level down to next to nothing now that the worst of it is over. I exhale, relieved.

"What did Demitri have to do?" Trey asks.

"He pulled the baby out in the palm of his hand," Tanner whispers, still in a state of shock.

Trey looks at Demitri, his expression grief-stricken.

"The baby was already gone, Trey," Demitri assures. "It had no heartbeat. That's the first thing I checked when I got here. At that point, it became a matter of keeping Melanie alive."

Trey looks at Demitri's arm that's stained a red tinge. "Thank you, Demitri. You definitely got the worst end of the helper jobs on this one." He shakes his head and halfheartedly jokes, "Bet you didn't wake up this morning planning to turn your Fraggle into a ventriloquist doll."

The tension breaks, and everyone chuckles quietly.

"I'm no stranger to pain, but you took that shit to a whole new level," I tell Demitri.

Demitri turns to lean on my dresser. His head hangs, and I'm scared I've lost my best friend. He's run from a deeper connection with me before, and this nightmare is more than I should ask of my teenage friend, old soul or not.

"Is Melanie going to live now?" Zane tearfully asks.

"Yes, honey." Mabel compassionately scans the room as all the guys exhale hard. "Melanie's in the clear. The one-for-one trade had to be the baby."

"Darren commented that her energy wasn't humming, and then found an energy hum in her gut when she was trying to save Zane," Demitri says. "I guarantee that was the baby's energy." He puts his hand on my stomach, and the pain improves a bit. "I got the bleeding to slow," he informs. "I need a few days to recharge before I can fix this, though."

Mama Mabel takes off her medical gloves. "I'm going to call Dr. Fontaine for a round of antibiotics." She looks into my eyes. "You're going to be okay, Melanie. He'll come check you." Mama Mabel crosses to the intercom and pushes a button. "Constance, I need a fresh mattress and linens from storage brought to the Valdez room, please."

"Good job, love," Zane says. "You got through it."

Trey stands, motioning for Tanner to hold my hand, and crosses the room. He kneels in the corner while he internally loses his mind. Without Trey's help, pain hums and throbs through me, but it's nothing compared to what I just felt.

Arch crosses the room to help Trey.

"Tanner, we need to clean up," Destiny says as she gestures my way subtly. "Arch, keep Trey facing the corner, okay? Demitri, don't turn around."

"I've already seen all of it," Demitri says. He turns from the dresser and passes the cleanup process to sit down next to me. He leans to block my view, and with a dejected smile, adds, "I'm proud of you."

I hear rustling as Destiny and the three other girls scurry about.

I close my eyes and think, *Are we going to be okay after this?* I put my hand on Demitri's chest and send the memory. He watches it and takes my hand, squeezing gently. I take the offered memory.

He thinks, *'We'll always be okay, Melanie. I know you didn't want me to see or do any of what I just had too. I knew I could fix you, but I apologize I had to hurt you to do it. I want you to understand that I will never intentionally hurt you or do something you aren't okay with again. The ONLY reason I did is because it was a matter of life or death.'*

A fresh round of tears streams down my cheeks. I'm shivering as Demitri pulls the edge of the blanket over my chest.

"I'm covered in blood," I protest. "I'll ruin the blanket."

"It already needs to be thrown away," he reassures me. "Don't worry."

"I promise I'll pay for it," I whimper to Mabel.

"No one is concerned about the bedspread," Mama Mabel says. She wipes sweaty strands of hair from my forehead.

Through our open connection, I hear Trey whisper to Arch, "I promise I've got her. I need Demitri to back off."

"He's not usually that blunt, but Melanie nearly dying threw him off," Arch whispers back. "Cut him some slack. He's not going to give up being her best friend, Trey. With that said, I don't think he'd interfere in your relationship under normal circumstances."

Trey's shoulders hunch, and I feel a wave of heartbreak over losing the baby pour from him. I block the connection between us, giving Trey what little privacy I can while he breaks down.

I squeeze Demitri's hand and send him the memory of Trey and Arch's whispered exchange. He watches it and nods to himself.

Demitri scoots off the bed and pats Zane on the shoulder. Rocco puts an arm around Demitri and guides him into the other corner to quietly talk. Demitri breaks down, and Rocco hugs him.

Zane gently scoots out from behind me and kneels next to the bed. He holds my hand. "I'm so sorry that you lost the baby to save me," he says through tears.

My face falls, and Zane cups my cheek.

"I didn't want a baby, Zane. I know that's terrible of me."

"Hey, hey, hey," Zane quietly replies, "It's okay that you feel that way."

Guilt radiates from me.

"I didn't want this either, Melanie," Trey says. "I've never been so relieved. You're alive, and the exchange that was looming is done. I've never felt more guilty in my life."

"You're on the same page," Rocco says. "Everything you're both feeling makes so much sense."

"Nice work keeping it together, Rocco," Arch compliments stoically.

With the same stoic gravity that some of the guys have dropped into, Rocco nods his appreciation Arch's way.

Trey's head drops, and he starts sobbing again. Tanner hugs him while Arch stands vigil for a long stretch.

CHAPTER 25

Frustration wars with my shocked state. I've been stuck here for fifteen minutes, lying in blood and drying vomit while Mabel fusses with my lady parts. The guys are all either rallying or falling apart. Trey's emotional meltdown has consumed Tanner and Arch. Rocco's busy flustering between Demitri and Zane, who've set up trauma camps on opposite sides of the room. Demitri's energy backlash raged up twenty minutes ago, and he collapsed. Sapphire had to abandon her assistant duties to use smelling salts to revive Demitri, who is now under her watchful hawkeye. Destiny double-timed it to assist Mabel because her other two girls cratered and had to leave the room. The problem is that no one has helped me cope with all of this. I've been resigned to a body being worked on while the mortified sixteen-year-old part of me dejectedly spirals through humiliation.

"Arch, we need Trey," Mama Mabel says when Destiny finishes cleaning up.

Trey's shoulders hunch, and his back flexes while he works through what he's dealing with internally. Arch looks back at Mama Mabel and shakes his head.

"Trey needs a minute, and I need to go deal with the potentially dead assholes in my parking lot," Mama Mabel says to me. "Who do you trust that hasn't already been through hell to help you shower?"

"I would like to help Melanie," Adam announces as he slips back into the room. "There aren't words to express how sorry I am for leaving at the worst time."

He's clearly distraught, but I can't deal with him right now. I ignore Adam's offer.

"I need Finley, please," I request.

"I'll get Fin," Arch quietly says with conviction. He focuses on me, and his expression compassionately slacks. "I'm so sorry, Mel. Love you."

"Love you too, Arch," I whisper back, my voice wobbly. "Thank you for helping."

"Warn Finley," Tanner requests.

Arch nods and heads out the door.

"Thank you for helping Melanie," Tanner says to Mabel. "I know Trey will thank you when he snaps out of it."

"Melanie and Trey are going to need you. They're both traumatized," Mama Mabel says.

'Nice of her to notice,' I sarcastically think, earning a side-eye from Adam, who picked it up across our connection.

"You and Finley are welcome to stay in the guest room across the hall, if you're up for helping them," Mabel offers.

Tanner agrees as Mama Mabel leaves and closes the door behind her.

"How bad is the room?" I ask Tanner.

"Mama's girls have cleaned up the worst of it, other than the destroyed bedding that we'll handle while you're in the shower. You look like you've been through a war, though, and it's shocking. Finley can handle it, if she's prepped. We'll get you cleaned up."

Finley walks in, surveying the scene, but to her credit she doesn't fall apart or panic. She leans her head out the cracked door. "Melanie's not going to be up for visitors tonight. Absolutely no one comes in this room without permission."

We can overhear people clamoring on the other side of the door.

"Enough," we hear Arch authoritatively say in the hallway. "What Melanie just went through is going to give me nightmares. Their room looks like a Civil War battle triage unit. She's covered from head to toe in blood. All of us are covered in vomit and blood. She nearly died and Demitri had to save her. If Melanie didn't have magical friends, we'd be calling the coroner right now. I assure you that Melanie and Trey have earned privacy. They need time, and Melanie needs rest."

"How did Demitri save her?" we hear Victoria ask.

"Here we go," Demitri mutters as he gets up from the floor and crosses to the bed, taking my hand.

"He had to force her body to cooperate, and he pulled the baby out," Arch informs.

"If she's pissed, will you be okay?" I ask Demitri.

"I don't give a shit if she's pissed. I wasn't going to leave you in a deadly situation because my girlfriend wouldn't approve of what I had to do to help you."

"I'm glad he could help," Victoria says.

I'm surprised by her response, but Demitri still rolls his eyes. I look up at him quizzically, and he squeezes my hand. I take the memory of him thinking, *'I guarantee she'll eventually decide she's pissed because I had to see you undressed. I don't care at this point. I'm over her.'*

"You guys need to go home," Finley informs the hall dwellers, using the "mom voice" we regularly tease her about. She closes the door and locks it.

"Fin, I need to get in the shower," I inform, wanting to get on with this so I can finally get dressed. I've endured my "naked spectacle role" in this macabre farce for as long as I can muster. "Can you handle helping me?"

Finley surveys Trey, who's sobbing on his knees in the corner. She hits Adam with an icy stare. If looks could kill, he'd keel over dead.

Adam shakes his head, his face a mask of agony, and starts to speak.

"Shut up, Adam!" Finley snaps, being uncharacteristically nasty. She turns her sky-blue eyes my way. "Of course," she says.

"Thank you," I whisper as post-trauma tears roll calmly down my cheeks.

"Everyone in the parlor heard the screaming," Finley enlightens. "We knew we needed to go outside and get the Reapers carted off, but we couldn't bring ourselves to leave in case any of us proved to be useful."

"There wasn't anyone outside when I got here," Zane informs.

"I told all of them about what you've been through lately," Finley continues. "Trey filled me and Tanner in on the latest during the baby shower. Every single person is horrified that they weren't there for you when you needed them. They stayed, hoping to apologize. Obviously, now isn't a good time. Hence, why I sent them home, but they get it."

Finley gives Adam the full weight of her infamous disappointed-mom glare. "I plan to speak with you later," she tells him.

"I already know I've been an ass, Finley," Adam says.

"I don't care if you know or not," Finley rails. "I'm so damn mad at you that I need to get it out. Your selfish bullshit is bad enough, but you leaving Melanie stranded outside because you forgot to pass on a phone message cost Melanie and Trey their baby.

Meanwhile you and your selfish wife get to have two."

"I lost the baby because of a trade I made for Zane's soul," I inform. "We thought the trade was for my soul, but it wasn't."

"What are you talking about?" Adam asks.

"I'm talking about what you never took time to hear from Bear and Darren."

"Who did you make the trade with?" he asks.

"The gatekeepers in the spirit realm." I look away. "Losing the baby isn't on you, but leaving me outside and being so oblivious is."

"I hope that Karma drops you to your knees, Adam! Over and over! You deserve it," Finley says, trying to calm her tears of rage. "You're *so* self-centered!"

I didn't know Finley was capable of that level of brutality.

Finley surveys Demitri, who is clearly in shock. "Demitri, you've earned a breather," Finley softly says.

"Meley needs help," Demitri quietly replies, but his hands are shaking.

"I'll help her," Zane offers.

"You sure?" Demitri whispers, on the edge of tears.

Zane nods. "I've got this."

Demitri leaves the room, and I internally panic. *He's not okay.*

"I'm going to go talk to him," Rocco says. "I'm so sorry, Melanie."

Finley and Zane slowly help me up. I gasp, but I make it to my feet.

Zane gestures to Trey's office supplies on his nightstand. "Grab the scissors," he says to Finley. "Cut her sports bra down the front and back. The top is constricting. It'll hurt if we wiggle it off."

Finley cuts the blood-coated sports bra and slides each half down my arms. I hang my head, wishing I had more privacy than our situation allows.

Zane wraps his arm around my chest, covering what he can as politely as possible.

Adam rushes to the bathroom and comes back with a towel that he holds over me. Apparently, I sent my embarrassment down our connection without realizing it.

I hate needing help.

"I'm going to pick you up," Zane gently warns. "It's going to hurt, but I think walking will be worse."

"Wait," Trey interrupts with conviction. He pulls himself together and stands. When he turns to us, clarity is back in his eyes.

Points for him.

"I'll pull pain so you don't have to," Adam offers.

"Get OUT!" Trey roars.

"I'm sorry about earlier. I've got you. Let's get this done," Adam insists.

"Leave," Trey snarls, and Adam hesitantly does.

"Tanner, I know you'd be here through this till the bitter end if you could, but I'm worried about you," Finley says. "You need a break."

"Will you be okay if I step out?" Tanner compassionately asks me, but his eyes are still dilated with shock.

I nod. "Thank you for everything you did."

"Mama asked if we could stay here tonight," Tanner says to Finley as he heads to the door. "She's putting us in the room across the hall. Are you okay with that?"

Finley agrees and Tanner exits.

Zane heads into the bathroom, and I hear him turn on the shower.

Trey taps into our connection and completely blocks my pain as he lifts me. Finley lays the towel over me. Trey winces as he takes on the excruciating jolt that I don't feel. His forehead sweats, and he turns pale again. He freezes statue-still, all his muscles bunched, until my pain dissipates in his body.

When he's able to walk again, he carries me into the bathroom and hands me to Zane. Trey walks to the toilet, kneels, and throws up. Zane turns to block my view, and I sag with my head on Zane's chest. He puts his cheek on my forehead.

Zane turns to face Trey's way after the toilet flushes.

"Trey, I know this was a lot," I console. My forlorn expression matches Trey's. "I can feel that you need a minute. You can go."

"I'm not leaving you right now," he insists, but he looks dead on his feet.

"I need you to, because I also need a minute," I softly reply.

Trey gives into emotional exhaustion. "I'll be ready when you come out."

"Thank you." I watch as Trey slips out, closing the door behind him. I swallow hard.

"How about Zane holds you in the shower while I clean you up, and then I'll step out?" Finley offers, getting down to business. "It's going to take two people."

"Yes, please."

"Zane, are you comfortable with this?" Finley asks.

"Yes," he stoically replies.

Finley studies him. "It's weird. I know you're Zane Drell, but you also aren't, you know?"

"I used to be Zane Drell, and then that person was hijacked by a public image." Zane scrunches his mouth. "If it helps, who you're seeing is who I really am."

"I like that you're down-to-earth. Thank you for helping Melanie." Finley strips to her underwear and bra, prepping to get in the shower. Somehow, she seems unfazed by the oddity, but acting *normal* is the theme of this nightmare. I suspect Arch coached her when he retrieved her. "Melanie, can Zane set you down so he can get out of his jeans?" she asks with forced normalcy in her tone, confirming my suspicion of the coaching.

I love her for it. I'm out of room for anymore humiliation.

"Just unbutton me," Zane says while he lifts me a little higher.

Finley blushes, but efficiently unbuttons and unzips Zane's jeans. He turns, and she lowers his pants. She reaches toward the linen cabinet and takes out a washcloth before stepping into the shower in her underwear. "Just hold her so she doesn't have to stand," she tells Zane. "I've got it." Zane steps into the shower in his boxers. Finley squirts my vanilla-and-sandalwood soap onto the washcloth and instructs Zane to turn when she needs him to, while she cleans me up.

I cower, embarrassed for some reason about Finley helping with this. Through my hand on Zane's arm, I send a memory of me thinking, *'Somehow, Arch, Demitri, Rocco, you, and Tanner seeing me naked and vulnerable is okay, but Finley has me spun out.'*

"Finley, Melanie's struggling."

"I'm almost done. Look the other way, Zane." Finley says to me, her tone soft, "Deep breath. No embarrassment." I take the requested deep breath as Finley moves my knee. She gets to the worst of the cleanup.

I whimper, and exhausted tears roll.

Finley takes the showerhead from its holder and flips through the settings to the gentlest one. She tries that instead of the washcloth, and I exhale. "I'm sorry, Melanie," Finley quietly says.

I shake my head. "You're good, Fin. Everything just hurts."

She finishes her efficient cleanup job and grabs one of Trey's black towels before stepping out of the shower and drying herself off quickly. She leaves, and I bury my face in Zane's neck. We stood like this in the shower so many times while I was in the hospital after I broke my neck. I can fall apart with just Zane. Tears roll down my cheeks, and he patiently waits it out.

"I'm so sorry this happened," Zane says when I calm.

"I'm so glad you're alive, Zane." I look at him with big eyes.

"I never should have done what I did," Zane admits. "Had I known that you'd lose a baby . . ."

"I already know." My gaze drops. "I've seen the kids I'm supposed to have. The thought of that little girl being trapped by the gatekeepers is terrifying."

"You've seen your babies?"

"Yes. I'm supposed to have three." My expression crumples. "I don't know if I'm now having two." I look up at Zane. "The oldest is an actress. Would you like to see her?"

Zane nods. I send the memory of the pretty brunette, in her red dress, walking onto set with a script in her hand. She's confident, with old soul eyes. She's tiny, but a force to be reckoned with.

Zane closes his eyes, watching the brief memory, before looking at me again. "She's beautiful."

I nod, just starting to realize that I gave her up in a trade I didn't understand. "She's perfect."

"You love her so much in that memory," Zane says, a little choked up.

"She's my baby, even though she's my current age in that memory."

"The you in that memory is a good mom," Zane says. "You feel ready to take on the world for her."

"I hope she's okay," I whisper.

Zane slides down the tile wall and sits with me cradled in his lap.

"I've been through some tough things, but this? I'm sorry you walked in on that. I wasn't trying to reach you mind-to-mind."

"I know you weren't." Zane says. "I was hoping the connection would open when it was time. Rocco's been staying with me, waiting."

"I owe apologies to you, Rocco, Tanner, Demitri, and Arch." I say and shake my head in disbelief. "That was revolting."

"No," Zane replies, radiating honesty, "it was incredibly human."

"You say that now," I mutter, remembering that I can't trust Zane. I roll to my knees and slowly pull myself up by the soap shelf. "Your story will change when you tell it to Rachelle."

I discover that my legs work, and I'm relieved for only a moment, until I look down at Zane. His leg is covered in blood, and I grimace.

"I'm not going to gossip flippantly about this," Zane insists while he gets up. The only indication that he notices the mess is a slight turn in the water to tactfully rinse off. He gets an arm around me and opens the glass door, reaching for a towel.

He tries to wrap me in the towel, but I shake my head, caging down emotionally. "Get dried off. I'll get out in a minute."

Zane steps out of the shower and dries off. He turns his back to me, dropping the wet boxers and pulling on his blood- and vomit-stained jeans. I rinse off again while my legs shake.

"Please let me help you."

"I can do this, but thank you," I reply with a shaking voice. I can't do it myself, but I also can't depend on Zane. "I refuse for the end of your story to be that I couldn't even shower alone."

"Melanie, I'm not going to tear you down again with Rachelle," Zane desperately implores. "I know how it sounded when you got that memory of me doing that about the hospital."

"Will you please get Finley?" I request. Standing takes everything I've got.

Zane's eyes scrunch, but he heads to the door. Demitri comes in a moment later, and I wince.

"Hey, Meley," Demitri softly says. "Fin's talking to Tanner. Trey's in a shower. Will I work?"

I survey the clothes in his hands. "Just leave everything on the counter, please."

"You can hardly stand," Zane insists.

"I have to do this MYSELF!" irrationally screeches from me. Panic spirals as everything I just went through overwhelms me. My head drops. "Please," whispers out of me. "You have no idea how hard it is for me to be so helpless that I need people right now. I have to manage this."

Zane and Demitri exchange a pained look. "We'll be in your room," Demitri says. They leave, closing the door after them.

I swallow hard and manage to get out of the shower and dry off. I have to sit on the tile floor so I don't fall over as I reach for the clothes Demitri left on the counter. The effort makes me gasp. I lie on the floor, fighting to breathe around the pain. The door opens. I look up and watch as Zane and Demitri come in.

"You did good, Melanie," Zane softly says.

"Close your eyes," Demitri guides just above a whisper. I do, because there's nothing left of my energy, and they get busy efficiently dressing me. They communicate with quiet stoicism, saying cooperative things like, "Shift her."

"I wanted to do this myself," I whimper, as my shirt is pulled over my head gently.

"I'm sorry, Melanie," Zane says. "We couldn't handle that though."

I look up at him in the dim. "Why?"

Zane's head drops, his expression pained.

Demitri chooses to answer. "This is what the two of us have."

He looks so vulnerable. "We're the sidelined guys," he explains. "Trey deserves a few minutes to get it together. He left us here, knowing you'd need help. We'll be damned if we stand in the other room while you struggle on the floor. We need to do this. We all know you're a badass beast. You did your part, and we're doing ours."

Situated, Zane gingerly helps me to my feet. "I'll get things cleaned up in here," he says.

I wince, realizing the floor is a mess.

Zane smiles softly at me. "I've got this."

"Thank you."

Zane nods, clearly fighting tears.

I slide very young eyes Demitri's way. "Thank you."

"You're welcome," he quietly says. "Your room is ready. Would you like to lie down?"

"Yes, please."

"Can I carry you to bed?" Demitri asks.

I nod, my legs severely shaking, and he delicately picks me up. I wince from a jolt of pain. He carries me into the bedroom and pulls aside the sheet and new bedspread. A paper medical pad is on the bed. I blush.

"Don't worry about it," Demitri says. "Mabel's got this all figured out."

He sets me down on the paper pad and pulls the covers over me.

Zane comes in.

"Zane, you can go home," I inform. "I disrupted your evening. I'm sorry."

"I'd like to stay," Zane admits.

"I think you should get Rocco out of here." I grimace a little. "You're used to helping with my crazy, but he isn't. Thank you for coming here."

"You're sure?" Zane asks, his face slack and pale.

"I'm sure."

Zane slowly makes his way out the door.

"I know that I hate him for trivializing your hospital time." Demitri looks to the vacated door. "But damn, he's hard not to love."

"I know." I quirk my mouth. "The guy that just left is who I was sure he was. There's another side to him, though."

"Do you want him to stay?" Demitri asks.

"Yes. He's good at post-trauma aftermath, until he's not." My gaze drops. "I'm going to die of shame when he tells Rachelle."

Demitri sits on the bed and takes my hand. "This one was rough."

I nod.

"Thank you for trusting me tonight."

"Thank you for saving me."

The door opens, and Trey comes in wearing clean clothes. He has wet hair. "Hey," he softly says.

"Hey."

"Think we can try to sleep?" Trey asks.

"Yes, please."

Demitri stands, and he and Trey stare at each other. Their fight earlier worries me now that things have settled.

"Thank you," Trey expresses, albeit stilted.

"You're welcome," Demitri briskly replies before leaving and closing the door behind him.

CHAPTER *26*

I sweat profusely, my body feeling like I'm cooking from the inside, while simultaneously feeling like I'm freezing. It's been several hours since I was put to bed, but it feels like a million years.

"She's burning a wicked fever. I'm going to give her an IV antibiotic drip to deal with her infection," Dr. Fontaine instructs. He levels Mabel with serious eyes and adds with concern lacing his tone, "She's going to need surgery."

Mama closes her eyes and mournfully shakes her head.

The doctor starts an IV line in my hand and hangs a bag from the metal stand that Destiny wheeled in. He levels me with serious eyes. "I need to adjust my protocols. Your blood test showed that you weren't pregnant, but you clearly were. Your body doesn't react to traditional medical testing. It must be due to your status as a powerful energy worker. I'm going to research and create a new standard where you're concerned."

"Thank you," gasps from me.

Trey refuses to leave my side, and he's holding my hand while he siphons off pain again. He's exhausted. His face is gaunt, and dark circles ring his eyes. Dr. Fontaine arrived to check me twenty minutes ago, and while not as bad as what I went through earlier, the exam is painful. Trey's doing everything he can to help, but the strain on him has me worried.

I inhale sharply as Dr. Fontaine does something that sends throbbing pain up my midsection. Trey gasps slightly with me, taking half of my pain to keep me from passing out.

Dr. Fontaine finishes his examination. "You're okay, Melanie. The bleeding should subside steadily over the next few weeks. I'll look into getting you scheduled for surgery."

I get a memory from the doctor of his thought during my examination, *'This is bad. I don't think her uterus is childbearing-viable anymore.'*

I close my eyes tight and fuzz out my connection with Trey to avoid him hearing the thought. Panic sits just below the surface, and I tamp it down. *One problem at a time.*

Mabel pulls the covers up after the doctor finishes his examination.

Dr. Fontaine turns to Mama Mabel. "No heavy lifting, or strenuous activity. Keep her on the pill antibiotics until they're done. I don't want her at school until I clear it. Have them send work here. If she can't handle doing the work, I'll call the school myself and get her an extension."

"That would be great," Mabel says. "Her parents left to help with a sick relative, and Melanie's staying here while they're gone. They called this morning and said they need to extend their trip. The timing is good because she wants to keep this to herself."

"We'll see how keeping it to herself goes," Dr. Fontaine says. "She may have a long road ahead."

"We need to switch her birth control prescription to something stronger. I had her on the lightest dose possible when she needed a new prescription." Mama Mabel says. She raises an eyebrow, looking from me to Trey. "I should've known better."

"No intimate anything for four weeks, and I mean that," Dr. Fontaine sternly tells Trey. He turns back to Mabel. "I'll switch her prescription and call it in."

"Got it," Trey says.

"Trey, you need to get some rest," Dr. Fontaine adds. "You look like hell."

"As soon as her pain level drops, I will," Trey says.

"Pain pills are an option."

I shake my head weakly. "I've been down the pill road before, and I won't do it again, but thank you."

"Trey, your blood pressure is through the roof," Dr. Fontaine warns. "I need you to take a breather and get some legitimate sleep right now. I'm serious."

Trey glances at Mabel, and she nods. "It does no good if you collapse trying to help Melanie." Mabel asks me, "Who do you trust to come in here and help you sleep? You need to rest."

I slide blunt eyes Trey's way, and he snorts. "Is Demitri still here?" he asks Mabel.

"He is. Bear and Darren are helping Tanner, Arch, and Demitri work through everything in the parlor."

"Is he in good enough condition to help Melanie fall asleep?" Trey asks.

"Honestly, he's a nervous wreck because he's not in here," Mabel bluntly informs. "He keeps pacing like a dog with a burr up its butt. He'd likely be much happier if he could be of use to Melanie."

Dr. Fontaine removes my IV needle and packs up his stuff. He says his goodbyes, with a promise to return tomorrow, and takes his leave.

"I'm going to go get Demitri," Finley says. "I'll be in the parlor if you need me."

"Finley," I call as she starts to walk away.

She turns my way.

"Thank you. I know this was a lot."

"You're welcome. Tanner and I will be here with you every step of the way," Finley promises with a smile. She leaves.

"Are you okay with Demitri doing this?" I ask Trey.

Trey rubs his face hard. "We're in survival mode, and he's the best choice. So, yes."

There's a soft knock on the door, and Demitri comes in.

"No offense, but you look like shit and I'm loving it," Trey razzes. "Mr. Perfect finally got pushed over the edge."

I'm relieved because I didn't know how it would go when they saw each other again.

"Today's been a lot," Demitri says with a laugh. "I've got dangerously low energy reserves. Makes my usual shimmering glow a little less vibrant."

"I too have lost my usual shimmering glow," I joke. My exhausted eyes sparkle, amused.

"How about we all settle for being human for a minute instead of hot superheroes?" Demitri smirks.

Trey squeezes my hand before scooting off the bed. "I'm going to crater if I don't sleep off some of my energy backlash. I can't curl up with Melanie because my pain siphoning ability won't shut off if I'm touching her when she's this injured. Any chance you'd be willing to hang with her so she can sleep?"

"No problem," Demitri says with relief.

"I'm nervous about seeing Tanner and Arch again," I admit. "I was scared to see you again. I don't do vulnerable gracefully. I didn't realize how intense that whole episode was going to get, or I wouldn't have dragged you, Arch, and Tanner into it." I look at Trey. "We would have dealt with it on our own."

"You would've died. It took all of us." Trey looks at Demitri. "How are Tanner and Arch holding up?"

"Exactly how you'd expect," Demitri says. "Tanner is finding ways to be amusing, and Arch is quietly pondering. They're both fine. They're also both fully aware that Melanie's going to be a weird mess."

"To alleviate weirdness, you and I are good." Demitri addresses me directly.

"Please make sure Trey sleeps," I tell Mabel. "I'll be okay. It sounds like me and D are in a good place."

"How long can you stay?" Mabel asks Demitri.

"Victoria left, and my dad is out of town," Demitri responds. "I refused to leave in case Melanie needed me. I'm good with whatever."

Mama Mabel nods.

"Panic room the door," Trey requests. "I can't be knocked out cold if I don't know she's locked up tight. I'm going to ask the guys that are still here to stay and keep an eye on the place while I'm unconscious."

Mabel and Trey leave, and Demitri opens the panel, pushing the panic room button. We listen as the locks slide into place.

I grimace grandly as I realize something humiliating.

"What's up, Meley?" Demitri asks.

I swallow hard as a mortified crimson blush creeps up my neck and engulfs my face. "I need something, but getting up is painful and I'm not wearing anything." My eyes slide to the blanket covering my waist.

Without hesitation, Demitri opens my dresser and grabs some shorts, handing them to me.

I wince. "That's part of what I need," whimpers from me.

Demitri pulls a pair of panties from the next drawer, after

searching through a few. I let him poke around because I'm going to faint from humiliation. He starts to hand them to me, and I whimper, "Umm. . . Doctor Fontaine had to do an internal examination. Mabel took my. . ." I trail off.

Demitri ponders a moment, because I'm being less than helpful. "Aaahhh," breathes from him before he disappears into the bathroom. I hear paper pulled from the sticky tape and I'm both relieved, and extra horrified, that he figured out my problem.

He returns with the panties clutched in his hanging hand. He cocks a hip in a perfect imitation of Tanner. "Be NORMAL," flamboyantly flusters from him.

I crack up laughing and cover my bright red face with my hands. "I'm sorry, Demitri."

"Look at me, girly," he says. I do, and he chuckles. "A few hours ago, I was stuffed elbow deep in your ya-ya. I think I can handle a pair of panties and a pad."

"This has been the single most humiliating day of my life," I gossip, grateful that he's taking the edge off with humor.

Demitri nods. "Yup. That's totally understandable." He takes a comically deep breath. "Now, you're going to act like it's totally normal while I help you, because for me, it actually feels normal. I've seen the show." He gestures to the blanket covering me, but he uses the panty-holding hand, causing the panties to flap about and me to peel laughter. "I've seen my fair share of what you sport. It's all very normal. I'm about to do this for you, because I'm dead tired and I can't handle watching you struggle in pain."

"Thank you," I say appreciatively. "You know I love you, right?" comes from me unintentionally, and in my most sincere tone. For a heartbeat, I'm embarrassed, but then I decide to go with it, because it's not like I can stuff the statement back in my mouth hole.

Demitri's expression slides stoically. "I love you too. Now gut up for some normalcy." He pulls the blanket aside and slides the panties over my ankles while I cover my face and blush so severely that I feel like I'm going to pass out. Demitri's arm slides under my back, and he lifts my tush slightly from the bed while shimmying the underwear in place with his other hand.

The bedspread covers me again, and only then am I willing to drop my hands from my face. "Thank you," I whisper.

"For what?" Demitri asks casually, like he didn't just do any of this. He moves a chair next to the bed. He sits and laces his hand with mine before propping his feet on the bed with his ankles crossed.

"You're going to hurt sleeping like that," I inform him.

"Doesn't matter. I just need to know you're okay." Demitri's head flops back against the top of the chair. "Love you, Meley. Goodnight."

"Love you, too, Demitri. Thank you for helping me," I mumble as I fall asleep.

CHAPTER 27

I wake to the sound of movement. My eyes snap open and I sit up, ready for a fight. I groan as pain radiates through my abdomen.

"It's just me, love," Trey says as he pulls on a T-shirt. He clicks on the nightstand light and smiles at me. Steam pours from the bathroom from the shower he must have just taken.

Demitri shifts in his chair and sits up. He stretches and asks Trey, "What time is it?"

"Noon."

"You okay, Trey?" I ask. "How did last night go?"

"Mabel gave me sleeping pills. It was weird. I just felt totally gone, but I feel better today." He sits on the bed and puts his hand flat on my stomach to do a pain search. "It's still bad, babe," he says.

"The pain is so much less than what it was at the worst of it that it just kind of feels like a relief."

"I'm going to get cleaned up and handle some stuff," Demitri says. "I promise I'll be back to help you, okay?"

"Thanks, Demitri. I know it's been the weekend from hell." I smile and hug him.

"That's kinda how it goes with this group, you know? Could be worse. We could be planning your funeral." Demitri looks down at his hand, and dried blood is still under his fingernails.

I scrunch up my face and pout.

He glances my way and jokes, "It was purely selfish on my part. I didn't want to get partnered with Justine again if you died."

I crack up.

Someone knocks on the door, and Trey opens it. Tanner struts in, surveying Demitri shirtless in the chair. "Aaawww, yeah!" he says, shimmying his shoulders. "Get it, get it, get it."

Finley starts to smack Tanner on the arm for being crass when she sees Demitri. Her mouth drops open. "You have to be the HOTTEST guy on the planet," she blurts.

"I prefer to focus on my personality," he replies with an eye-roll. "Looks are a coincidence, but thank you."

Arch comes in, assesses the situation, and nudges the door closed with his foot.

"Can we just get this out of the way now?" I ask Arch and Tanner with a vulnerable look. "Is shit weird with us?"

"Lady parts don't freak me out," Arch replies, deadpan. "Death does, but that was narrowly averted. You and I are fine."

I blush, and everyone laughs quietly.

"Watching Demitri lose his hand in your Bermuda Triangle was eye-opening, but not friendship losing," Tanner tells me. He looks at Demitri and jokes, "Glad you didn't disappear, and congratulations on that particular skill set. I wouldn't have known where to start."

Me being called the Bermuda Triangle that everyone fears, and my soulmates get lost in, never to be emotionally stable again, has been a running joke.

"Losing a hand was less of a practiced skill and more of a necessity, but thank you." Demitri says and turns to me. "For the record, and never to be mentioned again, I'm sorry. I know that hurt."

"You okay?" Finley asks.

I nod. "I'm over the humiliation phase." I look at Demitri and add, "And, yes, it hurt. Asshole."

Everyone laughs.

"Normal squaaad," Tanner sasses, earning exhausted chuckles from the rest of us.

"Now for the bad news," Arch says. "Victoria is here to talk to Demitri. She wants details on what happened. So far, she's only being mildly bitchy, but the day is young."

"I need my shirt," Demitri groans.

I scoot out from the covers and bend to get Demitri's shirt for him. Blazing pain rips through my abdomen, and I gasp.

"Seriously, Mel?" Trey says as he leans to pick up the shirt. "You have no business helping anyone right now."

I tip my head back and whimper. I know I'm pale, covered in a cold sweat. Trey eases me down on the bed.

Demitri tugs on the shirt before putting his hand on my stomach. He sighs. "Meley, this pain is going to take a lot to fix, and I need another day before I can attempt it."

"I'm okay," I whisper. "I just need a minute."

"Demitri, I think you and I need to talk before you meet with your girlfriend in the parlor," Arch guides.

Tanner takes his room key out of his pocket. "I'll let you two into our guest room."

"Demitri will be there in a minute," Trey says to Arch. "We need to talk."

"I'll go chat with Victoria while you guys talk," Finley says.

"So much talking needed," I grumble. I scrunch up my face like a Fraggle, and Demitri pensively chuckles.

"You doing okay, D? Real deal, no bullshit," Trey asks after the others leave.

"Nope. Not one bit. What we all went through yesterday . . ." Demitri looks at me with an expression edged with grief before focusing on Trey again. "Victoria's pettiness was already hard to deal with, but after watching Meley get beat half to death by bikers, and almost die on your bed, I can't even stomach the thought of a conversation with Victoria."

"Victoria's gonna lose her shit when she hears that you turned Melanie into a hand puppet and snuggled her all night," Trey remarks.

Demitri and I crack up, and I gasp, "It hurts to laugh. Stop."

"We didn't snuggle all night," Demitri assures. "I held her hand. That was it."

"How did your shirt end up off?" Trey asks, seeming vulnerable instead of angry.

"I burn up in a backlash state," Demitri informs. "I wasn't attempting to woo your passed-out girlfriend. Melanie slipped into a backlash coma moments after you left."

"Makes sense," Trey replies, barely over a whisper.

"Are you and me okay, Trey?" Demitri asks.

Trey hits him with a sincere expression. "Hell yes, we are. You saved Melanie. Frankly, I'm impressed that you challenged me. I'm the bruiser of our group, and you're passive. Melanie needs people in her life that are passionate about doing what they think is right for her."

Trey pauses for a long stretch, his gaze drifting contemplatively. "A warning that I'm out of tactful fucks to give, so I'm throwing the real deal out on the table. The three of us need to discuss this," Trey finally says and looks Demitri in the eyes. "I'm sorry that you're stuck in the position you're in. Adam and I have both been there, and it's damn hard to be sidelined when you love Melanie. You have my word that I respect your friendship with her. With that said, I'm not going anywhere."

I exhale hard and look from Trey to Demitri.

"I appreciate that," Demitri says. "I know you aren't. You need to know that I'm also not going anywhere."

The two guys stare at each other, and the air is stiflingly heavy. It's not laced with challenge as much as it's laced with reality.

"Fan-fucking-tastic," I snark, rolling my eyes. "Now, you two are all worked up."

Trey hits me with a heavy stare. "Can I ask you a couple questions?" he asks, and I nod. "I want honest answers, Melanie."

"I've only not been a hundred percent honest with you about Demitri one time," I taunt him with a mischievous smile.

"When?" Trey asks.

Demitri looks at me nervously.

"You asked if I loved him, and I distracted you from the question by telling you I wrapped my legs around him."

Trey's mouth drops open, but he can't help laughing. "You distracted me with Mr. Perfect's dick, so you didn't have to tell me you loved him?" he asks.

"Yup," I amusedly reply. "I wasn't ready to even *begin* to broach the topic. Sorry, but I saw it more as a distraction than a lie, so I went with it. I don't lie to either of you."

"All right," Trey says to me. "Now we're clear. You love him."

"Funny thing is, the two of you are a perfect balance," I say contemplatively. "Demitri's calm. He heals and sees the best in people. You, Trey, are harsh and pragmatic. You protect and handle brutality like a champ. Realistically, the two of you are exactly what I need. If I could mash you into one person, I would."

"What's Adam?" Trey asks.

"Adam's a selfish ass who's great when things are good, but I guarantee he'll hang me out to dry every damn time when being there is inconvenient," I say. "Yesterday proved that. He needed to stick it out for ten more minutes, and he cratered. Him leaving made things substantially more painful for me. I recognize that I'm not his problem anymore, but sometimes good people give of themselves to help others. He isn't good people. At least, not right now."

"What is Zane?" Trey asks.

"Demitri, will you please fill him in?" I say as I close my eyes.

"He doesn't know what happened?" Demitri asks.

I shake my head, and Demitri blows out a big breath. He fills Trey in on Zane gossiping with Rachelle about my hospital time.

Trey's mouth drops open. "Unreal," he says when Demitri gets to the end of the tawdry tale. He slides forlorn eyes my way. "I'm so sorry he did that, Melanie."

"Thank you for never betraying me like that," I quietly say to Trey, before looking to Demitri. "The same goes for you."

"I never would," Demitri replies.

Trey doesn't say anything, instead staring off into space again. It makes me suspiciously nervous, but he's been through so much that I brush it off.

I take the silent opportunity to really study both guys. "I'm forced to be and do the unthinkable," I share finally. "There's nothing exciting about being hunted, threatened, and stalked. Evil is attracted to me because there's something alluring about taking me out. I need Trey to protect me, and he's good at it. I need Demitri to let me be me. You keep me mentally safe because, at some point, I must be allowed to be a little quirky to decompress. I need the person who curls up with me and hands me a fresh box of crayons and a Care Bear coloring book."

"Seriously?" Trey asks. "Coloring? You level mobs."

"She does that because she has too," Demitri says. "She colors because she wants too."

"Wait, she *actually* colors?" Trey asks, incredulous.

"I have a picture of Laugh-A-Lot Bear framed in my bedroom that she colored for me for my birthday," Demitri says. "She was also at my house coloring when my dad was getting ready for a big casino design proposal. She colored a Good Luck Bear and gave the picture to him. He still has it on the refrigerator."

"She knows your dad that well?" Trey asks.

"Yes. He adores her and nicknamed her 'Little Imp.' He harps on me to date her all the time." Demitri crosses the room, unzipping my dance bag. He pulls out my Care Bear coloring book and the crayons he got me. He hands them to me. "It's a good day for coloring," he says.

"You got her a coloring book and crayons?" Trey asks.

"She likes the box with the sharpener built in, even though she never uses it." Demitri chuckles. "I have a Transformers coloring book in my dance bag that she got me. We ditch and color in my Jeep, while we listen to music and she eats SweeTARTS. I've always got a fresh box of them in my glove compartment."

"I was fine with him stuffing his hand up my favorite part of you," Trey tells me. "I was fine that he held your hand all night. Coloring books and SweeTARTS make me jealous, though. I didn't even know you like SweeTARTS."

"They're my dad's favorite candy." I shrug. "Demitri found that out when we went to see *Jurassic Park* and started buying them for me."

I flip through the coloring book and show Trey two pages. "You have a choice between the Care Bear Cousin, Noble Heart Horse, or Grumpy Bear," I tell him. "You get a picture to frame too."

"I like the grumpy one," Trey huffs.

"I'll color the picture for you."

"Don't forget that I got a picture first," Demitri says with a mischievous grin.

"How the *hell* do you have time to color with her?" Trey questions Demitri. "You're as busy as I am!"

"I make the time," Demitri replies. "I live for the moments when her anxiety level drops and she's happy. She laughs, and everything in me synchronizes."

"Shit. You really do love her." Trey intensely studies me. "What we dealt with yesterday aside, are you emotionally okay in general?"

"Now that you aren't being mean, I am," I reply. "But I want to level with you that I wouldn't be okay without Demitri. Frankly, you and I don't have a lot of fun. Our lives are painfully adult. You're always working, and all we do is battle evil. Demitri makes me feel like a normal teenage girl. We get ice cream. We go CD shopping. We color."

"It sounds like a relationship to me," Trey says.

"It's not, in the way you're insinuating, because you know how my dark-water side works," I explain. "Unless that riveting delight with his hand yesterday counts, he's never taken a spin with me. Without that, it's not a relationship in my world. He's legit my friend."

"Being honest, I'll never make time for shit like coloring," Trey tells Demitri. "It's just not who I am. Do me a favor and keep making her happy by fulfilling those types of things. She obviously needs it, and I'll see it as nothing but an annoyance."

"I will," Demitri states with a nod.

"It's weird realizing that Melanie needs both of us so deeply," Trey admits. "I didn't grasp that before this conversation."

"Thank you for accepting my friendship with Meley," Demitri

says. "I'd be devastated if I lost that with her. I spent a lot of time lonely before Melanie and I became friends. People are weird around me, and I hate it. If they aren't drooling, they get all tongue-tied and act bizarre. Melanie lets me be normal."

"You don't get caught up in his jaw-dropping perfection?" Trey asks me.

"I'd have to be dead not to notice," I joke, "but generally, not really. The one exception are his abs that render me brainless."

"That's true. She traces them absently when she reads with her head on my leg during studio breaks," Demitri reveals.

"You don't tell her to stop?" Trey asks.

"Nope. I love it," Demitri confesses.

"Sorry. It's a thing," I tell Trey, shrugging playfully. "Anyhow, his appearance made me nervous right up until I got to know his goofy side, and I see him totally different than everyone else does, now. He's funny and nice to me."

"You two spend a lot of time together. I've worried about him being all smoke-show smoldering around you," Trey admits.

I grin at Demitri and cross my eyes, squinching up my face comically. He laughs and makes the same face back.

"That's the smoldering smoke show that you're worried about," I tell Trey.

"There's nothing sexy about that, Demitri," Trey informs.

Demitri rolls his eyes and gives me the smoldering look Trey's harping on.

I cover my mouth, trying not to laugh.

Demitri shifts to a look that renders most people speechless, but I'm not most people. I bust up laughing.

"It's so ridiculous, I just can't." I wave my hand Demitri's way while telling Trey, "That does nothing for me. I like his silly faces a lot more."

"She's LITERALLY the only girl who has ever LAUGHED at my looks," Demitri says. "I freaking love that about her! I'm so sick of being stared at all the time."

"You want me to feel sorry for you because you're drop-dead gorgeous?" Trey scoffs.

"It's really lonely looking like this, Trey," Demitri says. "I'm not an egotistical supermodel in my head. I'm a quirky Fraggle. I finally found another quirky Fraggle who happens to love dance as much as I do. We both like SweeTARTS and TERRIBLE horror movies. We both like to read. We both think Elvis is way cooler than the Beatles."

"You like Elvis?" Trey asks me.

"My dream vacation is to tour Graceland," I say.

"If someone quizzed me, I'd say your dream vacation was somewhere tropical."

I shake my head. "I hate bugs, muggy weather, and extreme heat."

"Did you know that about her?" Trey asks Demitri.

Demitri nods. "My dad took me to Graceland, and I bought the tour video for her. We watched it together at my house one evening, and she was mesmerized."

"Of course, Mr. Perfect found a way to take Melanie on her dream vacation without ever leaving California," Trey mutters.

"Thank you for discussing all of this with me." Demitri pats Trey on the shoulder. "I'm going to go talk with Arch. Melanie, you need to stay in bed and rest. And Trey, I'm going to go home after I finish dealing with Victoria. Call if you need me before I come back to heal her."

Trey nods his agreement.

Demitri kisses me on the forehead and leaves.

CHAPTER 28

I take a gasping breath as I accidentally shift in a particularly painful way. It's late, and my pain tolerance seems to severely diminish at the end of the night. I'm not pleased that Adam interrupted the chat Trey and I were about to have with Mabel, who had just sat down at our little dining table when he slogged in. Resigned to this, I stare at Adam, hoping whatever he wants is quick. I'm not in the mood to deal with him. I want to talk with Mabel and then attempt to sleep through the night.

"What did the doctor say?" Adam asks.

"None of your damn business, Adam," I snap. "By club edict, I'm declaring Retribution Clause against the Stones. Let Valerie know I accept her challenge."

"That's not necessary," Adam insists.

I can feel his panic thrum under the surface. "I should have never gone to you for help in the first place, and I apologize for it." It's easier just to level him with reality. I smile with a hint of malicious evil. "I want to thank you for breaking my heart by proposing to Valerie. I dodged a serious bullet because you would've been a shit boyfriend." I meet Trey's gaze across the room.

"I love you so much, Trey," I say. "Thank you for not leaving my side even though it was impossibly difficult for you to make it through the nightmare. I definitely landed in the right set of arms."

I watch heartbreak fill Adam's eyes. Trey's and Mabel's eyebrows shoot into their hairlines as they exchange a side-eyed glance. Trey works through what I've said. I note something alarming about his expression, but I don't have the gumption to unpack it right now.

"I love you, Melanie," Trey sends down our connection. *"I'll always be here. Come hell or high water, I've got you."* Both Adam and I can hear this.

I smile down the connection with Trey, sending love and that I feel safe with him. Simultaneously, down my connection with Adam, I radiate finality laced with sadness.

"Valerie and I had a long talk," Adam says. "I was brutally honest. After a whole lot of reflection, she's mortified. She's been so caught up with her own struggles that she lost sight of a lot." He shifts apology gears to Mama Mabel. "With the utmost sincerity, I apologize on behalf of both Valerie and me. You've been incredibly generous, and we're both ashamed of how we took advantage of you." Adam looks to Trey next, but Trey cuts him off.

"I don't care what you have to say," Trey snaps. "Save it."

Adam turns to me again. He takes a breath, trying to work through the swelling emotions I can feel through our connection. "Melanie, there aren't words to express how sorry Valerie and I are," he declares. "Val cried harder than I've ever seen her cry when she realized that she had you running like mad when you were faced with all the side effects of pregnancy, your energy issues, and all the haphazardness that hit with your gifts going haywire. I've never seen her this upset. I promise that she doesn't want a battle with you." He sends a pulse down our connection, begging me to understand how sorry he is that he didn't pass on the message that I was coming to Mabel's instead of going home.

"You just made what I'm dealing with about Valerie," I scold. "I appreciate that you feel bad, but I'm done, Adam. I don't give a damn how she feels. Valerie and I are through. We'll see about that fight she's working to get out of. She won't be pregnant much longer, and then it's fair game."

Adam appears both distraught and scared. "I wasn't trying to make what you went through about Valerie. I apologize. Melanie, she doesn't stand a chance against you. I'm asking you not to attack her."

I raise my eyebrows. "I'm not the one who leveled the threat, Adam," I remind him. "She is. She invoked Retribution Clause."

"She didn't mean it as a Retribution invocation." Adam grimaces. "Valerie was just being a bitch. It seems she decided she was queen bee and forgot reality. I've admonished her at length about that."

"She's yet to come in here and discuss this," I remind with a laugh that holds no humor.

"She's on bed rest orders like you are," Adam explains.

"Thank you for talking with us, Adam, and thank you for your help during part of it," Trey interjects. "Getting Melanie through the initial medical nightmare would have been much harder without you, even if you were only half in the battle. I understand that not all of us are built the same though, and I can't expect you to gut up when you aren't strong enough."

Mama Mabel whistles low, reacting to Trey's brutal jab.

"There it is!" I crow. "I knew a 'Trey moment' was coming."

Mama Mabel snorts.

"Trot off and play fetch for your wife like a good dog." Trey waves Adam away dismissively.

Adam leaves, and my heart hurts from the dejected look on his face as he closes the door.

I exhale. "That was harsh."

"It needed to be done," Mabel assures. "Let it go. If it was the wrong move, I would've stepped in when you did it. You two need to get some rest."

Mama Mabel makes her way out the door as Trey and I look at each other, buried under the weight of more than we know what to start with.

"I was really hoping Mabel would talk with us," I admit. "We need help."

"I'm not ready to deal with any of what happened," Trey says, rubbing bloodshot eyes.

He might not be ready, but I called Mama Mabel in here for a reason. I'm losing my mind not working through everything that has happened.

CHAPTER 29

"Only Bear and Darren are left," Finley announces as she comes into the room with Tanner. "Have a talk with them, and then you can rest."

I close my eyes, exhausted from the steady stream of visitors this afternoon. Our friends are all desperate to talk to me and see firsthand that I'm alive. I appreciate their concern, but it's been a lot, and all I want is to try to process things with Trey. We hardly slept last night because I was in pain, and he couldn't shut down his siphoning. We're both running on fumes, and my anxiety is on overdrive.

"They're insisting on talking to Melanie alone," Finley says apologetically and shakes her head in mild disgust.

"You have to be kidding!" Trey protests. "I'm pain sharing with her so she can get through this. If I leave, she's going to hurt worse."

"Why do everyone else's needs always come first?" I ask.

"Because we can feel from here that Trey needs a break," Bear calls from the other side of the door.

"You're the biggest know-it-all EVER!" I jokingly yell back.

"Hey, wait a minute!" Darren yells. "What about me?"

Bear's trademark laughter booms. Finley opens the door for the guys.

"I know we've heard she's okay, but I feel better now that I've seen it myself," Darren tells Bear as they walk into the room.

Bear rounds the bed to Trey's side and motions for him to get up. Trey stands and Bear lies down, taking my hand. He sends a fresh stream of energy, and I close my eyes.

"Trey, I'm okay," I say after a few moments. "Bear's whole Zen vibe isn't the same as your pain syphoning, but it's helping take the edge off."

Trey gives me a contemplative look.

"You need to go get some air and take a breather from pain sharing. You're using energy faster than you can recharge." I smile compassionately. "We're in a marathon with this pain issue, and I need you to take care of yourself through this. I'm seriously okay. Take an hour and chill."

"I hate to admit it, but I need a few quiet minutes where I'm not funneling pain. The lady parts I don't have hurt, and it's disorienting." Trey rushes to add, "I know that's not fair for me to say because you don't get a break from the pain."

I smile at him, feeling unbelievably calm from Bear's energy. "I need you to take a break now so you can pull enough pain to get me to sleep later," I implore him.

Trey grabs his smokes and lighter from the drawer in his nightstand. "I'll be on the back porch. I won't be long."

"A heads-up that Adam and Valerie are on the back porch 'getting some sun,'" Tanner warns.

"Of course, they are." Trey rolls his eyes.

"I'll ask them to leave the porch," Finley offers.

"Don't bother, but I appreciate the offer," Trey tells her,

radiating irritation. He turns to Tanner. "I'm going to grab lunch for us. Getting out of the house might be my best bet. Can you stay and watch over the place while I'm gone?"

"Of course," Tanner replies.

Trey takes a deep breath and starts to give a list of instructions.

"Yeah, yeah," Tanner interrupts. "If there's a riot, use the Vault system. A home invasion? Panic room system. Don't open the windows because someone might crawl through. Lock the door behind you, and double, then triple-check it. If anyone breaks in, kill them. Don't answer the door until you get back, and I need to call immediately if anything happens. Did I cover it?"

Trey is a bit sheepish while he laughs.

"He's Mabel's head of security for a reason." I rally on Trey's behalf.

"Yeah, because he's bat-shit crazy," Tanner retorts jokingly.

Trey kisses me on the forehead, before heading out the door with Tanner and Finley.

Darren lies down on my other side, taking my free hand. He sends Zen energy that mirrors Bear's.

"We had a lengthy discussion with Adam and Valerie," Bear reveals.

I stiffen defensively.

"Valerie wasn't intending to invoke Retribution Clause," Darren softly informs. "Adam is terrified that you believe that."

"Did you really come in here to talk about Valerie?" I ask.

Darren sighs. "You can't try to kill Valerie."

"But it's fine for her to threaten me during the hardest thing I've ever been through?" I snap back.

"She's remorseful like you wouldn't believe," Bear assures. "She didn't realize what was happening when she had her fit."

"Get out," I order, fed up.

"Melanie, please. We're sorry that we took Adam and Valerie's side," Bear quietly says. "We've got the big picture now."

"Instead of coming in here out of concern for me, you're here advocating for Valerie. That's another strike against her," I coldly say.

"We *are* concerned about you," Darren assures me. "I apologize. We should have talked about that first before mentioning the other issue."

"Let Adam know that he and Valerie greatly overstepped again," I warn.

Bear and Darren stand and move toward the door. I roll carefully to my side, wincing, but I don't want to face them.

"We apologize," Darren says. I hear the door open and close as they leave.

There's conversation in the hall. The only part I can clearly hear is Adam passionately bellowing, "Damn it!"

— —

"Babe, I'm home," Trey calls out from the hall as he bypasses our room.

"Bet you he's going to check the security monitors in his office," I tell Finley and Tanner knowingly.

They both laugh, and Tanner flips a page in the magazine that we've been reading.

"I love these quizzes," Finley squeals. "Let's take it."

I'm reading the first question of the quiz to myself when I hear Trey walk in. I look up to see him smiling softly at me with a lunch bag in his hand.

"I thought we'd have some lighthearted fun," Tanner says with a shrug.

"Bear and Darren already left?" Trey asks.

Tanner flamboyantly grimaces as a warning, and Trey rolls his eyes.

"I don't even want to know," Trey mutters.

"Come take this ridiculous, 'Have You Found Your Soulmate?' quiz with us," I chirp, reaching for Trey's hand.

He snorts. "Thank goodness we have the magazine to offer us insight into *that*!" He gestures to the bag that he sets on the little dining table. "I got us all lunch."

Everyone grins as Trey joins our pile on the bed, lounging next to Finley who scoots to make room for him.

We each take the quiz and share our results. We're all laughing and exclaiming over Trey's answers that indicate I'm 'definitely not a match,' when Mama Mabel breezes in with a fresh stack of toiletries.

"That's a sight for sore eyes!" she says. 'You okay?'

I nod enthusiastically, and she winks at me.

"Thank you for letting Fin and Tanner stay," Trey tells her. "We needed this."

"If their parents are okay with it, I'm fine having them over tonight also," Mabel offers.

Finley squeals and claps her hands.

Mama Mabel exhales, realizing that things are getting back to normal. She leaves, pulling the door closed behind her.

CHAPTER 30

Finley and Tanner took their leave thirty minutes ago. Spending several hours with them was a good reset, but I'm exhausted. Trey and I have just started fitfully sleeping, hoping to knock out early even though it's only six at night, when we're disturbed by a knock at the door.

"What nooowww?" he groans.

"This place is like a damn airport." I sigh, close to tears with frustration. "I've never seen so many people come and go in my life."

Trey stalks to the door in his boxers, not bothering to put on a shirt and shorts, and yanks the door open. I hear murmuring and put my arm over my face to block out the sound.

"This is an interruption you'll be happy about," Trey says.

I sit up in my tank top, holding the bedspread to my chest. "Toss me those shorts," I request, pointing to a pair folded on top of our dresser.

He tosses them my way, and I pull them on, wincing as I shift too much. I close my eyes, my expression pained. When I open my eyes, Demitri and Victoria are standing at the open door.

I smile and hold out my hand. Demitri crosses to me, and I subtly flick my eyes Victoria's way. He squeezes my hand, and I take the memory of him thinking, *'She's legit not pissed. She wanted to check on you and Trey, so I agreed.'*

I sigh. I have no interest in her watching me struggle.

"I've spent several days in meditation topping off my energy tanks," Demitri states, before giving me a wry look. "Not all of us can black out all of Hollywood when we need a boost."

We all quietly chuckle.

"Anyhow, it's time for me to see what I can do to fix the damage."

"Do you think it'll work?" I ask.

"It's never failed me yet," he proclaims.

"Please try," I say.

"Do I need to pull pain while you jam your hand up her ass this time?" Trey jokingly asks.

"You aren't seriously putting your hand up my ass, right?" I squawk. "I have freaking rules about that!"

Demitri and Victoria both laugh.

"Everything I'm about to do happens with my hand on your stomach," Demitri assures us.

Trey puts on a pair of gym shorts. He and Victoria lean against the wall. He relaxes a touch. Victoria takes Trey's hand and leads him across the room to where they can sit on the floor and still see what Demitri's going to do. I toss a pillow their way as she crosses her legs. She puts the pillow over her lap and pulls Trey down. He lies down with his head on the pillow, and she starts running her fingers through his hair. I'm guessing this is a throwback to their dating days. Trey needs to relax, and being near me has been nothing but work for him while he siphons off my pain. The tension completely drains from him, leaving a calm hum down our connection line.

"Are you okay with this?" I ask Demitri as he looks at Victoria and Trey.

"If Victoria can help ease Trey's tension, then I'm good with it," Demitri says. "Everyone in our group is desperate to help, and we're no exception. We've got a collective plan on who checks in when, who passes on info to who, who yells at Adam again." We all laugh, and Demitri continues, "Those of us with abilities are obviously in the game, but everyone else is handling anything they can. If Victoria is the 'Trey Whisperer' then so be it."

"Help Melanie. I've got Trey," Victoria says, smiling at Trey. She switches to lightly scratching his back slowly with her nails, and his eyes close.

"Does it hurt sitting cross-legged?" Demitri asks.

I try and I'm fine. I settle into his requested position.

"Close your eyes, drop your shields, and just trust me," Demitri says. "I'm going to assess you first."

Demitri puts his hands on either side of my face and tips my head down, resting his forehead on mine. I feel him energetically scanning my body. It's disorientating but doesn't make my constant pain worse. A memory unexpectedly jumps from him. I fuzz Trey out and watch. It's of Demitri and Arch talking in the guest room across the hall after Demitri and I woke up the day after my miscarriage.

Demitri turns to Arch in the memory. "I don't want this talk discussed with anyone, except maybe Melanie."

"That's a given," Arch assures him. "Obviously, there's a lot going on with you and Mel. Spill it."

"I've been in love with her since I started dancing with her. She's aware, and we have firm boundaries," Demitri says. He's exhausted and far more open than he usually is.

"Where does Melanie stand?" Arch asks.

"I hesitate to speak for her, but she's admitted she's in the same boat. We spend a lot of time not discussing it, and we're good at the whole quirky friend route."

"How much does Trey know?" Arch asks.

"He's aware of that part. We've talked. He's not aware that we went on a date to Disneyland. I think only Presley knows that. I don't think he's aware that Melanie and I had a spirit-guide bond with each other that I managed to dissolve without realizing it."

"What?" Arch asks, stunned.

Demitri's head drops. "Pierre revealed that after he died." He looks at Arch, and his gaze feels haunted. "No one knows this, but I have a soulmate point in me now with Melanie. She doesn't have one. I'm being torn apart on the daily."

"Does Melanie know?"

My heart constricts with that news, and I remember that damn boom I felt when Pierre threatened to level the playing field. I let the memory continue.

Demitri shakes his head, swallowing hard. "I dissolved my spirit-guide eternal bond with Meley for a soulmate connection with Victoria."

Arch's mouth thuds open. "Why?"

Demitri shakes his head slowly in disbelief. "I didn't know I was doing it at the time."

"Can you hold it together after what happened?" Arch asks.

"I'm not losing my friendship with Melanie. It's all I have, and I have to have something."

Arch gives him a pointed look. "Can you seriously handle what you had to do?"

Demitri's expression crumples, and I feel blazing unhappiness rip through him.

I study his feelings in the memory and find that he's mortified that he had to hurt me and scared that I'll fear him if we ever land in an amorous relationship.

Arch hugs him. "You handled that shit like a champ. It was the most horrific thing I've ever seen someone do."

Demitri gasps out through his sobbing, "I'll never get the sound of her screaming out of my head, Arch. It's going to haunt me."

"Can you live without her and be happy with Victoria?"

"No and no. But those are two distinctly different questions. Victoria is a time-passer. Nothing more. Melanie is my girl, and I've accepted that she's taken. I respect Trey, and it's better that I'm friends with him and keep solid boundaries. I love Melanie, and I won't do anything to further complicate her life."

"What's your plan today?" Arch asks.

"I'm going to go home and cry myself sick."

"You've got it bad, D."

"All I can say is, I'm damn good at controlling my emotions and compartmentalizing."

"When do you let go and deal, then?"

"When I'm alone."

"I can stay at your house tonight in case you need to talk," Arch offers.

"I appreciate that, but I need to deal with this my way." Demitri blows out a rough exhale. "I can't handle talking to Victoria. Can you put her off for me?"

Arch agrees. Demitri heads up the hall, the opposite direction of the crowd in the parlor. He slips through the gym and out the back hallway to a side exit into the parking lot, wincing at the afternoon sun. He unlocks his Jeep and gets in. Alone, he sobs, torrential tears pouring down his cheeks. He collapses around his seizing lungs.

Pulling me out of the memory, Demitri inhales and takes his forehead from mine. I open my eyes and blink back tears. He looks at me quizzically, and I avert my gaze while I try to pull it together. Knowing that Demitri is so full of anguish, fear, and heartbreak leaves me desperate to figure out how to help him.

"You've got a lot of internal injuries from being punched by twelve men. I'm going to start with those because I can clear them easily," he explains.

He squeezes my hand, and I take the memory of him asking, *'What happened just then?'*

I send back my memory thought to Demitri, *'Don't worry about it.'*

Trey's staring at Demitri with fear in his eyes, his head still on the pillow on Victoria's lap. "How bad is the other damage?"

"I'm not going to lie to you, Trey. It's bad," Demitri says.

Trey tenses.

"Relax, Trey," Victoria coos. "I'm telling you that Demitri won't stop until he fixes Mel. We've got you."

Trey closes his eyes, and Victoria resumes her back-scratching.

"Thank you for not being mad. Tori's the only one, other than you, who can get me to breathe," Trey sends through our connection.

"Uh huh," I send back.

"There it is," Trey snorts in my mind. *"That's my girl! Cynical and jealous."*

I flick my eyes his way, glaring, as he raises an eyebrow at me.

"I was waiting for it." Victoria chuckles. "Don't pick a fight with Trey over this. I don't know what you two are yapping about in each other's minds, but I'm sure it's snarky." Victoria hits me with a challenging eyebrow raise.

"Uh-oh. Victoria's up to no good," Demitri says.

"Might I remind you that I watched you grind my boyfriend

into the ground during the Star Shine Grant Competition duet, and I didn't get mad?" Victoria challenges.

Both guys snap their eyes to me in unison, radiating amusement.

I relent with a sigh. "Damn it! You win. Carry on."

"Yesssss," Victoria hisses. We grin at each other. We're well matched in the catty-snark arena, and we love a good standoff with each other.

Trey cracks up and lies back down for Victoria to continue her back-scratching.

Mama Mabel comes in and assesses the situation.

"Lie down, Firebird," Demitri instructs. "I think I can fix it, but it's going to hurt like hell."

"Let's do this," Trey says and stands up to help siphon the pain.

"Are you sure you're up for this?" I ask Trey. "Your energy reserves are still bottomed out."

"I'm fine," Trey says. He turns to Mabel. "Any chance you have another dose of sleeping pills?"

Mabel nods, and her eyes flick from Demitri to Victoria. I glance at Demitri, who stares at me pointedly. I close my eyes and energy-scan the house for Finley. She's in the guest room with Tanner. I tap into my noncorporeal ability to send a voice into their room. *"Finley, can you entertain Victoria for us? Take her to a movie or something?"*

I subtly put my hand against Demitri's leg and give him the memory of what I just did.

"Vic, this is going to take forever," Demitri says. "You'll be bored."

Before she can comment, someone knocks on the door, and Finley enters the room.

"Hey, guys," she says. "Whatcha doing?"

"Healing Melanie," Demitri replies. "We're in for a long night."

"Victoria, wanna hang with me instead of being bored while they do their hocus-pocus thing?" Finley asks. "Tanner and I are going to see the live *Rocky Horror Picture Show* at the Santa Monica Playhouse. We can drop you off at home after."

"Think it's okay, babe?" Victoria asks Demitri. "I can see you at school tomorrow?"

Demitri smiles and nods.

She hops up. "Trey, can I talk to you for a minute?" she asks as she heads to the door.

I didn't expect that. He follows her. Finley winks at me before closing the door.

I look at Demitri with narrowed eyes. He glances at the door and settles his gaze back on me.

"What do you think that's about?" I ask.

"No clue," Demitri says with a shrug. "She's been all concerned about how you and Trey are doing. Maybe she just wants to check on him."

"Tap into your connection and eavesdrop, Melanie," Mama Mabel suggests, sounding suspicious.

I try.

"He's got me Fort Knoxed," I tell them. "Iron shield on his side."

"Any previous cause for alarm?" Mama Mabel asks us.

"They seem to be busy a lot at the same time," Demitiri admits. "It's why Melanie and I have a lot of time to hang together, just us."

"Uh-huh," Mama Mabel says but she doesn't get to discuss anything further because Trey comes back in. We all look at him with caged expressions.

"What?" Trey asks.

"You want to explain your little private chat?" I inquire with an eyebrow raised.

"Tori wanted to hear my side of why Demitri stayed the night with Melanie," Trey explains. "You know how jealous she gets."

"You told her what exactly?" Demitri replies with a guarded tone.

"I told her we're in survival mode and I needed help," states Trey. "I can't be any good to Melanie if I crash and burn. I just explained that I asked Demitri to keep an eye on Mel while she slept so I could get some shut-eye."

My intuition nags gently at me. I try to tap into Trey's memory center, but he has me blocked.

"It was nothing," Trey continues as he walks to my bedside. "Just typical Victoria. I'll give her credit because she seems to be aiming for maturity about this."

We all exhale, deciding we're worried about nothing.

"Can you stay tonight and zonk out Mel?" Trey asks. "Neither of us has gotten enough sleep."

"Me neither," Demitri admits. "I can stay. Both of our reserves are going to be catastrophically low after this, and we'll need Melanie's help."

"I can't sleep when I'm with her, and you can't sleep without her. This is greaaaat." Trey rolls his eyes.

"It'll all level out," Mama Mabel assures us. "The three of you took the brunt of what happened. Just get through the recovery."

Trey lies next to me on my right, and Mama sits on my left.

"I need more access to her," Demitri says.

I solve that problem by shifting to sit up and motioning him forward. He scoots closer and sits cross-legged. I sit on his lap, wrapping my legs around him. Mama Mabel lines two pillows up to support me. I lie back and wince from the pain, as I settle into them.

"Are you okay with this?" I ask Demitri.

"It's perfect because I've got your energy around me. It'll

help me gauge if I need to stop because you can't handle the pain. Melanie, your only job is to lie there and try to relax," Demitri instructs. He carefully places his hands on my abdomen.

I nod, close my eyes, focus on my breathing, and drop into a trance state as I feel Trey's hand over my chest, ready to pull pain, and Mama Mabel's hand on my arm.

I drift away on a wave of calm. The combination of Mabel's, Demitri's, and Trey's energy is unexpectedly soothing, but I don't know why I'm surprised. They're three of the most energetically grounded people I know.

— —

"That's unbelievable," Mama Mabel says. Her voice brings me back from my trance.

I feel Mama Mabel and Demitri both remove their hands. I open my eyes, a little woozy. Demitri's covered in sweat like we just had a two-hour dance rehearsal.

"Are all of you, okay?" I ask.

They nod.

"You helped a lot more than you know," Demitri tells me. "I've been mentally preparing all day to drop into your inferno. I didn't know you could trance like that, and it took nearly all the edge off."

I close my eyes to focus my energy on my stomach. After a long moment, hope rises. I open my eyes.

"Trey, how much pain are you pulling right now?" I ask.

"I'm not," he says with a smile. "I just wanted to feel your heartbeat and decided not to take my hand away."

Mama Mabel and Demitri smile at us. Guilt bubbles up about my suspicion earlier.

I look at Demitri. "You did it. My stomach literally doesn't hurt at all."

I exhale, closing my eyes, and send relief through to Trey that's so strong it makes him exhale hard. Trey puts his hand over my stomach, closing his eyes and searching for pain. His eyebrows furrow. "Her gut pain is gone, and her energy doesn't go haywire in her gut anymore."

"Lie down flat and slip into a trance again," Demitiri requests, tapping my leg. "I've never done this healing with someone who can trance out like that, and it makes it a lot easier. I can heal everything else before I crater instead of dividing this into two sessions."

Trey grabs me under the arms and pulls me backward so Demitri can get up.

"Can you work on her while she lies back on me?" Trey asks. "I think I can help you."

Demitri shrugs. "Sure."

Trey props up with pillows and settles. He pulls me, and I rest the back of my head on his chest. I exhale.

"Drop in with me, babe," he says. "See you on the flipside."

He laces his fingers with mine, and we both drop into a meditative trance, meeting in the common place in our collective minds. I open my eyes in my mind's eye and Trey's there. He sends, *"I've got an idea."*

I raise an eyebrow at him suggestively and he laughs. *"We can't do that for a month,"* he reminds.

"The doctor didn't say anything about not energy sharing in our minds for a month," I tease.

"That solves that problem. Later, though."

He gestures for me to lie down, and the "me" in our minds complies. He puts his hands flat on my chest and stomach. *"Pulse your energy."* I do, and he studies it. *"Hang tight."*

I feel him split his psyche between our minds and reality.

"Right shoulder. Spleen. Broken rib third down on left side. Giant bruise on her tush. Some kind of damage to liver or kidney, I can't quite tell," Trey tells Mabel and Demitri.

"Oh, honey," Mabel says, concerned. "She hasn't complained of any of those injuries."

"Damn! Nice work, Trey," Demitri exclaims. "That's saves me from having to search."

"Tell me where you're headed," Trey requests. "I'll 'watch' and let you know if anything needs more work."

"Broken rib."

I pulse energy to that area, and Trey puts his hands over my rib cage on the 'me' in our psyche.

"A little to the left," Trey guides Demitri. Demitri goes the wrong way, and Trey chuckles. "Your other left."

"Typical dancer," Demitri says. "I'm awesome in the studio but have zero sense of direction in real life."

We work in tandem. Trey searches for injured spots and guides Demitri to pinpoint exact issues. I pulse my energy. Demitri heals me.

After a long stretch of cooperative effort, every sore spot feels better. Relief floods through me. No longer being in pain has made me so sleepy. I instinctively reach for the Trey in our shared psyche space, taking his hand and trying to pull him down to curl up with me in our trance space.

Trey disappears from our shared space while I try to stay awake. I roll on my side in reality and reach absently. Someone hands me my favorite throw blanket, and I snuggle with it like a sleepy toddler.

"Looks like we did it." Demitri chuckles. He sounds far away.

"It's such a relief to see her finally relax," Mabel says. "You're remarkable, Demitri."

"Thank you for coming here and helping her!" Trey says with conviction.

"Trey, now that she's not in pain, I don't think you need the sleeping pills," Mabel says. "Demitri's going to have backlash issues again, and you'll both need Melanie to recharge you."

"I love you, Mama Mabel. I don't know what we'd do without you," Trey says. His voice wobbles.

"Oh, honey. Come here," Mama Mabel coos.

Trey says something I can't hear.

"I know you do," responds Mama Mabel. "I have an idea, but we can discuss it when you're not so tired. You've been terrified, and you're worn out. It's midnight and you all need solid sleep. I'm not going to wake you three up. You can go back to school on Tuesday, instead of tomorrow. Frankly, you've all been through hell and, while the dynamic is bizarre, all three of you will be better off if you sleep this off together."

Somewhere in my lethargic state, I realize that Demitri arrived six hours ago. I feel bad that he healed me for so long, but I feel so much better that it was all worth it for him to drain himself to nothing.

"You up for this weird shit?" Trey asks Demitri.

"My energy reserves are bottomed out again, and I've already got a migraine starting," Demitri shares. "I'm still in survival mode. I'm fine if you are."

"Melanie's already half asleep," Trey says. "I'd rather we both stay here in case she wakes up in pain again."

I come out from my trance space, needing to check on them. I sit up groggily as Mama Mabel closes the door behind her. Trey crosses to the control panel and pushes the panic room button. We listen as the locks slide into place.

"Do either of you want food?" Trey asks.

I shake my head, hardly able to hold it up. "Just sleep," I mumble.

"Demitri, take the other side. She'll refill your drained reserves faster if she's behind you. You're in worse shape than I am. Shirt off."

"This should be weird," Demitri says.

"Yeah, it should, but it's not, so whatever." Trey pauses a moment and asks, "Melanie, are you okay with this?"

"I need both of you. The past few days were really scary," I reply. Fear burns through my sleepy fog.

"I hate when she's scared," Trey tells Demitri.

"Me too. Frankly, all three of us have spent the past few days scared. I couldn't sleep by myself. I had nightmares about what happened. As much as I hate to admit it, I'll sleep better knowing nothing will get through you if anyone breaks in here, Trey."

"Your whole calm vibe might be the only thing that can get me to sleep tonight," Trey confesses to Demitri.

I feel the bed shift on both sides, and Trey curls up behind me. Demitri scoots, pressing his back against my chest.

I feel completely content for the first time since this nightmare started. "I've seriously never been happier," I mumble.

"Shit, Melanie," Demitri says. "Don't piss him off now. There's no way I can drive home this tired."

"I just want her to be okay, D," Trey says with a chuckle. "I'm not kicking you out. Sleeping next to a happy Melanie is unreal. You'll see. Her energy hums when she hits a deep sleep. It's hypnotic."

Trey doesn't know that I've slept the night at Demitri's house before, and neither of us mention it.

"I'll get my shit together sooner rather than later," Demitri promises. "I don't fall apart often, but this whole episode threw me off. Not even my calm ability could fix it."

I wiggle happily.

"Trey, do you know how long you've been her soulmate?" Demitri asks. "There must be a backstory. It's weird that she has that bond with you and Adam."

"No clue. I've known her from past lives. I knew that the first time I saw her in the hall at school."

"Literally the second I took her hand to partner her the first time, I knew we had danced together in a past life," Demitri informs. "Memories from that lifetime come to me in dreams."

"You're kidding?" Trey says.

I lift my head, baffled. "You've never told me that, D." I hold my hand out over his side. "Give it." I open and close my hand like a toddler wanting snacks.

Demitri laughs and takes my hand. I pull the memory and send it to Trey. Demitri doesn't let go of my hand, and I settle in again. We all watch the memory from that lifetime together.

Demitri is a strawberry blond, and I'm a lithe blond with a permanent serious expression. We're on a stage, getting our asses handed to us by a choreographer that we apparently are both exhausted with.

Demitri turns to me in the memory and mutters, "Let's just do it his way. I can muscle you through it. I want to get this over with."

Memory me sighs and backs up, prepping and leaping his way. He catches me and adjusts his hand when he doesn't get the placement right. He hefts me up and glares at the massive wedding ring on my finger. *This woman is going to be the death of me*, he thinks. *I'm so sick of her husband. What does she see in him, other than money?* He sets me down and glares at a blue-eyed man standing at the edge of the stage.

Mr. Blue Eyes growls at the choreographer we don't like, "This show better be ready, Charles, or you're fired and I'm hiring a new choreographer." The blue-eyed guy looks my way. "You're the only saving grace in this fiasco, my love."

In the memory, Demitri waits until the blue-eyed guy, who's clearly Adam, walks away, before wrapping his arms around memory me. "You aren't seriously going home tonight, are you?" he asks.

Memory me looks up at him, and his breath catches slightly.

"Eventually," I reply coyly.

We come out of the memory, and Trey cracks up. "You had an affair with Melanie when she was married to Adam?"

"Apparently," Demitri says, amused. "That's the only memory that had any clue alluding to that. The rest are all boring rehearsals. The show was a classical ballet. Melanie didn't talk much in most of the memories."

"I thought you weren't that guy?" Trey sarcastically admonishes.

Demitri rolls over on his back, resting on the pillows. "I'm not that guy with you, Trey," he assures. "I don't give a shit about doing the right thing with Adam. If Meley was with Adam, I'd have cannonballed them the first day."

"See!" Trey exuberantly expresses. "I knew we were meant to be friends. Anyone who hates that fucker is great with me."

Demitri chuckles.

"Some people love him," I huff. "Bear and Darren weren't coming in here to check on me. Valerie and Adam sent them to bully me into letting Valerie's threat go."

"Excuse them!" Trey gets up, jabs the panic room button, and leaves. I watch through the soulmate connection as he stalks to Adam's door and pounds. Adam answers, and Trey points to Valerie, who's in the bed. "If you ever *speak* to Melanie again, I'll kill you myself," he threatens. "Sending Bear and Darren to bully my girl is the last straw."

"We weren't commissioning bullies," protests Adam. "We were trying to get help."

"So, instead of visiting Melanie because they care," Trey retorts, "they visited in honor of Valerie?"

"They hadn't visited before?" Valerie asks bashfully.

"Nope."

I get up and grab a marker and paper. I write on the paper, before taking a butterfly knife from Trey's nightstand drawer.

"What are you doing, Melanie?" Demitri asks, alarmed. He follows, as I make my way to Adam and Valerie's room.

Without a word, I step into the room, place the paper against the wall, and drive the knife through the note to stick it to the wall. I turn to storm out to the sound of a gasp.

Adam rushes after me, making the mistake of grabbing my arm as I get to the doorway. I whip around and hit him with a gut punch that drops him to his knees. Valerie screams from her bed vantage point, and I grin sadistically.

Tanner, Finley, and Mama Mabel pour from Tanner's guest room.

"Guess who's healed, BITCH," I bellow as I set my sights on Valerie. I feel my humanity slipping away. My head tips, and a desire to kill her nearly rattles me into insanity.

"Melanie, no!" Mabel grabs me from behind and starts to pull me back. That's when I realize I was stalking toward Valerie without knowing it.

"I'm sorry," Valerie gasps as desperate tears pour down her cheeks. She moans and doubles over around her full-term stomach.

"You don't get to be sorry," I snarl, dark and gravely. "Stand by your threat."

"Melanie," Adam hoarsely says, still wincing from the gut punch.

I slide evil eyes his way. "Have you really been with this shallow Normal for so long that you forgot who we are? WHAT we are? You think encouraging her to toy with me is smart?"

"I never encouraged it," Adam insists.

My dark-water intensity fills my eyes. "I'm going to kill her," I growl gutturally. "That's a promise, not a threat." I point to the knife-embedded paper, and everyone reads the words, *Stand your ground.* "It's coming, but I'll let you sweat first," I taunt Valerie with a smirk. "I'm not killing you today, because one day, you'll push me so far that Adam can't hunt me for taking you out." I lean my arms on the bed.

Valerie shrinks back.

"I'm going to make it slow, and excruciating. If you're lucky, I'll make your kids watch. That is if I don't decide to kill one of them also."

"What?" Valerie screeches.

I nod, slow and calculated. "Adam locked me out, and I lost my child. Per Retribution Clause that YOU invoked and old-world rules, I have the right to balance the scales."

Adam sharply inhales.

"Don't worry," I tell him. "You're having two babies. You'll still have one left."

"Not to be the crab apple in our barrel full of delicious insanity, but when did Melanie start flippantly threatening to murder babies?" Tanner panics into the mix.

"Scale balancing," I say as I swing my insane expression Tanner's way, "can be messy."

"This is a new level of ratchet," Tanner breathes in disbelief.

Adam and I stare intensely at each other for a long moment.

"In all our lifetimes," Adam says with slow conviction, "you've never been a child killer."

My body rattles with rage as one of the past life memories that haunts my nightmares swarms up in my mind. Suffice to say, it's horrific, and one of my deepest regrets. "Not true," vibrates from me on a wave of thick emotion and hatred for Adam.

He blanches when he realizes his mistake. We don't discuss the incident with Antrell, my daughter from so many lifetimes ago. It destroyed us.

"I'm sorry," Adam breathes out heavily.

"Someone care to explain?" Tanner asks, earning an arm smack from Finley so he'll hush.

"No," Adam says, trying to curb this. He knows that adding the Antrell disaster to this moment is surely a death sentence for him, his wife, and his children.

"It was you and me for over two hundred lifetimes," I remind him. "Is Valerie that captivating that she can render you so brainless that you forgot how this energy worker shit operates?"

Adam knows that I'm alluding to what happened so long ago, and he blanches pale.

I point to Valerie after I'm certain that Adam grasps the depth of how badly this could go. "Set her straight," I order Adam. "Do it quickly and be thorough, because that bitch is so damn dumb that she thinks she and I are equals. We aren't." I pull the knife from the wall, flip it, and catch the handle. I whip my gaze to Valerie and throw the knife. It spirals so fast that it's a blur. It embeds in the headboard, inches from Valerie's head, with the paper still stuck to it.

Valerie screams. Adam nearly throws up, and Trey belts satisfied laughter.

I pan a slow, sadistic, gaze to Mabel. "You no longer get the privilege of teaching these two assholes to behave," I inform her. "Now *I'm* going to do it."

"I think you two should move home," Mabel advises Adam with a panicked flutter of her hands.

"You've been checking on me all day," Valerie pleads. "That's what's kept me going."

"I made a mistake with this," Mabel says. "You have an ob-gyn who can see you."

"Every time I leave this bed, I have contractions! I need to make it another couple days before it's safe to deliver," Valerie sobs.

"Threatening Melanie about your baby shower being cut short, while she was in the middle of a miscarriage, after your husband failed to pass on that she was coming here . . ." Mabel trails off, in disbelief of Adam and Valerie.

"I was venting my frustration to my husband," Valerie says defensively, albeit in a kindly way. "I didn't march into Melanie's room and scream at her while she was in agony. I could hear Melanie screaming, and felt the earthquakes, but I didn't understand what was happening."

"My soulmate connection was shut down for months," Adam bashfully interjects. "I was so out of my mind when I got back in here that I forgot that I needed to block my side. Valerie started screaming, then your pain crashed in, and Trey took the flippant threat of Valerie's as real. Melanie, I'm sorry."

"I didn't mean it," Valerie jumps in. "I've been miserable, and huge, and stuck in bed. I looked forward to the baby shower. The moment Adam blocked his connection, he explained what I'd just done. I wasn't really threatening you, but even if it had been a real threat, I wouldn't invoke THAT clause. I think of a tiff as two people being bitchy to each other. You seem to believe it's a fight to the death."

"Do you not understand that the Reapers came for me in that parking lot?" I ask. "THAT is what my life is. I let them live, after

THEY attacked our home during the earthquake aftermath. I lost a baby because of my compassion. I assure you, I will never overlook a threat again. It's my aggressor or me, and I choose me."

"Can you accept that Valerie wasn't actually threatening you as you perceive it?" Mabel asks.

"No."

"Adam, you and Valerie created this mess by being so self-centered," Mabel guides. "The staff that haven't already quit are fed up. Destiny is ready to quit if you two stay. Melanie is ready to kill Valerie for a threat Valerie heartlessly made. As the owner of this home, I must ask you to leave."

"Right when we realize it, and are trying to make amends?" Adam asks, making one last attempt at rationalizing.

"You realized it too late," Mabel compassionately expresses. "I'm proud of you for realizing it, though. Maybe that will help you do right the next time someone tries to help you."

Adam's eyes close. He knocks on the blockage between us. I open my side, and he sends, *"I can't handle Valerie on my own right now. I apologize on behalf of both of us. I'm begging you to help me here."*

"You bailed when I needed help, but expect me to compassionately help you?" I send. *"You left me screaming in agony so that you could see if Valerie needed her pillows fluffed, right? What you were really doing is hauling your gossiping ass into your room so you two could plot against me."*

"I wasn't," Adam sends. Considering that it's close to impossible to lie mind-to-mind, it seems he's telling the truth. *"I couldn't handle watching you go through that."* Adam slowly shakes his head. He's in a traumatic place. *"I was watching MY girl, my soulmate of my entire existence, screaming on a bed. If I hadn't screwed up, this wouldn't have happened to you. I left you, for Valerie. I married her, and she's a monster. I've never been this trapped. I hate her and my marriage, and I've regretted this choice more often than I can express."*

My expression softens against my better judgment.

Adam swallows around tears. *"I can't watch you writhe in pain. I can't handle that you lost a baby, hurt like that, or that Trey screwed up so bad with my girl. I wasn't abandoning you. I was mourning that I let this happen to my other half."*

"She's your other half now," I remind him.

Adam looks so young and scared. It's a rarity for him. *"I can't do this, Melanie."*

"You may not have to, because I'm going to lose the battle eventually."

"You won't lose against Valerie," Adam sends.

"I'm referring to the battle against my morality," I clarify. *"I truly don't care that she's sorry. I feel nothing about killing her beyond eliminating an irritation. You chose her, and you can go against me in a battle to the death to protect her. I'll be ready."*

"I won't fight you," Adam sends.

"Then she'll die," I gravely reply.

"I don't think I care."

"Inquiring minds want to know," Tanner hesitantly says into the silence the others are experiencing. "Care to fill us in?"

"I created this, and I'd like to formally apologize," Adam says to the room. "I allowed a lot to happen that never should have." He looks to Valerie. "We need to move home."

"Because of the conversation you and Melanie just kept from the rest of us?" Valerie replies, clearly angry.

"Well, Valerie, you didn't let me get to the unveiling," I sarcastically sugar her way. "It's not a secret." I blast the memory of the conversation Adam and I just had into everyone's minds.

"Damn it, Melanie," Adam barks.

"What? Valerie doesn't like secrets," I cattily retort.

"That was between us."

"Was it?" I reply with sweet sarcasm. "I'm *so* sorry."

It doesn't take long for everyone to review the memory. When they blink back to reality, Tanner whistles his surprise. Finley winces. Demitri's eyes are huge. Adam revealed a great deal, and I was out of line for sending it, but I'm flat done. Valerie needs to know her place.

"Ummm . . . ," Tanner hums into the silent shock. "Are you planning to wait for the slaughter until after she has babies, or before?"

I slide hard eyes Tanner's way. "Does it matter?" I rumble evilly.

He draws back his head and scrunches his face in return. It would be hilarious if humor was an option in this grave moment.

"Hush, Tanner," Finley whispers insistently.

"Just saying," Tanner mutters, "that we'd need to dig a hell of a hole to bury a 'pregnant with twins' body." Demitri and Trey try desperately to curb their spurting laughter, earning a quirky look from Tanner. "Might need a backhoe," he hisses at Trey.

Trey loses his battle and laughter foghorns while Valerie appears beyond offended. Tanner's wit does nothing to soften my rage.

"I," rumbles from me, deep and deadly, "have tried. Over and over, through horrors you've all been there for. Did you really think I'd remain sweet, shy, insecure Melanie through rape, attacks, gut punches, stalkers, and biker-fueled miscarriages?" I whip my rattlesnake gaze to Valerie. "Welcome to the Thunderdome. I've got a lot of unrectified grievances with the evil fuckwits of the world. I've chosen to start by dealing with *you*."

"Melanie, you can't do this. She apologized and seems sincere," Demitri implores.

I smirk his way as my dark-water side thrums. "Demitri, humans evolve and learn for a variety of reasons. Case in point, we're all evolving right now. None of us are coming out of this experience the same way we went in. I, for instance, pulled into Mabel's parking lot a pitiful shell of a pregnant teenager three nights ago. I came out of my miscarriage a new incarnation. Take it or leave it, but I suggest everyone be mindful that I'm not to be toyed with." I point toward Valerie. "She went too far because she's a Normal, a bitch, a selfish monster, and has always been on a tough-girl pedestal." I tip my head, radiating pragmatic insanity. "I've grown weary, and the past two years feel like a million lifetimes. THIS is our new normal, and my morality and ethical threshold has shifted." I smile as I ground my primal rage down and out, settling into what is intended to appear a bit more like the me that they know. "Understood?" I politely ask.

My inquiry is met with caged fear and stunned shock. Silence prevails.

"I'll take that as a yes." I pan a pleasant gaze Adam's way. "Best get to that packing."

"We're discussing what you sent to her when we get home," Valerie snarls his way. It's bold, considering that she faces certain death, but that's Valerie for you.

"Well," Trey chirps, oddly enthusiastic for him. "I, for one, am thrilled to watch Melanie kill Valerie. I think she should do it for the snack-cake theft infraction alone."

"Hence the backhoe need," Tanner mutters.

I spurt laughter while Valerie cowers, her snarky bravado from a moment ago evaporating again.

Trey scrunches his nose cattily at Adam. "Your wife is a peach."

I nod congenially. "Who would have ever seen this coming?" I shake my head. "Tsk, tsk. You never really know a person until they hit rock bottom." My expression slides deadly serious again as I look at Valerie with slow malevolence. "I don't share my snack cakes, my miscarriage attention, or tolerate catfights." I smile with the weight of ancient pain and regret. "The good news, for you at least, is that I don't want Adam. You can have him, you lowlife bitch." I belt laughter that bubbles up, uncontrolled. "My daughter, Antrell, wasn't so lucky. I wanted Adam then, and so did she." I give Valerie a very pointed look. "You need to learn to bow down," gravels from me.

"Sorry, but I have to know," Tanner interrupts, waving his hands about. "What did you do to Antrell?"

I steer my no-nonsense vibe his way. "Liquified her," I inform, blasé. "Blast, splat," I add while rattling sarcastic jazz hands.

"Holy shit," Tanner breathes on a wave of morbid fascination.

Adam grandly winces, deeply pained to this day by what happened so many lifetimes ago between him and my grown daughter. "Melanie, please," he pleadingly whispers.

What happened was so much worse than I just downplayed. It's cruel, but I can't emotionally dive down that rabbit hole. Detached flippancy is my only option, but it cuts even deeper for Adam that I diluted the incident in such a manner.

"So sorry," I offer Adam, my tone detached. I snap back to amusedly cute Melanie and dip into an exaggerated curtsy. "Thus concludes Melanie Slate's performance of 'No Fucks Left to Give.'"

"Sometimes I forget that you aren't like the rest of us." Finley surveys me with haunted blue eyes. At my askant look, she explains, "I'm busy being a teenager. Meanwhile, you're carting around so many lifetimes of horror. I don't know how you make it through Algebra class on a Tuesday."

I scoff at the thought. "I'd rather murder Antrell in her bedroom a thousand times than face that damn class." I smile congenially, while intentionally ignoring the distraught vibe rolling from Adam. "And we're off!" I lace my arms through Trey and Demitri's elbows and comically spin us around to face the door. "Gentleman, it's time for bed."

Trey belts full-bodied laughter as we exit the room.

CHAPTER 31

I hear a soft knock on the bedroom door.

"Come in," I invite.

The last person I expect walks in with Mabel. I'm relieved that I put on a dress and a little makeup today.

Mabel smiles at Zane's mother, Cindy. "It's so nice to have met you," she remarks politely before stepping out and closing the door.

"Hi, honey," Zane's mom says softly now that we're alone.

"Can I help you?" I ask, caged. I really don't like this shallow woman, and I'm not in a good emotional place for this right now.

Cindy holds up her hands in a peace gesture. "We got off on the wrong foot. I'm here for several reasons, but they're all to your benefit. I ask that you hear me out."

My eyes narrow. "You and me," I gesture between us, "aren't copacetic."

Cindy smiles, looking down. "I was warned that you might tear my ass apart."

This admission surprises me, as does her cussing candor. "By?"

"Zane, but I had to try." The look Cindy gives me cuts through my defenses far quicker than I expected.

"Don't give me that look right now, please," I request.

Cindy laughs a little. "I'm not a shallow ungrateful monster. I'm a mom who was processing my dead son when I met you." She gestures from herself to me. "I suspect you may be able to relate now."

My eyes close as heartbreak bubbles up. It's always just under the surface, and I'm not handling the loss of the baby well.

"I'm sorry I said that," Cindy gently backpedals.

I stuff down my discontent, deciding to give Cindy a chance because it's a good distraction from what I haven't dealt with yet. "I take it Zane blabbed?"

"He wasn't blabbing." Cindy says compassionately. "We all know you made a trade to give us back Zane. We've all been worried sick about you. We knew the end of the life-for-a-life deal had come to fruition the moment Zane and Rocco came through my door."

"They went to your house when they left here?" I ask, as I invite her with a gesture to sit at my little dining table.

"They needed to cry and feel safe. They weren't aiming to gossip about you," she explains as she sits gingerly.

"It was traumatic. I get that." I hang my head, fighting a whirlwind of emotions.

"I encouraged the boys to allow me to gather the group who were there for Zane's miracle," Cindy admits. "I know you hate Rachelle, but she's changed a lot since you last saw her. She grew up far more than I expected."

"I guess that's good," I awkwardly mumble, not really wanting to talk about Rachelle.

"I'm here to thank you on behalf of all of them," Cindy claims as she takes my hand, seeming to get my shutdown and pivoting the conversation. "You gave me back my baby and lost your own as payment. I'm so sorry it came to that, and relieved that you're okay."

"Thank you."

"Rocco's pretty sure you and him are friends again," adds Cindy.

"We are."

"What about you and Zane?" she asks.

"I appreciate how he helped me."

"I don't think you understand how much he loves you," Cindy says. Apparently, she's getting to her point rapidly. It's a quality that I like, and I relax a little.

"I'm blunt," I caution.

"I was warned. I am too, and I'd prefer bluntness, if it helps."

"For the record, I'm aware that I'm sixteen."

She gives me a knowing look. "There's nothing *sixteen* about you."

I duck my head and blush.

"Don't you dare drop your head, ashamed," she admonishes. "Chin up. I won't have it."

"Thank you," I say, rallying. "That means a lot."

"Give it to me straight, Melanie."

"Zane says he loves me, but his gossiping actions speak otherwise." I fidget with a lip gloss on the table.

"Can I see what happened a few days ago?" Cindy requests, to my surprise.

"It's not a tidy memory," I warn her.

"I gathered that based on the condition of Zane's clothes when he arrived at my house," Cindy softly says. "Opening the door to my son covered in dried blood was scary. I gave up on his white tank top and tossed it, but it came clean from his jeans." Her expression morphs sad. "I Q-tipped blood out of his right ear. He said he showered."

I blush but decide to trust her. "He was covered in blood by the time it was over. He had to do terrible things."

Cindy doesn't flinch. "He wouldn't have had it any other way."

Deciding that the woman in front of me seems much kinder than who she seemed to be when Zane was dead, I touch her arm and send the hellacious memory. I don't close my eyes with her. I have no interest in reliving that nightmare.

Cindy's expression morphs through a series of emotions as she watches the memory. Finally, she opens her tearful eyes. She gets up from her chair and rounds to my side of the table. She kneels and hugs me. When she pulls away, she takes my hands in hers. "I'm so sorry, Melanie. Being a girl sucks."

I laugh, having not expected that. Cindy smiles.

"It really does." I sigh. "How did everyone take the news?"

"Maturely. My husband was there, and he cried. I know you've never met him, but he acts like you're one of his kids now." Cindy squeezes my hands. "I don't think Zane's handling the possibility that you're out of his life well. He wants a relationship with you. My family would be thrilled."

"I appreciate your support." I smile a little. "Zane is a good catch, but he's not my catch."

"Can I please see the memory that ruined everything?" Cindy asks.

I touch her arm, sending my discovery of Zane and Rachelle's crap-talking-affair-nonsense. She closes her eyes, and silence sits between us for a stretch.

When her eyes open, she blushes. "He told me he gossiped about you ONCE," she remarks. "You found the *one* time."

"The guys in my life will tell you I'm good at that." I laugh awkwardly. "They hate it."

"Nothing destroys a mother's heart like seeing her children make a mistake that she can't fix," asserts Cindy.

"Why do you think it's okay?"

"I don't," Cindy says and pats my hand. "I promise it was just an immature moment from Zane. He didn't mean any of it. Rachelle was a very shallow person. Everyone was used to gossiping with her. She won't stand for that kind of talk now, and all of us have grown because of you. Getting called out brings clarity. You won that battle, Melanie."

"I'm not trying to win," I reply. "I respect what you're saying, though. I appreciate that he learned from it. The next girl will benefit from him being his kindest version."

"He doesn't want another girl," Cindy implores. "It's important that he regains your trust."

"I've never trusted anyone like I trusted him," I explain. "That's why I can't. I forgive him, but I'll always wonder if he'll betray me. Zane wasn't a flippant connection for me. The direction I was headed with him doesn't have room for this hurdle."

Cindy smiles sadly. "Zane's always seemed older, but he's only twenty-one. You taught him an important lesson that he *learned*."

"I didn't want him there for what I faced in the hospital because I knew how gross it was. I asked him to leave, and he refused over and over. He promised that it was okay." I look down at the table. "He did exactly what I feared, after swearing he wouldn't."

"I know, honey," Cindy says as she rubs my hand with her thumb. "He knows that also. Zane betrayed his own integrity about something that deeply mattered to him. It obviously wasn't worth it."

"Thank you for telling me."

"You're welcome . . ." She trails off.

"And?" Cindy gently prompts when I don't respond.

"And what?"

"And you're going to forgive him?" Cindy coaches. "And you'll hold his hand and skip on the beach? You will be with him forever and ever, because you're his fairy princess, and he wants to be with you for the rest of eternity?"

I laugh. "I'm not a fairy princess, but thank you. I appreciate that he's sorry. I just miscarried Trey's baby. I need to focus on that relationship."

Cindy seems to sag in defeat. In the brief time I've known her, it's becoming blazingly obvious that she moves mountains for her two boys. It's a quality I respect.

"I've never cared about what someone thinks like I cared about that with Zane," I admit.

"Then you need to put your all into rebuilding with him," Cindy insists.

"I can't. He was sincerely repulsed by me when he gossiped to Rachelle," I whimper pitifully. I hate the sound of it.

"I think he needed a moment to decompress," Cindy softly says. "Repulsed by you isn't his usual."

I shake my head, more to myself than anything.

"He wasn't repulsed by your miscarriage," Cindy assures me. "He was terrified. Seeing his girl covered in blood, and screaming, is a hard thing."

"I'm certain it was," I remark. "Everyone is struggling. They're all having nightmares."

"Are you having nightmares?"

"No. Trauma isn't new or exciting. If I give in to nightmares, I'll go insane. I just get through each new hurdle with focus."

"Like you did when you saved Zane?" she softly asks.

"Precisely," I reply, emotionally exhausted. "Focus on the task and push through until it's over."

"I've never seen anyone do what you can." Cindy waves a hand about. "I'm not talking about the metaphysical miracles. I'm talking about the extreme focus. Zane told me that's how you were in the hospital."

"It was Zane's determination and focus that pulled off that miracle," I reply.

"All the more reason to forgive him for having a weak moment," she attempts to guide. "That brand of miracle isn't his everyday experience. I know it's nothing in your world, but for a Normal, there's a lot of stress and trauma that comes with that kind of focused long-term miracle. He talked to me about how he would watch you follow his coaching and how he marveled when it worked. He had no idea what he was doing, even though he seemed like he had it together. Watching a miracle unfold, that you're blindly guiding, is a big deal." She gives me a motherly look. "Part of his response to that trauma was giving in to his shallow side for a moment with someone who didn't know you at the time and was shallow enough that him being shallow was acceptable. He's not shallow now, and really wasn't then. He was a floundering kid on the inside through that mess."

"You can tell the measure of someone's constitution by seeing them at their worst," I retort with an eye roll.

"My point exactly," Cindy says. "He saved the shit part of him that needed to bellow 'what the hell' for someone shitty. He gave you his best, and Rachelle his worst, because that's what you both deserved. Rachelle will never see Zane at his best."

"I'll think on that," I reply. "Thank you for being the one who came to talk to me. I wanted to end on a good note with you.

I was greatly bothered by our conflict. I care about Zane and would like a respectful relationship with his mother."

"So, that's it?" Cindy asks, flummoxed.

"That's all she wrote."

Cindy's eyes narrow with a hint of mischief. It clues me in yet again that there's more to her than our first interaction revealed.

"Have you been gifted a celebration for *Glamour* yet?" Cindy unexpectedly asks with a sparkle in her eye.

"You're crafty," I compliment. "Nice shift of tactics." Cindy laughs as I shake my head and remind her, "I've been a little distracted with my teen pregnancy, Zane's suicide, and trying to avoid the death sentence by the suicide blobs."

"No one took you to dinner, or anything?" she prods.

I shake my head, curious where she's going with this.

"Are you going to the prescreen and media question-and-answer panel for *Glamour* today at four?" Cindy asks.

I wince. "I completely forgot about that," I confess. "No. I don't think I'm going."

"That's understandable, but would you go to Surfrider at eight? Bring your surfboard."

"What's happening there?"

"Let me be your mama for one night," she says, all bubbly.

It's nice to get a glimpse of her fun side.

"It'll be special. I promise."

"Umm . . ."

Before I can answer, the door opens, and Trey strides in. He stops and studies Cindy. "Hello," he says, a bit guarded. He's not accustomed to strangers in our room.

Nervous, I clamp down tighter on my connection with Trey so he isn't clued in about how conflicted I am. "Trey, this is Cindy, Zane's mom. She came to check on me."

Trey knows Cindy wasn't nice to me, and it shows in his body language, but he aims for polite. "I wasn't trying to interrupt. I didn't know you had company."

"We were just wrapping up." I stand, saying formally to Cindy, "Thank you so much for coming by. Please thank Zane and Rocco for me."

Cindy stands. "It was good to see you, Melanie," she says, sounding unsure.

"You too. Have a good day." I head to the door, and Cindy follows. I walk her to the foyer door, opening it.

Trey follows, and Cindy looks from him to me. "Please call Zane," she says finally.

"I'm sure I'll run into him at the Beach Bar sometime."

"I'm glad you're okay, Melanie," she says as she steps out, and I gently close the door.

"What was that about?" Trey asks.

I sigh. "Cindy helped Zane and Rocco with the aftermath. She was worried. I'm just glad we got that talk over with."

"What did she say about Zane?"

"Just that he's struggling." I shrug. "He's helped me through too many difficult things. It upsets him."

"Are you okay if I get in some work?"

I nod, relieved because I need time to think.

Trey kisses me before making his way through the parlor. I exhale hard as soon as he's out of earshot.

CHAPTER 32

Cindy left an hour ago. Somehow that talk settled some of my overwhelmed mental state. I need to handle a few things that have been nagging at me, and I finally feel up to it. The gym is the only place I can find privacy at Mabel's. While my room is an option, I don't want to handle this task there because it'll haunt me every time I walk through that door. Adam and Valerie are a screaming mess, but that's my own fault. Revealing that private talk spurred World War III for the Stones. Valerie is so upset that Dr. Fontaine has ordered that she not be moved. We're stuck with her until she delivers.

I set down the tote bag on a weight bench and close my eyes as my pulse thuds. Now that my body is healed, it's time to deal with my heart.

Tears well up, and I allow them to silently stream down my cheeks. I know that bottling up the tears will bottle up my anxiety and heartbreak. I release my jagged emotions and wait patiently until I'm emptied enough to have control.

When I'm ready, I take two white pillar candles from the bag and carefully set them on a little table in the corner. I pull a smaller pink candle out of the bag, and a fresh wave of tears flow. I hold the candle to my chest, and my head drops.

After a long moment, I hear movement behind me and turn to see Trey pushing away from the wall he was leaning on to walk toward me. Arch, Demitri, Finley, Adam, and Tanner are standing near the doorway with tears in their eyes.

"Now isn't a good time, Adam." It's rude of me, but I don't want him here for this moment, in particular.

"I can feel your pain from across the house," Adam softly informs. Distraught, he shakes his head. "You're right that I bail when it counts, but I've got my head on straight again. Please, Melanie. I need to help you."

My head drops as I consider this. Deciding that I've tortured him enough, and got to terrify Valerie, I opt to let my anger with Adam drop. "Okay."

Adam's shoulders relax and he mouths, "Thank you," silently.

"Can I join you?" Trey asks.

I lean my head against his shoulder and crumple. He wraps his arms around me and holds me up, waiting until I pull myself together.

When I open my eyes, our friends cross the room to us. Trey and I turn to the little table. Finley and Demitri step behind me on my right, and Tanner and Arch mirror them on Trey's left. Adam hangs back respectfully. I set the little candle on the table in front of the two white pillar candles.

Trey shifts to face Tanner. I watch out of the corner of my eye as Trey's shoulders cave in. Tanner puts his arms around Trey. Arch sets a hand on his back. My expression collapses, and Finley pulls me in to hug me. Demitri puts his cheek on the top of my head. I can feel our friends looking at each other. Finley's breath shudders a bit, and I get a twinge of guilt for putting our friends through another round of emotional torment.

"I'm sorry. You've already been through so much with us," I say.

"We're here through all of it," Finley reassures me.

"We love you guys," Tanner says. "Let's do this for my niece. She deserves it."

Trey and I both take a deep breath, and our friends let us go. I cross to the cabinet above the stereo system and open a bag of little tea lights, pulling out five. I walk back to the table and set the candles on the table with the others.

I kneel and rummage through the tote bag. Frustration mounts, and I whimper, "Where is it?"

"What are you looking for?" Adam asks from across the room.

"I need to go get a lighter," I whimper pitifully.

Adam produces two from his jeans pocket and crosses the room, handing them to Trey.

"Thank you," Trey says through tears, as I stand.

Adam draws Trey in, hugging him with a compassionately stoic, "I'm so sorry you lost the baby, bro." There's an odd dynamic between Trey and Adam. They hate each other, but there's also a deep respect. It's been like this for many lifetimes.

Adam lets go of Trey, who faces me. Both of our faces are shiny with tears.

Trey and I take a shaky collective breath. Silently, we step up to the candles and each light a large, white one. We step back and hand the lighters to Tanner and Finley, who approach the table, hold hands, and light two little tea lights at the same time. They pass the lighters to Arch and Demitri and make room for them to light theirs. Trey hands his lighter to Adam, who lights the last little candle. We wait a moment watching the flames flicker.

Trey takes my hand, lacing his fingers with mine, and we light the pink candle together.

I've stood vigil over the candles for four hours, waiting for the pink candle to burn down. I'm not leaving this room until the flame flickers out. "Trey, it's time," I say through the intercom in the gym.

"I'm on my way," he replies.

Trey walks into the gym, and I'm waiting by the door. He holds his hand out to me, and we walk together to the little table with our candles. Trey drapes his arms over my shoulders, lacing his hands with mine. We watch the candles together.

Our friends' little candles burned out long ago. Mine and Trey's larger candles are still going strong. The baby's candle is down to the tiniest bit of pink liquid wax. The wick barely flickers. It delicately goes out, sending up a waft of smoke.

Trey unclasps our hands, and we blow out our two candles together. I close my eyes, and my heart squeezes tighter.

"I thought I'd feel better after this, but my heart still hurts."

Trey sends back, *"Mine does, too. It'll take some time."*

My jaw sets in a clamp.

"I need to talk about something with you." I work to keep my rage tightly held. It's not time for that yet, but I know it's coming.

Trey meets my stone-cold gaze.

"I originally felt a touch relieved because I didn't think we were ready for a baby," I share. "I've spent four hours in here thinking, and I'm not relieved anymore. I asked Mama Mabel what would've happened if we had ended up having the baby. She said she would've moved us in full time and switched us to the large suite that has two bedrooms. She also said she would've hired a nanny to take care of the baby while we were at school. We could've done it. It wouldn't have been easy, but nothing about our lives is easy."

"I've had a similar change of feelings," Trey admits. "I would prefer to wait, but we could've handled it."

"I'm, ashamed that I didn't even fight back in the parking lot when Mack attacked me," I confess. "Our baby deserved more from me."

"You had none of your abilities. You were helpless. There's nothing you could've done differently. Everyday sixteen-year-old girls don't take on a whole pack of bikers and win, Melanie." Trey looks to the side, radiating humiliation. "I'm to blame for this. Locking you out was an oversight that will haunt me forever."

I clamp down on my anger that spikes to prevent it getting to Trey through our connection. "I need you to understand something," I say. "Obviously, we're going to have kids. We've seen them. All my abilities are going to go haywire again when I'm pregnant. I'll need you to back me. I really am completely helpless."

Trey nods. "I won't abandon you again like I did the past few months," he promises. "I apologize for being so dismissive. I've got a lot of guilt I'm struggling with over that."

"I'm invoking Retribution Clause against the Reapers as my right through club edict. I'm avenging the baby," I assert, looking penetratingly into his eyes.

Trey's mouth drops open, and he radiates fear. "If you lose, they'll kill you," he warns.

"Then I better win," I reply. "This is my right as the mother of a murdered child according to the edict. It's the only thing I can do for her, because we both know I'm not going to kill Valerie and her babies."

We hear someone sharply inhale and turn our attention to the door, realizing Adam, Demitri, Arch, Finley, and Tanner are listening.

I choose to look away instead of responding.

"God help the Reapers," Trey says. "I'll talk to Big Joe and let him know what you're doing so the Hellhounds are aware."

"Are you in?" I ask him.

Trey's eyes morph steely. "We're cracking skulls."

Arch cracks his knuckles. "I'm calling in the Hellcats. This became family business the moment we all heard Melanie scream in agony."

"We make a battle plan," Trey growls.

We all look at each other as the energy amps up in the room.

"Wait, wait! I know the next part," Tanner says breaking the pensive silence. He hops in front of Demitri, imitating him with an over-exaggerated, sexy smolder. "You can't DOOOO this, Melanie. You're so tiny, and I need to rescue you," Tanner says in his best Demitri interpretation. "Huge muscles, smoldering gaze, backflip, tank top," he adds flippantly.

We all exchange glances, trying not to laugh.

Tanner points to Trey. "What's the matter, Peter Pan?" Tanner says with a deeper voice. "Can't find your balls and enjoy the dark side? I wear all black, and I'm evil. Neck crack. Knockout bad guy."

We're all covering our mouths, spurting laughter.

Tanner points at me and cocks a hip. "Don't underestimate me, Demitri," he coos in a seductive, babydoll voice. "I'm mean and nasty even though I'm sooooo cute." He wiggles his hips and pretends to toss long hair. "Blast seductive dark-water energy that gives everyone raging erections at parties."

Everyone doubles over laughing.

Tanner points at Arch. "Gut up," he orders. "We can argue about it later if we live through this. I wear a trench coat and run this shitshow, even though I know I'm the captain of the *Titanic* and all we do is hit icebergs." He points to Adam next and makes a stupid face. "Duuuhhh," rumbles out of him.

Even Adam howls laughter.

"Melanie's letting Valerie live so she can torture you for years, Adam," Tanner sassily informs. "Melanie was crafty with that supposed blessing that's really a punishment."

"It's working, if it helps," Adam grumbles.

Tanner points at Finley last and gives an exaggerated sigh. "Hush, Tanner," he admonishes in a fairy voice. "You're always stirring the pot. Let them have their moment. This isn't about you! 'I'm so pretty and have a disappointed mom look.'" Tanner grins vibrantly. "Did I get it right?" he crows like a proud third grader as he bounces on his toes.

We're all laughing, except for Demitri.

"Those assholes tried to kill Melanie," he growls. "If Trey doesn't kill Mack, I plan to."

I snap an amusedly shocked look Trey's way, who smirks.

"Well, look at you Laugh-A-Lot Bear," he says. "It's all fun and games until you love her, isn't it?"

"Precisely," Demitri replies gravely.

"Wait, you two are hunky-freaking-dory?" Arch asks. He snaps his baffled gaze to Demitri. "Didn't you threaten to take Trey's girl a few days ago before you got stuffed in her Venus flytrap while she screamed?"

Demitri and Trey both laugh.

"We have a solid understanding," Demitri informs.

Arch looks at Trey. "What?" he scoffs. "He apologized and you accepted? There ain't NO way."

"We resolved our issues because of a coloring book," Trey tells Arch.

"What the fuck?" Arch exclaims.

"Yup. You heard me right," Trey says. "If D wants into the battle, then he's in. He has a score to settle."

"Thank you," Demitri stoically says.

"Plot twist! I love it," Tanner crows and points at Trey. "Mark my words, you'll regret letting Mr. Perfect into your fold. He's gonna do another magic trick with the Queen of the Damned, but he isn't gonna lose a hand this time."

Demitri inhales to speak, and Tanner rolls his eyes.

"Yeah, yeah. We all know." Tanner poses like a sexy *GQ* model and smolders out, "I'm not that guy."

We all dissolve into laughter.

The others take their leave, but Adam stays behind. He stares in my eyes before wrapping me in a hug.

I stand still, here for it, but unsure.

When he lets me go, there are tears in his eyes. "I'm proud of you," he whispers, and then he leaves the room.

CHAPTER 33

The scent of the ocean greets me as I shut off my car. Staring out at the moonlit water, I gather my resolve. An invitation like Cindy's is hard to resist. I open my door, and my flip-flop-clad feet hit the sandy pavement. I have no idea what this invitation entails. I brought my board and have my swimsuit on under my floral dress.

Nervous, I make my way to the beach, finding a few tables and a small group. It's dark enough outside the party area, despite the outlined perimeter of tiki torches, that they don't see me as everyone chats and laughs. SWV's "Weak" thrums from a boombox. The vibe seems relaxed.

Cindy spots me first and quietly slips from her conversation to make her way to me. "You came!" she exclaims, sounding happy about it.

"You know that offer that you'd be my mama for a night?" I ask.

Cindy melts a little.

"My mom's been out of town this whole time. I need a mama for a second," I add in a rush.

Cindy wraps me in a hug. "I'm so proud of you, Melanie. *Glamour* is fantastic."

"You saw it?" I bashfully ask, relieved that she brought up a positive topic.

Cindy cups my chin. "They showed it before the press event," she informs me. "I swear every question was about you. I wish you had been there. The press is enamored with you."

"Are you upset because the movie is naughty?" I ask.

Cindy laughs lightly. "I learned a long time ago to separate my son from his movie characters. I guarantee you're going to win an award for that death scene. Everyone in that theater cried." She glances at the party over her shoulder. "I wish my husband was here. My daughter has a cheer competition in Sacramento. He's looking forward to meeting you."

I spot Zane and feel like I'm crashing the party as people who are clearly close with each other interact across the way. I'm second-guessing my decision to come. "I forgot something in my car. I'll be right back," I tell Cindy.

Cindy makes her way back to the party, and I scurry to my car. Just as I start to get in, I hear a voice behind me.

"Don't even think about it."

I whip around, not having expected that.

"I apologize for startling you," Rachelle rushes to say.

"Hi," I say, unsure.

"Hi." She smiles again, but it has a big sister energy to it. "Where are you going?"

"To a gas station." I wobble my head. "A bathroom. I forgot something. I don't feel good. I need to get home. I have homework." I shrug one shoulder, feeling silly. "Pick one. Any excuse will work."

"No running away." Rachelle rounds my car, pulling my

surfboard through the open passenger window. She carries it to me, but I don't move. Rachelle gives me a look. "Zane's earned a night of watching you be alive. Cindy and I have earned the opportunity to spend a little time trying to make amends with you. YOU have earned the opportunity to celebrate the best damn movie performance I've ever seen."

"You saw the movie at the screening we were both at," I remind her.

"No, I didn't," Rachelle replies. "I was such a nervous mess that day. I was embarrassed, and very uncomfortable. I *just* actually watched it, and you blew me away."

"Well, thank you," I reply, pulling it together.

"You're welcome," she says. She hands me my board. "Zane looks like shit. Everyone's worried about him. He can't sleep since you almost died the other night. I'm so glad you're okay." She lets me set the pace back to the party, which turns out to be a slow trudge. Understanding my hesitancy, Rachelle stops and says, "Brian and Zane are in counseling."

"That's good," I meekly reply.

"Full disclosure, I've been at two of the sessions," Rachelle adds. "The therapist wanted to get a handle on the dynamic. We decided that we all needed to try settling back in the roles we're most comfortable in."

I stare at my feet. "What roles are those?"

"Those roles are me being Brian's girlfriend, and Brian and me being big brother and sister to Zaney."

I look up at the taller girl as Rachelle's eyes crinkle at the corners.

"He was eleven when I started dating Brian, but I've known the family longer. He's been my little brother up until about eight months ago. I'm very uncomfortable with him being anything else.

We're much happier with the old dynamic," she shares.

I bite my lip wanting to ask stuff, but none of it is really mine to ask. I avert my gaze, pondering.

Rachelle saves me. "I didn't take you and him serious enough, but I do now. The look in both of your eyes when those Ani DiFranco songs played . . ." She trails off.

I slide huge eyes up to meet hers, and her expression melts around the edges.

"I've never seen Zane look that way. I knew I screwed up by overstepping. Obviously, it's torn the Drell family, you, and me apart. I know he's grown, but that day I watched little Zaney stare into the eyes of the woman he wanted a forever with, while they were both destroyed over my actions that NEVER should have happened in the first place. That's what hurt me the most. My kid brother deserves you. He offers everything, except a clean slate. I tarnished that. If it weren't for me, and a little time for you to get older, he'd have it all. I want him to have it all because Zaney has always been one of my very favorite people. I used to babysit him. He always wanted to watch *Teenage Mutant Ninja Turtles*."

I giggle, charmed by that tidbit.

"He even had the turtle-shell backpack and eye-cover bandana thing," she divulges, crinkling her nose at me.

"Which one was he?"

"It was orange," recalls Rachelle.

"Michaelangelo!" I feel my smile light my eyes. "He's the funny one."

"That look, right there, is priceless." Rachelle smiles. "You really do love that he dressed up like the funny turtle, don't you?"

I nod. "That's why I love Zane. I don't give a damn about his money or resume. I love that he has Spiderman boxer shorts."

"You have to be kidding?" Rachelle gapes.

"About the boxer shorts, or that I love them?"

"The boxer shorts," Rachelle says, amused.

I giggle. "He also has Lucky Charms ones. Complete with rainbow and leprechaun."

"No way. Why do you know that?" she gossipingly whispers my way, but it feels friendly instead of sinister.

"He stayed with me for a long time in the hospital," I remind her. "I know the man's underwear."

Rachelle puts an arm around my waist, guiding me toward the party. "You never have to worry about anything involving me again," she assures, before smiling encouragingly. "You like tacos, right?"

"There are people who don't like tacos?" I give her the look the question deserves.

"Cindy had tacos catered. Welcome to the party," Rachelle replies with a giggle.

Brian sees us and rushes my way. He scoops me up.

"I'm so glad you're here," he says. "Are you holding up okay?"

"Your mom invited me tonight." I wince a little. "I needed some fun. Things haven't been fun, you know?"

"We can provide fun." Brian appears a little surprised. "Zane didn't tell me you were coming."

"I don't think he knows," I say, unsure.

Brian guides me through the little twenty-person party and taps Zane on the shoulder, while pulling me to hide behind him.

"What's up?" I hear Zane ask but can't see him because, apparently, I'm hiding.

"There's a girl here to see you," Brian informs him.

It makes me nervous. I have no idea what Zane's going to say.

"That's a big goose egg," Zane says. "No girls. No thank you. I've got zero left in the tank on that front."

"The girl who wants to see you is all tiny and adorable," Brian says. "I think you'll like her."

"I already have one of those," Zane replies, "but thank you."

"Sorry. He's not interested," Brian says, leaning back to talk to me over his shoulder.

"Who's behind you?" Zane asks, sounding annoyed.

"Too bad," I chirp back. "Cindy said she'd be my mom tonight, and I need that." I peek around Brian to talk to Zane. "Guess I'll have to eat tacos alone."

Zane grabs my wrist and yanks me to him. He picks me up and crushes me to his chest. His face buries in my neck. I wrap my arms around his head, letting him hide. He's massive, but he has these really innocent moments when he's emotional. Even huge guys need to hide sometimes. We've done this a lot, and he's admitted that he loves it.

Everyone at the gathering watches us. Some I don't recognize, but all have a sweetness in their expressions. Cindy gets that mom look that all moms have when their kid has a lot happening in their lives. I smile at her, and she mouths, "Thank you."

After a long moment surrounded by silent support, Zane takes a deep breath and sets me down carefully. "How are you?" he asks.

"Better," I whisper back. "Demitri healed all of it."

"Like, you're better better?"

"Everything's better except the swelling. I'm not likely to take off this dress and reveal a bikini with this gut I'm sporting."

"No one cares about that," he assures me. He hugs me again, swinging me back and forth. "You invited Melanie?" he asks his mom.

"No one did a celebration for her. It's her first movie." Cindy grins. "Firsts are important."

"Thank you," Zane says. "Did you add me to the catering count?"

"Yes. I added Melanie also," Cindy says, laughing. "Sixteen tacos."

"Sister, you're insane," a man I don't know remarks. "You think that tiny girl can eat eight tacos?"

"Melanie, meet my Uncle Sylvester," Zane says.

"Call me Sly," Zane's uncle offers.

"It's nice to meet you," I bubble happily. As much as Zane and I have had our problems, when I'm wrapped up in his arms, I'm always happy.

"Twelve of those tacos are for me," Zane claims, and gives me a squeeze. "I guarantee this little sprite will rachet down four tacos."

"You're so much tinier in person," Uncle Sly marvels.

"Zane has that effect." I giggle. "Perspective." I crank my neck to gaze up at Zane. He crinkles his nose at me before kissing my forehead.

"The movie was beyond good," Sly compliments. "I feel dirty talking to you, though."

"Eh." I shrug. "It's just work. I'm glad you liked the movie."

"*That's* just work?" Uncle Sly bellows Zane's way, earning laughter from those who got to preview the movie.

"I love my job," Zane says with a grin.

"Yeah, I would also if my job involved all of that," Uncle Sly chides. "You lucky shit."

Zane rubs his nose on mine.

"Everyone, this is Melanie," he announces to the party. "I'll bring her around to introduce you in a few. First, I have to feed her."

I get quite a few welcoming hellos before everyone goes about their business.

"I'll be relieved to see you eat," Cindy tells Zane.

"I'm better when I'm with her," Zane responds.

Cindy imploringly stares in my eyes. "Skip, hold hands, fairy princess. Told you."

I laugh while we traverse the distance to the banquet table. We fill our plates, and Zane guides me to one of the many blankets spread about on the sand. Rocco joins us and silently side hugs me while I take a beef taco bite.

Rocco stares at me, but it's not rude. He's earned the right to see that I'm okay, and I think that's what he's pondering. "Thank you for coming tonight."

I smile his way and lean my back against Zane's chest. I watch a taco venture to Zane's mouth. "I'm okay, Roc," I say. "Thank you for helping. I know that was a lot."

Rocco sighs. "I'm just glad you're not under a death sentence anymore."

"That had me so bunched up," Zane admits.

"Oooooooh, chicken taco," I happily exclaim.

Zane lowers his taco for me, and I take a bite.

"Demitri couldn't have gotten through helping her if you hadn't kept him going," Zane tells Rocco, while I side-eye him mischievously and take another taco bite.

"The things you sacrifice for her," Rocco teases Zane.

Zane puts his forehead on the back of my head. "Whatever it takes," he says.

I stealthily take another taco bite.

Rocco grins. "You two are really cute," he comments.

I nibble the last of the taco from Zane's fingers.

"You brat," he jokes as he realizes I just gobbled up his taco. Rocco chuckles.

"I like chicken," I say and bat my eyelashes at Zane.

He snuffles behind my ear. He loves the vanilla pheromone I exude. I snuggle up closer while he puts his plate down on the blanket and leans back so I can settle against his chest.

I eat another taco while Zane and Rocco happily banter. I lift it to Zane, and he takes a bite without missing a conversation beat.

Cindy and Rachelle catch my eye as they watch us across the way. Cindy winks at me, and I smile happily as Zane's arm absently drapes over my chest. His hand lands on my stomach, and my eyes contentedly droop. When I open them, Cindy appears sad.

"Babe," I say quietly.

Zane lowers his head to mine, catching my intimate tone.

"You need to talk to your mom. I think she's got an unfounded assumption about us."

Zane glances from his hand that's on my stomach to his mom. He doesn't get a chance to reply.

"The baby was Zane's right?" Rocco asks.

"No," Zane replies. His tone cages.

I look up and find his jaw tight. His hand splays wider on my stomach, doubling down on his commitment to what just happened a few days ago.

Rocco and I exchange a stealthy side-eye.

"Talk to us, Zane," Rocco encourages.

"I don't want you with Trey," Zane says to me.

"Why?" I ask. "I mean, I know why, but it also seems there's a specific why that's new."

"You can't have a baby with someone who's an energy worker," Zane says.

I snap my gaze to Zane, not expecting that. "I wasn't aiming to have one in the first place," I protest.

Zane meets my gaze without hesitation. "I'm serious, Melanie," he warns. "A child with the ability of two energy workers is going to kill you before you make it to forty weeks."

"I take it you're offering a baby?" Rocco tactlessly asks.

"I'm not having this conversation tonight when she's earned a stress-free evening," Zane tells Rocco. "I'll tell you this much, though. I'll never watch her coat a room in blood again. You don't deserve that, Melanie. Everything that Rocco and I rushed into the middle of was wrong."

"I made it, though." I smile, but it's sad. "I always make it, Zane."

"Is Trey at least upset?" Zane asks in disbelief.

"In his way," I reply. At Zane's askant look, I clarify. "Trey isn't talking much about it, but he's attentive."

"I'm surprised he was okay with you coming here tonight," Zane huffs.

"He's at his parents' house. He hadn't spent any time at home in a long time. It cleared me to come here," I explain. "I was scared to be alone and thought time with you would be nice. I didn't come here to upset you."

"I'm not upset at you," Zane replies. "I'll go talk to my mom."

I let him up, and when he's out of earshot, give a groan.

Rocco rubs his forehead. "Zane's really screwed up, Melanie," he confides. "I watched his face while you went through the final push. It was horrible."

"I was hoping you didn't watch any of it. Your vantage point behind Demitri was horrific," I exclaim, mortified.

"Demitri leaned over you, and blocked the graphic view," Rocco says, "but I had to make sure Zane was okay. He was broken."

"That's horrifying. Do you think he's repulsed by me now?" I whimper.

"Definitely not," Rocco compassionately says. "He's having a hard time with it though."

"I'll talk to him," I promise. "What's happening?" I ask, unable to see Zane and his mom from my angle.

"Worried faces from Mom," Rocco fills in. "Zane is yapping."

"Lovely," I sigh. "Maybe I shouldn't have accepted the invite."

"You needed to accept the invite," Rocco insists. "We all need to work through this. If that means you steal tacos, Zane protectively clutches your stomach, and the rest of us ponder Zane's baby-daddy status, so be it."

"I've only kissed Zane," I say.

"Even with all that hospital naked-shower time?"

"I was naked in a lot of showers because of my injuries and issues," I share. "Zane rarely was."

"You're kidding!" Rocco exclaims, baffled.

"Nope. He's either the ultimate gentleman or prefers showers in boxers, like a weirdo. Or he's really not that into me."

"He was being a gentleman." Rocco chuckles. Rocco looks disdainfully toward the boombox as a new song comes on.

I squeal.

Rocco reaches to change the song.

"Don't even think about it, Roc," I loudly command as I hop up.

He looks at me like I've lost my mind, along with everyone else at the party.

"1989 called, and they want my fifth-grade recital piece back," I announce.

Zane cracks up as he and his mom make their way back to us. The guests look at me curiously. This group seems open, and I grin Zane's way.

"It's bubbling. I feel it."

Zane chuckles. "Please tell me you're about to dance to Debbie Gibson's 'Electric Youth.'"

I chortle. "Are you prepared, Zaney, for the fifth-grade extravaganza that I had the lead in?"

"She's so WEIRD," Rocco blathers, while Brian laughs adoringly.

With a grin, Uncle Sly hoists a video camera to his shoulder as I start the dance. It's a 1980s intermediate kids' jazz extravaganza, and the whole crowd is suddenly smiling as I bop and glide, slide and jazz-hand shimmy.

"What are you wearing for this amazing piece?" Zane inquires.

I hop from foot to foot, punctuating the air with dramatically splayed jazz hands. "Pink bedazzled tank top, knotted at the side, purple sports bra that fifth-grade me did NOT need, blue biker shorts, and purple leg warmers."

"I love her," Zane adoringly informs his mom.

I very properly prep a turn with exaggerated technique. To Zane's amusement, I execute a single pirouette. "Only a clean single, because that's what we can pull off." I grin at Zane as I hitch-kick before jazz splitting to the sand and lying on my stomach, kicking my pointed feet. "That's what Ms. Georgette said every single rehearsal."

We hit the breakdown in the song. "Dramatic girl boss poses to the keytar," I announce.

"Naturally," Zane agrees enthusiastically. "It's the only choice."

"Big finish," I crow as I wave jazz hands rapidly in front of my face before sliding into a split with my arms over my head on the last note.

Raucous applause rings out. Zane takes my hand, spins me on my tush, and helps me stand. He guides me around him with a noble air before presenting me with a dramatic flourish to my adoring audience. I deeply curtsy with a comedically humble hand to my chest as I receive a standing ovation. I come out of the deep curtsy, and Zane belts laughter while he hugs me.

"I love you to the moon and back, Melanie," Cindy exclaims.

"You're the cutest thing I've ever seen," Uncle Sly chimes in.

"Thank you so much," I breathe, like a diva receiving admiring praise.

Everyone laughs.

I turn an over-exaggerated look Zane's way and challenge him. "I formally request that you top that recital masterpiece."

"Oh," Zane says with haughty amusement. "Can I ever! Picture it." He sweeps an arm, painting the picture for us all. "Sixteen-year-old Zane. Already the coolest guy in the studio, and then, a fresh miracle happens. Recital piece selection reveals that I get the lead in Ms. Nanny Nannette's advanced hip-hop extravaganza, 'Hangin' Tough.'"

I giggle and Zane smolders my way.

"That's right, a New Kids on the Block dream come true was mine," he brags.

"Please tell me you remember it," I say.

"I do, and I'll never do it again."

"Bet you will," I suggest with twinkling eyes.

"Nope. There's not a damn thing you could say to make me do that piece."

"It'll make me haaappy." I flutter girlishly.

Zane's expression comically slides deadpan, and I giggle.

"Rocco, I'm about to hang tough, aren't I?" Zane says.

"Yuuuppp," Rocco foghorns. "That's the cutest expression I've ever seen on that girl."

"We don't have the music," Zane says, pretending to be crestfallen.

"Now, Zane," Rocco says with a grin, "I'm disappointed in you." He points to Brian, himself, and a guy I don't know. "Do you not recall our talent show piece at the Beach Bar three years ago?"

"Don't even think about it," Zane hisses, glaring at Rocco.

"The pretty girl showed up this time. Do the piece, or you'll cry all night," Cindy teases.

Confused, I swing my attention Cindy's way.

"Zane invited Penny Plonze to see him be the ultimate teen fantasy," she informs the crowd. "She didn't show up because she decided a guy named Luke was a better choice. Zane cried for days."

I rudely spurt laughter, and Zane gives his mother an aggrieved look.

"Really MOM! You had to reveal *that*?"

I scan the crowd, sighting a friend of Zane's that I've yet to meet, who appears amused. "Luke?" I call out with terrible romance intentions.

"Name's Toby, but after seeing your movie, I'll be Luke," he answers with a grin.

I laugh before carefully contorting my expression back to girly flutter. "I'm sorry," I expel with a huffy huff, "but only Luke will do." I scan the crowd before settling my gaze on Zane. "And then, she saw him. The toughest hang in the crowd."

Zane blusters with barely contained laughter as I grab Cindy's and Rachelle's hands and skirt the performance area. I shoo back Uncle Sly and pull the ladies down to sit on either side of me on the blanket at front row center.

I fan my face and fluster like a teen nightmare. "Thank you so much for coming to the show with me! You won't believe this guy," I coo at them and toss my head back. "He's dreamy."

"What about Luke?" Rachelle asks with feigned girly eyes.

"Luke WHO?" I moan like every tween-age girl. "There's only one."

"And then, the lights dim," Toby dramatically narrates as he crosses the performance space. "Luke arrives." He snaps a debonair look my way, and I toss my hair with a snotty nose to the air.

"Don't look, girls," I chime. "Luke's no one now!"

Cindy and Rachelle dramatically avert their gaze as the spectators crow laughter.

"That's when it happened." Toby continues his trek with a wide arm sweep. "The curtain opened."

I obnoxiously fan my face as the beatboxing starts. Brian, Rocco, and their friend give it hell singing "Hangin' Tough," while Zane does the single worst recital hip-hop piece I've ever seen. Rachelle, Cindy, and I make quite the production of squealing and carrying on through the whole debacle. Zane does his part, smoldering and being oh-so-tough. Zane ends the piece on one knee with his fist under his chin and a raised eyebrow.

I applaud with gusto, along with all the other spectators, who are beside themselves laughing. I hop to my feet and bounce around while Cindy, Rachelle, and I squeal and have fake vapors.

Zane, laughing, stands and takes a bow.

I rush to him and boing up into his arms. He catches me, and I smile bigger than I have in so long. He hugs me tight.

"I adore that he plays with me," I exclaim to Cindy.

After everyone but the inner circle goes back to their own thing, Zane looks to his mom. "Can I have a sleepoveeer?" he asks like a fourth grader.

Cindy gives him the funniest confused look. "Well, dear, I don't know. Who did you want to have over?"

"My friend, Mel. We want to sleep in the pool house and watch scary movies all night."

"Honey, Mel needs her parents' permission," Cindy says.

"No," I retort bashfully. "I actually don't. You see, my live-in boyfriend is at his parents' house. I suppose I could ask the madam at the brothel I live at, if that would please you."

Rocco caws laughter.

"Brothel?" Cindy asks.

"You visited me there," I remind her. "Mabel is the madam. I just accepted the job as events coordinator."

"What kinds of events?" Cindy asks, while rapidly blinking.

"Stripper reviews, bachelor parties, coordinated orgies, the occasional birthday party," I answer with a shrug. "Brothel stuff."

"Is it an intern*ship*?" Cindy asks quizzically, trying to wrap her mind around the oddity.

Rocco, Zane, and Brian guffaw as Rachelle and Cindy give me mom looks.

"Nope," I chirp. "I'm making sixty thousand a year, with paid room and board."

Cindy's mouth drops open. "At sixteen?"

"I made five hundred thousand straddling your son, but I can't touch it until I'm twenty-one." I choke on my own warped sense of humor. "The money, I mean. I can touch Zane at eighteen."

Cindy howls laughter while Zane rubs his neck, amused and blushing.

"Can we have a sleepoverrrrr?" I childishly repeat Zane's question.

"I never thought I'd hear those words again from my boy," she says and gives me a confused look. "Or his girl. Yes, you can have a sleepover in my pool house."

I squeal and hug Zane. "We have to do all the things," I tell him.

"Awesome," Zane responds, purse-lipped.

"Popcorn," I suggest.

"Gremlins movie," Zane says with a manly smolder.

"Pillow fight," I add to the list.

Zane nods with gusto. "Sneaking candy."

"I thought they were talking about sex for a second there." Cindy seems undisturbed by the notion. I like that she's so laid-back.

"Nope. They spend every minute acting like four-year-olds," Rocco informs Cindy.

"It's true. They watch cartoons and share Slurpees," Brian teases.

Cindy gives us an adoring look.

My phone rings and I sigh, pulling it out of my purse that's on the blanket by my feet. I answer, putting it on speaker, but don't get a chance to even say hello before Demitri barrels through.

"Where are you?" he asks angrily.

"At a celebration for *Glamour*. Why?"

"You're missing," Demitri accuses. "Everyone is panicking."

"I'm fine!"

"Arch got his ass handed to him," he growls. "Trey's stuck at dinner with his parents, but he ordered us to call in the Misfits and start a search."

"How dramatic," I huff back. "Clearly all you needed to do was call me. Is there a reason you called Trey in the first place?"

"Is there a reason you LEFT in the first place?" Demitri blisters back.

"I wanted to have some fun!"

"You need security," Demitri sighs. "You should have taken one of us with you. You didn't even leave a note!"

"Gee whiz, DAD," I bark.

Demitri clears his throat. "I'm sorry," he says, sounding a little more rational.

I can hear Arch talking in the background.

"Where are you?" Demitri asks.

"Surfrider, eating tacos."

"We're on our way," Demitri states.

"I didn't invite you. I'm FINE," I say, rolling my eyes.

"Sorry, Mel," Arch says over the phone line. "We're under orders from the boss. Full security detail is getting in cars."

"Don't you dare!"

He must have handed the phone back to Demitri.

"Trey asked me to stay with you tonight," he informs.

I rub my face hard. "I'm not coming home tonight. I need a breather."

"Then I'm packing a bag," Demitri replies.

"Now you want to trap me also?" I snap.

I'm met with long silence.

"We worry," Demitri says, sounding a little ashamed.

"Demitri, I drove to the beach at eight o'clock at night to go to a party with friends. I didn't go radio silent, skip town, or team up with drug runners. Do you understand how insane you're all acting?"

"Where the fuck is she?" Adam bellows before Demitri can answer.

"Surfrider at a party for *Glamour*," Demitri informs.

"That's not *missing*!" I hear Adam insist. "I was ready to destroy all of Los Angeles to find her!" His voice comes clearer. He must have taken the phone. "Hey, love, what the hell is happening?"

"I went to a party, ate tacos, danced on the beach, and then you lunatics called," I angrily inform him.

"She's fine. Everyone stop," Adam hollers. "Why didn't you answer?" he asks me.

"I did," I defend. "Demitri called, and I answered to all of you being insane!"

"Demitri, did you try Mel first, or did you call Trey, stir every-one up, and insight panic first?" Adam asks.

"Panic first," Demitri admits.

"You people are all nut jobs," Adam scolds. "Mel, are you safe with the Surfrider crew?"

"Yes," I reply, pissed.

"Go back to your party," Adam softly says. "I'll deal with the dictator. Go inside," he shouts at the others.

We hear motorcycles and cars start.

"Damn it, they're heading out."

"I can't live like this, Adam," I gasp around rising panic. I'm just now realizing how little freedom I've had for a long time. Because of all the danger, I'm under constant lock and key.

"I know you can't." Adam consoles me. "Demitri left his phone in my hand. He just sped out of the parking lot doing Mach 10. I'm going to catch up with them." His Harley roars to life, and he hangs up.

I rub my face hard before dropping my phone onto the blanket. "Apparently, the cavalry is on its way."

"You can't even have fun with your friends?" Rocco asks, astonished.

"Not without security," I grumble. I feel my cheeks burn. "I'm so sorry," I tell Cindy, who appears bowled over by all of this.

"I'll talk to them when they get here," Cindy offers.

"It won't help, but thank you," I doggedly reply.

"I can't believe DEMITRI is the one pulling this," Zane says.

"He's been a wreck. What went on really threw him off," I offer in his defense.

"I guess that's understandable," Zane concedes.

"From what we heard," Rachelle softly says, "Demitri handled difficult things."

"Demitri has an unfused soulmate point with me," I reveal. "I don't have one, and it made him crazy even before he detonated fireballs in my yoohoo."

"So sorry," Cindy says as she tries to curb a burst of laughter. "You're hilarious, even when you're sad, Melanie. It'll take the nut jobs time to get here. Grab your board and catch a night ride. Enjoy the party. We'll feed them tacos when they arrive, and maybe they'll see that you're safe."

"I'm not letting my psychos clean you out of the rest of your tacos," I exhaustedly say. "I'm going to wait in my car for them."

"I've got another hundred tacos in catering trays on that table. I'm feeding everyone and helping you," Cindy insists. "We'll get this sorted. Now, go night ride with my boy."

"Do you have your board?" I ask Zane..

"Always," he says, downtrodden.

"Why don't I watch you surf?" I suggest, realizing my stomach is really swollen.

Zane shakes his head while he stares in my eyes. "Nope. I'm not letting you do this. You went through a lot, Melanie. You earned the swelling. You aren't going to be a sixteen-year-old dancer forever, and this shame cycle ends now, before it gets a foothold. Forty pounds, scars, age, whatever. You're not allowed to be ashamed of any of it."

"Pierre said something similar," I quietly inform him.

"That's because he loved you for you." Zane hugs me.

Cindy is softly smiling at us. A quick scan around the group, and I see similar expressions from Rachelle, Brian, and Rocco.

"Yup," Cindy says, "I approve of everything about this." She happily sighs and walks off to conversate with others.

"Well, Mom likes her," Brian says.

"I'm surprised, given how tense things were when I was saving Zane," I mutter.

"I think that actually helped," Brian informs. "You don't take any shit and didn't give in to her. She respects that."

"I respect her," I assure. "But, no, I don't take any shit. When it comes down to retrieving Zane's soul from the gatekeepers, I'm in charge."

"I need to speak with Melanie," Zane says with a serious edge.

Rocco and Brian take their leave, and Zane hits me with penetrating eyes.

"What do you mean Demitri has a soulmate bond with you?"

"Pierre did it to teach Demitri a lesson about what he was taking for granted," I tell him.

"My dead best friend betrayed me?" Zane asks.

I wince.

"Get rid of it, Melanie," he orders.

"I'm not in charge of this, Zane. If it helps, I'm not pleased about it. The last thing I need is more complication." Even though I don't want to, I say, "Let's go for a night ride."

I walk to my surfboard at the edge of the party area. I strip off my dress, look up at the night sky and take a deep breath. I feel like I have only a few more minutes of freedom before I'm trapped again. It scares me. I exhale, snag my board, wade out, and paddle to the break line.

"Hey, Mel," Arch says, aiming for jovial as he approaches and I slip my floral dress back on.

"I can't believe you guys came here," I grumble.

"We couldn't miss out on tacos," Marcus says, trying to keep things light, as he holds up a heaping plate.

"This is ridiculous," Adam scolds. "You guys are now extensions of Trey's crazy!"

"I borrowed Trey's board. Want to surf?" Demitri asks.

"Not a shot," I coldly reply.

"You were just surfing," Demitri points out dejectedly.

"I was surfing with Zane," I retort. "I'm not surfing with you."

Demitri blinks rapidly, trying to wrap his mind around my brush-off.

"Way to go, Peter Pan. You violated your little Meley's sanctuary." Adam gestures to Marcus, Arch, Tanner, and himself. "You showed up with reminders of her painful screaming episode."

"I just want tacos and to keep my job. I wasn't involved in Melanie's torture chamber event," Marcus clarifies.

"Rocco and Zane were there, also," Demitri snaps back, ignoring Marcus.

"True, but they're from a different part of Melanie's life," Adam schools. "She's had ample opportunity to discuss what happened with all of us. She needed time with them, that you invaded."

"I'm sorry I overreacted," Demitri mutters as he rubs his pale face. He leaves mottled red lines when he drops his hands. "I found her gone when I got to Mabel's. I searched the room for a note and panicked. I immediately thought she'd been kidnapped, or vaporized, or buried alive."

"Vaporized?" I ask, amused despite my irritation.

"Hell, I never know at his point," Demitri grumbles.

"I didn't leave a note because Trey was gone for the night," I explain. "Had I known you were slated to be my warden, I would have left a note."

"I'm sorry I crashed your party," Demitri dejectedly says. "I'm going to have a talk with Trey, because acting like a crazy prison warden is his gig. I've always been a part of your fun."

"I appreciate that," I reply. "I realize you've had to save me over and over lately. It's been a lot."

"This has SUCKED." Demitri boils over.

"Let it out," Uncle Sly barks. He's tipsy at this phase of the evening and has proven to be as unhinged as I can be. I grin as Uncle Sly yells at the moon, "THIS HAS SUCKED!" He waves his hands about enthusiastically. "Everyone needs to help the hot guy release this. On three." Uncle Sly counts, and everyone, including Demitri, bellows, "THIS HAS SUCKED!"

"Thank you! I feel better." Demitri grins at drunk Uncle Sly.

"You gotta let it out," Uncle Sly crows. "Bottling it up just makes the suck fester! I hate a festering suck!"

"There goes your love life," Toby crows from the other side of the party, earning hilarity from the whole dancing bunch.

"To festering suck only when it's good, and releasing it when it's bad." Rocco sounds off.

"Cheers," emits from the crowd.

"A real sinister event," Marcus hisses to Demitri, who winces because they invaded unnecessarily.

I glance Cindy's way, concerned she'll be offended by the shenanigans. She winks at me before taking another slug from a sippy cup of wine. When I asked why she uses a toddler's cup, she explained that this bunch tends to spill her wine glass, and she got sick of it. I've decided she's exactly what I want to be when I grow up: a quirky, passionate, amazing mom who accepts her crazy with as much grace as she can muster.

"Grab a sippy cup full of wine and let loose," she tells me as she gives me a hug,

"She can't," Demitri says, albeit clearly sorry. "Mabel and Trey want her locked behind steel gates in a panic-locked room, and me in there all night to bodyguard. She has to drive her car home."

"She's allowed to have fun," Zane coldly insists. "She's staying with me tonight."

Demitri just shakes his head. He's clearly uncomfortable.

"You aren't even hired as a bouncer," I remind. "Since when are you a bodyguard?"

"Since this morning," Demitri reveals. "Trey hired me as your personal security anytime he can't be there."

"You aren't one of the fighters," I snap. It comes out judgmental because I'm flustered.

"I can fight, I just don't like to." Demitri sighs. "I can also heal you if anything happens. Trey is paying me fifty an hour to stick to you like glue. He figured you'd be thrilled. So did I, but you're clearly not."

"I liked you sticking to me like glue because you're my best friend. I'm not interested in being your chore."

"Melanie, the Reapers tried to murder you," he says, tipping his head back in frustration. "They obviously didn't succeed, and we're on high alert. Those assholes are still out there, likely plotting. Your plan to evoke Retribution Clause may get out."

Adam wraps his arm around my waist. His hand lands on my stomach. Concern wafts through the connection from him.

"Demitri, are you sure she wasn't pregnant with twins?" Adam asks, his tone cautious.

"I didn't check for that," he states as his eyes widen. "I was just trying to get the deceased baby out."

"I know pregnant," Adam warns.

"Her chest is swollen," Zane notes.

"How do you know that?" Adam asks, as his hand slides up to cup a knocker. I Fraggle my face at the invasion.

"I spent an entire movie shoot with my hands there because of union rules. We had to cover her chest in the naughty movie," Zane explains.

"He's right," Adam confirms.

Zane grimaces Rocco's way. In turn, Rocco gives Adam a questionable look.

"Okayyyyy," I warble. "Demitri, why don't you subtly check to see if I'm spawning a herd of hellions. Adam, thanks for the grope, but I don't think your pregnant wife would like that."

Adam's hand slides to my hip that he grips. It's possessive, but Adam seems to have taken to my reminder of what we were. I let it ride, because focusing on Demitri gripping my squashy gut has me more uncomfortable than Adam's attentiveness.

Demitri closes his eyes, and I feel his energetic search. His forehead beads sweat.

"You need to tell me what you're doing, please," I warily request.

"There's not another baby, Melanie," Demitri murmurs through extreme concentration. "I'm getting some of the swelling to go down. You're still infected. It's going to take time. You have two more weeks of antibiotics left. I need Dr. Fontaine to do another IV drip. I'll call him. The chest swelling is just residual pregnancy hormones. They take time to go away." Demitri opens his eyes but leaves his hand where it is. "Is that why you don't want me to stay with you tonight?"

"It's one of the reasons," I say, closing one eye in a comic wince. "I'm not real interested in curling up with you when I look six months pregnant. I also had plans already."

"You're okay curling up with Zane, though?" Demitri asks.

"I am."

"Why?" Demitri demands, but it's not harsh.

"Because Zane has supported me through a lot worse than a little squish."

Demitri gives me a challenging look. "So have I."

I roll my eyes, and he sighs.

"I need you to get past your belief that I require you to be perfect. I've told you that I've changed, but you continue to put that on me," he insists.

"I get that you've changed, D," I groan, not wanting to publicly discuss this. "There's still the reality that you're *you*, and I'm a big messy me."

Demitri drops his hand from my stomach. My empathy feels his panicked commitment to me rage through him.

"Zane, I'm sorry that your sleepover was invaded," Adam says, taking over this slog through awkward town.

"Me too." Zane glares at Demitri.

"How about I go back to the prison," I snark, "and Zane locks up behind closed doors with me?"

"Yup," Zane says. "That'll work."

"It won't," Demitri informs us, albeit apologetically. "Part of why I'm the chosen warden on duty is that I can do another healing round on you and then you can boost me while we sleep. If it helps, I don't want to be an unwelcome employee that invades your life. I plan to talk to Trey, but it needs to wait until tomorrow. He's busy being a teenage son of angry parents tonight. They don't know what happened, and he doesn't plan to tell them. They already don't like you, and word that you miscarried their grandchild is going to irrationally piss them off."

"Yes, of course," I snap back. "I intended to get the shit beat out of me by a biker gang." I narrow my eyes at Demitri.

"I didn't want to be the one to tell you that," Demitri says, "but I'm the one that knows."

"I preferred when you were my confident, instead of Trey's."

"So did I," he replies. "Trey's put me in a hell of a position I didn't expect. I should have, though. You much prefer to have a guy in your life that you choose, instead of one you are obligated to. That's always been my in with you." He slides a challenging side-eye Zane's way.

"All right, all right," Cindy interjects. "Melanie must head home tonight because her guardian requested it. We'll respect Mabel's wishes." She looks to Zane. "Apparently, Luke showed up after all."

Zane groans while I laugh with little humor. The guys that weren't there for our dumb recital showcase appear confused, but the comment wasn't for them.

"She's not leaving because she wants to, and therein lies the difference." Cindy slides her sad eyes my way. "I'm sorry you're controlled, but the day will come that you won't be. Hang on to that hope."

I attempt to smile.

"Hey, now, it's going to be okay," Cindy encourages me. "There are worse things than being locked up tight because you're safer that way."

"I'm not safer that way," I say, barely getting the words out around the lump in my throat. "I've been attacked while locked behind those very gates. I'm just easier to trap that way."

Zane rubs his face hard, while Demitri winces.

"Do you swear to me that you won't judge her tonight?" Zane asks Demitri.

"I never would, Zane," Demitri replies, appearing ashamed.

"I promise that the next night that I have free will be yours," I assure Zane. "We have a lot to discuss."

Adam and Demitri exchange a look that I don't understand, but whatever.

"Leave Trey," Zane requests with a ferocity that takes me off guard.

"I can't," I softly reply. "I have a baby to avenge."

"I'll hire out the hit," Zane replies.

Cindy's eyes widen. Clearly, she hadn't expected that.

"That kill is mine," I reply, deadly serious.

"Stop right there," Cindy insists. "I've seen what you can do, Melanie. I respect it, but we aren't doing any of that. We're focusing on big, exciting careers. Only positive."

The look I hit her with furrows her brow.

"While I appreciate the intent behind the sentiment, my life doesn't work that way," I pointedly inform. "The Reapers attacked me. I'm not just any run-of-the-mill energy worker, and they *will* bow down."

Cindy stares at me like she doesn't recognize me.

I nod, slow and deliberate. "That expression is correct. When I'm Melanie, I can consider and make right decisions. The Reapers didn't attack Melanie," I tell her. "They attacked La Diabla, and that's deadly in my world."

"You can't run about town killing people, Melanie," Cindy warns.

"I was in my own parking lot, minding my own business, and those assholes came for me in retaliation for THEM trying to pilfer my home during the earthquake aftermath," I assert. "They didn't get to rampage my home, because I stopped them, and they chose unwarranted revenge. That's on them. They murdered La Diabla's baby. That shit comes with a cost. They'll pay."

"What if it gets you killed?" Cindy rationalizes.

"Then Trey will kill them," I retort. "If they kill him, Demitri will step up, followed by Adam, followed by all the Hellhounds."

"How does a bloodbath help?" Cindy asks.

"This isn't about helping," I inform her. "There's no fixing losing the baby. This is about power, and hierarchy. I'm at the top of the metaphysical food chain. Bottom-feeders don't get to attack me. They WILL die. They must because if I let that go, I'm seen as weak."

Cindy's eyes close. "I know you love her, Zane, but you can't get so wrapped up that you start thinking like a mercenary."

"We need to talk to Trey," Adam mutters to Demitri.

"I'm staying the hell out of that," Demitri mutters back. At my quizzical look, Demitri just shakes his head.

"Melanie, you need to be careful," Cindy fearfully says.

"I'm sorry that I put you in this position with my suicide," Zane says, grief-filled. "I need to help you because it's my fault you lost the baby, were attacked, and these people are going to die."

"No, it's not," I softly reply. "If it's not this, it would be something else. It's always something, though. If I don't survive my retribution, it is NOT on you. I'm just glad you're alive."

"I can't keep watching her leave," Zane says desperately to his mom. "Especially not like this."

"I know you can't," Cindy replies. She grabs my arms. "If you need *anything*, you come to Zane. Do you understand?" I nod and she squeezes my arms.

"Thank you." I smile at Cindy. "I needed tonight so much. I'm sorry it was cut short, but reality always pulls me back when I'm happy. It's a sacrifice the universe seems to expect of me. I know better than to be truly happy." I gesture to Demitri. "Reality immediately chastised me."

"That is NOT what I want to be," Demitri insists, mortified.

"You chose to be this. Let's head out. We've ruined enough of this party," I tell him. I smile at Cindy. "Thank you for inviting me. I rarely get invitations. This meant a great deal to me."

"You can't leave just yet," she says. "We have cake and a gift for you."

"I really do need to get home," Adam apologetically says. "I can't leave Valerie for this long when we're so close to her due date."

"You can go, Adam," Demitri assures him. "I'll make sure Melanie gets home. I don't want her to miss cake and a present." He radiates guilt, realizing how innocent this evening is and how unhappy he's made me.

"We're being paid to show up here in force and leave as a unit," Adam reminds him, sounding uncomfortable.

Zane rolls his eyes, snagging his wallet from his back pocket. He yanks out a stack of cash and waggles it around. "Loyalty check," foghorns from Zane. "How many misguided Misfits think Trey overstepped by ordering you all to come here to kidnap Melanie from her fun and drag her back to her dungeon?"

Marcus, Adam, Demitri, Arch, and Tanner bashfully raise their hands.

"Very good," Zane chastises them. "Your suckage is huge!" He peels off a collection of bills and slams the money into Adam's hand. "You have a new boss. Congratulations, you're hired. I'm paying you to go away."

"Team Melanie," Adam caws before bowing in deference Zane's way. "It's an honor working for you, sir."

Zane chuckles as Adam happily walks away with a pocket full of cash.

"One down, four more to go," Zanes says. He peels off another round of bills. "Here you are, Tanner. You're hired to go away. Five hundred should cover a lot of lip gloss and sparkles."

"Ooo*ooo*hhh, hundooos," Tanner purrs, batting his eyelashes at Zane. "It's an honor to join Team Melanie as I accept my first assignment for Drell Inc. Thank you." Tanner sashays off.

Zane repeats this with Marcus and Arch, who leave together after proclaiming their allegiance to Team Melanie.

"Then there was one," Zane says to Demitri. He holds out a stack of cash. "I'm paying YOU a thousand to go away, and NEVER interfere in my time with Melanie again."

"I'm not getting paid after making her unhappy," Demitri says and looks at me. "I'm still on Team Melanie, though. I'd like to have cake and watch you get a present."

"Your attention, please," Cindy chimes in from across the party. "My family would like to thank you for being here on this special night. In honor of my kids, Zane, Rachelle, and Melanie, we appreciate you."

"I wonder what songs she picked this time," Rachelle whispers as we cross to join her.

Zane chuckles. I lean my back against his chest. He drapes his arm over my shoulder and puts his hand over my stomach again. His vibe is unexpected. There's a primal hum to him about my pregnant appearance.

"Melanie, we have a tradition, and this will be your first of these, but not your last," Cindy announces with a vibrant smile. "So, to explain for those that don't know, my husband and I choose a song that we gift our kids with at each new movie role celebration. Sometimes the choice is based on where they're at in life. Other times it's based on the theme of the movie." She holds up three items that look like key chains hanging from her finger. "This batch includes Beatles songs. Rachelle, Zane, and Melanie, congratulations on an amazing new artistic accomplishment. And, Melanie, congratulations on your first movie." Applause punctuates as Cindy crosses the party to join us. "Enjoy cake," she bellows to the crowd. She gets to us and hands Zane his present first.

"*A Hard Day's Night*, huh?" Zane asks as he reads the key chain.

"Your stepdad picked that one after you told the tale of your scenes with Melanie," Cindy shares. Zane and I laugh as she adds, "It's purely about title this time. That dirty old man thought it was funny." She turns to Rachelle. "Here's yours."

"*We Can Work It Out*," Rachelle reads when she takes the key chain. "Thank you." She hugs Cindy.

"You're welcome. And here's Melanie's." Cindy hands me a key chain.

"*Here Comes the Sun*." I smile softly while I stare at the gift.

"Push the button," Zane instructs me.

I do, and a snippet of the song softly hums from a little speaker embedded in the key chain.

"This is amazing! Thank you so much." I hug Cindy before turning to Zane. "I fear you wasted a bunch of money getting the others to go away, because I really should leave." My head drops. "I don't want to, but it would be rude to anger Mabel after everything she's done to help me." I offer Zane a sad smile, fearing it's edged with desperation. "We're going to head out."

"You aren't missing cake, Melanie," Zane insists.

"I am. My godmother requested me home, and I should go," I say as I hug Zane. "Thank you for reconnecting with me. I'm sorry it was cut short, but it started off exactly right. I got to breathe."

"Your palms are slick," Zane says fearfully.

"I'm not happy. I want to stay," I reply. "Unfortunately, I don't get that luxury. Though I'll take tacos, doing recital dance pieces with you, and getting to be carefree even for a few minutes." I squeeze his arms. "I love you."

"I love you too," Zane chokes out. Goodbyes are brutal for him.

I let him go and start walking.

Demitri jogs to catch up as I set a quick clip. "I'm sorry I sounded the alarm, Melanie," he says, yet again.

I don't respond, instead digging my keys out of my bag and winding the new key ring onto them.

As we get to the parking lot, Tanner is lounging against my car. He smiles sadly my way. "I told Marcus to head out," he explains. "He drove me. I'll drive your car back to Mabel's so you and Demitri can talk."

I hesitantly hand over my keys. I wanted to look at the new key ring closer when I got in my car. I really need the drive alone to think.

Demitri leads me to his Jeep. We get in, and he pulls out of the parking lot, following Tanner.

"The song choice was really sweet," Demitri softly says.

"There's no sun for me," I reply. "It was sweet, though."

CHAPTER 34

"Seriously?" I say when I walk into the room. Apparently the five minutes I spent rinsing off and brushing my teeth was too long. Demitri is comatose on the bed. I shake him a little. "D?"

A hand on his chest reveals energy depletion. That must be why he reacted like an irrational nut when he couldn't find me. Demitri's known for his metaphysical calm, but when his energy bottoms out, he gets wonky.

The drive home was a degraded mess, but I planned to talk to Demitri about it after we settled in. I'm feeling worse and worse. He intended to do another healing round on me, but it seems me refilling his energy tanks while we slept was his real reason for wanting to stay here with me.

A glance at the nightstand clock reveals that it's midnight. Mabel is known for being a night owl. I try the intercom to her office, but there's no answer.

You can take care of yourself, Melanie.

I find a thermometer in the medical kit Mabel keeps in the bathroom cabinet. I stick it under my tongue and watch, cross-eyed, as the red line rises rapidly. When it stops, I pull it, and my eyes widen. A hundred and three degrees is a spanking accomplishment.

I snag my phone and dial Zane. He answers.

"Any chance that you know what to do about a hundred-and-three-degree whopper?" I ask.

"Where's Demitri?" he barks.

"Passed out with depleted energy tanks. He won't wake up."

"Excuse the fuck out of him?" Zane bellows. "What happened to a healing round?"

"He didn't get around to that. I can't fill his tanks. I'm in bad shape, and this stomach of mine is now bigger." I slump into a chair at my little two-seater table. "I think I need to go to the hospital."

"MOMMMMMM," Zane cries.

I hear muffled conversation before Cindy's voice comes over the line. "Sweetheart, I want you to call an ambulance. We're getting in the car, and we'll head that way."

"Let's roll," Rocco belts in the background.

"Call and let us know which hospital they're delivering you to," Cindy orders. "We're going to head in your general direction."

"Okay, I'll let you know."

I hang up, and my head drops. There's no way I'm dramatically calling an ambulance. I grab my keys and put on sweatpants and my tennis shoes. A quick push of a few buttons, and the panic room lock disengages.

I pull into a parking spot at the hospital closest to Mabel's. I slump, profusely sweating. My vision is blurry, and my mouth is dry. Zane wrenches open my door and scoops me up.

"Run," Cindy orders when she sees my condition.

Zane takes off at a jog, barreling his way into the emergency room. Rocco and Cindy are close behind.

One look at me, and the check-in lady grabs the phone receiver. "Code seven," she relays through the phone.

Doors click and swing open. Two medical professionals push a gurney through the doorway. Zane lays me down, and one of the doctors asks, "Zane Drell?"

"Nice to meet you," Zane says, like he always does when he's recognized.

"Talk to us while we run," the doctor orders, snapping from starstruck awe to medical prowess.

I look up at Zane, unsure what to say. Through my hand he's holding, I send him a memory. *'I can't tell them I was healed by Demitri.'*

"She hasn't been feeling well," Zane explains. "Her stomach is swelling, and I think she has an infection. High fever, sweating, dizzy."

"What's your relationship to the patient?" the doctor asks.

"Partner at the Alice Agency," Zane explains efficiently. "Melanie's parents are out of town. She considers us family."

"You are?" the doctor asks with a glance Roc's way.

"Rocco Rutelle. I'm Melanie's brother."

"And I'm Cindy. Zane's mom."

"Patient's name?" the doctor asks after we've established our ever-morphing roles in this crazy game we play.

"Melanie Slate," I croak.

"Now I recognize you from an interview on the *Tradewinds* show," the doctor says as they wheel me into an exam room. He surveys my stomach and puts a hand to my fevered head. "Are you pregnant?"

"No, but I was," I admit bashfully.

"When was the baby born?"

I shake my head.

"Miscarriage," Zane answers.

"All right, I need everyone but Baby Dad and Melanie to step out."

"The baby wasn't mine," Zane corrects him. "I'm her closest friend."

"Oh, all right." The doctor gives a quizzical look. "Who would you like here, Melanie?"

"They're all fine," I reply.

Jelly stuff is slimed onto a wand, and Zane sits in the chair that's offered while he holds my hand. The doctor exposes my stomach. The wand is cold and greasy when it touches my midsection. I turn my head from the monitor and watch Zane while he watches the monitor image. His brow furrows. The moment is awkward. This is a very adult thing to go through, but Zane is here for it. I shift my gaze to Cindy, who has her hands on Zane's shoulders while she watches the monitor with him.

"It's going to be okay," she encourages with a soft smile.

"Was the miscarriage violent?" the doctor asks as he leans closer to the monitor.

"Yes," I whisper.

He hands the wand to the nurse and strips his gloves off before pushing an intercom button. "Prep OR three," he instructs. "Code one."

"What does that mean?" Zane asks.

"Emergency surgery," the doctor informs us. He places a hand on my leg. "You're going to be just fine."

"What's wrong with her?" Zane demands as he stands rapidly.

"She has an infected placenta that's still attached." The doctor holds up a hand to calm Zane. "It's rare, but fixable." He rushes out with the nurse.

A new medical person rushes in. "My name is Nurse Montreal. I'm taking Melanie to prep her for surgery. You're all welcome to wait in the waiting room. We'll have word to you within a couple of hours. In the meantime, we need paperwork and insurance information. The check-in desk will give you all the forms."

"Do you know your insurance information?" Cindy asks.

I shake my head.

Zane places a call. "No answer from Mabel," he snarls. He tries two more numbers, but there's no answer from Trey or Demitri either. Zane makes one more call. "Ms. Alice, do you have Melanie's insurance information on file?" he asks. He must get an affirmative, because he says, "I need you to fax it to County General as soon as possible." He hangs up and cups my cheeks. "I'm handling everything. Where are your parents?"

I fill him in about Uncle Vincent.

"They can't help from Montana, and it'll do zero good for us to worry them at two in the morning," Zane says. "Do you trust us to handle this?"

"Can Zane come with me?" I ask the nurse.

"I'm sorry, sweetheart," the nurse says as she shakes her head. "I'll stay with you and hold your hand while we put you under."

Zane leans down and kisses my forehead.

"I'll be in the waiting room. I'll see you the moment you wake up," he promises.

I swallow hard and nod. I'm terrified, feeling sixteen suddenly. I keep it in check, though. Zane feels like he's rattling, and I need to stay calm for him.

"Here we go," the nurse says with false cheer as she starts wheeling me out.

Cindy squeezes my arm as I pass.

Just as we exit the room into the hall, I hear Zane. "Moooommm," he whimpers desperately. He doesn't sound like a millionaire, A-list actor. He sounds like a scared kid.

"She's going to be okay," Cindy says. Her voice fades.

CHAPTER 35

"**U**ghhh."

The sound of a groan is annoying. I try to put an arm over my head to block it out so I can sleep again. Pain blazes. My eyes snap wide but can't stay open long. I see a fluttering image of a white tile ceiling. I groan again, realizing the sound is coming from me. *I know that ceiling.*

I feel hands on me.

"Shhh, baby you're okay," Zane consoles me. Hearing his voice in a hospital room is familiar enough that I'm able to relax.

"When is physical therapy?" I whisper.

"Wrong hospital visit, Mighty Mouse," Zane chuckles.

I grapple to open my eyes. He takes my hand.

"Sleepy," I whisper, while I tug a little at Zane. "Lie down."

"I can't this time," he says. My eyes flutter open, and Zane smiles softly above me.

"Explain?" comes a female voice. I turn my head to see Cindy.

"After she woke up from the car accident that killed Jet, she took to sleeping draped over my chest. It's the only way to get massive me in a hospital bed with her. Hospitals mean sleepy tights on my chest."

"Why am I here?" I ask. I'm so confused.

"Surgery," Zane softly replies. "You're on a constant antibiotic IV drip. Don't move your right hand."

"Ugh," I croak. "Hates it."

"I know," Zane commiserates.

"Gummy bears?" I open and close my left hand.

Soft chuckles meet my request.

"Not yet," Zane says. "We have to wait a little while before you can eat."

Something soft lands by my cheek, and I know it's one of the blankets Zane always had in the hospital for me after the car accident because of the Downy softener smell. I snuggle into it and open and close my hand again.

He squeezes it. "No gummy bears, Mighty Mouse. I have them waiting."

"Archie?" I hopefully lilt.

Zane laughs. "All right, but I can't put your hospital bed up for you to look at the pictures this time. You have to lie flat."

"Hate," I sneer up at him.

"I know," Zane says, like he's placating a child. He sits, and Cindy and Rocco pull up chairs. Zane puts his feet up on the bed and slouches like he's done a thousand times.

Before he can start reading, I crane my neck. I see that the floor is worn in the center. "Our room?"

"Yup. Same room," he says.

I sigh. "Hates it," I grumble like a toddler.

"I know," he says patiently before he starts reading the comic book. He must have had time to get stuff from his house while I was in surgery.

I wake with my face nuzzled in the Downy blanket and pressure on my cheek. It takes a moment to realize that the pressure is from my hand pressing Zane's hand into the side of my face. I gasp as pain boils in. It feels stronger the more awake I become.

"They're almost here," a soothing female voice says.

I let go of Zane and open my eyes with a moan. Zane shakes out his hand.

"I'm sorry," I whimper.

"This isn't new," Zane replies, unbothered. He scoots back his chair that's practically under my hospital bed and stands. He rounds to the other side of me and shifts my rolling bed so he can get to me. He takes my hand with the one that I didn't nearly break.

"The nurse is bringing in painkillers," he informs me. "Give it a few minutes."

"My stomach is on fire."

Zane kneels to be eye to eye with me. "Squeeze," he orders.

I do and clench my eyes.

"Deep breath in," he guides. "We're resetting."

I exhale, forcing my muscles to unclench. It leaves me frantically panting.

"Again," Zane instructs.

I do it again, and my breathing calms.

"Good. Keep your eyes closed." I feel Zane's thumb on my forehead. "Focus."

When I get to the state he's waiting for he makes a "foooo" sound and brushes his thumb up and away.

My body sags, and my head lolls. "I can't believe we're back to doing this," I whisper.

"Walk in the park," Zane calmly replies. "You and me.

We'll get a new routine down. This time will be a little different. We've got this."

"Goody," I whisper. "New hell."

"Just more self-control and patterns."

"Does stomach surgery mean bed crapping?" I ask.

"No clue, but we'll face everything we need too," Zane says with a laugh.

"Ugh," I groan. Chaotic energy rolls in my direction. "Nope, nope, nope," I fitfully whimper. "Stop that."

"Incoming," Rocco enlightens, because he's an energy worker who can also feel what I'm feeling.

"Take her hand," Zane says.

A female hand replaces his, but I don't open my eyes.

"Stop," Zane authoritatively says after I hear a door open. "Back up. We're establishing ground rules." He's met with a sputtering argument that he shuts down with a no-nonsense, "The hospital is my domain. You play by my rules, or you don't visit."

I hear the door shut and look up at Cindy with groggy eyes.

"Zane's got this," Cindy assures me. She smiles. "You two really do seem to have a routine down."

"A very clear one that I both love and hate," I tell her.

The door opens, and Zane leads Demitri, Mabel, and Trey in. They stare down at me with huge eyes.

"So sick of hospitals," Trey breathes, haunted by our hospital time a year and a half ago when I dropped from a mental breakdown.

I just roll my eyes.

"I'm so sorry I fell asleep," Demitri says.

"I don't think you could have fixed this one," I commiserate with him.

Apparently, someone notified someone, and all the someone's are now here.

I reach a hand D's way. "I'll boost you." Even from across the room, I can feel that he's still bottomed out.

"I've got it," Rocco offers and puts his hand on Demitri's back to refill his tanks.

"Valerie's in labor," Mabel says. "She's on the second floor. I'm going to check in with her, and then I'll be back." She looks to Trey. "Adam asked if you'd come with me and pain share with him until an epidural could be administered."

"Sure," Trey groans.

Zane's eyebrows fly into his hairline, but Mabel and Trey leave before he can say anything. He looks at Demitri. "Melanie's in a great deal of pain, and we've been waiting for pain meds for a while," Zane tells him.

"I'll be back," Demitri says.

He leaves, and Zane takes a deep grounding breath. "They didn't even ask how you are," he says. He digs a little deeper emotionally and settles at a new determined level.

"I don't want you to go through this again," I whimper.

"Over and over. Every time. Without fail," Zane insists stoically. "You know the drill. Get your head in the game, Melanie. Deep breath in from your chest, not your diaphragm."

I take the requested breath.

"Exhale," he coaches.

I do and reach a calmer state where I can climb above the throbbing gut pain.

The door opens, and a grinning lady pushes in a cart overflowing with flowers.

"Delivery," she says, chipper. She starts depositing vase after vase on the counter and table.

My brow furrows curiously.

The lady giggles as she studies her clipboard. "Pink bouquet,

Chelsea Alice. Purple bouquet, Piper from a place called the Beach Bar. Red bouquet, Pepe and Luis. Sunflowers, from Pepe on behalf of Pierre. Spring mix, from Jack Griffin." She smiles at me. "Now that I realize who you are," she says as her gaze snaps to Zane, "and who you are, apparently that bouquet *is* from the famous director."

"Nice to meet you," Zane says like he always does.

She flutters a bit. "All a twitter," she candidly says.

"Normal guy," Zane charms back.

"Not even remotely," she says with an amused look. "But sure, we'll go with that." She studies her clipboard again. "White carnations, Jayla Bethel. Tulips, Adam Stone. Big-ass fancy bouquet—that's what we're supposed to call it. We didn't choose that. That one's from Tanner and Finley. White-and-pink bouquet is from your NEW stepdad." She gives me an adorably confused look. "I was instructed to emphasize the word *new*."

"Did my mother get divorced and remarried in Montana?" I ponder.

Cindy laughs. "I guarantee that one's my husband." She crosses to the bouquet and pulls out the card. "'*Like a Surgeon*,'" she reads. "*Weird Al. Dedicated to my girl. Hang in there. Love you, kiddo.*"

I laugh a little because it hurts to laugh a lot. "You guys really are amazing," I say to Cindy.

"Last, but not least, the orange bouquet is from Dr. Fontaine," the flower lady says with a sigh. "You've kept us very busy, Ms. Melanie. Every call we got competitively demanded theirs be the biggest. I finally just resorted to telling everyone theirs was the biggest and made bouquets. To clarify, Jayla wanted hers filled with the most love. It was the others that were 'bigger is better.'"

"Typical," I giggle. "They're all crazy."

Trey rushes in, with Demitri quick on his heels. Demitri holds the door for the flower lady to wheel out her empty cart, after we thank her.

"I didn't realize you were hurting," Trey blathers. "I'm sorry I left to help Valerie." He grabs my hand and winces. "Damn, that's bad." He starts pulling pain, and I exhale, sagging. "I'm so sorry, Melanie. I should have put you first."

"Whatever, Trey."

"Don't brush me off," Trey manages through gritted teeth as he feels my pain in his body. "I should have asked before I left."

"You shouldn't have helped Valerie at all," I scold. "Adam left when I needed him to pull pain for me. Valerie will never get our help, in my opinion."

"Done," Trey says. He looks to Demitri. "Are you willing to go up there, and quietly let Adam know that I won't be back to help Valerie after Melanie gets her pain meds?"

Demitri purses his lips, nodding with an evil expression. "Considering how she's screaming, the timing is hilarious." Demitri offers a snotty look in my direction. "Adam tried, but he can only pull pain for you because of your soulmate connection." He grins sadistically. "That caused quite the fight when he had to admit it to Valerie. Anyhow, the anesthesiologist is backed up at least an hour. Valerie isn't handling labor gracefully." He swings his elation back to Trey. "I'd delight in this informative task, but I ain't quietly telling him. I want to see her panic." He saunters out egotistically, and I laugh.

The doctor comes in wheeling a little metal tray thing. He hangs a new IV bag, switches it out in my hand, and puts a syringe in the port. A quick plunger push, and my head lolls a moment later. Trey loosens his grip now that I'm not hurting.

"Melanie, I'm going to need to examine you," the doctor says.

He surveys the visitors. "I need everyone but Zane to leave. We'll let you know when you can return."

Trey starts to protest, but Cindy tactfully encourages him out the door as she herds them. The room clears out, to my relief. I don't want Trey involved in this round of medical intervention. I've settled into a hospital routine with Zane, and I'm not in a good place to tactfully consider Trey's position with me. I've earned the right to do this however I want.

The doctor pulls a blue covering from the rolling tray. One glance at what he's uncovered, and I grimace, changing my mind.

I look up at Zane. "I don't know if we're ready for this. We've handled a lot, but this one is a step beyond."

Zane surveys the tray and gives me an open look.

"I'll do this with you if needed," he says. "Let's try another route first."

"Not Trey," I whimper.

Zane gives me a baffled look. "Duh." He heads to the door and cracks it open. "Mom?"

Cindy slides in.

"This might be more your territory than mine," he tells his mom.

"I'm sorry," I whimper, humiliated. I really don't know Cindy. "This is asking a lot of someone who offered to be a mom for a night at a party."

Cindy surveys the tools on the tray and makes a face. "Mom duty, for sure. Zane, I've got it." She smiles at me. "All right, kiddo," she says as she takes a seat and grabs my hand. "Is this one new to you?"

I nod with big eyes.

"Here's the deal," Cindy says. "All women hate it. It never gets less awkward. Just stare at the ceiling and pretend it's not happening."

"What am I in for?"

Cindy shrugs. "No clue. Most women don't know what's actually happening, and never ask. We just suffer in silence and live in ignorance. It doesn't hurt, but it's invasive."

As Zane slips out, I exhale hard and look at the ceiling.

"What's happening?" I hear Trey ask from the hallway.

"Girl exam," Zane responds. "We're out here. Mom's got it."

The door clicks shut on Trey's arguing, and awkward misery commences.

CHAPTER 36

"I've got this, I promise," Zane assures Mabel. "Mabel, you're free to enjoy baby time in Valerie's room. We're in a waiting game now, and this will be easy."

"Melanie, are you okay with me visiting the babies?" Mabel asks.

"Yes," I reply. "Please snag a bouquet from the counter and take it up to the room."

"I think not," Mabel snorts.

I exhale, relieved, after she leaves. "Thank you," I say.

"You're welcome," Zane replies.

"Rocco and I are going to head home also," Cindy says as she pats my arm. "He needs to open the shop, and I'm going to get things cleaned up before the rest of the family gets home from the competition. I'll bring dinner tonight."

"Will you bring a pack of cards also?" Zane requests. "Melanie likes playing cards. Something new to do now that they've allowed her to sit up."

I pout. The nurse ordered me to sit up early this morning. It wasn't fun. Rocco and Cindy delicately hug me and leave.

Zane perches on the edge of my bed. "We've got the day to ourselves. Two *Gilligan's Island* episodes, *I Dream of Jeanie*, *Brady Bunch*, then lunch?" he suggests. This was our old routine.

"I was hoping everyone would leave so we could hang with the professor and Mary Ann," I reply.

Zane puts his forehead on mine, and we descend into our pattern of being what we are instead of what we're expected to be. I'm suddenly relieved to be back in this hospital room that offers a reality vortex we need, albeit a weird one.

Zane kisses my forehead hard before situating the blanket lower. "Close your eyes."

I do and feel him lift the hospital gown to my ribs while the blanket stays at my hips. Zane situates the gown again and pulls up my blanket.

"What's wrong?" I ask quietly.

"I needed to see what the incision looks like so I can track changes," he replies. "As usual, this place moves slow. I'll monitor for healing and infections."

"Humiliating," I whimper.

"How is a surgery incision humiliating?"

"Icky. There are weird stitches, aren't there?"

"There are stitches. There's nothing weird about it, though. The incision is low enough that it won't show in a bikini. They did a good job."

I slowly and painfully scoot to sit up. To Zane's dismay, I'm insistent that he settle behind me with me sitting between his legs like we used to in this room. I ease back to rest against his chest. He patiently waits while I settle, before putting a hand on my leg and getting comfortable. *Gilligan's Island* comes on, and we exhale together. I suspect I'm not the only one who missed this.

The door opens, but my back is to it. Zane is slow dancing with me to Ani DiFranco's "Hell Yeah." The song has just started. A little more able to move, I take his hand, and he turns me on the uptick. I see Rachelle, Brian, Rocco, and Cindy. We settle into movement that's a little more fast-paced.

"Don't push too hard, baby bear," Zane quietly reminds me.

He pulls me in as the music calms, and we go back to the swaying.

"She's supposed to move around a little," he explains to the others.

The music picks up again, and he spins me out and then back in, controlling my speed more carefully than usual. I lift my arms a little.

"I'm not tossing you around, crazy girl," he laughs.

"You're no fun," I joke back.

"If you pop those stitches, you go back into surgery," he admonishes.

"Fine, fine." I snuggle in, and he sways me gently.

"She's supposed to walk the halls, but the staff remember us and trust me not to let Mel get hurt while we dance instead," he explains to our guests. "I get recognized in the halls, and things get weird. We're stuck in here, just like last time."

"Amen, and yes to that," I happily say before quirking my mouth up at Zane. "Real-people clothes sounded like a great plan, but the waistband of these sweatpants keeps catching on the stitches."

Zane turns me and I face our guests, revealing Cindy holding out a Hot Topic shopping bag. "How about we try this?" she asks.

I pull out a really long T-shirt. I flip it around, and it proves to be a *She-Ra Princess of Power* nightshirt. I slide happy eyes up at Cindy. "Thank you," I chirp. "Hi, guys!"

"Let's get you changed," Zane says.

"I can help you," Rachelle offers.

"I need to check her stitches. I've got it," Zane informs her. "Thank you, though." Zane drapes his arm around my shoulders, guiding me to the bathroom.

Locked in the bathroom, I slowly lift my arms for Zane to help me out of my tank top. I wince.

"Stop there," Zane warns. "Don't stretch too far."

It takes but a moment to get me changed. The new nightshirt proves far more comfortable.

We join everyone in the hospital room, and Zane switches out the CD, while Rachelle says, "Cindy told me that you're in the same room." She ticks her gaze to the floor. "You really did wear the finish off."

Zane laughs. "Yup. I've danced more in this room that any studio I ever took lessons at."

Paul Simon's "I Know What I Know" comes on, and Zane settles on the bed. I ease on with him and get in my spot. He gets a pink squishy blanket to my waist before singing the song. We've always loved it, but it's now comical. We exchange a funny look when the lyrics mention meeting at a cinematographer's party. Our guests laugh as they get comfortable in the chairs.

"Can you eat again?" Cindy asks.

I nod. "I even got to have gummy bears. I'm happy."

Cindy pulls burger sacks from a cooler and gets busy serving all of us with Rachelle's help. I accept mine just as my doctor comes in.

"Anything to worry about?" the doctor asks.

"Nothing yet," Zane replies. "Her stitches look the same."

"I'm pleased with your progress, Melanie," the doctor says as he gently probes at my stomach while he stares at the ceiling.

"Swelling is going down. I think we're on the mend." He clicks his pen and writes something on his clipboard.

"How long will I be here?" I ask.

The doctor considers a moment. "Three more days, I suspect. Then you'll have some healing time at home."

I won't, because Demitri will heal the incision when I get out of here. He can't do it now because my surgeon would view that as very strange.

"Three days, huh?" Zane groans.

"We don't count," I remind him.

"I know," he dejectedly replies.

We thank the doctor, and he leaves.

"Eat, Zaney," I encourage him.

"Would you like to come back to my house when you're released?" Cindy asks. "You and Zane can stay in his old room while you heal."

"That's so sweet. I wish," I say. "The moment I'm out of here, Demitri will heal the incision, and I'll be back on my feet."

"You know, it wouldn't kill you to let your body heal on its own," Cindy says. "The rapid healing is a neat trick, but there's a reason we take time." She gives me a pointed look. "If it weren't for that rapid healing, the placenta issue likely wouldn't have happened. Demitri healed around it instead of letting it detach. The doctor pulled me aside about that when he finished your surgery. He thought it was odd, but I didn't fill him in."

"What?" I ask, baffled.

"Yup. The doctor found that placenta surrounded by healed tissue. It was infected and starting to rot," Cindy says.

"Why didn't the doctor tell me that?" I ask incredulously.

Cindy winces. "Because you're sixteen. I talked to Ms. Alice before she faxed your insurance paperwork to the hospital.

She added my name to the proxy guardian form that your mom filled out when you signed with the agency. I know it's unethical, but we were in a spot here because the hospital needed clearance. With your parents out of town, I was the obvious choice as your proxy guardian when all the surgery needs became an issue. Otherwise, the hospital was going to kick us out."

"That was a good solution," I assure.

I close my eyes and covertly pull Cindy's memory, watching the exchange Cindy privately had in the hall with the doctor. The news is a lot worse than what she just let on about. I huff when it ends and shift slowly. I'm emotionally dead, but I feel panic bubbling under the surface.

Zane knows what I want and loosens his arm, waiting until I adjust. He puts his arm around me again once I'm curled up with my cheek against his chest. He pulls the blanket up to my chin and holds me. "I'm going to talk to Demitri," he quietly says. "I'll give him a little time to get it together first. I get that he's good at what he does, but he made a serious mistake."

"He's usually flawless," I quietly reply, while internally grappling with the news Cindy is hiding. "He didn't mean to. Let's give him a pass," I add while my heart hurts.

"I can't," Zane says. "It almost killed you. If you had gone to sleep, you wouldn't have woken up."

"Thank you for meeting me here," I say softly. My eyes start drooping, and Zane instructs Cindy on the bed remote. We ease down as she lowers the bed.

"Curl up, baby bear," Zane quietly says, not wanting to disturb my sleepy state.

I shift carefully to lie chest to chest with him, and I exhale hard. My eyes slip closed, content. I hear Cindy and Zane talking as I fall asleep.

"Zane, I get your hesitation, but this is ridiculous. You need to just accept this. I'll help you talk to her parents."

"I can't," Zane replies. "It'll harm her career and mine."

Sleep takes me.

CHAPTER 37

I wake to conversation. Zane grabs the remote attached to the bed, and we ascend to sit now that my nap is over. He helps me shift so my back is against his chest. Situated, I smile as Rocco and Brian banter about some nonsense.

"You okay?" Cindy asks.

I nod and scoot slowly to the edge of the bed. Zane starts to get up with me, but I wave him off and head to the restroom. I manage to handle things myself.

When I emerge, Adam is slipping through the door.

"Hey, how are the babies?" I ask with a bright smile.

Adam turns with two newborns in his arms. I gasp.

"You okay if I brought them for you to see?" he asks.

"Of course! Let me sit down." I slowly make my way back to the bed. Zane gets up and helps me prop up against the pillows. Settled, I squeeze my eyes closed. I hurt. I sharply inhale, and when I open my eyes, Adam's staring at me like his world is ending.

"I'm okay," I assure him. I hold my arms out, and he hands me one of the little girls.

"This is Amy."

She fusses a bit, chewing at her hand. I gesture to his bag. Without a word, he plops it down on the end of my bed and takes out a bottle that he shakes. He hands it to me, and I plunk it in Amy's mouth.

"No more fuss," I coo at her before joining the conversation. Amy polishes off the bottle in record time, and my eyebrows rise. I wrestle it from her iron-suction with a laugh that hurts my stitches. "Dang girl, slow down." I get her to my shoulder and give her a well-placed little thump. She burps, and I give Adam a look. "This one eats like you."

The other baby sets to fussing.

"Girlfriend, give me a second," I joke her way. "Shake out the next bottle, and I'll trade you babies. Amy's sucked this one dry," I tell Adam. I hand the empty bottle to Zane while I hold her Adam's way.

"The next one is Anna," he informs while he takes Amy with one arm, and hands me Anna with the other.

Cindy gives me the next bottle, and I laugh with Rocco about him wrestling down a whole pack of shoplifters at the surf store. I go through the burping process, Anna proves to be a slower eater, but eventually polishes it off.

"Take over the second burping duty," I request, and Adam takes Anna while I cap the second empty bottle and toss it in the diaper bag. Amy is happily asleep in Cindy's arms. Rachelle takes Anna, who's far more interested in pulling her hair and gazing at Rachelle than sleeping.

"They're beautiful, and nothing alike," I compliment.

Adam plunks down and rubs his face hard. "They were born fourteen hours ago," he says, exhausted.

My brow furrows. "Talk to me, Adam. What's wrong?"

"I can't do this without you!" Adam passionately expresses, while drilling holes into me with his pointed gaze.

I rapidly blink baffled eyes. "You need to elaborate."

Adam looks like he's in shock. "I've never had babies with anyone but you."

I ponder a moment. "I don't remember past lives as clearly as you seem to."

"I don't remember all of them, but everything I remember, kids were with you," he says and shakes his head slowly. "Valerie's terrible at this, Melanie. Have you held a newborn this lifetime?"

"No," I reply. "I just know what to do. We've made an army's worth of kids over two hundred and three lifetimes. Feeding a baby isn't hard. I don't think I've ever used a bottle, to be honest, but it's not rocket science."

"She refuses to even try to breastfeed," Adam reveals in front of this room full of people he doesn't know all that well.

Things must be bad. "Don't get spun out about that," I encourage him. "I never used bottles, but they didn't exist for most of our lifetimes."

Anna sets to squalling, and I hold my arms Rachelle's way without even thinking about it. She hands over Anna, who I lay propped on my bent legs.

I rub her swollen stomach lightly and pump her legs a few times. "This one's going to have gas bubble issues, Adam," I warn. "You need to start triple burping her."

"Why aren't you burping her then?" Rocco asks.

"Newborns are dinky. The air is in her intestines now. It needs to go the other way," I inform him. I keep rubbing and pumping her tiny legs. "No being a lady right now. You need to let it go, girly."

She finally does, with gusto.

I take her little hand and fist-bump her. "There, that's better." I gather Anna up and put her on my chest. I rock her right and left while Adam watches me.

"Valerie has held the girls twice. One of those times was when she first birthed them, and they were put on her chest." Adam raises his eyebrows at me. "She asked for them to be removed and argued with the staff when they didn't want to."

"Maybe she just needs a minute," I say. Anna falls asleep, and I slow my rocking until I stop and lean back against my pillows with the baby on my chest.

"She doesn't want them," Adam says.

"Well, she has them," I retort. "She'll do this."

"They're incredibly fussy, and they irritate each other." It's the closest to a whimper I've ever heard from Adam.

"Clearly," I reply as I rub the silent baby's back.

"This is the first time those two have quit screaming," Adam remarks.

"Babies pick up on vibes," I remind him. "If Valerie's irritated, they're irritated. She needs to chill. She also needs to try to feed them without those bottles. That sleepy-time pheromone isn't in formula."

"She hasn't even bottle-fed them." Adam rubs his face.

"I know you're tired and scared," I softly say. "You need to teach her. Not everyone pushes out a baby and knows what to do with it. These two aren't any harder than other babies if you pay attention to the cues." I point to Amy. "That one eats fast, likely screams hard, and sleeps just as thoroughly. She's going to be the kid who knows what she wants and demands it." I gesture to Anna who's asleep on me. "This one is going to be indecisive, and get flustered when she's not understood, even though she doesn't even know what she wants."

"You're remarkable," Cindy breathes, while she stares at me in wonder.

I laugh a little, so I don't disturb Anna. "I'm good with kids," I say. "Ironically, I'm not generally a fan of most kids, but I've been a good mom when I have them. Adam's girls aren't some big mystery."

"Monumental mistake having kids without you," Adam claims. His face lands in his hands.

"Wrong," I reply compassionately. "There's a reason for this. You need to commit to your family, teach Valerie, and make this work."

The look Adam gives me is gut-wrenching, but now is the worst possible time for this. I tap on our blocked soulmate connection. He drops his blockage, blasting me with waves of everything I don't want to feel.

I gut up, knowing he needs help. *"You're going to be okay,"* I send. *"How did your surgery go?"*

I swallow hard. *"The problem was removed."*

"What was the problem?" Adam sends.

I fill him in as quickly as possible, knowing we're rudely silently communicating in a room full of waiting people.

Adam's mouth drops open, and he's so flustered that he bellows aloud, "He what?"

"I'm okay," I send.

"I'm going to fucking kill Demitri," Adam says, blistering mad.

Amy starts crying, startled by him yelling. I hold an arm out for her, and Cindy brings her to me. I get Amy situated on my chest next to her sister and rock back and forth. She quickly settles, and both girls are fast asleep.

"You aren't killing Demitri," I calmly say aloud. "He has no idea. I'll talk to him, but it wasn't intentional."

"Can you have kids?" Adam sends, getting control of himself enough to go back to mind-to-mind communication.

I subtly shake my head.

Adam's expression drops, and he watches me with his girls. "Cindy, can you take the babies?" he requests.

Cindy and Rachelle carefully take the girls, and Adam lifts the blanket from the side of the bed no one can see. He pulls up my nightgown and surveys my stitched stomach. He gets everything back in place, and his head drops to my chest.

I wrap my arm around his head. "None of this is your problem," I say to console him. "I need you to pull it together and handle your family."

He stares in my eyes, radiating horror, terror, and hopelessness.

I shake my head. "Don't you dare, Adam. I can't handle another round of saving someone from the suicide blobs. I have nothing else left to give. I'm asking you to do this for me. Pull it together, be a dad and a husband. You chose Valerie, and I need you to do right by that."

"What if I end up leaving her?" he asks, blinking in shock.

"Then you hire an attorney, and rock hell out of the single dad, joint-custody gig."

"What about you?" he asks.

"I'm not a dad," I respond. "I'm also not married, and don't have kids. The question is irrelevant in my scenario."

"That's not what I mean," Adam says.

"I know it's not," I respond kindly. "Adam, I'm covered up with a mess. I need to help Demitri with the fallout he's going to experience once he knows his mistake. Trey has shown up once and is MIA with phone calls. He has me blocked energetically. God only knows what he's doing. Zane is here and helping me. I don't have room for your panicked-husband regret, but I respect it.

I'm not raising your kids while Valerie makes our lives hell for eighteen years."

Adam has no sense in his expression. I can feel his energy tornadoing. "One bad choice," he grumbles. "One night where I missed a date with you, because I got caught up with Valerie, and it all spiraled."

"I gave you a chance after that night, and it spiraled again," I remind. "You're allowed to choose her, and you did. You need to get over this. I'm over it."

"You just had a screaming, knife-throwing, wife-threatening fit at me," he exclaims.

I chuckle, while everyone else appears scandalized.

"I got my point across," I say.

"How can you be over it? Us?" Adam asks desperately.

"I have self-respect," I gently inform him.

Adam finally seems to understand that we have an audience who he just revealed very personal things too. "I'm sorry," he says, while rapidly blinking. He leans back against the wall and turns ghostly pale.

"Zane, catch him," I plead.

Zane leaps up and catches Adam awkwardly as he falls. Zane can barely hold him up from the terrible angle. I scoot back to keep him from falling on my wound. I slowly get my legs out of the way and slide off the bed. Zane and Rocco get Adam settled on the bed. I take the chair Zane vacated, and my head hangs.

"Should we get a doctor?" Rocco asks.

"No. I've got this," I groan. "It's just shock. He locked his knees."

"How did you know he was going to pass out?" Cindy asks.

"No one knows Adam like I do," I reply. "Two hundred and three lifetimes really do make for a bond."

"Then why did he choose Valerie?" Cindy asks.

"Because she's a brass-balls bitch, and he likes that sort of thing," I reply, with my face in my hands. I look Cindy's way. "I am also, but at the time, I hadn't been jaded. I was still sweet and girly then. Now, I'm who he wants, but he trapped himself."

I heft myself up and put my hand on Adam's chest. I send a little jolt, and he gasps. "Hey," I softly say. "You took a snooze."

Adam sits up and blinks, in a daze. Demitri chooses now to walk through the door. Adam sights on him and lunges, grabbing Demitri around the neck.

He slams Demitri against the wall. "How dare you!" he snarls.

Demitri slides stunned eyes my way, and I wrench Adam away from Demitri, earning blistering stomach pain. I double over, and Zane grabs me before I can sink to my knees. He turns me so I'm facing away from the occupants and lifts my nightgown.

"Damn it," Zane exclaims.

I lean against Zane.

"Demitri, you need to heal me," I gasp. "I suspect I just popped stitches."

Demitri rushes to me, while Adam stares my way with huge-eyed unhelpfulness. Demitri kneels, lifting my nightgown. His head falls, and he grips my stomach. I feel heat and stand still.

"Don't you think the doctor is going to wonder why you're suddenly fine and dandy?" Zane snarks.

I slide a steely glare his way. Something about Adam's issues have spurned me back to my reality.

"We're blowing this pop stand," I say. "I have business to attend to. I need my phone."

Zane hands over my phone, and I dial a number, putting the call on speaker. There's no point in hiding my plan. Big Joe answers, and I gravel through rising dark-water rage, "I need intel. Mack. Get it now."

"What's the plan, Melanie?" Big Joe asks.

"We're balancing some scales," I say.

"Did something new happen?"

"Yes. Get me what I need," I demand and hang up. "Where's Trey?"

"We haven't seen him," Demitri says. "I figured he was here."

"He hasn't been here since the last time you were," I respond with cold eyes.

"Someone, tell me what's happening," Demitri requests, on guard.

Adam grabs my jaw, wrenching my head his direction. "What's the plan?" he demands.

"Your plan is to go snuggle with your wife and adorable children," I snarl back.

"There's no way in hell that I'm letting you walk into this alone," Adam insists, his head clearing as the severity of my energy affects him.

"I've said it before, but perhaps you don't understand," I growl, glaring at him. "You lost the privilege of battling with me when you chose Valerie. Now, go be a good lapdog to a Normal."

I expect anger, but instead, Adam leans his arms on the end of the hospital bed I no longer need. His head falls, and anguish rolls from him in waves. "I know this is my fault," Adam says in a grieving tone. "Watching you hold my babies when you can't have children is the worst nightmare I've ever experienced." He stands upright. "I should have listened. I should have been there. I didn't even know you'd made a trade for Zane."

"What the fuck do you mean she can't have children?" Zane breathes, while he yanks me to him, wrapping his arms around me.

I step back as fresh rage boils in me. I look into Zane's eyes. "The doctor talked to your mom. The damage done when he had to cut the placenta out rendered me barren," I tell him.

Zane's shaking hand rises to cup his mouth. He ungracefully plummets into his chair that's behind him. Cindy and Rachelle still have the sleeping twins in their arms. With their hands occupied, Rocco crosses to Zane and consoles him.

Demitri is staring at Zane in a state of shock. He snaps his gaze from me to Zane, and back to me again. "What happened?" he demands.

"The reason I had surgery was because you healed over my placenta that didn't detach," I explain. "It rotted inside a healed casing. That's why I swelled and got so sick. It was cut out, but the damage is severe. I can't have kids this lifetime."

Demitri sharply inhales and turns his back to me. Even though Adam just threatened him, he hugs Demitri.

"This is *not* happening," Demitri wails.

With everyone thoroughly occupied, I unzip my duffel bag and change into my black leather pants and a crop top. I ignore the newly formed scar, figuring I'll deal with that disgrace later. As I pull on my heeled motorcycle boots, my phone rings. I answer.

"I have an address, and confirmation that Mack is there," Big Joe tells me. He gives me the address and adds, "We're headed that way."

"He's mine," I snarl.

"He's yours, but we're going to be there to pick up the pieces," Big Joe says.

"There won't be anything left to clean up," I snarl.

"Fill me in on your plan," Big Joe requests.

"War," I growl through gritted teeth before I hang up.

"Trey, you need to decide if you still give a shit about Melanie," Adam says from behind me.

Slowly, I turn steely eyes his way.

Adam stares at me while he says into his phone, "La Diabla is going rogue. I can feel it from her. This is going to be bad." He puts the phone on speaker.

"Melanie?" Trey's voice blisters from Adam's phone.

"What?"

"I'm ordering you to stand down!" Trey commands.

"Fuck off," I reply with a snort.

"We'll handle this, but not this way," Trey insists.

"Go do whatever has you so conveniently distracted," I retort. "I'm sure she's riveting."

"I've been getting my head on straight," Trey insists. "Nothing else."

"Must be nice!" I snarl back.

"I knew Zane had you covered," Trey says defensively. "You were better off that way."

"She was told that she can't have kids," Adam informs him.

"WHAT?" Trey screams through the phone.

"You heard me," Adam says. "Lucky for you, Zane's currently sobbing in a hospital chair at that news. Looks like someone's grieving the loss of his future family. Just do what you're doing, Trey. I shouldn't have called you. You don't give a shit."

"Where are we headed?" Trey asks with deadly intensity, ignoring Adam.

I give him the address. "Are you close enough to Mabel's to grab my katana?" I ask.

"I'm in our room now," Trey says. "You sure?"

"Yes. Be careful. It's battle sharp," I warn.

"You're not bringing blades into this," Adam insists. "These guys play with firearms."

"Mack won't have time to shoot me," I reply. I gesture to Rachelle and Cindy, who have the girls. "Take your babies back to your wife's hospital room." I look to Cindy. "You, Rachelle, Brian, Rocco, and Zane need to go home."

"I'm going with you, Melanie," Zane says as he stands, pulling it together.

"And you plan to do what?" I ask.

"This is beyond personal," Zane says with blazing conviction. "I'll stay out of firing range, but I need to be there."

"This isn't for you," Adam warns. "I shouldn't have revealed the extent of Melanie's damage in front of you. I didn't understand that you see your future in her."

"This is my fault," Zane says, "and your fault, along with Demitri, and Trey. All four of us are responsible for Melanie's downfall. My suicide, Adam's oblivion, Demitri's healing mistake, and Trey's super-sperm. We all have to fix this."

"I can heal this," Demitri insists. "I won't stop until you can have kids, Melanie."

"Trey's going to do his part to make this right with you," Adam says. "I'm not going to do my part by going away. I can't."

"You have no choice," I reply. "You wanted a break this lifetime. You get the privilege of sitting on the sidelines, snuggled, safe, and warm. You get a wife that's whole. You get the kind of life where your biggest worry is that your workday is long, and you didn't have time for a lunch break on a random Tuesday."

"I didn't know I could be this unhappy." Adam stares in my eyes. "I can't watch you walk out the door to battle evil and not follow you." Adam shakes his head. "I can't be this guy."

"You chose to be this guy, Adam," I snap, and then soften my tone. "You've earned a weak lifetime. It's okay to be soft and hide behind your Normal. It's okay to make Normals and be normal."

Adam's breath catches, pained. "You think they're Normals?" he asks.

"I feel no energetic metaphysical spark in the babies," I compassionately say to Adam. I smile a little. "You did it. You wished for a normal life and created one."

"I was wrong," Adam whispers.

"Learn from that, Adam," I softly say back. "I need to learn to do this without you."

Adam's chin shakes as he closes his eyes. "I was always the one to step up and handle the heavy shit."

"You folded and gave up on the battlefield. Lucky for you, I'm a different me this lifetime." At Adam's aghast expression, I nod. "I'm a harsher, more deadly me, because I have to be." I tip my head. "Why do you think that is, Adam? Why would I have more deadly abilities? Why would I be harder, more pragmatic, and willing to kill?"

Adam swallows hard.

"Because I have to be," I say, answering my own question. "You won't be the guy who steps up and handles the heavy shit because you need a little breaky break. Enjoy it, without hesitation, because I don't need you this lifetime."

I know I just destroyed him, but that's the rub. Adam always wants it both ways. He doesn't get that privilege.

I straighten, swelling with arrogance. My expression slides cold. I non-corporeally send the audible mental thought into the room, *"We are who we align ourselves with. You're aligned with a woman who doesn't even want to feed her babies. Mediocre looks pretty mediocre on you."* I smirk.

"Does that make you a pathetic cheater who chooses bottom-feeding cheerleaders and hides from reality because he's a narcissist?" Adam bites back.

"Fuck you," I whisper. My voice rises as I add, "I'm not aligned with Trey. I'm trapped by him. Open your fucking eyes, Adam.

You're who always stood between me and the hell of life with Trey." I jamb a finger into his chest. "I'm aligned with YOU, but you fell. I don't fall, Adam Stone. I just get meaner, tougher, and more determined." I shove Adam back hard. "For you, I've become THIS because if I embody everything you used to be, then you can have this luxury lifetime of whining and bitching about that complacent waste you chose. You still live in me, and I'll give that part of you back the next lifetime, when you've finished your slog through complacency."

Adam starts to grab my arm, but I step back.

"You can touch me when I permit it. Know your fucking place," I command. I reach, and Zane's hand lands in mine. I pull his arm over my shoulder, putting his hand on my stomach that he grips. I'm healed now, but it means something to him.

"Take your babies and enjoy your evening, Adam. I've got her," Zane says.

"You're going to WHAT?" Adam blisters at me. "Teach Zane to use a katana?"

"What is a katana?" Zane asks.

"Technically, it's a wakizashi," I correct.

"A huh?" Zane asks.

"Smaller blade for ceremonial killings," I inform.

Zane rattles his head.

"Actually," Adam corrects with uppity superiority, "it's a fusion blade that I had customed for Melanie. It's smaller, like a wakizashi, because she's small, but needs the technical strike . . ." He trails off, waving his hands about. "Never mind, whatever. It's a sword. She can lop someone's head off with it. Big points for decapitation." He nods sarcastically at Zane.

"Decapitation points are a thing?" Zane shrilly screeches. "Why are we cutting off heads?"

I pan a baffled gaze Zane's way.

"The fuck?" I say and look to Adam.

Adam smirks. "He's a Normal," he reminds me. "Normals don't kill their enemies with double-sided, ancient murder-blades." He tips his head. "I *do*. I have the matching custom one to yours."

"You plan to cradle two infants while you cut a baby-murderer in half?" I snark. "I'm sure your Normal little bundles of joy will be ninja quiet while they get splattered with death."

"How is Zane going to help you murder Mack?" Adam asks with a sharp inhale.

"He's not," I snarl back. "He's going to realize that I'm not who he thinks I am. I'm not cute little Mighty Mouse who giggles at Weird Al Yankovich songs. You see, Adam, I wanted some normalcy also. There's only so much to go around in our world. You hogged it all up with your trash-can-to-the-curb chores, and mint-green-painting of the nursery."

"You *are* Mighty Mouse," Zane insists.

I step away and face Zane, allowing the full weight of what I really am to thrum in heavy waves through the room. It's suffocating suddenly, as arms goose-bump.

"I'm La Diabla, Zane," I say. "You're about to learn what a katana is. You can come with me, witness reality, and I encourage you to. You need to understand why I can't have children, be safe, or afford to giggle." I glare at Adam. "You're doing safety and giggles in doubles for us both." I smirk and flick my eyes to the twins. "Benchwarmer."

"You *bitch*," Adam says, exasperated.

"Don't forget it," I snip, before snagging my bag and heading out the door with purpose.

"Mom, grab the rest of her stuff," Zane instructs Cindy from behind me. "Leave the flowers. Get my bag packed. I'll head to your house when this is done."

"You aren't doing this," I hear Cindy insist.

"I am," Zane replies before jogging to catch up with me.

I need to leave at a quick clip before any of the medical staff can stop me. Per the usual, they prove to be sluggish, not realizing we're leaving. Demitri, Zane, and I load into the elevator. As the door closes, I stare at Adam in the hall while he holds two infants and looks like his world has crashed down.

"Well, you kicked him in the nads before we left." Demitri shrugs. "I can officially die happy when you attack Mack."

CHAPTER 38

Demitri's Jeep pulls into a little parking lot that is overrun with motorcycles, Trey's car, and Mabel's Bronco. Everyone has gathered. I step out, allowing Zane to get out of the back seat. Trey crosses to me, wordlessly holding the shoulder straps of the katana's harness out. I slide my arms through and shrug the sheath on. I reach over my head, testing the grip and pulling the katana. It slides out like butter.

Satisfied, I survey the crowd. "Stay here," I command.

I start walking, and an army of footsteps follow.

I stop and turn, meeting the eyes of over twenty people. "I said to stay here," I repeat.

"If you think I'm missing seeing you slice and dice Mack, you've lost your mind." Mercury grins. Considering that he's one of the deadliest of the Hellhound bikers, I'll take his enthusiasm. He may come in handy.

I roll my eyes. "Fine. Stay out of the way."

"You don't have to do this, Melanie," Mabel insists.

I slide haughty eyes her way. "How many times did you visit Valerie in the hospital?" I inquire.

"Three," she replies.

"How many times did you visit me?"

"One," she sheepishly answers.

"For how long?"

"A few minutes." Mabel sighs.

"Did you ask me if I was okay? Did you ask details? Did you do any of the mom stuff?"

Mabel shakes her head. "I was trying to give you and Trey space," she explains.

"Trey wasn't there. He stayed as long as you did." I raise my eyebrows Mabel's way. "I'm asking for space now, yet you and Trey, the space-masters, are following. WHY do the two of you insist on doing the opposite of what I want every single time?"

"You weren't with Melanie?" Mabel asks Trey.

"No," he answers with no explanation.

"I'm sorry, Melanie," Mabel says.

"I didn't invite you here," I reply curtly. "Why don't you go to the hospital and help Valerie get past her postpartum woes?"

Mabel's expression shrinks. "I've been counseling her through that. It's why I've spent so much time there."

"Whatever," I reply with zero care for her nonsense.

I continue my trudge down the alley. Mack's warehouse is in an industrial district that appears largely abandoned at this time of night. That's excellent news for me. The only lights in the whole neighborhood come from the warehouse we're approaching. I stop outside the door and stare at it.

I take long enough that Demitri speaks up. "What are we waiting for?" he asks.

"The song to end," I huff impatiently. I gesture to the warehouse that's blaring music.

"Why?" Demitri asks.

I give him the look that question deserves. "I'm not going to kill Mack to Warrant's 'Cherry Pie.'"

Quiet laughter spurts from many.

"It's not a bad song," Demitri hiss whispers.

"I'm not planning to flirt with him," I hiss back. "This isn't how I'm doing this."

"What if the next song sucks worse?" Demitri asks.

"Ughhh." I shrug. "We'll see."

The song ends, and L.A. Guns' "Sex Action" blasts from the warehouse.

"There it is," I say, satisfied. I gather a huge energy load, making sure to pass out cold anyone who is within the vicinity except for Mack and my people. Less chance of getting caught that way.

"Knock, knock," I breathe on a wave of power before I hit the industrial doors with a cataclysmic, invisible energy-cannonball. The doors blast from the hinges, flying across the warehouse. I step in and toss out an energy bubble that traps Mack.

Mack's eyes snap wide. "I didn't know when I came for you," he blathers.

"You said that already while I was coated in blood," I remind him. I look to Trey. "You want a crack at the baby killer?"

Trey shakes his head. "I'm here in case you need a second wave," he says. "He's yours."

"Ohhh, winner, winner, chicken dinner," I gravel on a wave of hatred. I flick a hand Mack's way, and he levitates, still trapped in the bubble, a few feet off the ground.

"I'm sorry! I'm sorry," Mack begs frantically.

"Shut the fuuuck up!" I shout and look to Trey. "Which fist did he gut-punch me with?"

"Right," Trey answers, clipped and to the point. Gotta love pragmatic Trey.

"Excellent," I breathe as I sight on Mack again. I strut forward, hips swaying, and reach over my shoulder, pulling the katana.

Mack stares at it with huge eyes and I cock a hip.

"I'm sorry," I chirp. "I was informed earlier that Normals don't know what one of these is." I tap Mack on the chest with it lightly. "This is a specially designed fusion katana. It originated in Japan in the 700s CE during the Heien period. Fascinating time. Warriors were disciplined, trained. And did you know, Mack, that katana masters passed that knowledge on for many, *many* years?" I feign innocence. "Do you know who was a katana master?"

Before I can enlighten him, Adam bellows, "I was."

I look over my shoulder, seeing Adam as he struts in through the destroyed hole in the wall.

"You're a benchwarmer," I remind him disgustedly.

"Every teacher wants to watch his student succeed," Adam replies, before turning his stone-cold, ocean-blue eyes Mack's way.

"She got the overhand strike down immediately," he informs the crowd. "She was quite skilled at it."

"Shall I demonstrate?" I ask.

Before anyone can stop me, I send out an energy snap, forcing Mack's right arm to stretch to the side. I raise my arms over my head and slash with perfect pull, bringing the razor-sharp katana down. It slices through his wrist like butter.

Mack inhales but is in such shock that he makes only a slight keening sound as he stares at his blood-spurting stump.

"Oooohhhhhhh, I love that *sound*," I breathe on a wave of thrilled obsession.

"You always have," Adam chuckles. He nods at Mack. "Not as much as she loves when her enemy squeals though."

I look to Adam. "Fist is attached to wrist, but forearm makes the fist punch," I recite.

"That it does," Adam responds, matter-of-fact.

"Let's try a diagonal strike this time," I suggest and bring the sword up over my left shoulder. I whip it down to my right side, severing Mack's arm at the elbow in the process. He makes a squealing sound, and I nod at Adam. "There it is."

"Nice work," Adam says, as if we're in a lesson. "You've still got the cross-body strike down."

"With all the dance training I now have, I bet I can finally do the up and under."

"You should try," Adam encourages.

"Everyone clear, jussssssst in case I don't have it down. It's been a long time, after all," I say. I bring the sword whirling overhead, gaining momentum as I lunge and artfully cut low, so rapid that the movement appears almost flowery to the untrained eye. It takes Mack's legs off at the knees, but he doesn't fall because I still have him suspended energetically.

Adam's applause is cut short as Mack starts screaming.

"You're a tough guy," I remind Mack pointedly. "No screaming like a scared baby." The screams become more desperate, and I huff. "You need to be quiet." When he doesn't, I drive the tip of the sword into Mack's throat before yanking it out. I got the hit just right, destroying his vocal box.

He wheezes and gasps, but the screaming stops.

"That's better," I chirp, while surveying Mack's pieces that are all floating with his dissected body.

"Nice hit," Adam compliments. "That requires centimeter precision."

"Who's ready for the big finish?" I ask.

"I am," Mercury happily announces. I look his way, and he's grinning from ear to ear, loving this.

"Slow or fast?" I ask Mercury.

"Katana work, traditionally, is about quick cuts in rapid succession," Mercury informs the group.

"Let's do the art form justice, shall we?" I ask, before whipping through the fast series of artful katana strikes that I remember from the ceremonial katas I learned during the lifetime Adam trained warriors. When done right, it resembles a graceful, albeit lightning-fast, dance. I make it to the last move, whipping around to face my audience while I drive the blade into Mack from my hip, at the perfect angle. The sword slides into his heart just right, and I smile, satisfied.

"That's my girl," Adam says proudly.

I yank the sword from Mack's dead body and release the energy suspending him. He thuds to the pavement with a series of wet splats.

"Well, I said we were here to pick up the pieces," Big Joe announces, unfazed. He gestures comically to Mack. "Let's get to it, Hellhounds."

Most of our group laughs. Demitri, Mabel, and Zane appear horrified. Adam and Trey are stoic.

"I'm not done yet," I snarl, causing the Hellhounds to back up.

"She's not done yet," Stubbs, one of the more amusing Hounds, comically says to Big Joe.

"Best day ever," Mercury happily expresses.

I hand the katana to Adam before turning to Trey. "Pocketknife, please," I request.

He pulls it from his front jeans pocket and opens it. I take it, slicing my palm. Trey holds out his hand, and I slice his palm. He doesn't flinch.

I kneel by Mack's torso and cut open his shirt, leaving his chest exposed.

I glance to Adam, who smiles adoringly. "She intentionally left that undamaged space on his chest," he marvels to our spectators.

"The rest of him is sliced and diced," Mercury says with admiration. "Why did you intentionally leave that section unharmed?"

"For this," I whisper as I carve *Abigail* into his corpse before standing and clasping bloody hands with Trey. We hold our hands over the name of the daughter we lost, and blood runs from our hands onto Mack. We let go, and Adam takes off his T-shirt, ripping several long strips from the front. He ties a strip around my hand, before repeating the process with Trey.

"*Now* do we clean up?" Big Joe asks.

"Do you not understand a blood-and-fire ritual?" I ask, exasperated.

"Fire?" Big Joe asks.

"Yeah, fire," I say as I look to Adam. "Normals don't do blood-and-fire rituals on the dead bodies of their enemies?"

"I don't know," Adam answers, as if I'm an inquisitive child. "Let's find out." He looks to Zane. "Do *you* do blood-and-fire rituals on the dead bodies of your enemies?" he cheerfully asks.

Zane's eyes are huge as he stares at the piecemeal body of Mack. He opens and closes his mouth a few times but can't make sound.

"Silence speaks volumes," Adam says as he sweeps an arm to Zane. "I believe Normals don't do this."

I make a hacking sound. "They should. It's satisfying." I hold my bandaged hand to Trey, but he shakes his head.

He unwraps his hand before unzipping my leather pants.

"Hell, yes," Mercury chortles. "Is voyeuristic, public display a part of a blood-and-fire ritual?"

"It's not, but those two march to the beat of their own crazy," Adam informs.

Trey's eyes don't leave mine as he pulls my pants down enough to reveal my surgery scar. He presses his bloody palm to the scar while he stares in my eyes. "I love you," he says. "I'm sorry it came to this. You took out Mack. I'll take out the rest of the Reapers."

I shake my head. "We take the rest out together."

"They're going to come for us," Trey warns. "We can't hide this."

"I don't plan to hide it," I reply. "I plan to hang a flashing neon welcome sign."

Trey kneels and kisses the scar, coated in his blood, before standing, pulling up my pants, and zipping them. I kneel, running my fingertips through the blood oozing from Mack's severely gashed thigh. Trey closes his eyes without being asked, and I slowly drag my fingers from Trey's forehead to his chin, leaving a fingertip blood trail behind.

He opens his eyes, staring at me for a moment before looking to Mack. "Burn in hell," he gravels. He drapes an arm over my shoulders, and we strut out the destroyed wall to the alley.

Our people follow us.

"They're wild," Mercury says. "What's up with the bloodlines?"

"Ritual," Trey gravels primally.

I send out an energetic search, finding the area devoid of any aware life. The few that were in the area are still out cold from my energy pilfering when we arrived.

I face the warehouse. "Everyone needs to head up the alley and get ready to leave," I request.

"We're not leaving you here," Demitri says.

"Walk away," Trey orders. "This is ours to do."

The group walks partway up the alley before watching Trey wrap his arms around me from behind, putting his hands on my stomach.

I inhale and narrow my eyes as I hyperfocus on the building. I find the spark in me that's always fueled by rage. "Abigail, we never intended to sacrifice you," I whisper. "You will be avenged. I traded you without understanding. I'm coming for you. I won't leave you there."

I flick a hand, and a spark appears that drifts lightly into the building. I inhale slowly before blasting an energy wave into the spark. The whole building engulfs with such ferocity that all the people in our peripheral vision shy away. Trey and I don't flinch.

"And so it is," Trey rumbles.

I send one more blast into the inferno, and it burns so hot that the windows high up start to warp. Adam steps up next to us.

"If it's hot enough to melt glass, is it hot enough to destroy Mack?" I ask.

"He's liquid," Adam assures.

Trey guides me down the alley. Adam follows with a hand on each of our shoulders. We all gather by our vehicles, and Trey's already on the phone with Tanner.

"Vault down. Full sweep of Mabel's. Search every closet, corner, and behind the furniture. Hunker down and be ready," he orders.

"For what?" I hear Tanner ask.

"War," Trey replies.

"Nerf war, Uzi war, or firework-energy-ball war?" Tanner asks.

"Our kind."

"Well, fuck a duck," Tanner exasperates. "I have a fashion line to work on, Trey."

"War," Trey repeats, hyperfocused on his mission.

"Yeah, yeah, war," Tanner snarks before hanging up.

"Little Mighty Mouse is nifty, huh, Zane?" Adam asks, while clapping Zane on the shoulder. At Zane's stunned expression, Adam happily exhales. "I love when she minces people." He nods jovially at a very unhappy Zane. "You should see her take down six fuckers with that routine she did in the warehouse. It wasn't nearly as impressive as it can be, considering Mack couldn't run or attack back." Adam gives me a look when Zane doesn't respond. "Holding Mack frozen? Really?" he asks.

"Efficiency," I reply. "I've earned that today." I look up at Zane, but there's no sense in his glazed eyes. "Come on," I say, blasé. "We need to get back to our cars at the hospital." I look to Trey. "Don't lock me out in the parking lot this time, Mr. Vault System."

"I won't." Trey sighs. When I give him the look he deserves, he tosses his hands. "We'll talk."

"Yippee!" I roll my eyes and address the crowd. "Thank you for spectating. I'm so glad I could entertain you this fine evening."

"We thought you'd need help," Big Joe informs. "You didn't, but we're here when you do. We'll always show up."

"Nifty concept," I say to Trey and gesture at Big Joe.

Trey just sighs.

Demitri guides zombie-Zane to his Jeep and helps him in. He closes the door. "Oh boy. Zane's about to crater," he says.

"He didn't have to cut Mack off at the legs," I reply, blasé. "He's fine."

"Looks like Mel has a little meltdown coming also," Demitri remarks with widening eyes.

"I'm fine, Demitri," I reply. "Fifty more fuck-sticks to go."

"*Then* she'll melt down," Adam informs. "We're mid-mission. Meltdown is a little way off."

"*I'm* mid-mission," I retort. "You're mid-invasion of a mission that's not yours."

"Now, now. I can be a part of the mission," Adam chides.

"No, you can't. Stay in your lane," I lecture. I get in the Jeep, and Demitri hops in a moment later. He reaches for his travel CD case and pulls one out, putting it in the dashboard slot. He rolls down the windows as Talking Heads' "Burning Down the House" blares. The Hellhounds crack up as we pull out of the parking lot.

We pull up to the hospital and find Cindy and Rocco waiting by my car. Brian and Rachelle must have already left. Cindy rushes our way but stops short as she surveys my blood-splattered state. I start to pull the katana from the Jeep, but Demitri stops me.

"Transfer it at Mabel's. Cameras," he warns.

"What happened?" Cindy asks Zane, as Demitri helps him from the back seat.

Zane holds up his hands and just waggles them about.

"He's a little fluster-gusted currently," Demitri explains.

Cindy hugs her son while she studies my and Demitri's stoicism.

"You two aren't buster-rusted," she remarks.

"Fluster-gusted," Demitri corrects.

"No, we're not," I reply calmly. I hold my hands to Rocco and Cindy, internally cringing because I'm covered in dried blood. They take them, and I pass them the memory. "Don't review that memory until after you've driven home and are seated," I instruct them. "It's disturbing, but you need to understand why Zane's gusted." I smile at Cindy. "Thank you again for helping me. I'm sorry that I'm not the girl you think I am."

I get in my car and Demitri follows me out of the parking lot in his Jeep.

CHAPTER 39

Trey comes in and surveys me lying on my side with Demitri spooned against my back. Demitri has his hand on my stomach with his eyes squeezed closed while he pours sweat.

"Any progress?" Trey asks.

"With my gut, or my intel?" I ask.

"Both."

Demitri exhales hard and rolls onto his back while I sit up.

"Regarding the gut, I can see the problem. I'm working on it. This is going to take time," he informs us, gasping from extreme energetic healing effort.

I hand Trey a file folder. "My research has been long, annoying, but fruitful. I've got the information I need on the Reapers. That's Mack's second in command," I say. "He goes by Thud. They seem to prefer them thick."

Trey peruses the contents of the folder before handing it back.

I hand him another. "Clench. Third in command. Not impressive. More big boy."

Trey blows out a solid exhale after surveying the folder's contents. "Do you know enough for us to deal with them?"

I shrug. "Your dumb infiltration plan is a waste of time, I've decided." At Trey's askant look, I roll my eyes. "He's brought every loser he can find into the Reapers. I don't need to comb through them to sort the good from the bad. I'm just going to take out the whole kit and caboodle. I've earned brevity at this stage of 'what the fuck.'"

"Planning to invite them all to a tea party?" Trey sarcastically asks.

I purse my lips, responding, "They have a bowling league in Reseda on Sundays."

"Oh," Trey sarcastically says with a brightly smug expression. "Blowing up a bowling alley in the heart of the Valley won't gain you a death sentence in the California State Penn." His face drops with deadpan disgust. "You can't blow up the *other* fine bowlers of Southern California. That's ludicrous, Melanie."

As we continue this illustrious debate, Demitri scurries about the room, pulling my dining chairs and producing a blue blanket from the bathroom cabinet.

"What are you doing?" Trey asks, as Demitri drapes the blanket over the end of the bed and back of the chairs.

"Blanket fort," Demitri announces, while he writes on a paper with a Sharpie he snagged from the pencil holder on Trey's night-stand. He tapes the paper onto the blanket.

"*No Grumps Allowed*," Trey reads aloud.

"I'm allowed in the clubhousssse . . . and, you're nooot," Demitri singsongs at Trey, while dancing around like a toddler.

"Woo-hoo!" I chime. "Capital plan, Demitri." I grin at Trey. "I'm tired of adulting. I'll plan Reaper mass murder later."

"We need to handle this, Melanie," Trey insists.

"No thanks," I chirp, handing Trey a framed Grumpy Bear picture that was sitting on the bed.

Trey takes it with a laugh, having not expected a colored picture. "You two seriously plan to crawl in there?" he asks, gesturing to the makeshift blanket fort.

"Yup," Demitri crows. "I need this. We've been adulting too long."

I crawl in after Demitri finishes filling the fort with pillows and snuggly blankets. I rush back out. "Hang tight," I order Demitri. "I have fun surprises." I snag a bag from the closet and rush back into the blanket fort. "SweeTARTS," I squeal when Demitri hands a box of them to me from his backpack. I rattle the box about as I open it.

"Pull tight on three," Demitri instructs.

We both pull on the hoods of our sweatshirts. He counts off, and we pull the drawstrings tight.

"You two are the cutest thing I've ever seen," Trey says as he peeks into our fort and smiles adoringly. We look at Trey and make silly faces.

"You ready to actually see the cutest thing ever?" I ask.

I pull two Fraggle coloring books from the grocery bag and hand one to Demitri.

"No way!" he exclaims. He's so excited that he dives at me, tackling me with a hug. "Thank you! We need new crayons!"

I grin at Trey. "He's adorable when he gets surprises," I inform. I pull out two fresh boxes of crayons. "We have a rule. New coloring book means new crayons. It's a thing."

Trey looks at Demitri like he's nuts. "How can you go from the version of you that had to save Melanie, to this?"

"The same way that Melanie goes from slicing up an idiot to this." Demitri gestures to me while I pop a SweeTART in my mouth and bobble my head.

"That oddly makes sense, I guess. Are you like this with Victoria?"

Demitri looks at Trey like he's nuts.

"Hell, no," he exclaims. "You're literally the only person, other than my dad and Meley, who knows I'm like this."

"Damn it, you're impossible to hate. It's nice that you trust me. Thank you," Trey says, gesturing to our happy little blanket-fort reality. "In light of this bizarre situation, I have a favor to ask."

"Okay," Demitri says curiously. "Hit me with it."

"I've got to get the schedule out to my bouncers," Trey says. "I'm buried in piles of paperwork that are waiting on my desk. Think you can hang with her for a while?"

"I would love that." Demitri grins.

"Thank you, Trey," I chirp.

"You might have to rearrange your blanket fort a little," Trey tells us. "I'm about to steal Melanie's coloring-book-present thunder."

"Why?" I ask. "I like it like this."

Trey laughs and disappears from the little doorway between the chairs. After a few moments, he lifts the edge of the blanket wall and slides our little room TV perched on top of the VCR through the gap.

"Demitri and I rarely watch TV," I tell him. "We talk instead."

"Bet you a week's salary that I can get you to watch TV," Trey challenges.

"I love winning bets against you, and I guarantee we won't watch TV, so it's on." I laugh.

Trey peeks through our little door again and hands in a Tower Records shopping bag. I reach in the bag and pull out a season one VHS box set of *The Fraggle Rock* show. I squeal.

"This is *seriously* the best present ever," Demitri says. "You got Melanie the show?"

Trey grins. "I got it for both of you. I wanted Melanie to be happy, but I also tend to spoil my closest friends. Tanner loves being my best friend."

"It's true. Trey's always taking him to concerts and stuff," I tell Demitri.

"Thank you, Trey." Demitri unwraps the cellophane and reads the back of the box. He looks at me. "We've got five hours of episodes! So many blanket fort days!"

"Nope," Trey says. "You don't." He slides three more shopping bags through the opening and laughs while we pull out seasons two, three, and four.

"I'm ordering takeout," Trey announces. "What do Fraggles eat?"

"Pineapple and Canadian bacon pizza. Sprite and chocolate chip cookies," Demitri and I announce at the same time.

"Gross. I'm on it," Trey responds.

"Also get a salad for Demitri, please," I request.

"If you want to join us, I'll take down my *No Grumps* sign," Demitri calls after him.

"I'm not about to wallow around on the ground watching dancing puppets in a hoodie," Trey says.

"They're Muppets, not puppets," Demitri schools him.

"You two are Muppets," Trey jabs back. "Have fun."

We hear the door close, and Demitri looks at me with sparkly eyes. "Your sugar daddy is *the best*," he says.

"He comes through on occasion. This was purely selfish, though. He wants me out of his hair so he can happily glare at his piles of paperwork all night." My expression softens. "Thank you for this. I need a fort and coloring night so bad."

"I know you do." Demitri pops the first tape into the VCR that's under the TV. He hesitates, his energy shifting as he slides stoic eyes my way. "Meley, I'm sorry."

My head ducks. "I know you are."

"I healed you too fast," Demitri confesses while cupping my cheek. I gaze up at him while he explains, "I was exhausted and really emotionally overwhelmed when I healed the miscarriage damage, but I couldn't wait any longer. You'd been in pain for days, and I needed to help you." He blushes a slow, deep magenta. "I obviously wasn't in my right mind for the task, because the error I made was rookie-level incompetence." He clears his throat awkwardly. "After I found what the surgeon had to fix, I did some research."

"On?" I prompt when he silently stares at the blanket-fort wall behind me for a long stretch of time.

"Female anatomy," he bashfully admits while he deeply blushes. He closes his eyes, his head sagging, as he continues. "Placentas and pregnancy are new to me. I've studied anatomy at length, but forgot the part about how pregnant women grow an organ that doesn't exist all the time." He shakes his head mournfully while he stares at his hands in his lap, clearly humiliated.

"Ah yes," I tease. "The old forgotten placenta." At Demitri's puppy dog expression, I giggle. "You're seventeen. What happened was ridiculous by any standards. Yes, you're a healer. With that said, you didn't go to medical school, aren't trained technically, and aren't a fifty-year-old practiced surgeon with a calm, cool head about the patient you don't know who needs help." I squeeze Demitri's hands that I take as he tears up. "Demitri, you were healing *me*," I softly say. "It was scary, very personal for you, but you stepped up and did it. That means a lot. Thank you."

He clears his throat, trying to hold it together. "When I put my hand on your stomach right after I got the baby out, I sent a healing blast to slow the bleeding. That prevented the placenta from detaching." Demitri shakes his head in disbelief about his error. "When I got around to the big healing episode . . . The way that I heal is to run an energy search to find the damage. I found it and started the healing process. The thing is that I regularly mentally refer to anatomy diagrams in my mind." He shakes his head. "A placenta wasn't on that diagram because the diagram I referred to wasn't of a pregnant woman. I assumed it was just swollen tissue, but it didn't feel damaged, because it wasn't. Technically, under other circumstances, it would have been the right call. In your case, it was a deadly error."

"There's a reason why trauma surgeons have specialties," I console. "We ask the impossible of you—healing people you love, in high-pressure situations, with the weirdest ailments." I rub noses with him before smiling as I look in his eyes. "You're remarkable, Demitri. I'm not mad at you for it."

"I would never hurt you that way," Demitri whispers, distraught.

"I know." I smile compassionately. "We're okay, Demitri. I talked to Adam, Zane, and Trey about it, and they get it. No one is mad now."

"Thank you," Demitri mumbles. He clears his throat. "I think I can fix your issues, if you want children."

"I do, desperately," I admit as my heart sinks.

"The process is going to be ugly," Demitri informs me stoically.

"Does it have to happen now?"

Demitri shakes his head. "It'll take time." He winces. "Several unpleasant times."

"Then we worry about it later." I wiggle my shoulders, and Demitri looks at me adoringly as the mood brightens. "Muppets," I remind, and he chuckles.

He hits *play* on the VCR. We get pillows situated, and Demitri holds his arm out so I can curl up against his side. The theme song starts, and we bop our heads and smile.

"This must be good if you dragged me out of my office," Mama Mabel says, bringing me out of my slumber.

I blink and squint at the light from the TV. The Fraggles are scurrying about on the screen. I look at the opening of my blanket fort, and Mama Mabel and Trey are smiling. Mabel looks around in the fort, surveying the pizza box, soda cans, open cookie packages, empty SweeTART boxes, coloring books, and blankets.

"Hi, sweetheart," Mabel softly says to me.

"Hey," I bashfully reply. We've had a rough run of it lately, and I don't know if Mabel and I are okay.

"I'm sorry that I wasn't there for you in the hospital," she says.

"Valerie has been such an attention suck," I mutter. "Her being needy in the hospital makes sense."

"I'm working on doing a much better job of balancing that," Mabel promises.

I nod, hoping Mabel will make time to help me work through losing the baby soon, but now isn't the time to bring that up.

She smiles softly at Demitri, who's out cold. I'm curled around his side, and he has his arm around me. I pick up a picture of Red the Fraggle.

"Do we have a spare frame?" I ask. "D colored me a picture."

"I'll have Constance frame it for you," Mabel says as she sets it aside. "You're seriously not bothered by this little display?" she asks Trey hesitantly.

"I got so much work done while they sat here and sang Fraggle songs," he explains. "I'd sooner die than watch five minutes of that dumb show. She's all sparkle-eyed, and I didn't have to suffer at all."

"Let's see if he's sparkle-eyed, also," Mabel says.

I scratch my nails lightly on Demitri's arm. "D, wake up," I cajole. "Our mess is currently under scrutiny."

Demitri wakes up and tips his head Mabel and Trey's way. He sings the start of the Fraggle theme song, and we both head bob like morons.

Mama Mabel busts out in laughter. "If I didn't know the evil that lives in her, I would be worried for you," she tells Trey. "But I do and I'm not. She needs you when it's time to pulverize biker-ass. Let it ride. You got a friend out of the deal, and a babysitter when she's in toddler mode."

"I'm so happy . . . that I don't care . . . that she called me a toddleeer," I singsong.

Demitri laughs.

"Come on, you two. Time for sleep," Trey insists. Trey looks Demitri's way and adds, "It's pouring outside. Is your dad still out of town?"

Demitri nods. "I toss and turn at home," he explains. "I don't have nightmares here, but I feel weird imposing."

"Are they still about having to save Melanie?" Trey asks.

"Only now, I can't save her, and she dies in the nightmares," Demitri says. "I wake up in a cold sweat with my heart racing. It's horrific." He looks my way. "When she's curled up behind me, the nightmares don't seem to happen."

"If someone had told me a year ago that I'd sleep better with Demitri Cantrell on the other side of my soulmate, I would've knocked them out on the grounds of insanity," Trey remarks.

"We'll likely all get back to normal," I say. "Until then, you're both happier when we call it survival mode." I gesture Demitri's way. "He's still emotionally reeling from what he had to do. Technically, that's my fault. We can justify helping him."

The guys help clean up the mess in the blanket fort, and I head to the bathroom, close the door, and get ready for bed. I stare at myself in the mirror. I look surprisingly normal, given my numerous near-death disasters. I wash my face and ponder. I need to come to terms with being a mess, mainly because I'm both conflicted, and completely unstable about my life right now. The big issue . . . I'm not ready to face the reality that Zane is who I want.

CHAPTER 40

"Stop! Please," I beg through shallow panting.

Demitri's head sags as sweat drips from his forehead onto the sheet that's covering me. He takes a ratcheting breath. "Talk to me, baby girl," he manages to get out.

"I can't . . ." I trail off as I start to roll onto my side, forgetting that his damn hand is lodged in my unmentionables.

He puts his other hand on my hip and rolls me to my back again. The look he gives me is drained from both his energetic exertion and awkwardness. "Stay still, Meley."

I cover my face with shaking hands. "For one goddamn day, can I PLEASE be a giggly teenager?" I snarl.

Demitri chuckles halfheartedly. "If it helps, I'd like to be a seventeen-year-old guy who flirts with the pretty little powerhouse brunette instead of stuffing my hand up her nether region while she screams."

I laugh as his candor breaks some of the awkward tension. My hands drop from my face, and I stare into his pretty steel-blue eyes. "Can our friendship, or whatever this is, survive this debacle?"

I make the mistake of shifting, causing his hand that's in me to jostle. We both blush.

Demitri groans comically. "I'd like to make the rule that we lean on the quirky side of our relationship throughout 'the debacle.' This," he flexes and then relaxes his interred hand, causing me to laugh bashfully, "can fit into our quirky category, I suppose."

I reach, snagging the open box of SweeTARTS on the nightstand. I pop one in my mouth before putting a pink one in his mouth. "Sounds like the only reasonable route to me," I reply while I chew. The sour candy zings, and my eye twitches its involuntary response.

Demitri cracks up, resting his forehead on my sheet-clad thigh. After a silent moment, he says, "I have an idea. Hang tight." His expression morphs comically. "Scratch that," he corrects. "I have an idea. Hang loose." He taps my hip, and I relax my pelvis. His hand slips free with a tug, and I wince at the awkwardness as he gets up and heads to the bathroom.

"I've tried not to complain, but this 'healing' you're doing really is horrific," I belt as I hear the water running in the bathroom sink. "I'm on the edge of tears through it, but I'm not a wimp, I swear."

Demitri chuckles as he returns to the bedroom, drying his hands on a towel. He snags his cell phone and dials a number. The other person must pick up because he asks, "Are you over your bitty baby shock of the old slice-and-dice yet?"

The call is put on speaker, as Zane replies, "Screw you, assface! That was rough." I hear him blow out a big breath. "Yes, I'm over it."

"What are you doing?" Demitri asks.

"Sitting here watching cartoons in my jammies," Zane informs.

"How riveting," Demitri jokes.

"Another day living the dream," Zane replies. "What are you doing?"

"Oh, you know . . . Another day living the nightmare over here," Demitri quips. "I could use your help with Melanie's Venus flytrap."

"Come again?"

I giggle while surveying Demitri with no clue what he's up to.

"Think you're up for talking Melanie through my healing efforts of what she's started referring to as her 'no-no zone'?" Demitri asks.

"Didn't see that one coming," Zane muses through the phone.

"She wants kids," Demitri informs him. "While I've got a shot at making that happen, I have to stuff her like a Thanksgiving gobbler to attempt it."

"You want me to coach Melanie through a pounding by your hot ass while you attempt to impregnate her?" Zane sounds baffled.

Demitri chuckles. "We're not attempting impregnation. We're attempting the future possibility of children. My hand is the tool of choice. While I might be able to accomplish healing with my other tool, that would likely be deemed unseemly."

We hear Zane blow out a monster breath. "You do realize I'm generally peeved by you, right Demitri?"

"I don't particularly like you either," Demitri chimes back, albeit amused.

I prop up on my elbow while I enjoy their gossipy banter.

"Why don't you like me?" Zane asks with feigned innocence.

"Because," Demitri replies with bright sarcasm, "you're the only gorilla in her zoo who comes close to my hot-guy status that mesmerizes Meley."

My eyebrows rise as I delight in this rare display of arrogance from Demitri.

Zane howls laughter. "Oh please," he snarks back condescendingly. "I've got you beat by a MILE with her."

"How so?" Demitri inquires with an uppity look in my direction.

I giggle, right up until Zane drops the, "Have you wiped her ass repeatedly while she bubble-gutted in a hospital for a month?" bomb.

I grandly wince while Demitri howls with laughter. He asks me, "How do ya feel about that, Mighty Mouse?"

"Shit!" Zane belts. "Am I on speaker?"

"Yuuuuuup," Demitri foghorns.

"I hate you, Demitri," Zane blisters, before switching gears with a singsongy, "Love youuuuu, Mighty Mouse."

"Yeah, yeah," I mutter. "You two can squabble while you help with this nightmare. Get over here and fight with D in person. It'll distract me from the excruciating pain he creates while he loses a hand in my Bermuda Triangle."

"On my way," Zane says. "I'm at my apartment. Be there in five minutes."

Demitri hangs up, and I mutter, "If I crap the bed while you torture me, Zane cleans it up."

Demitri's face scrunches with a dramatic grimace. "You've got a deal." He brightens. "Promise you'll foul the bed?"

I jokingly glare at him, earning a chuckle while he adjusts my sheet covering before taking a load off next to me.

— —

The door opens after a tentative knock. Zane enters, closing and locking the door after him.

"We're the only ones here," I inform him. "Hence doing this now."

"Where's Trey?" Zane asks.

"School," I reply.

Zane glances in the general direction of the parking lot outside. "The main door was unlocked."

I nod sarcastically. "Trey's out of sorts." I smirk. "Violent miscarriages and enemy dismemberment don't mix well with his habit of avoiding or dealing with trauma. He's been a real dissociative treat—hence forgetting to lock the front door when he left for school."

"You're playing with Melanie's no-no zone while Trey's at school?" Zane quizzically asks Demitri.

"He doesn't know we're doing this," Demitri offers. "But we're not doing *that*."

"Why?" Zane asks before rattling about his hand. "Why doesn't he know, I mean. Not the this or that thing."

"Because," I interject, "I'm not doing this for him. I'm also not thrilled with how dismissive and MIA he's been lately."

"How so?" Zane asks with a scrunched forehead.

"Setting aside what an MIA ass he was for months before my pregnancy was confirmed . . . I've been out of the hospital for two days." I give Zane a pointed look. "Trey's barely spoken to me, and when he does, he's generally aloof and unfocused. I feel like he wanders around avoiding reality, and I'm sick of it. Now that I'm not in life and death danger, he's falling right back into his old patterns. He's yet to discuss losing the baby, and every time I try to broach the topic, he scuttles off with an excuse of work." I scoff. "I've checked his office. He wasn't there."

Demitri scoots off the bed, seeming oddly caged.

"What?" I ask him.

"Nothing," Demitri replies with a hesitant undercurrent.

"What are you hiding?" I press.

"Meley," Demitri sighs out, "Let's stay focused on the current disaster."

I let it go, assuming he's overwhelmed with his monumental healing hurdle. The thought of getting back to the dreaded task makes me blanch with a cold sweat. "I'm scared to try this again," I admit.

Demitri looks to Zane. "Hence why you're here. What I'm having to do hurts." He glances my way before focusing on Zane again. "A lot."

Zane exhales, grounding in a way I depended on during my hospital stints. "All right," he says. "Pain protocol, my girl." He crosses to the far side of the bed and lies down next to me.

Demitri settles by my legs. "Bend, Meley."

I squeeze my eyes closed and bend at the knees, putting my feet flat on the bed, causing the sheet to tent. Demitri's invasion starts, and he sighs. I open my eyes to, "Meley, I need you to relax."

"Tall order," I snip back. "This isn't exactly a good time."

Zane gives Demitri a curious look.

"She tightens up," Demitri informs politely.

"Every time you do this, not only is it excruciating, but I feel like I'm going to crap the bed," I say defending myself.

Zane chuckles while he heads into the bathroom. We hear the sink run before he returns and stops by Demitri. "Shall I show you why?" he asks, amused.

Demitri stands, facing off with Zane defensively. "Planning to heal her, are ya?" he sarcastically asks.

"No," Zane retorts with a smirk. "It sounds like you could use a lesson though."

"Fine, what?" Demitri relents.

"Welcome to awkward town, party of three," Zane crows before smiling my way. "It's gonna get weird, but we're all going to act like this is normal. I've decided we're all okay with it." Before I know what's even happening, Zanes hand disappears under the sheet and secretly presents itself in a way that makes my eyes snap wide. Zane steers his condescending gaze Demitri's way. "You planning to join the voyage, Captain? Or are you going to spectate?"

Demitri rolls his eyes, and his hand disappears under the sheet. It's also found as I squeal. The guys ignore me as Zane does something that brings a spirited objection from me.

He asks me, "Is that what you feel when you say you're going to fog the bed?" I frantically nod, and Zane offers a demeaning smirk for Demitri's benefit. "That's the wall between her bowels and her lady parts, numb nuts." He smiles sweetly at me as his and Demitri's hands emerge from under the sheet. Zane heads back into the bathroom, while asking, "Melanie, do you feel like you have to use the restroom when you aren't being probed by Captain America's digits?"

"No," I reply meekly.

"Excellent," Zane says as he emerges from having washed his hands. "During labor, the reason most women announce that they're going to crap is because the baby's head puts pressure there." He gives Demitri a haughty look. "Is her injury there?"

"No," Demitri defensively replies.

"Then don't put pressure there," Zane condescends.

"That's a little hard to do," Demitri snarls back. He gestures my way. "She's tiny."

Zane smirks. "Quit packing her hand deep." At Demitri's flustered expression, Zane chuckles. "As you just learned, fingers suffice. You can get anywhere you need to that way."

"Easy for you to say," Demitri defends. "You weren't trying to heal her just then."

"Well," I mutter into the mix, "it was an improvement over Trey's wanderings, so whatever."

Zane gives me a look. "What the hell is wrong with your men?"

My face scrunches. "Considering that you're 'Rachelle hot water swimming,' you might want to can it."

"I'm trying to help here," Zane says defensively.

"Not all of us have explored every starlet in Hollywood." Demitri piles on, unwilling to let Zane's indiscretions gracefully pass.

"Oh, ewwwwww," grumbles from me.

Zane winces before glaring at Demitri. "Shut up, asshat."

Demitri shrugs. "Just pointing out that you gained your knowledge via hoeing."

"I don't want kids anymore," I spout while sitting up and reaching for my shorts. "I'm good."

Zane gives me a look. "Lie down. You want kids. I can teach Demitri about the intricacies. I assure you that I'm drawing from common sense. I have no hands-on knowledge."

"Liar," I accuse, but it lacks heart.

"I'm not new." Demitri defends himself. "Healing that mess is a little different than playing with it." He flips a hand toward my waist.

"Hey now," I bark, offended.

Zane shrugs. "Sounds like Trey's set the bar low. If you'll back that wrist up, you've got a shot at impressing our little squirrel."

"Oh ugh," I groan around an involuntary wince of disgust.

Zane and Demitri share a look, and I slam a fist down on the bed like a petulant toddler. "Trey's not bad at this." I defend him, not really wanting to, but here we are.

"Uh-huh," Zane placates, not believing me.

I flop back and thud my feet in the requested 'knees bent' position under the sheet. "Let's get this over with, Demitri. I want to watch cartoons."

Zane chuckles while he strides to my collection of VHS tapes. "*He-Man?*" he inquires my direction.

"*She-Ra,*" I request.

Zane grumbles, and Demitri snidely informs him, "She loves *She-Ra.* Her stepfather is an animator on that show."

I nod sweetly as Zane surveys me. "It's true. He worked on *He-Man* also. It's all right, I guess, but *She-Ra* is way better." I tip my head curiously. "Did you know, Zane, that I'm the one who suggested they add the circle to Orko's magician's robe?"

Zane chuckles. "I wasn't aware of that, Mighty Mouse."

I nod adorably. "It's true." My expression drops deadpan. "For the record, that little treat with your fingers does NOT COUNT!" Zane blinks his confusion my way, and I clarify, "I don't want that to be a first with us."

"So sweet," Zane says adoringly as he pops a VHS tape into the VCR.

"Excuse me!" Demitri blisters into the mix. "Nothing I've had to do counts either!"

"You've had to do a *lot,*" I remind him with a childish wince. "That's gonna be harder to ignore."

Demitri hits Zane with an icy glare. "Stuff your hand in her hee-hoo," he orders with a stern finger jab my direction.

Zane hits *play* and struts my way as the theme song of *She-Ra* starts on the TV. He pats my hip. "I would never hee-hoo you," smolders from him, earning my giggle in response. "Now," he guides as he lies down next to me and snuggles against my side, "watch the show, my girl."

Demitri grumbles and blusters while he takes the unfortunate spot by my knees again.

"Breathe, Melanie," Zane insists frantically. We've moved past the point that he can work with his thumb-whooshing trick on my forehead to relax me. We left that helpfulness in the dust ten minutes ago, and we're deep in the shit at this stage.

"Don't MOVE," Demitri bellows, as I involuntarily thrash.

Zane gets to his knees on the bed and holds my shoulders down.

"Talk to me, Zane," Demitri snarls through gritted teeth. "Is she okay?"

My psyche tornadoes, and I shriek.

"You can hear! Seriously?" Zane yells over my cacophony. "You've got one shot at this part, because she's not going to be willing again. Get whatever you're doing DONE!"

Zane thumps a knee over my side and straddles me. His arms bunch as he fights to hold me down.

I've experienced pain before, but this time it's so intense that all rationale is obliterated. I open my mouth to scream, but the most pitiful keening sound escapes instead. It hits an octave that shouldn't be humanly possible. I feel an energy detonation building that I can't stop. My eyes flutter open, revealing Zane's tear-streaked face. The intensity of his upset dissolves the building energy crisis, and my muscles all slump in unison as the energy detonation wooshes down through the bed, grounding out into the building's foundation. The foundation rumbles with earsplitting sound before shaking, deep and terrifying.

Zane lays his upper body down, encasing me, while he whispers frantically, "Good girl, Melanie. Breathe with me."

The ground quits shaking as the energy dissipates.

I inhale and exhale with the rise and fall of Zane's massive chest. My arms wrap around him, squeezing tight. It's not until I feel something oddly sticky on my fingertips that I realize my nails have punctured his skin. "So-r-r-y," I barely get out through chattering teeth.

"Whatever it takes," Zane pants through fear.

The searing pain ends suddenly, just as pressure is released. We hear a primal exhale from Demitri, and Zane looks over his shoulder. He shifts and turns to straddle my legs, facing away from me. I watch as his arms wrap around Demitri, who slumps into Zane's chest and sobs.

"You did good," Zane murmurs. "You're okay." Demitri continues sobbing as Zane looks over his shoulder. "Talk to me, Melanie."

"It's getting better," I pant out through massive breaths. "I just need a second."

Zane returns his attention to the sobbing heap that's collapsed against him. "Everyone take a moment and catch your breath," he coaches. He guides Demitri to lie on his side at the end of the bed. "Wait there, D," Zane says before scooting from the bed and hitting the *power* button to turn off the TV. Zane's head hangs for a moment before he takes a massive inhale. As his head rises, there's an authoritative sense in his expression. "Okay," he calmly guides, "we're okay. You both did good." He sits on the bed between Demitri and me, placing a hand on D's back and another on my hip. "I'm sorry I downplayed this. I had no idea what I was getting into. Ignorance was bliss, but very shortsighted of me."

Demitri manages to sit up as his tears slow, but his posture slouches exhaustedly. "I'm so sorry, Melanie."

"I'm okay," I assure him, but it comes out hollow.

Zane surveys me before taking my hand in his. My head lolls as I roll to my side. I wince as my gut burns.

Zane gestures for Demitri's right hand. His trembling hand is covered in blood as Demitri moves it closer.

"Okay," Zane mumbles. "All right," he adds through the shock, getting up and hurrying into the bathroom. He comes back with two wet washcloths, handing one to Demitri before moving to the opposite side of the bed. He tactfully reaches under the sheet, cleaning me up. "Have you done what you can today?" Zane asks Demitri as he makes his way back to the bathroom and returns without the gory washcloth.

"I'm burned out, but she's got an open internal wound I had to create," Demitri says. "I need to sleep for a few hours with her to refill my depleted energy store before I can finish that part."

"Is she going to bleed to death if you do that?" Zane asks.

Demitri shakes his head lethargically. "The bleeding isn't life-threatening."

"Let's get things situated, then," Zane guides. He helps Demitri up and settles him into my armchair I like to read in, before crossing to the bed and scooping me up, careful to keep the sheet over me. A quick cross to Demitri and then Zane bends and carefully sets me, cradled, in D's lap.

"What are you doing?" I ask, as Zane moves back to the vacated bed.

"Getting the sheets changed, and the bed prepped." Zane slides distraught eyes my way. "You don't want Trey to know, and the bloody sheets are a big hint."

Grateful, I sag against Demitri, while saying, "Thank you, Zane."

"You're welcome," he mumbles back while he efficiently pulls the bedding, tossing it in a heap. He makes quick work of retrieving a fresh set of linens from the bathroom cabinet and remaking the bed. Medical pads, leftover from the miscarriage mayhem, are spread in the center of the bed before I'm scooped up from D's lap and carefully deposited on the bed again. Zane makes his way across the room and scoops up Demitri in the same fashion, as if the massive guy weighs nothing. Demitri is so out of sorts that he doesn't fight the help. He's deposited next to me, and we roll to our sides with me wrapped around his back.

"Didn't expect that," Zane remarks about our chosen position.

Demitri melts down cataclysmically as I grip him protectively from behind.

"It's okay," I softly say as I hold on tight.

"It kills me to hurt you, but it's the only solution," Demitri barely manages through a horrific bout of tears.

"I know," I assure him. "You would never do this if there were another way."

Zane sits on the bed behind me and rubs my back while I hold on to Demitri. It takes a long while before Demitri slumps into an exhausted deep sleep.

When he's out, Zane gathers me into his lap. He rubs the back of my head, requesting, "I need to be here when he does this, Melanie. It's going to take all of us."

"It's so bad," I whisper.

"I know," Zane whispers back. "You're doing good through it, but if it's too much, I'll counsel you through not having kids this lifetime. We'll . . ." Zane trails off, before correcting himself. "You'll come to terms with it."

I swallow hard, choosing to ignore his "we" slip because I flat don't have the mental space to grasp what it means. "Thank you for helping me," I whimper.

"Thank you for trusting me with this," he replies. He doesn't let me go until my crying is relieved by exhaustion that takes over.

I'm unaware that I even slip into a deep sleep.

CHAPTER 41

My phone rings, and I glance toward it. I'm not in the mood. This morning was a new level of horrendous, and I'm still in shock. We're three days into my "healing." While we're making progress, I've screamed myself hoarse through it, and I hurt. Considering that Zane didn't show up for this morning's healing round, it was considerably more traumatizing, and I was left reeling.

I answer, and am bowled over by Zane's anger.

"How fucking DARE you!" he rages.

"What's wrong?" blathers from me, stunned. Zane's never talked to me like this.

"You were staying in a hospital with me just five days ago!" Zane blisters. "I watched you murder in cold blood and still stuck by you!" Zane takes a gasping breath and plows on before I can say anything. "You're a conniving, backstabbing, HARLOT!"

My eyes fill with tears, and my heart races.

"Don't EVER come to me for anything again!" Zane screams before hanging up.

I'm left staring at the phone with zero clue what to think. I sink to the Victorian love seat. My face lands in my hands. "What did I do?" I whimper. I rack my brain, finding nothing.

"Melanie, can we speak to you?" Mama Mabel asks as she crosses the parlor with Trey.

Trey holds a hand my way, and I stare at it. My cheeks are coated with tears.

"What's wrong?" Mabel inquires.

"Zane's mad at me. I don't know why." I fitfully inhale.

Mama Mabel has a glint in her eyes. "We're not going to worry about that right now."

Apparently, the fact that I'm very worried about that makes no difference.

"Have I ever told you that I'm a pagan priestess?" she asks with a mischievous tone.

"You haven't," I whisper, wanting nothing to do with this conversation.

Mama turns to Trey. "Shall we?" she asks.

Trey takes my hand and leads me to our room. He pushes open the door, revealing a smiling Tanner and Finley. Their expressions slide with concern as they take in my emotional turmoil and tearstained face.

"Tell her," encourages Mama Mabel.

Trey looks down at me, saying, "Hi," nervously.

I raise my eyebrows, still unsettled and having a difficult time making the shift to whatever this is. "Hi, Trey."

Trey looks at Mama Mabel. "*How* does she still make me nervous?"

"Because she matters to you." Mama Mabel chuckles.

"Trey, whatever it is, it needs to wait. I'm in the middle of a meltdown." My head sags.

Tanner and Finley exchange a pensive look.

Mabel waves her hands about to clear the air. "We have a surprise," she says and gives me a mysterious look. "It's a ritual. You'll love it."

I scrunch my face and hesitantly reply, "Okay."

"Finley's going to get you ready," Mama Mabel informs me and scoots Trey and Tanner out the door without so much as a backward glance.

Finley and I stare at my reflection in the mirror. Apparently, Trey had a custom dress made for me with spaghetti straps and a dangerously draping chest line. The white satin fabric hugs my sides. My entire back is exposed, and I fight not to hunch. I feel blazingly vulnerable. The dress flows long with a little bit of a train that drapes on the floor and a slit up to my hip on my right side. The entire dress is covered in sparkly little clear gemstones, spaced just enough apart to pick up the light and give some shine. It's racy and suggestive, and I'm beyond uncomfortable being this exposed.

"You look beautiful," Finley encourages me.

Tanner opens the door and slips in, closing it behind him. He turns, and his mouth drops open. "You look like magic embodied, Melanie," he exclaims.

I blush a touch from the compliment. "No, I don't," I whisper. "Why did Trey have a weird fairy-hooker pageant dress made for me?"

Finley and Tanner exchange unsure looks.

"The sparkles are so pretty," Finley encourages.

"What is this about?" I ask. I shake my head. "I don't want to do some ritual. We've done all the rituals I can stomach. Will one of you please go tell Trey no to whatever this is."

"Oh dear," Finley says, flustered.

Tanner crosses to me and plunks me down in the dining chair. He spreads out all sorts of compacts and tubes on my little dining table, before rapidly getting to work on my makeup and hair. "You're going to love it," he assures me. "You need a fun night. It'll be fine."

I want to run as Tanner puts dark-red lipstick on me.

"You ready?" he asks after a scrutinizing look-over of his glam handywork.

My eyes glaze with shock, but he pays my mental state no mind as he hoists me up, and we start a trek to the banquet hall. Mama Mabel stands in the hall by the double doors. We stop, and Mama nods at Finley. Finley goes into the banquet room and comes out with my parents.

I turn stunned eyes Mama Mabel's way as my heart pounds.

"I've filled in your parents," she informs me. "They got back into town two hours ago."

"You're doing this in the hall?" I gasp.

My cyclonic jumble of emotions tears through my connection blockage with Trey, and he's watching all of it unfold with his mouth hanging open. My terror and mortification are on full display.

I hear through his ears. "Shit! Mabel just blindsided Melanie with her parents in the hall," he says. "I planned to talk to her parents about her getting pregnant right after the ceremony so that Melanie wasn't on the front lines."

Trey frantically fuzzes me out.

My mom and Rich hug me.

"Before you lose it, Mabel worked us through our initial shock at the news," my mom says, "and our anger that you got pregnant, and heartbreak about everything that happened. We're not upset."

"Thank you. I'm glad you made it home safe." It takes everything I have to talk about this right now.

"Are you okay?" my mom asks me.

"I am," I lie. "Mama Mabel and Demitri handled the worst of it. Tanner, Arch, Zane, and Finley also helped get me through it."

"Thank you for helping her," my mom tells Finley.

Finley nods and hugs Mom.

"Why don't you make your way inside?" Mama Mabel suggests. "We'll be there shortly."

Mom, Rich, and Finley scoot through the door, leaving Mama Mabel and me in the hall.

I tip my head back, exhaling. "I wasn't ready for that conversation," I tell her. "I needed Trey with me. I had a whole plan on how I was going to talk to them about this."

"I'm sorry, Melanie." Mama Mabel sighs. "I didn't think about that. I should have asked you."

"Is there a reason Trey just threw me to the wolves with my parents?" I ask her desperately. "There's no excuse for him to make me handle that discussion alone."

I feel dismay rip through our connection, and hear through Trey as he tells Adam and Demitri what I just said.

"Honestly," Demitri says, "I couldn't figure out why you were just standing here instead of rushing out there to talk to them."

"Because I'm not supposed to see her."

Adam's mouth drops open. "The sixteen-year-old mother of your dead child just had to face her parents, and you stood here like a gutless moron because of a superstition?"

Trey fuzzes me out again.

"What is going on?" I demand of Mabel as dread bubbles in me.

Mabel ignores my question and gives me an anticipatory grin instead. She pulls the door open with a sweep of her arm. I take a deep breath while I walk in. Haunting classical music wafts through the open door. I round the corner and pass under draped white fabric arches with white, twinkling lights. Smoke wafts, blocking the view.

I step through the smoke into Mama Mabel's banquet hall, that's completely transformed into a gaudy wonderland. Wafting fog floats as I survey white fabric draped everywhere with shimmering lights coating the ceiling. Sounds good, right? It's not. The display is beyond tacky with abundance.

White and burgundy stargazer lilies in huge silver bouquet stands grace the room, their heady aroma filling the air. My heart clenches at the reminder of Pierre and my villa that was full of these flowers. That scent always reminds me of him, and I avoid it because it hurts.

I slowly try to back up. Mabel puts a hand between my shoulders and guides me to the center of the huge, crowded room. I fight not to cry because I'm so uncomfortable with the scrutiny.

Mama Mabel crosses the room to Trey as I scan the faces of all my Hellcat friends, my parents, Mr. Isley, and all the Hellhounds. A lot of people brought dates with them, whom I don't know. Panic rips through me.

I whip around and survey who's behind me, uncomfortable having people at my back while I'm this vulnerable. Everyone watches my reaction, unsure what's happening.

"You're okay, Melanie," Big Joe says. "I've already checked, and everyone here is safe."

I swallow hard as my gaze lands on Rocco, Brian, Ms. Alice, and Zane's mom. They all look pissed.

"What is happening?" I gasp at Zane's mom. My eyes plead. and her expression morphs from pissed to stunned.

"Does she not know?" Cindy demands of Trey.

"It's a surprise," Trey replies.

"Oh my God," Cindy mumbles while we stare at each other. She looks to Rocco.

"Wait, she doesn't know this is happening?" my stepfather bellows.

"Oh no," Mr. Cantrell mutters.

Trey smiles at me softly. He's wearing a black dress shirt and black slacks.

I swallow hard and send through our connection, *"Hi."*

"Hi, love. That dress is everything." He studies my expression, seeming elatedly oblivious to my discontent.

I lock eyes with Rocco again as my head spins. I blink, trying not to pass out while he stares at me, horrified by my expression.

"Moment of truth," Tanner interrupts. "Before we get down to business, everyone in the room has serious money on the line. Now it's time to play . . ." He pauses dramatically, and like a game show announcer, crows, "Melanie, can you name this song?"

I rattle my head, trying to wrap my mind around this turn of events. It's a good distraction though, and I decide to play along. "Trying to stump me, huh?" I tease.

"You're doing this NOW?" Trey hisses.

Tanner ignores him, looking at me mischievously.

I take a deep breath, switching into performance mode, and hold my hands out to my sides with a flourish. "Drumroll please!" I request. Everyone drums on their legs, and I dramatically announce, *"Lux Aeterna* by Gyorgy Ligeti."

Tanner looks shocked. "HOW do you know that?"

I raise an eyebrow at Tanner. "I played Titania in a TERRIBLE dance version of *Midsummer Night's Dream*," I share. "Guess what song my dramatic forest solo was to? The choreographer screamed maniacally at me every time this song played. I swore I'd never listen to it again when that production ended."

"Damn it. I lost the bet," Tanner says. "I'm sorry, Melanie. I picked the song." Tanner sweeps his arm Mama Mabel's way. "Without further ado."

Mama Mabel raises an eyebrow, torn between amusement and irritation. "Well! Thank you, Tanner," Mabel says and smiles at me. "Please join Trey for our ritual."

I flick my eyes to a random woman I've never seen. I send to Trey, *"Who is that?"*

Trey subtly glances her way. *"No clue. She's Stubbs's date."*

"Is there a reason that Stubbs is here? I don't do rituals in front of just anyone."

"This one you will," Trey assures me.

"What is this about?"

"We're getting married," Trey sends with a huge smile.

My stomach nearly heaves as panic boils.

I snarl, "WHAT?" in disbelief.

Trey's eyes widen. It's more than obvious that I don't want to do this.

"All our friends are here." Trey gives me a hopeful look, but it's edged with desperation.

I tip my head pointedly. *"I don't share my special with everyone I've ever met."*

"I'm sorry, Melanie. I definitely got this part wrong."

I nod. *"Very much so. If you'd like a wedding, I recommend that you ask Victoria, at the very least, to leave."*

Trey's head hangs dejectedly. *"I can't do that, Melanie. Tori worked her ass off decorating this place. She volunteered to be Mabel's right hand and outdid herself."*

I smirk. *"Well, that explains why it's so tacky in here."* Trey's expression falls, but he chose to bulldoze me with this, and honesty is all I have to offer. *"This is horrendous."*

Trey glances around the massive room. "*It's a lot, I guess.*" He gives me a searching look, but his next thought is interrupted.

"What's happening?" someone asks.

I look to the invading voice, and it's the woman I don't know. Stubbs shushes her, explaining, "They can speak mind-to-mind. They're chatting about something."

The woman looks at him like he's crazy. "They can WHAT?"

"Don't EVER reveal my personal business to some random again," I bark at Stubbs.

His eyes widen.

I look to the woman. "Get out!"

"Melanie, please!" Stubbs protests. He looks like he wants to fall through the floor. "I'm so sorry."

I hit Trey with a deadpan expression. "*You invited people to our WEDDING that don't even know about our soulmate connection? What the hell is wrong with you, Trey? Start marching people out the door, please.*"

Trey gives Stubbs a look.

Stubbs winces.

Trey's gaze settles back on me. "*I apologize, Melanie. I know it's a lot to ask, but will you please make it through this, as is? Everyone's been really excited.*"

"*How nice that everyone but me got to anticipate excitedly.*"

Trey appears baffled. "*I thought you'd love this.*"

"*Not even remotely.*"

Mabel starts to speak, and Trey holds up a hand. "We need a minute," he says aloud. "*Get it out on the table. Be honest,*" he sends through our connection.

"*The time for my opinion has passed. I'm wearing what you want, in a room full of people you invited. I walked through the door. That's all I was supposed to do, right? Show up?*"

Trey side-eyes Mama Mabel.

"Shit," Mama Mabel murmurs.

"Here we go," Adam says simultaneously.

Trey sends, *"Are you nervous? The only thing that makes me nervous is whether we're going to survive this ceremony. The Reapers are trying to kill us, and I'm waiting for disaster to strike. That's why I agreed to have everyone here. I initially wanted just us, I swear to you."*

I narrow my eyes. *"Am I nervous? I'm TERRIFIED. I didn't get to experience the butterfly flutters and nervous wedding jitters. I'm sorry, but can we please turn off this song? It gives me raging anxiety."*

"Dante, can you fade this out?" Trey asks.

The music fades, and Trey turns back to me. *"Continue, Melanie."*

"I have a massive meltdown looming, and that's what I needed to handle tonight."

His mouth drops open. *"I wanted to give you some fun, so you DIDN'T have to deal with grief."*

Knowing that I need help, I survey the crowd. "Where is my dad?" I ask. "I'd like a minute with him."

"Rich is here," Trey says.

I give him a pointed look. "I appreciate that."

Trey seems baffled, and Demitri clears his throat. Trey glances his way.

"I believe she's referring to her biological father, who lives in Texas," Demitri says.

Victoria looks up at Demitri with wide eyes and then at me. Even she seems to understand the issue, and I've met potatoes with more savvy than Victoria. Trey looks like he just got smacked.

"Melanie, I'm sorry," Trey says. "I didn't even think about that."

I put my face in my hands, trying to curb the massive meltdown that roars up. *I don't want to get married without my dad!*

I hear footsteps, and Demitri's arms wrap around me. He puts his hands flat on my back and sends a calm wave into me. He takes a deep slow breath, and I breathe with him. We exhale together.

"This is a five-alarm disaster," Demitri mumbles.

My desperate, wide-eyed gaze slides up to meet Demitri's.

"If you need out, all you have to do is walk over to me, and we'll leave," he tells me.

I nod, and Demitri crosses to his spot by his dad.

I turn back to Trey. *"Face Mama Mabel, and let's get this nightmare over with. Everyone is watching me melt down, and the mood is turning tense. They want the big party they've been promised, after all."*

Trey shakes his head frantically. *"I want you to be happy at our wedding."* He glances around, flummoxed, before looking at me again. *"I wanted you to have a princess moment."*

I look down at my dress. *"This is what princesses wear?"*

Trey swallows hard while he surveys the dress. "Give me a minute, love," he requests. He points at Demitri and Adam. "I need to speak to you, and you."

"The wedding will be in an hour," Mama Mabel boisterously announces to the crowd. "Champagne and hors d'oeuvres are being served. Make yourselves at home."

Everyone exhales but me.

The staff breeze in with silver trays of champagne glasses and finger foods, as party music suddenly bounces happily through the speakers.

Trey crosses the banquet hall and heads into the catering kitchen. Adam and Demitri follow and close the door after them. Trey's left our connection open, and I hover in the back of his mind, subtly eavesdropping.

People start rushing my way, excited, and Mama Mabel distracts them politely.

I look at Demitri's dad, desperately.

He crosses to me.

"Will you get me somewhere where I can get my head on straight?" I ask quietly. My gaze snaps to Cindy, and she rushes my way.

"Of course," Mr. Cantrell replies. He puts his hand on my back, guiding me to the skate rental booth. We slide behind the counter. Mabel follows and watches me pensively.

I find my parents as I scan the crowd, but Rich is occupied with my mother, who is crying in the far corner.

"Shit," I mutter. "Mabel, my mother is having a meltdown at this surprise wedding from hell."

Mabel rushes that way.

I cross my arms uncomfortably over my skimpily covered chest and listen through Trey's ears and see through his eyes as the guys debate in the catering kitchen.

Trey points at Adam first. "Tell me where I went wrong."

"You literally didn't do anything right. This whole situation is the opposite of what she'd want."

"Do you agree with Adam?" Trey asks Demitri.

"Yes."

"Why didn't you tell me?"

Demitri exhales hard. "Because I severely overstepped when I invaded Melanie's beach party," he explains. "I promised her I wouldn't do that again. I hope you don't plan for her to profess her innermost feelings in front of everyone."

"Why?" Trey asks. "That's what this whole ceremony is."

"Do you know her at all?" Adam snaps.

Trey looks confused, and Adam and Demitri side-eye each other.

"She hates the dress. She almost cried," Tanner reveals as he slips into the catering kitchen to join them.

"What the hell do you suggest?" Trey asks.

"You have your wedding your way, because this certainly isn't Melanie's way," Demitri says.

"What's her wedding, her way?"

"Private," Adam answers.

"Casual," Demitri offers.

"No stress," Adam says.

"Where she feels like she's a part of things, instead of a prop in a play," Demitri adds and levels Trey with a narrow-eyed look.

"That's the opposite of how I wanted her to feel," Trey insists. "I thought she would feel special because she was surprised."

"If her opinion mattered, you would have asked it," Adam says. "It makes no difference that she just lost a baby. It makes no difference that you weren't there for a private discussion with her parents about the miscarriage. It makes no difference that her mom didn't get to go wedding-dress shopping with her. Did any of that occur to you?"

Trey gives him an overwhelmed and unresponsive blank stare.

Adam points to Demitri. "She literally clings to Demitri in her sleep. I came in to check on her with Mama Mabel, and she was latched onto him like he was the last lifeline to sanity, when you went to school, and he decided to ditch to sleep in with her."

"Did it bother you?" Trey asks.

"THAT'S your question?" Adam shouts like Trey is nuts.

"No, Trey, it didn't bother me," Demitri replies. "What bothered me was that she is only calm in her sleep when she is wrapped around me, or Zane. I find that to be telling."

"I appreciate you being there for her."

"What the hell!" Adam huffs before switching tactics. "Why did you rush this?"

"I rarely have a free night. I scheduled it when I could."

"When did you propose to her?" Demitri asks.

Trey's mouth opens and closes. "She has the promise ring," he manages to say.

"You didn't ask her to marry you?" Adam breathes through shock.

Trey closes his eyes tight and looks like he's going to be sick. "We've seen that proposal in one of her intuition pulses, but I forgot. It was supposed to be on Mulholland." He looks at Demitri and Adam, aghast.

"Who forgets to PROPOSE?" Tanner screeches. "Holy tacos and turkeys covered in tabasco!"

I close my line with Trey, not needing to hear any more. I swallow hard and open my eyes. "I need to show you what just happened," I quietly inform. "I don't want my mom and Rich involved in this humiliating mess, though."

Mama Mabel winces. "Well, they're currently holed up in my office. Rich is calming your mom down."

"Is she okay?" I ask.

Mabel purses her lips and looks down at the floor. "She's upset that she didn't get to plan all of this with you. Full disclosure, she feels like I took over the mom duties with you, and she's not taking kindly to that scenario. It wasn't my intention. This was Trey's thing, and I realistically just offered a location and let him run wild."

"He's certainly doing that." I offer my arm. Mr. Cantrell, Cindy, and Mabel latch on. I send the memory, and sink to my haunches, hiding behind the skate counter while they watch.

I feel blindsided and betrayed that Trey chose to spring this wedding on me instead of taking the time to talk through our incredibly complicated issues. My eyes squeeze shut, and my breathing hitches. I hear Cindy's voice.

"Honey, she didn't know," she says into her phone. "She's crouched in a slutty dress, hiding behind a roller skate counter."

"What?" Zane screams so loud that I catch it even though the call isn't on speaker.

"Trey decided to surprise her. They weren't even engaged," Cindy says. Cindy scans the banquet hall with horrified eyes. "I think you need to come down here." She listens again before squeezing her eyes closed. She hangs up and rushes away. I stand, watching as she gets to Rocco and Brian and drags them to the far corner.

Mr. Cantrell turns stunned eyes on Mabel. "How could you allow this surprise handfasting with Melanie's reservations and concerns?"

Mabel blinks rapidly, and Mr. Cantrell's eyes further widen. He slides that gaze to me. "Demitri filled me in," he says. "Has anyone counseled you through Trey's dismissiveness for months?" I shake my head, and Mr. Cantrell's breath catches. "Your parents were gone, according to Demitri. Has anyone helped you through losing the baby, or your surgery?"

I fight tears and shake my head desperately.

"What the hell is wrong with you?" Mr. Cantrell hisses at Mabel, furious. "A sixteen-year-old girl just went through pregnancy, a biker gang attack, a HORRIFIC miscarriage, slaughtering her attacker. . ." It takes Mr. Cantrell a moment to still his spinning emotions that we can clearly feel. Finally, he takes up the thread again. "Add to it the confusion of her original soulmate having twins with a woman who threatened her." He scoffs. "And the Demitri and Zane pressure on top of it. . ." The look he levels Mabel with could melt steel.

"Are you okay?" Mabel asks me as realization about how much she's overlooked starts to dawn.

I close my eyes and try to rally. "I appreciate everything you've done, Mabel," I say. "Thank you. I just need a minute." My tone betrays my fear.

"Cut the crap, Melanie," Mabel gently says. "You don't want to do this, do you?"

"No. I don't want to marry Trey. I apologize for the drama."

"I'm the one who needs to apologize," Mabel says. "I should have talked to you. The only reason I didn't was that Trey wanted to surprise you."

"You should have talked to her about a lot more than this ridiculous ceremony," Mr. Cantrell accuses.

"Shit," Mabel expresses vibrantly.

I turn to Mr. Cantrell. "I apologize that you're hearing all of this," I tell him. "I didn't expect things to go this direction."

"It's okay, Melanie. I worked Demitri through what he had to do, and I'm incredibly sorry that you lost the baby." Mr. Cantrell takes a grounding breath. "I'd like to get you out of here and talk to you for as long as you need."

Cindy rushes back around the skate counter and grabs my arms, interrupting.

"I know Zane called you screaming. He thought you hid this," she insistently informs me.

"Hid this?" I whimper. "I've been so busy trying to process losing the baby, all by myself, that I haven't masterminded a WEDDING!"

"I found time to talk to Demitri and Trey, but I never followed up with Melanie," Mabel mutters. "Damn it. Melanie, I'm so sorry."

My expression falls and I radiate desperation. "I'm being hunted by the Reapers. Demitri is doing healing rounds on me because of the damage. I . . . ," I sputter. It takes me a moment to gather my mind. Finally, I give Mabel a pointed look. "When the day comes that I get my head on straight, I'm going to dump gasoline on my life and light that shit up. Be ready. It'll be a doozie."

I turn to walk away, and Finley, Presley, Trey, Adam, and Demitri are standing there.

Adam smiles leeringly at Demitri. "Congratulations in advance for being the Phoenix who rises from a gasoline fire."

"Last time I checked," Demitri replies, "I'm dating Victoria."

"Get your head out of your ass, son," Mr. Cantrell scolds.

Adam cracks up. "Victoria!" wheezes from him, making Demitri kind of deflate. It really is ridiculous. She's such a waste.

I wince at the exchange. Mr. Cantrell has harped on D to date me for a long time. It's awkward, but not nearly as awkward as Trey already knowing this and saying NOTHING in this moment.

Adam looks at Trey, who's staring at me, totally oblivious to everything that's clear to be garnered.

"Nope," Adam says. "Still nothing."

I slide huge eyes to Demitri, who puts an arm around me, pulling me into a hug.

"I think you should marry all of them and let these jackasses have a duel in the parking lot while we eat wedding cake and cheer on their deaths." Presley smirks.

"Damn, this is awful," our usually sweet Finley says as she scans the room.

"It looks like the cast of *Footloose* had a rich benefactor and decided to really go for it," I marvel in horror.

Mabel cringes slightly as she surveys the space. "It really is a lot," she says. "The dress though? It's beautiful."

My eyes widen before my gaze slides down. I grimace. "I guess braless bride is a thing?"

"This is the kind of trash Victoria would wear," Presley snorts, giving my dress a snide look over.

Demitri's dad covers his mouth while he laughs. Demitri coughs awkwardly.

"No offense," Presley adds for Demitri's benefit.

"None taken. It's the first thing I thought when I saw Melanie in the dress," Demitri admits. He grimaces as his eyes slide around the room. "And when I walked in here."

Mama Mabel's mouth purses tight as she really studies the dress.

"Melanie is always in sports bras, Trey," Demitri reminds him. "Generally padded ones because she feels weird when stuff shows."

"I love her in stuff like this." Trey sighs.

I blush crimson.

"Every guy here can see why you like her in this stuff, Trey," Demitri's dad scolds.

Presley points at Demitri's dad. "Precisely," she states.

"How about I hand you back this dress, and you can stuff Victoria's knockers in it and marry her?" I say sarcastically to Trey. "That'd solve all my problems."

Trey looks shell-shocked.

"Wait, wait, wait," Adam jovially interrupts and turns to Demitri. "What would Melanie prefer to wear?"

"She'd prefer something ladylike and pretty," Demitri lectures. "She wouldn't choose something sexy."

"Why does every guy know your fiancée better than you?" Adam says to Trey, grinning like a nut.

"I'm not his fiancée," I remind.

Trey groans while Cindy gives him a disgusted look.

"I like the slit up to your hip," Finley suggests. "You wear it well. The little dance shorts were a good choice, though, because the slit gapes when you walk, and that ass of yours is playing peek-a-boo with every step." She turns to address Trey. "It's an interesting choice, given what she's been through. Way to get her back out there, though."

I give up on trying to cover my unmentionables. I flex, cracking my spine. "Thank you, Fin," I say. I give Trey a disgusted look. "This isn't who I am when I'm vulnerable and putting my heart on the line. Might I remind you that my stepfather, my ex-boyfriend, my AGENT, and Demitri are here. None of them need to see me look like this at my wedding."

"I'm great with you looking like a tramp," Adam interjects. "Boing! Turkeys are done. It really is cold in here." Everyone but me tries not to laugh as Adam juts his thumb Demitri's way. "It's Peter Pan that's likely bothered by it."

"Why is he here?" I demand of Trey while gesturing at Adam.

"I wanted to watch Ace crash and burn," Adam tactlessly says and looks to Trey. "This room smells like a French perfumery with all those stargazers. Has she shown you the album of her and Pierre's Hawaii trip?"

Trey nods, appearing baffled by why it's relevant.

"Have at it," Adam says pointing to Demitri.

"The whole villa was covered in these flowers when she was in Hawaii," Demitri explains, giving Trey a fed-up expression. "It was a big, girly moment for Melanie when Pierre surprised her with them. After he died, the scent hit her when she walked back in the villa to get her stuff. She attributes that smell to losing the love of her life. You filled her wedding with death, Trey."

Trey clears his throat, uncomfortable. "What would you have chosen?" he asks.

Demitri closes his eyes, his jaw tight. After a moment he opens his eyes. "I wouldn't have chosen flowers at all," he responds. "I would have married her on the beach with only our core people there. Flip-flops. Simple sundress. Bra of her choice. Sunshine. No pressure."

I roll my eyes while my heart secretly explodes. Of course, Demitri gave the perfect answer. Presley snickers. Demitri's expression strains around the edges while he slides off his suit jacket and drapes it over my shoulders. I close my eyes. It's warm and smells like Demitri's cologne. I draw the jacket closed around me, and my head drops.

"Thank you," I whisper.

"You're welcome," Demitri murmurs.

"It's a clue, Trey!" Adam crows while gesturing vibrantly at Demitri. "Why does Demitri know better than you do what Melanie needs?" Adam goads.

Trey just looks kind of dense.

"If she needs to, she can move in with us," Mr. Cantrell informs Demitri.

Everyone's eyes snap wide.

"You'd actually be okay with that situation, wouldn't you?" Adam asks, cracking up and gesturing to Demitri and me. He flourishes his hand comically to the fancy banquet hall.

"Absolutely. I'm expecting it," Mr. Cantrell replies.

Cindy squeezes her eyes closed. She's clearly expecting it also, but with her son. "Leave with me right now," she encourages me. "Zane will have an engagement ring within a day, I swear to you."

My head spins.

"I give you credit, Mel," Presley says. "They line the hell up for you."

"I know EXACTLY how to fix this. We can have an affair, and Trey will bail," Adam suggests and smiles at me exuberantly. "We're great in the sack. It'll be awesome!" He snaps his head to Demitri. "That okay with you, Peter Pan? I don't want to keep her. Just think of me as a ferry that she rides from one island to another."

"Adam is a good time," Presley jokingly says.

"That he is," Finley agrees.

Adam scrunches us up in his arms comically. "Aw, that's so sweet! We made some memories, huh, gals?"

Demitri's dad looks at all of us like we're nuts, Cindy appears thunderstruck, and Mama Mabel snorts laughter.

"We're like a bunch of hamsters, crawling all over each other and shitting everywhere," I inform the elders while rolling my eyes. I turn to Adam. "Thank you for that creative solution. I'm gonna pass."

"Just trying to do my civic duty," Adam remarks with a shrug. "You're always saying we must use our superpowers for good instead of evil."

Trey turns scathing eyes on Adam. "Can you not hit on my fiancée right now?"

"I'm not your fiancée!" I intensely hiss under my breath. "Also, YOU invited him to our magical public expression of love. This is on *you*!"

"Cut me some slack," Adam huffs. "I'm married and miserable." Adam gives Trey a pointed look. "It's a good time, let me tell ya. Besides, *I'm* not still in love with her." He looks amusedly to Demitri, but Trey doesn't take the hint. Adam wobbles his head about. "Eh. That's a lie. I'm still in love with her." He grins at me. "Wanna head to Vegas to get hitched?"

"You're already married, dumb shit," Demitri snarls.

I put my head in my hands. "My life is a circus."

"What do you need right now?" Trey asks me.

"What I need makes no difference because I get none of those things from you, lately."

Everyone sharply inhales.

"There it is," Mr. Cantrell encourages. "Finish the thought,

Melanie. This is the time." He side-eyes Adam. "Unless you want to hop on the sexy-time express for a ride from Oblivious-Ville to Dreamland."

I shake my head, still staring at Trey.

"Melanie, look at me," Mr. Cantrell says with a serious tone.

I shift scared eyes his way and swallow hard.

"You are the silliest, giggliest little critter I've ever met. Every time you come to my house, you and Demitri spend the whole time laughing until you cry. My metaphysical abilities specialize in emotions. How you're feeling right now scares me. I thought you were usually a happy, bouncy, teenager who drinks Cactus Coolers and says 'boing' when you hop off my front steps. I showed up tonight and watched a pensive, caged woman fight to be heard. You can't live like this. It's obvious that you didn't want to get pregnant, Melanie. You also clearly don't want what we're all standing in this damn banquet hall for. You need to be brave enough to spill it."

When I say nothing, Mr. Cantrell viciously turns on Demitri. "You need to haul Melanie out of here! I can't take this. She doesn't want to do this, and from everything I've heard, TREY," he stabs a finger Trey's direction, "is a dismissive, oblivious, dangerous DISASTER!"

"I can't," Demitri breathes, blasting out a wave of fear about losing me to this wedding, fear in general about my relationship with Trey, and monumental unresolved emotions about what he had to do to save me from the miscarriage. Trey, Adam, Mr. Cantrell, Mabel, and I can clearly feel what he's exuding.

"BIG clue? Yes?" Adam jabs at Trey, who stares at him blankly. "Wow," he marvels at Trey's obliviousness.

"You're enjoying this entirely too much," I admonish Adam with a glare. I turn my attention back to Mr. Cantrell. "I'm a beacon for evil," I confess. "I know you think I should walk away from this mess, but it's not that simple. I'm always being attacked. I need Trey to keep me alive. Demitri is my happy zone where I get to actually be me. He doesn't stop the evil, though. I need Demitri and Zane to keep me sane. I must choose being alive because being happy makes no difference if I'm dead. This isn't a simple matter of who makes me smile. The fact that Trey and I don't work right now is irrelevant."

"Melanie! You're still friends with Demitri. Us getting married has nothing to do with that," Trey says and wobbles his head. "I'm glad Zane's gone though."

Everyone looks at Trey like he's nuts.

"Holy shit, Trey. Are you really not understanding what's happening?" Presley asks.

"She's talking like things are going to change with her and D," Trey says. "That's not going to happen. I've never asked that of her."

"I love my life," Adam mutters. He bobbles his head at Trey. "Yo, numb nuts! Melanie feels trapped and ambushed. She wants to haul ass out of here, change into sweatpants and a hoodie, and cry herself sick with either Demitri or Zane. Zane isn't here. I think Demitri wins."

"Kick ass," Demitri snarks. "I'm the runner-up at the wedding."

Cindy pulls out her phone, hitting redial. "You need to get here," she hisses into the phone. She wanders to the corner. Her tone is lecturing, but I pay it no mind.

I lean on the counter, hunkering around my collapsing lungs. Demitri's jacket falls from my shoulders to the floor.

"Your boobs are falling out of your lingerie dress, Mel," Adam informs me. "Stand up straight and be distraught."

"All right," Trey sighs. "The dress is too revealing. I apologize, Melanie."

Cindy rushes back into the mix. "Come home with me," she demands. "Zane can't get here. He drowned himself in a bottle of tequila. He'll sober up and marry you."

"I don't want to marry *anyone!*" I toss my hands, my mind a swirling mess. "I guess if I have to pick . . ." I look at Demitri before looking to Cindy. "Well, Demitri doesn't want me, because he likes tacky sleazoids. Zane's drunk and doesn't approve of me dicing assholes to death with a katana."

"*Why* do you have to pick one?" Presley asks, baffled.

"There's a wedding, Presley," I reply sarcastically, waving my arms about.

Mr. Cantrell takes me by the shoulders. "I will personally walk you out the door and buckle you into my son's car. Then I'll come back in here and deal with any fallout."

"You're not leaving here with Demitri," Cindy insists. "You leave with me, and we sober up my drunk son."

Everyone looks at her like she's nuts.

Cindy sighs.

"Keep locking me into desperate situations," I challenge Trey. "Keep shoving me further and further over the edge. I dare you. At this point, I hope evil takes me out, because I can't keep doing this, but I'm trapped."

"She can't bring herself to do what she needs too. You need to do it. Can you love her enough to do that?" Mr. Cantrell questions Trey.

"What do I need to do?" Trey asks.

Mr. Cantrell sputters before hissing menacingly, "You two need to be done, Trey! This is madness! You and Melanie have had nothing but problems. She can't seem to leave, and you can't seem to live in reality long enough to get it! She's not property! I'm flat—"

"Enough!" Demitri booms, interrupting. He slides fierce eyes my way. "Trey wants you, and I think you should give him *all* of you."

Suddenly, I know what to do. I close my eyes, gathering and grounding out my rogue fear and desperation. I smile and it turns into a weighted laugh as I peer at Trey through my lashes. "All of me is now *yours*," I coo with a bounce and flutter. "I don't want to melt down after the wedding any more. I want to watch *Fraggle Rock*! I'm so excited that you got me four seasons of it. Let's lounge around in bed all day tomorrow and watch it while we color."

Demitri laughs.

"That's your best-friend gig," Trey says, turning to Demitiri with huge eyes.

"Nope," replies Demitri as he scrunches up his mouth, amused.

Adam, Presley, and Finley look like they're gonna bust.

"I need you to quit working late, Trey, because I get lonely and sad," I say, and scrunch my shoulders with feigned innocent happiness. I saunter across the tight circle and then whip back around, elated. "Oh, and one more thing. I want you to quit shutting off from my tantric side because you can't handle heavy emotions. You'll be fine. Just muscle through your misery."

I lean against the counter seductively and smirk at Trey, not giving a damn that I'm revealing our private problems. I take a deep breath and unleash my dark-water side. "What's the point of having superpowers," I gravel deeply, "if you won't let me make you *scream* that you love me?"

"Holy crap, she's wicked," Demitri's dad gasps.

"She's adorable, until she's not," Demitri replies. "That's when it gets interesting."

I slowly slink Trey's way, working his sexy, custom dress within an inch of its life while his eyes widen. I get to Trey and smile seductively as my dark-water side fills my eyes. I put my hands flat on his chest and run them slowly to his shoulders. "Emotion, Trey," I purr. "You need to give in because I feel like I'm trapped in a dismissive void with you." I've had enough of him avoiding me, and if he wants to trap me in this fake wedding bullshit, then I'm trapping him into facing harsh reality that he can't avoid because we're in a crowd of people he invited. "You need to quit running from us working through things." My head tips suspiciously. "Why do you run?"

I grab his neck, and his eyes widen. "Oh God. Please, no, Melanie," Trey gasps. "Don't do this right now. I'm a confused mess."

"You aren't going to continue to hide behind your rules, because I know why you do it," I say, leaning so close to him our lips almost touch. "It's hard to be honest when you have shit like your Tiffany affair to hide."

Trey's eyes widen fearfully.

I smile evilly. "I'm not the only one who needed to discuss our reality before we get married, but don't worry. You can handle this. It was your idea, after all," I purr.

I kiss him, unleashing my tantric side, and his knees give out. He catches himself on the skate shelf. I tip my head back, taking a gasping breath. I smile deviously as Trey falls to the ground, panting, and looks up at me with a pained expression.

"What the fuck has been happening behind closed doors between you two?" Adam asks, completely serious for the first time during this exchange.

I pan stone-cold eyes Adam's way. "Trey spends an ungodly amount of time mysteriously MIA. He doesn't answer his phone and blocks our soulmate connection for long stretches. When he *is* around, he dodges serious topics."

Adam's eyes narrow speculatively while he stares at Trey. "That's not new, Melanie. He's done that in past lives."

"I don't remember past lives like you," I remind.

"So help me, Trey," Adam growls. "If I find out you're screwing Melanie over, you'll deal with me."

I survey Trey lying in a pathetic heap on the floor. He appears traumatized on a lot of levels.

"Are you back in your body yet?" I ask sweetly as Trey gasps.

He takes a deep breath and nods, but it lacks umph.

"You asked what I need." I raise an eyebrow. "I need to be heard, respected, worthy of your time. I need laughter and your presence during the simple things in life. I need a partner who respects that my feelings are valid. I need connection. I need you to be honest and transparent." I tip my head and ooze out, "Do all of that, and we'll be fine." I smirk as my suspicions breeze up. "Unless you ever cheat on me again. If that happens, you're likely to burn to death in our bed while I rage." I shake my head sarcastically. "I'm sure you wouldn't hurt me like that again. You learned during the Tiffany affair."

Trey stands, radiating terror. "Melanie, we——," he starts to protest.

"Marriage! I'm so excited." I cut him off, smiling girlishly with a bouncy giggle.

"She's got this wife shit *down*." Adam laughs and looks at Trey. "And you look miserable. I tell you what, you two are gonna be great at marriage."

Presley and Finley giggle while Mama Mabel's eyes nearly pop out of her head.

"Melanie, wait," Trey says.

"We have a wedding to get to, silly," I chirp, shaking my head at him innocently. "There's no time to talk. You're fine!"

"No time, Trey," Demitri says with a laugh. "These things move quickly. You don't need to talk. Just jump in like you always make Melanie do. It works out so well, every time."

"Are you muscling through this mess, or are you taking control of your life?" Presley asks me.

"Muscling through. Trey needs to learn, and I think trapping himself in a marriage he forces is the perfect teacher."

Trey looks petrified.

"We need twenty minutes," Presley announces and slides an arm around my hips. She turns to Finley. "Get Tanner. Melanie is changing, and I need him to Fairy-God-Tanner some magical bullshit together." She turns to Demitri. "Fix this music disaster. I'm not letting Melanie walk down the aisle to anything but a song she loves." She turns to Adam. "Talk to Rich and tell him he's walking his daughter down the aisle." She thinks a moment and adds exasperatedly, "Make an aisle happen!"

"We've got this," Demitri says to me.

"Do you need a song suggestion?" I ask.

Everything is revealed on Demitri's face that he's feeling. "No," he answers quietly.

Finley rushes to get Tanner, and Presley guides me out of the banquet room to the sound of Adam's laughter.

CHAPTER 42

"That's my girl. You look beautiful," my stepfather, Rich, says as he takes my hand and spins me around in the dressing room.

Tanner dug through wardrobe storage at Mabel's and found a white Jessica McClintock prom dress. Turns out it used to belong to a girl that worked for Mabel a few years ago. Mabel gave us permission to have it, and Tanner whip-stitched the straps a little shorter. It fits perfectly. Spaghetti straps, with a heart-shaped top that's got just enough sparkle to be ladylike and pretty. The skirt is fluffy tulle. Tanner changed my makeup to an ethereal light-honey pink. I don't feel like a sleaze anymore.

Rich opens the door, and the sound of "Can't Help Falling in Love" by Elvis wafts in. I instantly tear up and stop for a second to pull it together. Demitri's song choice is perfect, but I'm marrying the wrong guy to it.

We walk through the fogged archway and see rows of chairs. Everyone stands and turns to look at me. All the girls gasp.

"Now, that's our Mel," Presley says.

Trey sees me and tears up. Tanner fist-bumps him.

I have our connection fuzzed out, and Trey doesn't know what

I'm thinking, but I prefer it that way. I walk down the aisle with Rich and pass a teary-eyed Adam. He nods at me, clearly approving of the shift. Demitri and Victoria are next to Adam, and Demitri winks. He's misty-eyed, and my heart hurts looking at him. I get to Trey, and Rich hugs me.

"I've always got your back," Rich whispers. "No matter what happens."

I work to curb the looming tears. Rich takes his leave, and I face Trey. He taps his temple and I un-fuzz my side of our connection.

He looks me up and down. *"You're beautiful,"* he sends. *"I'm hoping tonight will be perfect now."*

"Trey to my right and Melanie to my left," Mabel instructs us.

We step into place. Each of us stands in front of a little table with a candle and a lighter.

Mama Mabel lights a candle behind her, murmuring quietly as she starts the ceremony. She calls in the four directions and traces a protection symbol with her hand over each of us as she sets her circle. She closes her eyes, takes a deep breath, and lights another white candle. She opens her eyes. "The circle is set, and no harm shall come to the occupants as we gather today to honor the bond of love shared between Melanie and Trey," she announces. "I ask that all our guests wait in patient silence as I guide Melanie and Trey through this ceremony in their way." She turns to Trey. "Please begin."

"We're doing this our way because I don't want to hold anything back," Trey sends through our connection. *"Can you meet me in our energy space?"*

"Absolutely not," I say aloud. My eyebrows rise.

Trey looks to Mabel before staring at me.

"I thought we'd make promises to each other mind-to-mind," he whispers for only Mabel and me to hear.

"No thank you," I whisper back.

Trey's mouth drops open. "Vows, Melanie," he protests quietly.

"You and Mabel called this a ritual. Vows have nothing to do with a ritual," I state.

"Vows are a part of a wedding ritual," Trey whispers back. "I have a whole thing prepared to tell you."

"Must be nice," I say quietly. "I have nothing prepared because I didn't know about this. I'm not going to make up some bullshit to put on a show for these people. Clinical ritual. That's it."

"Let's do the ritual part," Mabel murmurs. "You two can exchange vows privately later."

Trey swallows hard but relents.

Mama levels me with a weighted look. "Melanie, are you committed to this pact that, while not bound by *law*," she pointedly emphasizes the word while tipping her head slightly, her eyes lancing, "is bound by sacred union sanctified by the witness of your friends and family?"

My eyes narrow. *Not bound by law . . . Mabel just gave me the intel I need to get through this.*

"Yes," I answer willingly now that I know this isn't legally binding.

"Melanie, light the candle on the table in front of you," Mabel instructs.

I take the lighter and light the candle.

Mabel shifts her gaze to Trey. "Trey, are you committed to this pact that, while not bound by law, is bound by sacred union sanctified by the witness of your friends and family?" she asks.

Trey smiles at me, putting both hands on my cheeks. "I'm Melanie's heart, mind, body, energy, and soul," he professes.

I melt a little.

"Trey, light your candle," Mama Mabel says, and he complies.

"Trey, Melanie, cross your arms and take each other's hands."

We do as she's asked.

She takes a length of red cord and a length of black cord, wrapping our hands and wrists together. Mama Mabel studies Finley on my side and Tanner on Trey's side. "As witnesses of this bond, can you attest to this union?" she asks them.

"We can," Tanner and Finley respond in unison.

I feel a ring slipped onto my finger, but I'm such a mentally scattered mess that I don't even look at it.

Mama Mabel scans our gathered friends and family as she knots the cords. "With these cords I bind you together in a handfasting marriage. May these cords be knotted in your hearts until you choose to unknot them," she advises. "You are bound by your words, promise, and the love you share. Hold each other in joy and sadness, fear and elation, danger and safety. Take care of each other and love fiercely in your way." Mama Mabel smiles first at Trey and then at me. She picks up her lighter and looks to the crowd. "As they have proclaimed, the universe recognizes this union of two souls that were joined long ago and found each other in this lifetime," she announces to the crowd before she turns to light a silver candle on the table behind her.

Trey yanks his wrists to pull me to him. He leans in and kisses me delicately. The crowd erupts in cheers and clapping. Trey twists around behind me so that we face the crowd. He lifts our tied arms over our heads, and we both flash devil horns. All our people throw up devil horns with a roar. The Hellhounds throw their heads back and howl.

Mama Mabel does a brief ceremony and unties our hands. I turn to Trey and start to say something, but Hiram's voice through the speakers interrupts me.

"Firebird, this is from Shivers," he proclaims.

"Seriously?" I mutter to Trey, who winces.

"How Do You Talk to an Angel," from *The Heights*, wafts through the speakers. Trey reaches for my hand, turns me around twice, and pulls me in to dance right there in our ceremony spot.

Everyone pairs up, dancing and laughing. Some of Mama Mabel's staff begin handing out champagne glasses and wandering the crowd with a fresh round of fancy appetizer trays, while other staff clear the chairs awkwardly in the middle of the dancing because there's no transition from wedding to reception.

"The song is a nice choice," I compliment.

"I was interested in what you were about to say before Hiram interrupted," Trey prompts hopefully.

"It was one of those works-in-the-moment things, but it'd be weird now," I respond with a shrug. "Just a girly sentiment. I was feeling bride-like for a moment."

"And you don't now?"

"No." My expression cages. "Hiram interrupting was perfectly in tune with all of this. I don't get to be a bride."

"What have you looked most forward to about a wedding?"

I scrunch my mouth. "Inviting all the girls to do the ladies' brunch and wedding-dress shopping with my mom, and my future mother-in-law."

"Damn it," Trey mutters. "The girls asked me if that was possible, and I said no because I didn't want the surprise ruined."

"Where are your parents?" I ask, looking around.

"They didn't approve, and I didn't invite them," Trey admits.

"I'm sorry they don't like me," I say as I blush.

"I am also, Melanie." Trey's brow furrows. "This isn't exactly how I imagined our first dance at our wedding."

"Well, had Hiram given us time to walk down the aisle holding hands, this wouldn't be an issue," I say.

Trey gives me a quizzical look and I sigh.

"Here's how it works," I explain. "The couple kisses, they whisper a little, they take hands and exit the room together. That's when the reception is prepped. The couple take pictures with a photographer and talk for a while before coming into the reception, being introduced, and having a party."

Trey stops dancing and looks so sad. "That sounds really nice," he says, dejected. "I didn't know weddings go like that."

"None of this is how weddings go."

"We've never discussed what you'd want for a wedding," Trey sheepishly admits.

I look down at my hand for the first time. I have a pretty little solitaire ring on, and I ponder it.

"Do you not like it?" Trey asks.

I laugh a little before scrunching my face Trey's way. "It's beautiful. You're an odd one but thank you for all of this."

"The ring is odd?" Trey looks at the classic solitaire.

"It's an engagement ring, not a wedding ring," I explain. "I guess we got engaged at our wedding?"

"What's the difference?" Trey asks.

"An engagement ring is this beautiful diamond that was really thoughtful of you." I smile softly at Trey, trying to take a little of the sting out of this. "A wedding ring is a wrap, or row of diamonds that goes up against an engagement ring as the next step."

"Oh," Trey says while he studies the ring. "My parents just wear gold bands." He ponders a moment. "My mom has two thin gold bands now that I think about it."

"You aren't wearing a ring. I guess I'm the only one who's marked with the married title."

Trey closes his eyes. "I didn't think about a ring for me."

"That's part of that pre-wedding, giggly couple's stuff," I

remind him. An idea to save this poor mood of mine comes to me. "Can we get to the cake, even though dinner hasn't been served? I'm really excited about cake."

"Cake?" he asks.

My eyebrows rise. "Big, fancy tiers with candy pearls and red-icing roses. I assure you that if this is my wedding, THAT cake is in THAT kitchen." I gesture the direction of the catering kitchen.

"There isn't cake, Melanie," he says, wincing. "Victoria handled the food. Madeleine cookies, shrimp cocktail, puffed-beef pastries."

"Well, I like beef pastries."

"You don't like Madeleine cookies or shrimp cocktail?" Trey asks.

"I can't stand either, but this isn't my wedding, right?" I raise my eyebrows, giving in to my displeasure. "I assume we're having a plated dinner, and tables are going to be awkwardly rolled out at any moment?"

"No," Trey dejectedly says. "We're just doing the finger foods you don't like."

I toss my hands.

"Cake and dinner are important?"

"Wedding cake and dinner are the best part of a wedding," I huff.

"Shrimp cocktail or salmon croquettes?" a waiter offers as he breezes up to us.

"No thank you. I despise seafood. I'd like the beef pastry, please," I request, as politely as I can muster.

"My apologies," the man replies. "We served those during the cocktail hour you requested earlier."

"Of course, you did," I grumble.

The waiter walks away, and I finally let the full weight of my irritation show.

"Seafood, Trey?"

"I forgot that you hate it."

"If Madeleine cookies are served, I'm dissolving this handfasting. This is absolutely asinine. Send Victoria into that kitchen and have her force the staff to create a plated ribeye dinner for everyone and a wedding cake."

Trey's mouth drops open.

The happy song, "Brown Eyed Girl," comes on next, and I smile across the room at Rich.

"Go on. Get to it." I prod Trey. "Victoria's magic, after all."

Rich says something to my mom before making his way across the crowded dance floor to me. "May I?" he asks Trey. "This has been our song since she was little."

Trey gives my hand to Rich. Rich starts breezing me through the song. I smile up at him as he turns me around him.

Trey talks to Mabel, and a moment later we hear her bark, "She doesn't like SEAFOOD?"

Trey shakes his head and murmurs something else.

"A cake?" Mabel asks, while she looks at me, forlorn. "Victoria said the cookies were the perfect idea."

"Melanie hates Madeleine cookies," Trey admits.

"Did you know that?" Mabel asks.

"No."

"Shit," Mabel hisses. "We screwed this up, Trey."

We're interrupted as our chef, Randall, stops Rich and me from dancing. "Melanie, I'm so sorry," Randall says. "Brian just filled me in. I had no idea you dislike seafood."

Trey, Mabel, Adam, and Demitri join us.

"Well, Randall," I retort rudely, "you didn't bother asking, did you?"

"I was told Victoria was the wedding planner," Randall says with a grimace.

"VICTORIA?" Rich screeches. Luckily, he lowers his voice as he snarls at Trey, "You let someone Melanie despises plan this?"

"What?" Randall asks in disbelief.

"I thought Melanie and Victoria were on better terms now," Mabel says, attempting to cool things down.

"Just because two people can sit in a high school auditorium without killing each other doesn't mean they can plan a wedding for each other," Rich says, glaring at Mabel like she has shit for brains. He shifts his fed-up gaze to Randall. "Ribeye dinner. Loaded baked potatoes. Brussel sprouts with sea salt and a honey drizzle."

"I would have loved to serve that, but we don't have the supplies for it," Randall says and sadly shakes his head. He smiles softly at me. "Everyone seems to like the food. I apologize that it doesn't work for you. What can I make you that would appeal?"

"Peanut butter and jelly, I guess," I huff.

Rocco steps into the group. "Hang on a second." He whips out his phone and places a call. "Hi, Greco. I need ten number ones delivered to . . ." He looks to Mabel, who gives him the address. He listens a moment and then nods. "Yup. I'm sorry about this, but I'm standing in the middle of a debacle you wouldn't BELIEVE! There are a handful of us who are going to refuse to eat seafood at a wedding from hell." He hangs up.

"Who did you call?" Mabel groans.

"The regional manager of In-N-Out. They're Melanie's favorite burgers," he states.

"Well played, Roc," Rich commends Rocco, and they fist-bump. "I don't suppose YOU would like to marry Melanie?"

"Perhaps after a first date." Rocco chuckles. He looks around. "Not in this strange situation though." He rattles his head, looking like he smells something bad. "I've NEVER seen a more hideous . . ." He trails off.

Mabel vibrantly blushes.

Randall blushes to match. "Please don't serve fast food burgers to the bride," he pleads. "I can figure this out without resorting to that. This is a wedding."

"Like hell it is," I snap. "This is a spectacle of *some* sort, but it isn't MY wedding, I assure you. Figure out a cake, Randall. I'm dead-ass serious."

"Wedding cakes take an entire day to make," Randall sighs. "I'm sorry, Melanie."

"If anyone eats Madeleine cookies, I'm going to burn this building down," I snarl back. "This is RIDICULOUS."

"I made six hundred Madeleine cookies, with almond extract I flew in from PARIS," Randall hisses at Mabel.

"Nasty," I snap back. It's rude, but I've had enough. I can apologize later.

"She doesn't like almond cookies?" Randall asks Mabel, boring holes in her with his eyes.

Mabel shakes her head sheepishly.

Randall jabs a finger in my direction. "She is my favorite resident here. I've been thrilled to do this for her and busted my ass. My reputation is on the line, and this is humiliating."

"I make not a damn bit of difference, Randall," I inform him. He turns soft eyes my way and I nod. "None of this was about me. It was about Trey, Mabel, and Victoria. They're all thrilled with the food, along with these guests, ninety percent of whom I would have NEVER invited. I'm now the events coordinator, and you can let the waitstaff know at the end of the evening that they're fired, because I won't have employees on my roster that cater to Victoria. I've never been madder than I am right now, but I must get through this."

The look Randall gives Mabel could ice a forest fire. "This is a nightmare. I didn't realize that Melanie is now MY events boss," he says and looks to me. "I'm so incredibly sorry."

"Thank you for acting like you give a damn," I scoff. "You're another of Victoria's lapdogs, though." My statement is harsh. Randall has never been anything but nice to me.

He swallows hard. "I don't even like Victoria," he admits. "She's rude, crass, and treated the staff like they were pond scum. I only tolerated it because this wedding was for you."

"I apologize Randall."

"I promise this mattered to me," he professes. "I put my all into it. I trusted my employer. We've never had this happen here, and I'm mortified."

"Please don't serve those cookies," Trey requests. "I really think Melanie might leave me for it."

Mabel squeezes her eyes closed, pained. Randall dejectedly goes back to the kitchen, motioning the waitstaff to follow him. Trey looks like he wants to die. Rich is newly furious. Adam gleefully grins.

I notice Victoria across the party and launch an invisible energy ball her way. It hits her in the chest, and she flies through the swinging catering kitchen doors. I send into the kitchen the audible mental scream, *"Throw them away, bitch!"*

We hear my scream over the music, all the way from here.

Adam roars laughter.

I look to Trey. "Just a warning that I plan to kill Victoria."

Trey's head drops.

Mabel waves her hands about. "I swear she tried. I promise."

"Dead. Stone cold. She knows I wouldn't want her to do this, yet she did," I gravel back, my eyes full of dark-water rage. "I'm the event coordinator here, NOT Victoria. Not only is she Trey's ex, who I do NOT get along with, but she's also a nasty snake who's clearly gunning for my JOB!"

"Victoria is your ex?" Mabel breathes out to Trey, astonished. Trey just pitifully nods.

"I can't breathe!" Adam wheezes out through his yeehaw laughter. "Holy crap, this is hilarious."

"Well, someone's having fun," I snarl with a disgruntled hand flip in Adam's direction.

"Best night of my life." Adam happily sighs as his chuckles calm. He looks to Demitri. "Peter Pan, when you marry Melanie, remember, no Madeleine cookies."

Demitri snorts, seeming not at all bothered that I just insulted his girlfriend. "Melanie hates all spongey cookies. The texture makes her make a . . ." He offers a lizardy-tongue grimace and one fluttering eye. " . . . face. They really are nasty. They always taste like wealthy-people food. Unsatisfying, but served at parties because they're a fancy shape." He slides an exhausted gaze Trey's way. "Victoria's been anorexic for years. How she stays so curvy is beyond me. She lives off Jolly Ranchers and a handful of pretzels here and there. She was the worst possible person to plan a menu for Melanie, who delights in food."

"I didn't know that," Mabel admits.

Demitri nods. "The menu Victoria suggested is what her mom's personal chef serves at all their awful parties. She just copied it because she had no clue but would never admit it."

"Shit," Trey mutters.

Adam heehaws again.

"You seem to understand a lot more about Melanie than Trey does," Rich says to Demitri.

"I would hope so," Demitri says. "I'm the one she shares everything with."

Rich holds his hand out in front of Demitri's chest. "I have to know."

"Stop, Rich," I rush to say. I turn to Demitri. "He can search soul-intent. It's painful, and your deepest intentions will be on full display."

Demitri puts his hands out to his sides. "I have nothing to hide, and I'm not scared of pain. Do what you need to."

Rich puts his hand on Demitri's chest, and Demitri's breathing never falters. My mouth drops open.

When Rich is done, he says, "You're a beast, Demitri. I've never had anyone stand, rock steady, while I did that." Rich looks at me. "You're up."

He puts his hand on my chest, and I squeeze my eyes closed, wincing as the inside of my chest suddenly feels like it's being twisted.

Rich drops his hand with a heartbroken expression. He turns to Adam. "Now you."

"How am I involved in this disaster?" Adam asks. "My only job is to think it's hilarious."

Rich gives him a look. "You're always in the middle of Melanie's unhappiness."

Adam huffs. "Go for it."

Rich puts his hand on Adam's chest, and Adam says, "Damn, Reckless! That hurts."

When Rich is done searching Adam's dirt, he says, "You're disgusting, Adam! Good Lord!"

Adam cracks up as Rich turns to me. "You have a soulmate bond with him?"

I nod.

Rich points at Adam. "No more hanging out with this walking porno!"

Adam and I both laugh.

"He's one of your best friends, Rich," I remind him.

"Now I know why. He's sick and so am I." Now Rich snaps furious eyes Trey's way. "Your turn."

"No," Trey replies, taking several steps back.

Rich's eyes narrow with fury. "You sackless piece of shit. Step up like a man."

We all gape, and Trey looks overwhelmed.

"I can't," Trey pleads.

Rich grabs Demitri and me by the elbows and pulls us across the room. He stops in a spot away from the party, leans in, and says quietly to Demitri, "Say it."

"I love your daughter," Demitri says. "I fully admit that I've made mistakes with her, and I apologize for them."

Rich nods. "I saw that." He looks at me. "Demitri is truly remorseful for his mistakes that sabotaged the relationship you two likely should have already had." He smiles at me softly. "I'm getting it out on the table." He looks to Demitri. "Melanie may thoroughly be Zane's, but I'm not sure. It's a toss-up. You and Zane have been a big source of inner debate and turmoil for Melanie."

Vibrantly, I blush.

"Choose me," Demitri says intensely.

I swallow hard, and after a moment of contemplation, look up at Demitri and nod.

"What do you think Trey is hiding?" Demitri asks.

I shrug a little.

Rich shakes his head. "No clue. He just lost my trust. I give it six months, and this marriage will implode."

Demitri bends at the waist. Panic radiates from him. He gasps desperately, "How sure are you?"

"I'm intuition-sure." Rich stares absently at nothing for a moment before adding, "I'm letting this ride only because Melanie is being hunted by the Reapers. We have to keep her alive, and Trey's good at that."

With monumental effort, Demitri manages to stand upright.

Rich gives me a soft look. "If it helps, you don't need to cook up a gentle way to tell Carol and me when the tables turn. We won't be shocked or upset. We just want you to be happy."

Demitri takes a rattling breath.

"You listen to me," Rich expresses intensely. "I am ORDERING you to follow your heart the moment you can't handle this marriage. You should have come to me the moment you couldn't handle this wedding. I know you were scared because we hadn't discussed the miscarriage, but I would never hang you out to dry." Rich's jaw hardens. "I suspect that Trey loves you, but he's got some seriously bad defense mechanisms where emotional pain, fear, and vulnerability are concerned. I can assure you that Demitri loves you. Adam loves you too, but he's *busted*." His expression sobers. "Zane didn't bother to show up and fight for you. In my eyes, he's out." Rich stalks away, radiating fury.

Adam walks up and hands me a bottle of tequila. I slug a huge gulp and rattle my head hard. Demitri takes the bottle and guzzles. When his dad joins us, Demitri hands him the bottle next, and he takes a pull.

"I've got a trashy dress to put on," I inform.

"You're full of tequila, so you can handle it," Adam says. "Go put it on, but ditch the shorts this time. I want to see that ass."

"You're a naughty boy," I purr at Adam.

He grins at me mischievously. "That's why you love to hate me. The affair offer is still on the table. I'm miserable, and so are you. Just saying."

I smirk up at him. "I'm not going there at this phase of my nightmare."

"You might want to walk away," Adam warns Demitri's dad. "I'm gonna be me."

Mr. Cantrell looks at me. "Do you care if I'm here? Frankly, it's been a rough night, and Adam's funny. I could use a laugh."

"Nope. You can stay, but a warning that I'm buzzy right now, and that makes me candid."

Mr. Cantrell grins at me. "You're candid sober, Melanie."

"Good point." I turn to Adam. "Fire away."

Adam's gaze snaps to Demitri. "Is she saying that you two have never taken the plunge? I was convinced the baby was yours!"

Demitri laughs, his head dropping. "Nope. Never."

"You've got to be kidding!" Mr. Cantrell quietly exclaims. "I thought the same thing!"

"I really do mean it when I say I'm not that guy."

With a naughty smile, I gaze up at Demitri. "It's freaking annoying, let me tell ya. Things got carried away on the dark stage after 'Throb' when I was *single*, and he *still* chose Victoria."

"Are you stupid?" his dad asks him. "Holy crap! You left that part out of that story."

Adam hands Demitri the tequila. "Your willpower is astronomical." He scrunches up his face. "You picked Victoria over wonder tush over here?"

Demitri sighs. "I was trying to be a good guy and didn't want to cheat on my girlfriend any more than I already had. Good intentions, horrific choice."

Adam says to Demitri's dad, "Buckle up. Here it comes." He juts his chin my way as he says to Demitri, "It would be worth bending your Peter Pan rules for a throw with her. My mind exploded, and I begged her to marry me."

I crack up. "That was actually really sweet, for the record."

Adam rolls his eyes. "I blame YOU that I got Valerie pregnant.

I was just diving into a constant distraction from losing you."

Demitri's eyes are huge. "Wait! Did you actually do that in the sack?"

"Technically it was in the ocean, but whatever," Adam clarifies. "Yup. While my entire body exploded. Her tantric dark-water shit is no joke. The side effect where you spill all your deepest thoughts is worth it. If you ring the right bells, and you can get her to blow with you, it'll liquify your brain. I saw stars and nearly passed out. It's been my running alone-time fantasy for over a year."

"Aw, babe," I say. "That's so sweet!"

Adam rattles his head. "Girl . . ."

I saunter away as Adam and Mr. Cantrell laugh and Demitri takes another gulp from the tequila bottle.

CHAPTER 43

"**W**hy did Melanie attack me?" I hear Victoria whimper, just before I round the hall corner. I stop and eavesdrop. It's a terrible habit.

"Melanie's been through too much lately. She has no patience left. She hates everything about this wedding. Considering that it's her big event and girls dream of this stuff, she's on edge," I hear Trey say.

"What do you mean she hates it?" Victoria's dismayed voice replies.

"We got it all wrong. She wanted an understated, private event."

"Oh no," Victoria breathes. "There's nothing understated about what I did in there."

"I know you worked hard on this," Trey replies. "I wanted to warn you that Melanie thinks you intentionally destroyed her wedding."

"I swear I didn't try to ruin this," Victoria replies, panicky.

"She put up with the décor and flowers that couldn't possibly be more inappropriate but finally snapped when she found out we served seafood and Madeleine cookies. She despises both."

"She hates seafood?" Victoria gasps, sounding legitimately upset.

"Yes," Trey answers. "I think that was just the final straw. Food and cake were really important to her, but I had no idea. We've never discussed what she'd want for a wedding."

"I would have never made a menu that included seafood, if I had known." Victoria whimpers fitfully. "Is her wanting cake why Randall threw the whole cookie display away?"

"Yes," Trey replies. "He's furious. He thinks you and Mabel railroaded him."

"Trey, this isn't cool. I was hoping to impress Melanie, and that she'd hire me as her events coordinator assistant. I really wanted that job."

"Don't even mention that," Trey instructs. "You need to stay away from Melanie. She's not rational right now. She views everything she hates in there as your vindictive doing. The truth is that you're just very different people, and this is what you would have wanted."

"I thought it looked amazing in there," Victoria says.

"I know. I appreciate how hard you tried," Trey replies. "Melanie disappeared. I need to find her."

I round the corner, having changed back into the dress Trey designed for me. He stares at me across the distance. Sound apparently travels well down this tiled hall, but he'd never expect I could hear them from this range. He didn't hit on Victoria, and my concern that they're having an affair is somewhat alleviated.

"Head back in," Trey says to Victoria.

She glances down the hall, and her expression slumps when she sees me. She starts to say something, but Trey shakes his head.

I refuse to move until Victoria goes away. After she's gone, I make my way to Trey.

"Hey, I was letting her know to leave you alone," Trey says as he hands me a fancy white plate with a burger and fries artfully arranged on it.

"Randall plated my In-n-Out?" I ask.

"Furiously, while cussing." Trey sighs. "Victoria is mortified. She truly didn't intend to ruin this wedding. When I told her you hate all of it, she almost cried. Please don't kill her. This mess is on me."

"I don't want to discuss Victoria," I reply curtly.

"I know you don't, but you're mad enough that I needed to say something."

I plop down and kick off the heels that hurt like the devil. I pick at my food, not hungry anymore.

Trey sits next to me. "Would you rather eat inside? The beach crew are all eating in there," he coaxes.

"No thank you. I'm stalling as long as I can before I must walk back in that room," I reply. "How long is this mess scheduled for?"

"Another three hours," Trey dejectedly says. "Dancing and an open bar are in full swing."

"Then they're all happily distracted."

"I really hoped you'd dance," Trey says bashfully. "Tanner had a whole plan for Dante to play some of the songs you all have routines to. Impromptu fun show."

"My gut still hurts when I move too much," I mutter. "Why would Tanner expect me to do that?"

"I didn't think about that." Trey sighs, rubbing his face hard.

I take a burger bite while Trey stares at his hands that are propped on his knees.

"While you were in the hospital, I launched myself into

planning this and pretending everything was fine," he confesses. "I needed to focus on you instead."

"Everyone says you disappeared," I quietly say.

"I didn't," he defends. "I was going over lists and helping Victoria order all of this. I spent the whole time in wedding mode."

"Well, ordering and setting up that extravaganza would certainly take time."

"You're right that it's horrible," Trey grumbles. "I was relieved there was so much to do with the decorations because it kept me occupied. I never once actually looked around. I just kept doing and doing. I lived in that banquet hall day and night. When I wasn't there, I was driving around picking stuff up from vendors."

"Thank you for trying so hard," I bashfully say, realizing what distracted him so much. "Your heart was in the right place."

"It wasn't," Trey says. "This was selfish of me. I want to work through everything we've been through."

"Let's get through tonight." I grab my shoes, slipping them on. "I can avenge the baby legitimately now."

"What do you mean?"

"I'm a Valdez now," I reply. "The baby was a Valdez. I want to do her justice."

"Melanie," Trey says, while he grabs my hand, "you didn't have to be a Valdez to do that."

"I don't want to be the hoe who avenges a baby out of wedlock. It's the only reason I went through with this."

"Do you really not want to be married to me?" Trey pitifully asks.

"I don't want to be married at sixteen!"

"You were married to Pierre," Trey breathes in horror.

"Pierre was Pierre," I reply. "I don't want to be married just because the concept exists." I give Trey the look he deserves.

"You missed out on all the marriage experiences when Pierre died," Trey says. "I wanted to give you that."

I irrationally crack up. "Pierre would have walked in that room, if he was the groom, taken one look at that mess, and walked right back out."

"I'm classier than this, I swear. When Victoria volunteered, Mabel and I were excited because Mabel needed to help Valerie. We figured that Victoria has all those rich-girl parties at her house and knew how to do this. It seemed like the perfect solution."

"Victoria is lazy to a fault." I give Trey an amused look. "I guarantee she does nothing more than attend those parties. She doesn't help the staff set them up."

"I see your point." Trey grimaces. "Mabel finally walked in right before we went to get you. She looked like she'd been stabbed through the heart with your katana. The woman turned fuchsia. She prides herself on nice events. She wanted to fix it, but people were already starting to arrive."

"She didn't like it?"

Trey shakes his head. "She was nice to Victoria about it, but when it was just her and I, she muttered, 'Holy tits and gravy. For the first time, my brothel looks like a brothel.'"

"You let a whore decorate," I softly say, feeling more compassionate toward Trey.

"You really think that about Victoria, don't you?"

"Everybody does," I respond. "She's the trashiest person I know."

We're interrupted as Dante nearly falls over Trey's legs while he rushes around the corner.

"Hey," he says. "I was coming to find you two."

"Found us," I mutter.

Dante sits next to Trey. "Mabel talked to me and Hiram about how this was supposed to go," he tells us and winces. "I don't think any of us are getting the jobs we were hoping for."

"You were hoping for jobs?" I ask.

Dante nods. "Hiram wanted to stage manage events here. I wanted to be the deejay. Mabel told us, Victoria, and a bunch of waitstaff, that this was our audition."

"Shit," I mutter as guilt bubbles up. "I didn't know how much was on the line."

"My fault," Trey says. "I shouldn't have put everyone in this position."

"Anyhow," Dante says, "I've got one of my mixed CDs rolling so I could come get you. Hiram is behind the skate racks. He's wrecked. Mr. Cantrell is talking to him. Mabel is hiding in the corner of the kitchen, having vapors. Randall left. Victoria is crying in the storage closet while Demitri talks her down. We all know we screwed up." Dante laughs a little. "I knew we were doomed the second I saw the fountain with a naked baby angel pissing."

My mouth drops open. "We have a fitting mascot."

Trey puts his hands over his face. "That fountain pisses?" he asks. "I'm the one that hefted it in there, but I didn't know that."

"If you turn it up high enough, it pisses *on* people, completely missing the marble bowl," Dante informs us. "Adam and Stealth figured that out. They're blasting people as they walk by now that they're drunk."

Trey vibrantly groans.

"We feel terrible that you didn't get to do the whole post-ceremony thing," Dante shares. "Mabel was mortified when Hiram cut Melanie off. We'd like to introduce you and start the reception over the right way. Would you like a proper first dance?"

"No thank you," I reply.

"I'd like to," Trey dejectedly says. "I've always wanted that moment of walking through the door and having my wife introduced with my last name. I just didn't know the order of how that worked."

"None of this is real, Trey. Mabel said it's not bound by law," I reply softly. "You can have that moment when you actually get legally married."

"It's real to me," Trey whispers.

Dante clears his throat. "Trey's been very excited about marrying you."

"She just admitted to me that she only did this as a symbolic gesture so she could avenge the baby as a Valdez," Trey informs.

Dante winces.

"I want to be a real person that's respected," I kindly explain. "Women love planning their wedding. I was an afterthought in this, ignored, oblivious, and left out of all the fun stuff. The man I really marry won't do that to me."

Trey further slouches, completely crapped out by how this is going.

"Melanie, how are you feeling?" Dante asks. "Jayla told me you had surgery."

I take my hands from my stomach, revealing how swollen I am. "I'm in bad shape still, but apparently a revealing dress, pissing angel fountain, and Victoria's dream wedding are what matter."

"I'm never going to live down Victoria helping with this, am I?" Trey dejectedly asks.

"Absolutely not," I mutter.

Dante grimaces. "That was a questionable choice, Trey."

"I've gathered that," Trey mumbles.

"I'm sorry, Melanie," Dante says. "I knew this was a mistake but didn't want to be the asshole that derailed things. The Misfits talked, and everyone's in the same boat. We all wanted to stop it but didn't know how."

"That would have meant a lot to me, but it's done now." I smile. "This all ends soon, and then I'm hoping no one ever mentions it again."

"What ends soon?" Trey asks.

"Avenging the baby," I reply. "Once that's over, we can dissolve our handfasting. Like I said, it's not real. We're married until we decide we aren't. It's why I agreed to it."

"I'm asking you to take this seriously and give me a chance," Trey insists, suddenly bolstered by my flippant take. He grabs my arm. "I heard everything you said before we went through the ceremony. I get it, but the only way I can prove it to you is if you give me a chance."

I ponder this deeply. My gaze drifts to Dante, who smiles with soft compassion.

"You love Trey, or you wouldn't have stuck it out," Dante says. "I know things have been rough lately, but if Trey's willing to try, I think it's worth a shot. He's your soulmate, after all."

"True," I whisper. Love for Trey swells in my chest. I look at him. "Please be present, trustworthy, and all in with me."

"I will," Trey says, seeming to mean it.

I stand and hold a hand to Trey. My mood has taken an upswing. "Okay. Let's get back in there and enjoy this party."

The look Trey gives me helps solidify my resolve.

"I'll kick everyone out that you don't want here, and we can have the reception with just our inner circle," Trey offers.

"There's no need," I reply. "They're all having fun." I give Trey a look. "Nothing else goes wrong, though. If we're going to try, then things improve as of right now."

"Done," Trey says, standing with Dante.

"Head inside," Dante encourages. "I'm going to talk to Trey." Dante winks at me, and I suspect he's going to give Trey some guidance. Dante has helped us before. He's really good at this.

I open the door and walk in. The music fades.

"Now introducing Mr. and Mrs. Valdez!" Hiram exuberantly crows through the speakers.

All eyes turn to me, and here I stand alone.

"Phenomenal," I say into the silence, my bolstered mood plummeting. While irrational, Trey JUST promised things would improve. Now I've been whammied again.

"Oh LORD," Adam barks. He gives Hiram a look. "Did you check to make sure they were ready?"

"No," Hiram says into the microphone.

A collective groan emits from the crowd. I flop my hands. A waiter walks by, and I attempt to stop him. He ignores me on his mission toward the kitchen.

"I can't even get something to drink around here!" I scoff.

"That's not true," Adam belts. "I gave you a bottle of tequila you slammed back half of."

"My apologies," I reply with sarcasm. "I was, indeed, offered a beverage."

"No one from this waitstaff offered you a drink?" Mabel asks angrily.

"Nope." I smile at her. "I'm sure Victoria told them not to."

"I swear I didn't," Victoria whimpers.

A throat clears, and we look in that direction.

"You must be six months pregnant," a woman I don't know says with motherly care. "You shouldn't be drinking, even at a special occasion."

Gasps emit from my closest friends as I look down at my swollen stomach. I choose to just address the issue head on. "I'm not pregnant," I announce. "I just had surgery. Apparently, my husband, who designed this lingerie nightmare, didn't account for the fact that I swell when I move around too much." I smile at the lady, but it's edged with tacky. "So, while I appreciate your concern, you can mind your own fucking business."

"I'm so sorry," the woman apologizes. "I assumed that's why you were getting married."

"I'm sure a lot of you did." I smirk at the crowd before glowering at Trey, who's standing under the draped arch by the double doors. I'm about to go off the rails, but I feel like he just set me up for failure with his promise that things would go well when I came back in. I've had enough of this charade. "This crowd of besties you invited didn't even know I've had surgery. I don't appreciate being chastised by a stranger for drinking because I'm apparently pregnant."

"I've never been more horrified," the woman breathes.

I sweep a flourishing hand to the fountain. "Don't be upset," I coo at the woman. "This is classy shit, after all."

Adam hits the button with a grin, shooting a stream of water halfway across the room.

Mabel slides astonished eyes Victoria's way. "We do not have urinating décor at my event center!" Mabel proclaims.

Victoria turns a vibrant shade of humiliated.

"I love the fountain." I request of Adam, "Shoot it again." He does and I giggle.

Cindy rushes my way, handing me a water bottle. "I asked the waitstaff for a water, and this is what they gave me."

I take a swig from the plastic bottle.

"Everyone else has glassware. Apparently, a plastic bottle is what your staff think Melanie deserves, though." Cindy smirks at Mabel. "I have eight events this year. I was thinking that I'd contract them with you, but I don't do Tammy Faye Baker bashes."

Mabel looks like she just got gut-punched.

"Thank you for getting me water," I reply into the awkward silence.

Trey rushes my way with an empty glass. He takes the bottle and pours water into the glass before handing it to me. "I heard the announcement and nearly died," he says. "I had no idea we were about to be announced when we came back or I would have entered with you."

"Just more of your planning perfection," I comment with a nod Victoria's way. "You're good at this." Victoria blushes vibrantly as I glare at Trey. "You promised nothing else would go wrong."

Trey takes a slow breath. He gives Victoria, Hiram, and Dante harsh looks before settling on me again. "I apologize. Apparently, my team didn't have my back."

"Good to know," I chirp, fully aware that the 'team' are hoping for jobs. "I'll keep that in mind."

Dante is the only one in my line of sight. I watch him wince.

"Have no fear," Adam crows. "I'm on Melanie's team." Adam hits the button on the fountain, soaking the front of Trey's pants. I howl laughter, leaning against Adam.

He grins at me. "You've been blessed, my child," Adam says to Trey.

Chuckles start spurting from the guests, and then the tension breaks as raucous laughter explodes.

"This is the trashiest fun I've ever had," Rocco caws, while he leans on Brian, enjoying his laughter.

"Gerald asked me to marry him last week," Stubbs's date announces.

Apparently, Stubbs's actual name is Gerald. Who would've thunk it?

His trashy fiancée continues, "I was thinking we'd get hitched at a demolition derby event in Duarte, but this place is our speed.

We'd like to get hitched here. Hot dogs and Coors Light."

I study the woman, baffled, but it appears she's serious as she smiles at Mabel.

"I told you you'd love it here," Stubb whoops. He looks to Mabel. "Can you do a demolition derby theme?"

"*Hell*, yes!" I fire off. "I'm the new events coordinator. I've got you!"

Mabel looks like she wants to die as all the Hellhounds bellow, "Cheers," and down their beers in one gulp.

I flourish my hands. "It's a Melanie wedding," I blister with feigned thrill. "I'm so honored."

I hit the furthest fountain button, and the angel sprays water halfway across the room.

Mabel storms over, unplugging it from the wall. "That is NOT here," she blathers and huffs as she flounces off. "It doesn't exist. I have NEVER!"

I plug it back in after she leaves.

"It's here, because I like it," I say as I test out a different button on the back. My mouth drops open jubilantly. "Well, would you look at that," I caw as we all watch the angel's wings and eyes light in red.

Adam high-fives me.

"Demonic little fucker," he says. "*Now* it's a Melanie wedding."

Trey wilts.

CHAPTER 44

Adam joins me in the corner. Everyone is having fun, and the lady who accused me of being pregnant apologized so sincerely that I accepted. Now that the evening has settled into an actual party, I'm catching a moment to breathe.

Adam wraps me up in his arms, putting his hands on my back. He pulls pain, and I sag against him. "It's bad, Melanie," Adam softly says.

"I'm aware," I acknowledge and smile sadly up at Adam. "I need to rest. Demitri's attempting to heal me so I can have kids. The work he's doing requires him to tear stuff apart and rebuild it. It's horrible."

"Does Trey know that?"

"No," I reply. "He's avoided discussing the miscarriage with me. In this case, it was convenient, though. I didn't want him to know the extent. I just want it fixed." I quirk my mouth. "I'd like children."

"I know, honey," Adam says.

A hand lands on my arm, and Trey starts pulling pain, working in tandem with Adam. "Why is the swelling so bad again?" Trey asks.

"You can't hurt Demitri if I tell you," I implore to Trey.

His brow furrows with worry. "Okay. I won't," he promises.

"We had a long talk, because he can fix me, but he has to turn me into a hand puppet to do it at this phase."

"Why didn't you tell me?" Trey's eyes widen. "I'd be there to pull pain and supervise."

"It's awkward," I say, shaking my head. "I didn't want you there. We have a good routine. He heals for as long as he can before he nearly burns out because he wants this to take the least number of sessions as possible."

"It's not intimate?" Trey asks.

"No. It's horrendous." I swallow hard. "Our deal is that I cry while he fixes me, and then he completely melts down after, and I hold him." I look up at Adam. "You told Trey that you walked in on Demitri and me wrapped around each other asleep. He did a two-hour healing round on me that morning. He was so upset that it made him sick. That's why I was curled around him like that."

"I had no idea," Trey says.

"I know. I want kids one day though. Demitri is my only shot at fixing this, and I had to try."

Trey waves Demitri over, and he joins us.

"I was just filled in on the healing you're doing," Trey informs him.

Demitri's face slackens, all happiness dropping from his expression. "Okay."

"Why are you doing it?" Trey asks.

"Because, while you were busy hauling angel dick fountains, Melanie opened up to me about how upset she was." Demitri's eyes close. "I knew I could help her."

Trey seems suspicious. "How does this work?"

"From your perspective, the same way it did with the

miscarriage. What I'm actually trying to accomplish is very different, though."

"So, it's not an intimate thing?" Trey asks.

"That'd be a hell of a lot easier," Demitri scoffs.

"How do you feel about me not wanting you to do this?" Trey asks Demitri.

"Conflicted, but I heard Melanie out and agree that it's her body," Demitri replies. "She may not always be with you, Trey. I owe it to whoever she lands with to do this."

"After everything we've been through, you aren't doing this to help me?" Trey asks.

"No," Demitri answers honestly. "I don't approve of this wedding. I don't approve of how you trapped her." He gives Trey a pointed look. "You really do owe Zane. You've done nothing to help Melanie in comparison."

"Zane's mad at me, but Cindy told him I didn't know about this wedding," I inform them.

"I know," Demitri says. "I called him last night to ask if he'd come over this morning and help you. He told me to F off. I had no idea why until now."

"I called Rocco yesterday and invited Cindy, Brian, Roc, and Zane to the wedding," Trey says.

"It was so much worse without his help," I quietly say.

"I know it was, but we're going to get through it," Demitri says and wraps his arms around me. Demitri surveys Trey. "Melanie needs Zane. You need to come to terms with that."

"You, yes," Trey says. "Zane, no."

"I'm not going to be around, Trey," Demitri says.

"What?" Trey asks.

"I can't," Demitri says. "I need distance now that Melanie is married. I'll finish healing her though."

"You're still her best friend," Trey insists.

Demitri steps back and releases me from his arms. "There's only so much I can take," he quietly confesses before walking away.

I swallow hard, suddenly feel trapped in a new and profound way.

CHAPTER 45

I nod, but my response is cut off as my intuition nearly knocks me off my feet. I gasp, doubling over, grabbing for Finley's hand. She steadies me as I nearly crater.

"SOMEONE TURN OFF THE MUSIC," Trey yells.

Everyone looks our way and quickly deposits their plates and glasses on tables before they gather around as they music cuts off mid-song.

"Send it," Trey orders. I send an intuition bubble down our connection, and his eyes unfocus as he studies it.

"We're finishing this. Now," Trey snarls.

I nod, the intuition pain dropping away on a wave of rage.

"Listen up. Adam, take Melanie's mom, and anyone else who isn't up for a fight, to the security office. Lock yourselves in and press the panic room button for that room." Trey levels Adam with a deadly look. "If anyone comes through that door, take them down."

"How bad is whatever's coming?" Adam asks.

"It's not coming," I growl. "They're here."

"It's bad," Trey says. "Run, Adam."

Adam runs with my mom and a few others through the double doors, heading to the security office.

"What are we up against?" Big Joe asks.

"Retribution for the death of Mack. One of his ranks is a special prize for me," I say.

"You two don't need to deal with this," Big Joe insists. "Mercury, Stealth, and I will."

I shake my head and meet Trey's eyes.

"No. The Reapers are ours," Trey growls.

"If you kill him, we'll deal with the cleanup," Big Joe assures.

My dark-water side slides behind my eyes, and I let it fill me.

"Holy shit," Demitri's dad mutters. "What's happening?"

"You're about to see why Melanie needs to be kept safe," Demitri informs.

"Trey and Melanie Valdez have invoked Retribution Clause against the Reapers for the murder of their child," Big Joe says with an official tone. "Their declaration is warranted, and I'm authorizing it. We're going to back them."

The Hellhounds all throw their heads back and howl.

"Can you handle this?" I ask Rich.

"The Reapers killed my grandchild," he says and looks at me with haunted eyes. "I'll kill them for you myself. You don't have to do it."

"Trey and Melanie have the right to do this," Big Joe says to Rich.

"I'll back you. Do what you need to," Rich concedes. He turns to Trey with conviction. "You stay with my girl and fight like hell. If you don't make it, I'll kill them."

"I appreciate that, but my backup plan is already set." Trey turns to Demitri. "If I don't make it, you take out the new leader of the Reapers."

Demitri nods, and his dad's eyes are huge.

"Everyone needs to stay away from me when we get outside," I announce. "They've brought someone with them to challenge me to an energy battle." I turn to Mama Mabel and instruct, "I need someone on staff to turn on the house generator, quickly."

Constance races away to handle my request.

"Bear and Darren, I need you to shield the group when this starts," I order. They agree, and I continue, "Once I've dealt with the Reapers' special guest, you're all free to flatten anyone you please."

I feel the generator kick on. "Trey, backup. I'm going to pull power, so I don't black out most of Hollywood again."

Trey shakes his head. "I'm going to fill up and act as a power source for you."

I smile, a touch sadistic. "You're filling up with me?"

"You bet your ass I am."

I close my eyes, opening a line to the generator. I gasp as I pull electricity directly from the source. My back bows, and I shriek. Bear holds me up. My psyche blazes white hot, and I work to wrap my mind around it as I fill every energy reserve I have until I'm quaking. I open my eyes when I'm full. "Trey, you can't handle this," I fight to say. "It's about to burn me up."

"Send it," Trey growls.

I send the white-hot energy to him, and his eyes snap wide. His mouth drops open, and he looks terrified.

"Hang on, love," I snarl.

I drop his hand when he's full, and Arch holds him up while he gasps and tries to work his buckling psyche around the pain.

My dark-water side rages, making the power fit. "Pull it together, Trey," I implore harshly. "They're in the parking lot. We need to move, NOW."

Trey moans and stands. He turns to Dante, who's still in the deejay booth. "Put on Metallica's 'Wherever I May Roam' and turn it all the way up," he tells him.

I raise an eyebrow. "Dramatic! I like it."

The music suddenly hums from the speakers, and Trey and I turn together, facing the doors to the parking lot.

"Leave the doors propped open," I instruct. "Music fuels me, and I'm going to need every tool in my arsenal for this."

Trey takes my hand, and we walk with rage-filled purpose to the double doors, shoving them open as the drum kicks. Hiram props the doors open behind us as we stride to the middle of the massive parking lot. The Reapers are standing in a line that spans its entire width.

Trey checks that everyone's in place and sends to me, *"Game on, Melanie. Get your revenge. I'm right behind you."*

A man steps forward and starts to introduce himself.

I wave my hand about. "You're officially Fat Fuck. No one cares. Get on with it."

"Introductions are part of retribution," the man retorts haughtily.

"Whatever, Fat Fuck. What do you want?"

"Did you light Mack's warehouse on fire?"

I give him a pondering look, choosing not to answer.

"Where is Mack?" the man demands.

"Looks like his body melted in the fire," I send to Trey. "I don't keep track of you morons," I reply. "Cut to the big show. The foreplay's tedious."

"I don't know what you mean."

"You brought a special enemy just for me." I scan the Reapers. "Step forward!"

A slight man steps from the line and crosses to Fat Fuck. I feel his energy probing me, and I slap it away.

"This is who you want me to battle?" he asks in disbelief. "She's a tiny teenager."

I let my dark-water side shine through my eyes. I gather energy from my first reserve and send out a mental blast that booms like a verbal explosion as the music swells. *"The Valdez family invokes Retribution Clause on the grounds of the murder of our child. IF YOU RUN, YOU DIE! STAND YOUR GROUNDDD!"*

The Reapers' lackey gapes at me. I feel doubt radiating from him in waves.

Fat Fuck waves his hand dismissively in my direction. "Nothing but parlor tricks," he scoffs.

The lackey looks like he's going to be sick. "You're a corpse if you can't feel what's rolling from her," the slight man gasps.

I smile sadistically. "What's your handle?" I ask him.

"Warlock."

"Oh, she cares about *his* name," Fat Fuck blathers, insulted.

I grin. "I'm Firebird, but the Reapers know me as La Diabla," I say. "In a moment, you'll see why."

"It's nice to meet you," Warlock politely replies out of habit.

I send to Trey, *"This idiot is way out of his element."* My face contorts with rage, and I send out a blast of fury. It terrifies Warlock, and he reactively flings what I can only describe as an invisible energy bolt my way. I throw up a shield around Trey and me, and the bolt absorbs harmlessly. "Cut the crap and get to it," I demand. "You've got one more shot before I level you. Choose carefully because I'm not going to play slap and tickle."

Warlock expands his invisible energy shield rapidly, and I counter, expanding mine. I pull from my energy stores, emptying the second of four. I use the energy recklessly, knowing that if I must, I can drain the whole city. The parking lot audibly hums and crackles. I study his shield as mine reaches his. I send to Trey, *"He works in air and lightning-like energy. I work in fire and steel. We're well matched."*

"Can you best him, or do I kill him with bare hands now?" Trey sends.

"I've never been this mad. I've got a shot."

Warlock is studying my energy shield just as I was studying his. His eyes narrow, and he pushes as hard as he can, energetically shoving me backward. My heels skid on the asphalt, and Trey braces behind me, pushing me back as he expands a shield I've never felt before to reinforce mine. I close my eyes and study Trey's shield. It's made of something close to invisible granite.

I open my eyes and send to Trey, *"That's new and about to come in handy. Let's lay this asshole flat. On three."*

"I'm with you."

"THREE."

We both expand our energy shields like growing bubbles. Trey's lining mine, and I drain my third power reserve as I aggressively stalk forward. The bubble hits Warlock and plows him over, obliterating Warlock's protection shield. Trey walks next to me, and we keep pushing until we've shoved all the Reapers to the far side of the parking lot. We stop and shrink our shields down while the disoriented Reapers try to stand. One of the Reapers jumps to his feet and attempts to run to his motorcycle.

"HELLHOUNDS," I yell.

The Hellhounds surround the man.

"If you run, you die." I repeat the edict. "Stand your ground! You chose to bring this fight to us."

The coward backs up to his fellow bikers and holds his ground but looks like he regrets his choice to participate in this madness.

Without warning, Warlock gets under our combined energy bubble and hurls. It takes a moment to wrap my mind around the fact that I'm flying backward through the air, my dress whipping over my face. I slam into something and look over my shoulder. Demitri's got me. He sets me on my feet. I yank off my heels and drop them as Trey lands hard next to me.

"They want an energy fight," I send to Trey. *"They'll get one, but let's handle this our way. Knock Fat Fuck out as soon as I get to Warlock. I bubble, you don't."*

Trey sends back, *"Let's do this,"* while he chuckles.

"I can't keep calling you Fat Fuck," I inform Fat Fuck. "It brings a sense of hilarity to this battle. What is your handle?"

"Gut Buster."

"See! I was right." I sarcastically gesture. I scan the enemy crowd. "You're the second in command."

I point to the guy who I know is Thud. Thud ducks his head a bit.

"Fat Fuck battled his way up the hierarchy," he confesses. "I surrendered. He's in charge."

"New intel," I acknowledge. My expression brightens, and I smile pleasantly at Warlock, who's patiently waiting as we hash this out. "I'm still learning how this crazy works. Hang tight. I love how patient you are."

Warlock politely nods, despite the fact that we were just battling. "Thank you."

I look to Big Joe. "Is that how this crazy works?" I question. "Fight up the ladder and win command?"

"You start at the bottom of the top ten. It's all fistfight. No weapons allowed," Big Joe responds.

"Phenomenal," I exclaim and scrunch my nose adorably. "I'd like to be in charge of the Fat Fuck Brigade. Say the official nonsense on my behalf, please."

Reaper mouths drop open while all the Hellhounds boil over with laughter and leg slaps.

"Oh my God, I love her," Mercury manages to gasp through his hilarity.

Big Joe fights through his yeehaw-good-time to say, "On behalf of Melanie Slate-Valdez, by biker code, she challenges the Reaper hierarchy to a duel to the death."

"The death, huh?" I remark with a face scrunch.

Big Joe nods. "An outsider doesn't have the option of surrender," he informs me.

I cross to Big Joe. All the Hellhounds lean in.

"No weapons, right?" I whisper.

More nods.

"Can I use metaphysical abilities?" I ask.

A debate starts among the Hellhounds.

"Fighting uses energy," Big Joe suggests. "Metaphysics is energy. I think it's a gray area, but we can argue for it."

I whip an elated look to the Reapers. "Best night of my life. You see," I profess with a sweet smile, "my life has been one real humdinger after another." I cock a hip in my slutty dress. "Top ten in the hierarchy, raise your hands."

Hands rise and I study them.

"Nice. You guys are impressive. So much snackage!" I tap a finger to my lips, pondering. "What about numbers eleven through twenty?" Those hands go up and I grin. "How many of you also want to be challenged?" All the hands stay up, and I giggle with a clapping bounce. I exhale hard. "I'll ask again after what I'm about to do to Warlock. You might change your mind."

Many Reapers exchange amused glances, still underestimating me.

"All ready for you," I jubilantly chirp to Warlock, who's staring at me in stunned shock.

"You plan to fistfight to the death with twenty grown men?" Warlock asks.

I nod exuberantly. "I'm on my two hundred and third lifetime. I've been every form of warrior you can imagine. I've always been female, as far as I know, but they let me play with the big boys. I'm *that* good." I grin mischievously as I survey the Reapers. "You see, when you came here and beat my ass in this very parking lot, I was a little out of sorts. *Now* I'm not."

Without warning, I drop the equivalent of a nuclear bomb over Warlock's shield. It dissolves in a brilliant flash that makes everyone shield their eyes.

"Let's get ready to RUMBLLLE," Tanner foghorns.

"I'm out," Warlock squawks. "She's got me bested."

"Well, he's no fun," Tanner snarks.

"Yeah," one of the Reapers says, "I'm not fistfighting her." He nods congenially my way. "I'm fifth in the hierarchy. You can cross me out. You win."

"Nifty, you giant P-word." I look to the slack-mouthed guests. "That's a reference to female anatomy, but it's crass. Best to abbreviate," I inform with a polite tone, earning chuckles from the Hellhounds.

Warlock compassionately stares at my swollen gut. My white satin dress shines in the moonlight.

"Are you sure you're not still pregnant?" Warlock asks.

My expression slides childlike, lost and scared. "I'm definitely not. Because of what the Reapers did, I can never have children again," I reveal. "I'm swollen from surgery."

Warlock looks to Gut Buster. "I'm *not* doing this," he insists.

"You will, or we'll kill you," Gut Buster threatens.

"I'll just let them kill me," Warlock says to me. "I'm not going to hurt you."

"Sorry, Warlock," I reply, "but you came here and threatened me by Retribution Clause. We're doing this." My chin wobbles.

"I have to do this. I owe it to the baby. Trey and I have seen our children." I gesture at Trey. "We just lost a beautiful brunette. She's really sweet and has an old soul."

Warlock's expression slides slack, along with several of the Reapers. "How old are you?" Warlock asks.

"Sixteen."

"I have a daughter your age," Warlock informs. "I'd kill anyone who did this to her. The surgeon said you can't have kids now?" I nod, and Warlock gestures to Big Joe. "I want you to stand guard. If at any point you think I'm going to harm her, you can kill me. I won't hurt her though."

Big Joe steps to my side.

"What the fuck are you doing?" Fat Fuck demands.

Warlock ignores him. "May I please come to you and touch your stomach?" Warlock asks me.

"Why?" I whimper.

"Can you help her?" Trey asks, radiating unchecked desperation suddenly as the fight seems forgotten.

Warlock nods. "I'm a healer," he reveals. "I should have never agreed to this attack. I didn't realize what I was getting into. I don't think I'm here to battle with you. I think I'm here to help you."

Demitri rushes forward. "I've been healing her," he blurts.

My mouth plunges open. Demitri keeps his abilities a secret.

Demitri and Mr. Cantrell both shrug out of their suit jackets, laying them on the pavement. Trey scoops me up before laying me down on them. Arch balls up his coat under my head.

I'm emotionally overwhelmed as Warlock kneels by my side. I ugly cry, unable to stop it. "Is this going to hurt?"

Demitri instantly doubles over, hysterical. "What I've had to do to her to try to fix this. . .," he gasps through traumatized tears.

Trey tips his head back while silent tears pour down his cheeks. "Please fix her," he begs.

"I'm not doing this, Gut Buster," one of the Reapers claims. "I can't attack a parking lot full of teenagers that are hysterical because they lost a baby."

Several others agree.

The one who proclaimed that heads our way and kneels. "I'm an ER doctor," he informs me. "I need to know exactly what you were told, and how the issue was described." He sits crisscross opposite Warlock.

"If I give you the memory of the surgery, and what I was told, does that help?" I whimper.

"You can do that?" the ER-doctor Reaper asks.

"Yes." My expression crumples. "I took the memory from the surgeon without permission, but I needed Demitri to see it in case he could fix me."

"Hey, hey," Warlock compassionately says. "You did the right thing. It's okay."

I put a hand on the ER doctor's arm, sending him both memories.

Warlock touches my wrist. "Send it to me," he requests.

I do, and they both close their eyes, watching.

Warlock's eyes snap open. "I see what the problem is. If I scan you, can you give the memory of your current condition to Scalpel?"

"I'm done with all this biker shit," Scalpel, the ER doctor says. "My name is Dr. Anton."

"Thank you for helping me," I whimper.

"I'm Jerry Smith," Warlock confides. "I'm a freelance healer, but my business is shrouded in religious healing miracles. It's shady, and I'm embarrassed to admit that to you."

"Do you actually help people?" I ask. "If you help people, then it's okay. I'm pretty shady too."

"Yes, I help people," Warlock replies, "but I charge an ungodly amount of money."

We're interrupted by Cindy, frantically panting into her cell phone, "Zane, listen," she fills him in quickly before putting the call she apparently made on speaker.

"Jerry Smith, can you fix her?" Zane blisters through the phone.

"Between me and Scalpel, I think we can," Warlock replies.

"I'll pay your fee."

"Sir, I doubt you can afford my fee," Warlock chuckles. "I charge a million a miracle."

"Done," Zane barks. "Get me the wire information!"

"Who are you?" Warlock asks.

"Zane Drell."

Warlock's eyes widen. "The *actor*?"

"Yes," Zane says. "Melanie is my partner at the Alice Agency. She's also my best friend. Please help her."

"Full disclosure," Warlock says. "I was hired to kill her. I can't do it. I'm saving her instead. I'm not charging for my services. I'm hoping me helping evens the karmic scales."

"Mom, does Melanie have people there to protect her?" Zane bellows.

"Yes," Cindy replies. "She's got an unreal number of people here, and the Fat Fuck Brigade suddenly seem interested in helping her instead of killing her."

"The WHAT?" Zane baffles.

"Hell," Cindy says, "I don't even know at this point. We got through the worst wedding I've ever experienced. Then, Melanie collapsed from some psychic whoopie. Next thing I know, we're in the parking lot while she and this Warlock guy shoot fireworks out their asses. Melanie's apparently still got a fistfight against twenty men coming, because she's decided she wants to be the tiny leader of the Fat Fucks."

"You need to drive faster, Pepe," Zane orders. "I've apparently got a fistfight with twenty guys looming."

"What?" we hear Pepe say faintly.

"The Fat Fuck Brigade showed up at the wedding to kill Melanie. Now, she's supposed to fistfight them. I'm going to do it for her."

"Where are you, Zane?" Rich asks.

"We were sobering up in a room at the Hotel Marmont," Zane replies. "I'm five minutes away."

"Get here," Rich orders.

Cindy hangs up as Warlock puts his hands delicately on my swollen midsection. He closes his eyes, and I feel a scan. It's worlds different from the scan Demitri generally does.

Warlock takes his time and finally opens his eyes. "Take the memory, Melanie," he advises.

I do, and pass it to the ER doctor.

"Fascinating," Dr. Anton murmurs as he reviews it. His eyes snap open. He looks to Warlock. "I need to get her to an operating room."

"I have a full battery of medical supplies," Mabel says.

"Do you have morphine and scalpels?" Dr. Anton asks.

"Yes."

"All right," Dr. Anton says, "I need all the Reapers to cease their nonsense. We're done with this."

Several argue, and I swallow hard, gutting up. I stand. "Line the fuck up," I snap.

"I'm not fistfighting you," snarks one of the Reapers who pushed back.

"We'll start with you," I snarl before rushing his way, as a car screeches into the parking lot. I hit him with a dark-water, rage-fueled uppercut that launches the mammoth guy six feet through the air.

He thuds to the pavement, out cold.

"Who's next?" I ask, as Zane gets out from the passenger side and struts into the middle of the crowd.

"Hoooly crap," a Reaper breathes. "It *is* him."

"Who's next?" I demand again.

"Enough," Gut Buster bellows. "The Reapers rescind our Retribution Declaration. I ask that you do the same, Melanie. We need to work together to fix you."

"I'm not fistfighting her, or *him*," a Reaper claims and points to Zane. "I want to keep all my teeth. They can have the Reapers for all I care." The man crosses to me. "I'm Olaf Herrera. I'm an anesthesiologist. I'll help you."

Zane surveys me with mortification. "Please tell me you didn't get married in that," he spurts out.

"No," I bashfully say. "This is what Trey had designed for me for the wedding. I refused but put it back on for the reception."

"No, no, no, no," Zane breathes while he looks at Trey like his heart is breaking. "Melanie doesn't wear that."

"This is a wedding?" Gut Buster asks, dismayed.

"Not really," I huff dejectedly. "There isn't even cake. Trey's ex-hussy screwed this whole surprise nightmare up four ways from Sunday."

"No cake?" Gut Buster asks, astonished.

"No," I whimper.

"What kind of wedding has no CAKE?" another Reaper boils out.

"The kind that sucks," I snark.

"Screw this," one of the Reapers says as he heads to his motorcycle.

"Where are you going, Rimshot?" Gut Buster asks.

"To the grocery store around the corner," the man who apparently goes by Rimshot says. "I'm getting her a cake. This is ridiculous."

Everyone chuckles.

"No chocolate," Trey yells. "She wanted red-icing roses."

"On it," Rimshot yells back over his rumbling Harley, before pulling out of the parking lot.

"I get cake," I chirp with a delight clap.

Adam, my mom, and the few who locked down in the security office, emerge. They've likely been watching on the monitors, and I'm guessing Adam deemed this not worth hiding from.

"So, this Rimshot guy," Adam inquires. "Did he earn that nickname from porn or is he a drummer?"

Everyone laughs.

"He teaches the drum line at State," Gut Buster tells us with a grin.

Adam's expression scrunches. "No offense, but you guys seem professionally on the up and up. You came HERE? Against us? Against HER?" Adam asks as he points my way.

"We're clearly idiots," Gut Buster snorts.

"I can't take it," Zane mutters and whips off his shirt. He pulls it over my head.

I put my arms through, and it covers me to my knees. "Thank you!" I exhale.

"In light of the fact that everyone seems to be getting along," Zane says, "can we go inside and get Melanie fixed?"

All agree.

I look to Trey.

"If any of you attack us in our home, you *will* die," he warns.

"Not an issue," Gut Buster proclaims, to the agreement of the Reapers.

CHAPTER 46

"You can have cake as soon as the morphine wears off, okay?" Dr. Anton says.

Rimshot returned with cake just as a makeshift medical triage was set up. None of the Reapers and wedding guests have left, and we now sit at 250 spectators. I roll my eyes at the intrusion.

"All of you who aren't part of the main medical catastrophe crew, take a load off across the room," I request.

No one moves.

"We're all in this now," Stubbs's fiancée announces.

"Go," Zane orders. "Hospitals are my turf." He gestures about the banquet hall. "This counts." Zane scrunches his face while he looks around. "GoodNIGHT, this is an abomination."

Most of the spectators head across the room, dragging chairs from the wedding with them.

I'm laid down on a hospital bed that Mabel pulled from storage. Unfortunately, because the deadliest people in the room are the ones who need to be involved in this surgery, the Hellhounds decided to stay to bodyguard. I'm less than pleased, but having no privacy isn't exactly new to me.

Zane grabs my hand on my right side, and Adam takes my left hand. Trey wraps his hands around my shoulders.

The anesthesiologist from the Reapers starts an IV drip. "I'm going to morphine you, Melanie. I've got the right dose."

Demitri reaches across the bed and wraps his hand around the capped syringe. He focuses hard before announcing, "There's no poison in it that I can surmise."

"We're not going to hurt her," Warlock assures.

"I watched him pull the dose from my stash," Mabel informs.

"We're going to try the metaphysical route first," Scalpel says. "If that doesn't work, then I'm going in." He's in a blue medical gown with gloved hands that he's holding up. Everyone scrubbed up, per his supervision.

The morphine is plunged into the IV port, and my eyes flutter.

"I'm right here," Zane quietly says in my ear, as my stomach is coated in something wet.

"She's disinfected. All right, Demitri," Warlock says. "Put your hands over mine and scan what I do."

They chatter as the morphine draws me deeper into a state of confusion.

"Don't leave, Zane," I whisper.

"I'm not." Zane puts his thumb on my forehead and makes the sound that always signals my head to loll.

It does, and I exhale.

"Good girl," drifts in.

After an indecipherable amount of time, I hear, "We can't get this done. We're going to tear her apart. We can heal her after though."

"We don't have the stuff to put her under," is said next.

"Can you dose her again?"

"No. She's the size of a ten-year-old."

"Twelve," I whisper. "Twelve-year-old."

Light chuckling drifts by.

"All right, Melanie, look at me."

I try to focus my warbling eyesight on the doctor.

"I'm the head of the ER department, but my initial career was in surgery. I've cut more babies out of women than you'd believe. I'm taking over."

Trey's panic whooms in, but it's confusing.

"I can't do this again," Trey cries out through what sounds like desperate tears.

"Someone, take him," I hear Adam say. "I'm going to pull pain by myself. Morphine is my wingman this time."

"Come on sweetheart," I hear Cindy say. "Let's let the others take one for the team this time."

Mabel's hands land on my shoulders. "Melanie, you have me, Demitri, Adam, and Zane, here," she reassures me. "Your mom and Rich are across the room with Mr. Cantrell. You're okay."

I faintly nod.

"Here we go," the ER doctor says.

Adam grips my right hand, ready. Zane leans over me, gripping my other hand while he blocks the view with his body.

"Move in," I hear Adam say, and a bunch of hands land on my legs. "Arch, Rocco, Pepe, and Tanner are the ones touching you, Melanie."

I feel sharp pain and start to tense.

"Relax," Zane says. "Let your muscles go."

I try but can't.

Zane kisses my forehead hard before staring in my eyes. "Walk in the park." He looks over his shoulder and blanches pale, but says calmly, "Hold." Everything stops, and he stares in my eyes. "Deep breath in." I take the requested breath and Zane nods. "Good. On the exhale, you need to let all your muscles go."

I exhale and slump.

"Good girl. You've got morphine in you, so you're not feeling most of it. Now we take away the rest. Ready?"

I nod lethargically.

"Okay, Melanie." Zane puts his fingers on my temples. "Focus on my fingers." I do, and he rotates them in a little circle. He looks to Adam. "Switch your hand to holding somewhere else." Adam's hand plops on my T-shirt-clad boob, and Zane rolls his eyes. "That'll work, I guess." He turns his attention back to me. "Squeeze my triceps. Your arms are the only part that you can tense."

I exhale, relieved to be able to tense something. I grip his arms the best that I can in my drugged state.

"All right," Zane coaches. "Here we go."

The doctor takes that as his cue, and I feel the sharp, fiery pain again. I grip Zane's arms hard. Adam pulls pain harder. I start to make a keening sound.

"Nope. We're not doing that," Zane says. "Open your eyes, Melanie." I do and he's directly in front of me. "You and me."

I match my breathing to his and feel the hands on my legs relax as I relax.

"Good, Melanie," the doctor says.

"Rocco, I need you over here," Zane calmly requests without taking his eyes off me.

Mabel moves from my shoulders, and Rocco takes her place.

"Put your thumb lightly on her forehead," Zane requests, unable to do it himself because of the death grip I have on his triceps. His hands are on my arms, and he spreads his fingers to cover more real estate. "Focus on Rocco's thumb," Zane instructs.

"Your thumb," I mumble.

Zane chuckles. "Fine, focus on my thumb."

"*Your* thumb," I repeat for clarity. My thinking isn't at all clear.

"Right." Zane nods. I close my eyes, and after a moment, Zane makes the noise, and the thumb brushes up and away.

My head lolls, and my grip loosens on Zane's triceps.

"Good girl," Zane whispers.

I drift above the pain.

"Look in here," the doctor says.

I grip Zane harder.

"Ignore them," Zane advises. "The doctor is showing Demitri so that he understands. He heals and needs to know what he's energetically affecting. The physical reality helps."

Warlock's voice joins the mix as he crash courses for Demitri on metaphysical healing.

"Yo, asshats," Adam grits out. "I'm over here pulling pain while you enjoy a tour through uterus-ville."

"I can dose her again now," I hear someone say.

A moment later, I completely relax as all pain disappears.

Adam's shaking hand stills as he exhales hard. "She's not hurting now," he informs, sounding exhausted.

I feel a tug.

"This is where the problem is," I hear someone say.

"What are they doing?" I mumble.

Zane glances over his shoulder before snapping his gaze back to me. He blows out a sharp exhale and turns gray. "Oh no," he mumbles before his eyes roll.

"Whoa! Big guy," someone barks, and Zane disappears from my view.

I hear a grunt. "Holy crap," Arch exclaims. "What does this guy weigh?"

"Ease him down." Tanner strains into the vocal mix.

"Mabel, smelling-salt Zane," the doctor says calmly. "Almost there, Melanie. Okay, Warlock and Demitri, I need you to thicken the tissue here. This is where the problem is."

I feel a tug and whimper.

Tanner pops up in my line of sight and gives me a comical smolder. "Looks like Trey is hysterical, and Zane's a limp tool," he updates me. "Think we could get married in this sanctuary of love?" He flourishes a flamboyant hand over his head.

I giggle through my drug haze, while spectators laugh from across the room.

Rich's hands land on my shoulders. "You're doing good, Melon Seed." I watch as he looks at what's happening. "Is her uterus on her stomach?" he asks.

"Yup," the surgeon says.

"Oh boy," Rich warbles, before he disappears, and I hear a thud.

I huff and give Adam a drugged scowl. "It's your turn to pass out now."

"I'm an actual man, thank you very much," Adam snorts.

Jayla Bethel's hands land on my shoulders next. "I've got you, Meley Bean," she says.

"How gross is it?" I ask.

Jayla shrugs adorably. "Looks like an organ to me," she states. "I want to be a nurse. I'm good."

"Are you okay, Demitri?" I wobble out.

"Rock solid, Meley," Demitri replies through gritted teeth.

"You guys can't profusely sweat in an open cavity," the doctor insists.

"Comes with the territory," Warlock informs.

"They shifted back a little," Jayla narrates.

I hear a groan. "Is that Rich or Zane?" I mumble.

"Zane," Jayla sweetly says. She looks toward the floor. "Hello," she chirps.

"Sorry," Zane groans. "Apparently, I'm all good until there's weird red blobs."

"Melanie's uterus is on her stomach," Jayla informs. "That's the blob."

"Uggghhhhh," Zane groans.

There's a sharp exhale. "I'm burning out. Check it," Warlock says.

"Almost there, but not quite," the ER doctor guides.

"I've got this," Demitri confidently says, before I feel a burning sensation.

I scream, and Zane suddenly appears above me. Adam takes my hand and starts pulling pain, while Zane coaches me with his back to what's happening.

"Don't stop, Demitri," the surgeon excitedly encourages. "You've almost got it. We'd refer to this as skin grafting, but it's impossible in the place she needs it." His tone shifts amazed. "Unreal. It's literally like watching three months' worth of healing in one shot."

Something new happens, and I scream while the ground quakes as I lose control over my metaphysical center.

"Roll her, Dad," comes Demitri's strained demand.

Fingertips land on my forehead, and my eyes roll into the back of my head. The ground stops shaking, and I hear a deep guttural moan.

"Tranced," comes through, but sounds like it's worlds away.

CHAPTER 47

I come to as hands tremble on my stomach.

"Almost there," someone says, sounding exhausted.

"I can't believe what I'm seeing," another claims.

"Metaphysical healing is a wild ride," Mr. Cantrell says.

Zane's watching what's happening, so I'm guessing my innards are no longer on the outside. He looks to me. "Welcome back, Mighty Mouse. Warlock's out cold, but Demitri's pushing through. He's drained Mabel, Rocco, Mr. Isley, Bear and Darren."

"That leaves Trey and Adam," I whisper back.

"Nope," Zane says. "Adam pulled pain until he keeled over. Trey passed out cold from shock when you screamed. We're on our own."

Demitri exhales hard, and I crane my neck, watching as his knees give out. Tanner catches him before he face-plants, easing him to lie flat.

"You," the doctor says as he comes into view, "are healed."

"Can she have kids?" Zane asks.

The doctor nods with a huge smile. "Collective efforts did the job," he remarks.

A cheer rings out from the spectators.

I tear up and gaze at Zane. His eyes get misty to match. He leans down. "I planned to pay anything and fly you anywhere to fix this," he whispers.

Zane's mom rushes up and hugs him hard with a smile that I swear lights her soul. Zane pours relieved tears, and she takes her son out of my view.

My mom and Rich join me. Rich helps me sit up after it's okayed by the doctor.

"No pain." I exhale hard.

"I'll drink to that!" Big Joe chortles, and everyone boisterously agrees.

Mom and Rich hug me. Both look absolutely exhausted.

"Now to handle the next step," I murmur. I scoot off the bed and make my way to Trey. I put a hand on his chest and give him a little energy zing. He inhales sharply, waking up. He's the easy one out of all the prone cases. He's just got a case of standard shock.

"Hey," I say.

"Hi," Trey replies.

"I'm healed," I inform.

Trey sits up and grabs my cheeks. "Really?"

I nod and smile, elated.

Trey kisses me hard. I help him up, and he rushes to the doctor to thank him. He hugs him, his hands shaking on the man's back.

"You're welcome," Scalpel says with a smile. "On behalf of the Reapers, we're so sorry. We hope this helps."

They chat while I make my way from one passed-out person to another. I refill their energy reserves enough that they revive. As I revive Demitri, he blinks up at me.

"Did it work?" he asks.

I nod. "Thank you," I whisper.

Demitri sits up, and I leave him with Arch after kissing him on the cheek.

"Holy fuck!" Adam gasps sharply when I revive him.

"I'm fixed," I say and smile.

Adam grips my cheeks before looking to Trey with a mischievous glance. "I'm gonna do it," he warns.

Trey rolls his eyes. "Go for it."

Adam leans in and kisses me on the cheek. He grins at Trey. "I'll remember that you gave me permission to kiss her for real. I'm going to save it for another time though."

"Asshole," Trey says, but it's lighthearted. "Thank you for pulling pain on my behalf."

"You're welcome," Adam replies. It's one of those weird moments between them. As much as Trey and Adam hate each other, they share a deep respect.

Adam gives Trey a pointed look. "Don't forget what I said earlier. Treat Melanie right."

Trey nods, sliding a bit downtrodden.

I stand and find Gut Buster with a scan of the crowd. "How do you want to play this?" I ask.

"Allies," he offers.

Big Joe steps to the center of the room and motions me to him.

"I lead the Hellhounds," Big Joe announces. "Melanie Slate-Valdez leads the Hellcats. We formally invite the Reapers into an alliance."

Gut Buster strides to Big Joe and puts out a hand. "The Reapers formally accept." They shake hands. An exchange of howls and Viking roars emit from the crowd.

Gut Buster pulls me into a gentle hug.

I smile up at him. "The Hellcats accep—," I start to say.

Gut Buster's energy flashes maniacal, and his hands snap around my head. All hell breaks loose as the Hellhounds, Adam, Trey, Rich, Arch, and Darren, immediately attack the Reapers. People scream and chaos abounds.

Big Joe suddenly has a .357 at Gut Buster's temple. He bellows, "Stop!"

"Who do you think you arrre," breathes from me on an audible mental wave. I snap an invisible shield around Gut Buster and lift him to float off the ground. Mouths drop open from most of the spectators who are new to my abilities. I survey the stunned room before my eyes light on Gut Buster. "You rescinded retribution. Explain yourself!" Gut Buster having gone back on his word so flagrantly is stunning in our underground biker world.

"I lied," Gut Buster snarls. "You'll never be in charge of the Reapers."

"Have you no honor?" I blister.

Gut Buster glares at me, still trapped and elevated in the bubble. It's ballsy of him. It's also incredibly stupid.

"The Reapers have proven not to respect our code," I announce when he says nothing.

I survey all the Reapers. "Now we do this my way. I invoke Retribution Clause on the Reapers. The difference, gentleman, is that I won't rescind, and I won't stop until every member of the Reapers is dealt with."

Fear quakes from the Reapers, but this is what it is. They chose this through the actions of their leader.

"Number ten, front and center," I bellow.

A man hesitantly crosses to me. He side-eyes the floating Fat Fuck before saying, "My handle is Coke Bottle because of my glasses." We all survey the man's thick glasses as he implores, "I don't want to fight with you."

"Too bad," I snarl. As Coke Bottle argues futilely, I send,

"Adam, go get my katana." I see from my peripheral vision that Adam saunters away.

I snap my hand out and send an energy wave that drags Coke Bottle, pleading and screaming, against his will to me.

"You all seem confused," I gravel, so full of my dark-water side that I'm shaking. "I look cute and innocent." My eyes widen maniacally. "I'm not. We were prepared to align. Now, I'm about to own your asses."

"Please!" Coke Bottle begs. "You win!"

"Indeed, I do," I agree, before sending out an energy flick that snaps his neck. He falls, and everyone gapes at his dead body.

I tip my head, surveying Gut Buster. "One down, quite a few to go. Number nine, you're up." No one moves, and I huff. "Number nine, Hugo Cervantes. You're up."

Eyes widen.

"How do you know his name?" a Reaper asks.

I survey the inquisitive man. "Well, Jacob Garr, I know all your names. I did recon on you. You, for instance, have a mother who's a Sunday school teacher. Rita, right?"

Jacob's eyes widen. He pleads, "I don't want to fight you."

"Then why did Gut Buster attempt to kill me after feigning niceties?"

"That's him! Not us! We thought we were aligning." Jacob is beside himself terrified.

"Is that correct?" I ask the Reapers. Heads frantically nod, and I look Big Joe's way. "You ready?"

"Ready and willing," Big Joe says, his tone rock solid with no doubt. He still has the .357 expertly aimed at Gut Buster.

I vibrate with the effort to heft the bubble that's trapping Gut Buster higher. I mutter through gritted teeth, "Damn snacks! You're chonky." I situate the bubble over the heads of the stunned

Reapers who are staring up at their leader. "Let me be clear," I gravel. "No one deceives the Hounds and Cats. Prove a point, Big Joe."

Big Joe squeezes the trigger without hesitation. I release the invisible bubble of energy, perfectly timed to allow the kill shot. Gut Buster's head explodes. Blood rains down on the Reapers as Gut Buster's dead body splats.

My dark-water side rages, forcing my boiling panic to the back of my mind. "This isn't a game, ladies and gentlemen," I announce gravely. "While the Reapers clearly have no honor, as displayed by their leader rescinding his word," I gesture to Gut Buster's headless corpse, "I assure you that the Hellhounds and Cats respect the Code."

A promise of certain annihilation hangs heavily in the air. Our Reaper spectators' terror ricochets through the banquet hall as realization sets in. One of the tougher looking Reapers makes a high-pitched keening sound. It causes Big Joe to side-eye me warily. I meet his gaze and pick up on his energy shift. We've worked together so long now that wordless communication is seamless.

"No one move," I bellow. "Nice and orderly."

The Reapers watch me with horrified eyes as I bubble an invisible shield around them.

Shock is so thick in the air in the crowded room that it's hard to breathe. This moment is pivotal. My decisions, here and now, will solidify the Hellcats' reputation, and I have little time to consider my options. The biker code of honor has two factions: the weak and the strong. Strength is a complicated category that the Cats *must* dominate due to our youth and status as a new club. If I decimate all the Reapers, there are two repercussions that become insurmountable. One, there will be no one left to tell the tale, which runs contrary to the purpose of word spreading not to fuck with us. And two, we will be seen as a threat so unhinged that we must be eliminated, putting us on the kill list of every club. That puts my people at risk. Maniacal killing for sport is viewed as weak in the grand scheme. The Hellcats have yet to be defined by the Underground, and being categorized as loose cannons will bring certain blowback we don't need.

I take a moment to survey the leaders of my Hellcats crew, knowing that my decision will affect them most severely. Adam returned at some point during this fiasco, and is lounging against the wall with the katana, unbothered by the happenings. A glance Trey's way reveals blank eyes. The man has hit his limit and truly can't take any more. If Trey is done, then we're deep into PTSD territory. Trey has the deadliest lack of compassion of all my guys, and I must take his energetic condition into account as I set the bar in this scenario. Demitri stands next to Trey, and he looks like death warmed over.

Shit. There's one more guy to consider, even though he doesn't really run with the Hellcats. His status as a public figure makes him a target though.

I snap my gaze to Zane, who looks like he's going to pass out. He's shaking while he stares at me in shock.

"I'm still me, but I must handle this," I calmly say to Zane. "I need you to take a deep breath." Zane does, and I nod. "Good. Arch, will you please stand with him?" Realizing that I dragged my Normal into this mess worries me, but that's a concern for later. I turn my attention back to the problem at hand and a direction solidifies in my mind. "We're going to try a new route. When I instruct, you come forward one at the time," I order. "Bear and Darren, step forward." They join me, and I request, "Check intent of each that I call forward."

I start pointing one at a time while Big Joe holds the .357 to the temple of each Reaper who steps up. I watch with steely eyes as Darren proves to be the voice of my two chosen proxies.

Darren deems the first three to be pure of intent regarding an alliance. They each step aside, and the Hellhounds keep them surrounded.

"I'm Sandman, and I'm with you," the fourth man to step forward says. Hands land on him. Darren looks my way and just shakes his head.

Adam starts to step forward to handle him, but I hold a hand up to stop him. Sandman looks down at me, and evil shines in his eyes, even as his expression remains friendly.

"Katana," I request.

The man and I never waiver eye contact. His nerves only show with one sweat droplet that slides down his temple.

Adam unsheathes the katana, handing it to me. Before Sandman knows what hits him, I whip the katana across his neck. His head lops off, and his body falls. I watch as his mouth opens and closes before his eyes slide dead.

"The brain," I announce with disconnection, "continues to function for a moment after being severed."

Everyone is staring at me with gape-mouthed shock.

I raise an eyebrow. "You're playing with death, gentleman."

Several frantically try to run, but crash into my invisible shield.

I point to them. "Gut up. Stand your ground and wait your turn. You brought this fight to us, along with the consequences of your actions."

"You just cut his HEAD off," Mr. Cantrell breathes.

I meet his judgmental gaze. "I lead my crew, and I *will* protect everyone that's mine, to the death, from these assholes. I gave up my daughter, and that's all they get."

"That price was too much," Trey says. "I vote we kill them all on principal alone."

Trey and I stare at each other wordlessly for a long stretch. We don't talk mind-to-mind because I refuse to hide anything in this process. I also refuse to take the opinion of my stunned cohort into account. Trey just revealed himself as the most maniacal of all of us, and I'm relieved. The Reapers will spread word that if I fail, Trey will decimate everyone in a blaze of revenge glory. I'm still in charge though. I've got a very clear head at this moment. I need to prove myself as the leader, to my followers and to the collective underground biker regime.

"I'm not ruthless," I finally say. "The Reapers deserve a chance to prove themselves." I look to the Reapers. "Anyone else want to battle me for top spot?" Heads shake frantically, and I smirk, realizing my plan is working. "Fuck the rules. I'm now your leader, simply because I declare it. If you're deemed worthy, you can refer to me as Reaper."

Respect shines in the eyes of several.

"May I go next? You're a leader I can follow," one man says as he raises his hand.

I motion him forward, releasing him from my shield bubble. Another man tries to escape.

I point, stoically ordering, "Shoot him."

Without hesitation, Big Joe takes a clean headshot, and the man drops, dead.

I survey the Reapers. "If you run, you die. Stand your ground," rumbles from me.

"He was with *you*," one of the Reapers gasps. "That's my brother, Walrus. He was just scared."

"If you RUN, YOU *DIE*!" I scan the Reapers. "That's the last reasonable warning you're going to get."

The Reapers all look like they're going to pass out.

"Oh my God," Zane gasps, slowly sinking to his knees.

I look his way. "Zane, I need you to gut up. My world is

different from yours," I remind him. I'm careful to use my most kind, calm tone. He looks my way, and I inform, "I'm the smallest in this underground biker world we live in. I lead a crew of the youngest. I have no choice but to prove myself." I raise my eyebrows. "We live by a very strict edict. The Reapers know the rules and ramifications. They brought this fight to us because they thought we were weak. They were wrong. Consequences exist, and they're facing those consequences."

"It's illegal to kill people," Zane whispers.

"We live by an old-world code of ethics, Zane," I guide. "My actions are on the side of morality and ethics, in this case. Would you rather I die waiting for the authorities who have failed to corral these assholes for many years?"

Zane's staring at me with huge eyes. I'm not getting through to him.

"I need you to look at Adam."

Zane snaps his gaze to Adam, who's casually leaning against the wall with his arms crossed over his chest.

I look to Adam. "Am I scaring you right now?" I ask him.

"No. I'm relieved to see you handle business because everyone underestimates you." Adam snorts. "I'd rather you kill all of them in a blaze of serial killer glory than watch you battle one at a time, regularly. The fuck-sticks that you let live will pass on the message to allllll the other fuck-sticks that you have no issue cutting off their heads, or shooting them at point-blank range, for breaking edict."

I'm relieved to have verbal confirmation of what I've been thinking.

Adam looks to Zane. "She's doing this right. I promise."

Zane's head falls, and Adam crosses to him. He sits next to him on the wood floor and puts his hand on Zane's back. "If I panic, you panic," Adam guides. "Deal?"

"Deal," Zane whispers back.

Adam's expression slides compassionately. "It's hard watching little Melanie do these things."

"So hard," Zane whispers back.

"It gets easier," Adam quietly says, calculatedly aware that there's a room full of people listening. Adam smiles compassionately. "After you see her kill often enough, you start to believe that she can handle it. You'll know she's going to win instead of being terrified. I've watched her do what you're witnessing for more lifetimes than I can count."

He slides hooded eyes to the Reapers, who internally cower as his warning sinks in that I'm not playing with a single lifetime deck of cards. I'm not new to this, like they ignorantly believed. My soul age gives me clout in the underground. Adam just offered a mysterious reputation boost that will further elevate me in the hierarchy.

"Is she going to win this time?" Zane asks with a shaking voice.

"Against THEM?" Adam asks, pointing to the Reapers. Zane nods, and Adam cracks up. "Oh please. Those morons have a better shot of farting to the moon."

"Gut Buster was huge compared to her," Zane reminds.

"She didn't just get lucky killing him, Zane," Adam assures. "These morons are flicking gumballs, and she showed up with a bazooka. The only thing you need to worry about is how many of these assholes have children who are going to grow up fatherless because they let Melanie's tiny exterior and body age fool them. They misunderstood her soul age." Adam offers the Reapers a knowing look.

Zane looks to the Reapers. "Please don't do anything else to challenge her," he begs.

Shit! "Let me be abundantly clear," I address the Reapers. "If any of you so much as speak Zane's name, I'll kill your children." Mouths drop open, and I nod. "Dead. In their sleep."

"Melanie," Zane whimpers, aghast.

I make eye contact with him. "Your compassion makes you a target. My enemies will use you to get to me. I know you want people to live, but not everyone can. For you, I will sacrifice their entire bloodlines."

"All this brutality must *stop*," Zane insists.

"It stops because I pull rank," I reply. "That's why I'm doing this. They now know that I'll do anything to keep my people alive. Their best bet is to stand down and steer clear. They'll learn, Zane." I turn a maniacal gaze to the Reapers, considering for a long moment, before looking back at Zane. I shake my head slowly, gazing into his eyes. "This is done," I gravel. "I can't chance it." I gather a massive energy wave, blacking out a mile radius.

Zane must see in my eyes what I'm doing because he barks, "No! Melanie, stop," as I sight on the Reapers, who all cower and crouch, covering their heads. Zane rushes to me. "Don't, please." He looks their way. "How many of you have children?"

Half their hands shakingly rise.

Zane asks, "How many have wives?"

Many more hands rise.

Zane grabs my cheeks. "We've been through torment getting you healed enough to have a family one day. Please don't repay them by destroying their families."

I ignore my internal panic that he revealed so much about how we secretly feel about each other while we're standing in my defunct wedding location with Trey watching. We have bigger problems because Zane won't let this go.

My gaze hardens. I send the memory through my hand on his arm of me thinking, '*I hear and respect you. I need you to stop, though.*

You're part of my soft side. They can't see that you love me. You'll die. You're forcing me to be more ruthless.'

Zane shakes his head. "I won't believe that. I can't because the world can't be this cruel." He surveys the Reapers. "If you're all deemed positive of intentions . . . when that happens, because I believe in all of you . . . *when* you're deemed positive, if I get Melanie to soften her stand, will you respect her perspective?"

"Absolutely," one of the men says. "I'm Dozer, and I'm glad you're okay, Melanie. Scalpel and Warlock did the right thing healing you. I wasn't there when you were attacked. I came here trying to stop Gut Buster. I'm fourth in command, and I planned to challenge him to protect you."

"Zane, most of us don't want to do this with Melanie," Rimshot assures. "Melanie has a reputation, but no one ever believes it because there's no way someone who looks like her could do what people say." Rimshot stares in my eyes from across the space. "You've thoroughly made your point. You have my word that I will personally spread that messing with you, or your people, is certain death."

"Gut Buster tried to kill her when I trusted him," Zane says, in disbelief.

"Zane, stop," I murmur.

Adam gets hold of Zane and pulls him back a few steps. He, Arch, Big Joe, Mr. Cantrell, Mr. Isley, and Mercury all step in front of Zane. The look they give the Reapers could melt steel.

I whip my gaze back to the Reapers. My tone hardens. "Back to business," I demand.

I motion again for the man who volunteered to go next to join us. He's scanned for intention and joins the other Reapers who get to live. One after the other, the Reapers are judged, and join the living. We make it through the rest with only one more death.

Finished, I flourish to the judged and saved Reapers. "Hooray for all of you," I say. "You get to live."

Collective exhales emit as the Reapers sag.

"Damn, was that one for the record books," Rimshot mutters with rapidly blinking eyes.

Another Reaper blows out a huge breath. "I thought a lie detector test with the FBI was scary," he says. "They ain't got shit on these people."

I feel my quirky side bubble up as the killer that lives in my psyche takes a blasé backseat. She did her job. Besides, the quirky side has a chance to further solidify that I have layers my enemies can't predict.

I quirk my head before wincing. I dig around in my ear, removing brain matter from one of the dead assholes. "Ick." I make a face, earning chuckles from Stealth and Big Joe. I focus again on the living Reapers. "We have an understanding, right?"

There are nods.

"Did I win?" I ask Big Joe quizzically.

Laughter spurts from the Hellhounds who are accustomed to my oddities. Big Joe nods. "They're all yours," he says.

I survey the Reapers, who appear just as confused. "I don't actually want them," I huff. "I just wanted to make a point." I give Big Joe a curious look.

He just shrugs.

I scrunch one eye closed. "Anyone else want them? I'll give them to you."

"Oh joy," Tanner snarks, earning snorts and chuckles.

I steer my confusion Adam's way. "You want them?"

Adam gets a scrunchy look that matches mine. "I guess they could clean my house." He tips his head. "Any of you good with newborns and a bitchy wife?"

The Reapers collectively grimace.

Adam shrugs. "Not my monkeys, definitely not my circus."

"I guess the Reapers are disbanded," I ponder. "None of us want you."

"What does that mean for us?" one of the Reapers asks. "I'm Twenty-Twenty, by the way."

I chuckle with raised eyebrows. "You can give up any future biker-club membership and exile yourself from our underground world?"

Worried looks are exchanged.

"I'm Sage, Ms. Diabla," an older man says, introducing himself. "Perhaps a little history will bring a solution. My father was the founder of the Reapers. We were a good organization for a long time. Mack and Gut Buster tainted us. It was originally just supposed to be a family organization. A majority of us never wanted to follow Mack and Gut in the first place."

"Who were the original members?" Ten hands go up, and I motion them forward. "Would you like the Reapers to still exist?"

Heads nod.

"Would you like Sage to lead you?" I ask.

Affirmative desperation emits.

"Sage seems chill," I tell Big Joe. "What do you suggest?"

"Sage was my father's friend," Big Joe says with a nostalgic smile. "He's a good man. We're safe leaving the Reapers to Sage."

I consider for a long moment. I finally say, "Sage, I'm leaving the Reapers to you. We've deemed all the living members to be free from deception. If you have further trouble, the Hellhounds and Hellcats *will* arrive to sort through the disaster our way."

"Understood and respected," Sage replies.

I scan the Reapers. "Let me be clear. You're all at the mercy of one. If one of you betrays this chance at life, you all die. Do *not* come for me, or my people. I'll kill all you for the infraction. Decide if you can trust each other now."

An intuition pulse nearly knocks me over. I fight through the pain in my chest, keeping my expression neutral. I spin the pulse, studying it at rapid-fire pace. It doesn't tell me why, but I'm certain that I need information immediately.

I put a friendly hand on Warlock's arm. "I appreciate you so much," I say.

He smiles at me, having no clue that I'm pilfering a lifetime's worth of healing memories from him in one pull.

The information overload nearly floors me. I hold a hand Demitri's way, and he crosses to me. I pass the memory to Demitri of me thinking, *'I'm sorry for this, but we need it for some reason. Brace yourself.'*

I send the cataclysmic volume of Warlock's healing memories to Demitri, who looks like he just got gut-punched. No one pays it any mind, likely assuming he's just overwhelmed with the trauma of the day.

"I want it clear that I will help you anytime you need me," Olaf the anesthesiologist assures. He looks Zane's direction. "I'll personally monitor the Reapers for any indication that someone has ill will toward Zane." He smiles at me. "It's true that he ousted far too much about how he loves you, but the Reapers really are a pack of softies. You've killed the most vicious members. The rest of us do things like play poker and work on cars together."

Rimshot waves Zane our way. Adam and Mercury bodyguard him while Rimshot puts a hand on Zane's shoulder. "Son, you're obviously well-off," Rimshot says. "We all heard you offer to pay a million to heal Melanie. You're tempting ransom material."

The other Reapers intently listen.

"I'm the equivalent of Mercury in the Reapers." Rimshot

smiles. "I don't want you to get hurt. You MUST either toughen up or lie low. Melanie was right. You were putting yourself in danger."

"I'm sorry," Zane says to me.

Rimshot pats Zane's shoulder. "What you watched her do was terrifying for hardened bikers," he says. "Melanie's vicious. Listen to her, stay behind the bodyguards, and follow her lead." Rimshot turns to the Reapers. "I want it clear that nothing happens to Zane Drell. I will help Melanie kill you and yours if you come for him. With that said, Zane isn't a good target because his famous ass will be missed."

"Understood," Sage says. He addresses the Reapers. "No one hurts Zane. Melanie needs someone who keeps her human."

"Ain't that the damn truth," a man says. He nods politely my way. "Guzzle. Nice to make your acquaintance."

"You as well," I reply, ignoring the oddity of this polite chat after the violence that just went on.

"Not to get all 'golly gee' on you, but you're my favorite actor of all time," Guzzle says and gives Zane a starstruck look.

"Thank you," Zane replies and looks my way adoringly. "You'll love *Glamour*. Melanie is my costar in it."

"I look forward to it," Guzzle says with adulation.

"Aw," a man says, "Guzzle is in love!"

"We all are, and you know it," Guzzle calls out to his crowd. "Zane's all teddy bear big and adorable!" Guzzle smiles at me. "He's so cute with his whole, 'No, really guys! Let's all just be nice!' nonsense after you took someone's head off."

"Thank you for understanding," I giggle.

"We can all get along, kiddo," Rimshot says with a grin.

I grin in return. "You're my very favorite of the Reapers because you got me cake. Please don't be a stranger. I could hang with you."

"Done," Rimshot says before carefully hugging me while saying to Adam, "Only a hug. No bad intentions."

"No offense, but you don't have what it takes to deal with an attack from me," Adam snorts.

"Truer words have never been spoken, I suspect," Rimshot concedes as he heads back to the Reapers.

I survey Sage. "What's the verdict?" I ask him.

"I trust everyone here. We're all willing to put our lives on the line to vouch for each other," Sage replies.

"Then, the Reapers are yours," I declare politely.

"The Reapers are here for you anytime you need us," Sage offers with a steady breath.

"Thank you," I reply.

"Back my van up to the door," Sage orders.

We silently watch as the Reapers get the van situated right up against the doors they open. The fact that they brought the van speaks to the level of violence they intended. Biker clubs cart off their dead.

While they get things situated, Sage gathers Zane and me up. "Why did you marry Shivers when you're clearly Zane's?" Sage whispers.

I look up at him with huge eyes. "To avenge the baby."

"You have no business being married to Shivers," Sage advises.

"I'm aware, but the Reapers completely altered every part of my life." I sigh. "To clarify, Shivers is my soulmate, but we're a mess. Zane is in my friend-zone because of age."

Sage looks me in the eyes. "Soulmates doesn't mean true love. Your daughter is avenged. I'm here if you need help untangling from this personal mess that the Reapers forced you into. I'm a lawyer."

"Thank you," I whisper back.

The Reapers with the toughest stomachs gather the bodies of the dead, loading them into the van. I side-eye Big Joe. He nods confirmation that this is going how it's supposed to go, and we continue to wait until the dead are no longer our problem.

Sage closes the van doors, and the Reapers leave.

Mercury and Stealth close the banquet hall doors and lock them.

Big Joe exhales hard. "Let me be clear," he says to our people. "We did everything we could. We tried to give them a chance and chose to take them at their word. Attempting to murder Melanie is a no-go." Big Joe scans the Hellhounds. "Melanie Slate-Valdez is the most ruthless of all of us. She's earned her La Diabla reputation, plus some. Melanie must be fiercely protected, but we all need to fear her. To anyone who ever considers turning on her, remember today." Big Joe clears his throat and continues his speech, "There are wives and girlfriends of my people here. I ask that you respect our code. There will be no discussion about this evening, post-wedding ceremony. It didn't happen. Are we understood?"

Nods punctuate the space silently.

"I've got your back, Melanie," Stubbs's fiancée shouts out. "I'm so glad you're okay."

"Thank you," I reply, exhausted. I slide tired eyes Adam's way. "Will you clean up the katana for me?"

"Of course."

Trey sags. I watch him, concerned.

"You've hit your max." Big Joe consoles Trey. "I'm going to handle the rest of our cleanup. We're all going to do your reception party justice while you guys decompress."

Adam puts an arm around Trey's shoulders.

"Thank you for attending our wedding. I know this was a lot," Trey says to the crowd. He looks to me. "Melanie, I need to lockdown."

"Demitri, Zane, and Adam, can you come with us?" I ask, receiving agreement.

"Are you okay?" Zane asks, hugging his mom.

"Hell yes, I'm okay." Cindy smiles. "My son will always be safe when Melanie is there." She gives me a smirky side-eye. "You cut that guy's head the fuck offffff."

"I did." My expression crumples as I survey the crowd. "I'm so sorry about this whole debacle. The wedding. The bizarre reception. The energy fight. Surgery." I whimper. "Murder." My gaze slides to Trey. "Really?"

Trey just shakes his head.

"We have you BACK," Rich says. "You're healed! You're alive! The Reapers are done hunting you!"

"That's true," I say and smile, even though I'm devastated.

Mom and Rich hug me.

"Demitri? Where are you going?" Victoria asks bashfully.

"Melanie needs to boost me," he replies with dark circles under his eyes. "You don't understand what healing her took."

"Okay." She quietly relents. It's out of character for her, but a smart choice. The way she so severely overstepped with this wedding planning will be dealt with later.

Adam guides Trey to the door as Zane puts an arm around me and his other arm around Demitri.

Mabel joins us. "I'm going to put you in the guest room that has two queen-size beds," she offers.

We follow her through the halls to the guest room. Tanner walks in after us and sets a box that has paper plates on top, on the dresser. He opens the box, revealing a sheet cake with white frosting and red roses.

"The whole cake issue is stupid," I scoff. "I don't know why I even cared."

"It wasn't stupid," Trey says, sliding exhausted eyes my way. "I should have had a cake."

Mabel leans on the dresser next to the cake box. "We got a lot of tonight wrong," she admits. "We never should have surprised you with this. I'm glad we did though, because word's about to spread through the underground that messing with you means certain death."

I shake my head. "I hope it's going to go down like that, but there will be a few speedbumps before things settle."

"Explain," Mabel requests.

"There's this thing about being the baddest mother in town." Everyone studies me with exhausted trepidation, and I nod to myself. "We just opened the challenge. Every ego-driven little rod with something to prove is going to come for me. I'll need to prove myself several more times before the onslaught simmers down."

"Then we take every single one of them out," Adam says.

Eyes snap his way that are full of fear.

Adam scans the inner circle. "They'll be doing us a favor. If they step forward, we don't have to ferret them out. Killing is the easy part."

"Maybe for you," Demitri says. "I don't want to kill assholes every weekend."

"Weekend?" Adam asks with a chuckle.

"People work during the week," Demitri explains. "They're tired, and their bitching-ass wives have dinner ready. They'll attack on the weekends."

Adam gives Demitri a doubtful look, and I get an irrational case of the post-battle giggles.

"I have school all week," I say. "Killing on the weekends works best for my schedule. I'll take it."

Laughter spurts from everyone but Demitri. Mabel takes her

leave. Tanner hugs me before heading out, and Adam engages the panic room locks.

The moment we hear the locks slide tight, Trey slumps to sit on the bed and rubs his face hard.

"What's your plan, boys?" I ask.

"Adam," Demitri says, "you need to get home to Val and the twins."

"They're at Val's mother's house," Adam says. "I told her I wouldn't be home. I planned to party, laugh at Trey, and sack out in a guest room." He looks to Trey. "I need to stay so that Trey can actually sleep. Someone bigger and badder needs to be between him and the door."

Eyebrows rise. None of us expected that.

"It's purely selfish," Adam informs. "Trey's a basket case when he gets worn down. I don't want to deal with his bitching and raging. I already have one of those at home."

"Thank you," Trey sincerely says to Adam, ignoring the jab.

"You're welcome." Adam grins mischievously. "Bet you didn't think you'd spend your wedding night snuggled up with me."

Trey's expression drops deadpan, and we all laugh.

"She has to refill Demitri tanks while she sleeps," Adam needles like a jackass. He points to Zane. "And he is going to curl up against her back so *she* can sleep. I tried to warn you in that kitchen, but does anyone listen to Adam? Noooooo." Adam nods matter-of-factly. "You got yourself hitched into quite the group-thing debacle, Trey." He gestures to himself, before flicking a wrist to Zane and Demitri. "We don't just go away because you got fake married."

"A handfasting is the deepest form of marriage, and you know it," Trey growls back. He's so worn out that it lacks the luster he intends.

"She didn't want to do it Trey," Adam reminds. He raises his eyebrows while he stares daggers into Trey. "I wonder why? Could it be that Melanie has poly needs this lifetime?" At Trey's stunned expression, Adam smiles, slow and maniacal. "Never occurred to you, huh?" Adam chuckles. "Your wifey could fuel Chicago with that libido of hers. And that temper? Woooooo, doggies! You think YOU can handle her alone? Shiiiiiit."

Trey slides stunned eyes my way, and realization seems to slowly dawn.

Adam claps him on the shoulder. "Just getting it, buckaroo? Let's make sure you thoroughly understand." Adam grins as Trey pans a shocked gaze his way again. "I," Adam says with amusement, "am her original soulmate. I screwed up, and yet sassy pants over there clings to me when I hug her. Demitri, though? Oh yes, he looks like a Greek god, AND he heals her. Your only saving grace with him is that he runs from her, and Melanie doesn't chase men. She's royalty now in our metaphysical world. He's the one she could give up if it were just about lust. She can't though because she ritually bleeeeeeeds everywhere regularly. Zane's the one you need to look out for. She doesn't give a damn about his money, or that he's a Normal." Adam nods with bright sarcasm. "The princess fell in love with a servant in our metaphysical kingdom. That sounds like a fairy tale to me. She actually loves him, soul deep. We're all fucked, because he's her guy."

"You're observant," I smirk.

Zane covertly rubs my lower back with his thumb.

Adam looks at me with amused eyes. "I pretend to be an idiot because it keeps people in the dark about me."

"You're an idiot, Adam," I snark back, "but you're right."

Trey glares ferociously at Zane, and I tip my head, radiating malice. "If you so much as yell at Zane tonight, I'll murder you in this bedroom, bury your body in the parking lot planter, and have that motherfucker repaved by morning." My eyebrows rise. "We need to expand the parking lot. Fancy event center, with a new coordinator who works like a demon."

Trey meets my gaze with wide eyes.

I smirk. "You wanted to marry me," I remind him, "but I don't think you understood who I am."

Trey's gaze shifts to the floor, submitting.

I roll my eyes. "This is gonna be greaaaaat," I sarcastically ooze.

"You ready to break off the handfasting yet?" Adam asks me.

"Nope," I reply.

Trey's gaze snaps up to me.

I raise an eyebrow his way. "You wanted to do this, and I'm going to try." I take a cleansing breath. "It's time for the last hurdle, and we can close this chapter."

"We need to sleep," Demitri insists.

"Pardon hell out of you, Sir Six-Pack," I bark at Demitri. "You don't get to dictate that. The most important part of this journey is finally here."

"What could POSSIBLY be left?" Demitri says, exasperated.

I scan my guys.

Trey and Adam appear equally confused.

I shake my head, disappointed.

"Come here, Melanie," Zane says as he sits on the floor, with his back against the dresser. "I'll hold you when your body goes limp."

"Limp from what?" Trey asks.

"The real reason she went through all of this," Zane says. He narrows his eyes Trey's way. "You, especially, should know."

Trey blinks dully in response.

I sit in Zane's lap, and he smiles softly at me.

"You really do know, don't you?" I whisper.

Zane nods. "She's trapped, and you need to go get her."

"Melanie," Trey breathes, horrified. "I'm sorry. I should have thought of that."

Demitri looks equally abashed. "I'm sorry. I didn't mean to suggest that your daughter doesn't matter."

"Her guy remembered," Adam snorts as he sits next to Zane. "She's good."

Trey rubs his face hard before sliding off the bed and joining us on the floor. Demitri joins us, completing the circle.

"I'd like to hold my fiancée while she does this," Trey says.

"She's your wife, Trey," Adam laughs. "She didn't get to be your fiancée."

"Wow, that was a hell of a slip," Zane baffles. He scrunchy glares at Trey. "You really aren't ready for this husband gig. I hope you understand that."

"I'm sorry, Melanie. I'm exhausted and really out of it," Trey quietly says.

"Whatever," I retort before curling up against Zane with my head on his chest. I close my eyes and meditate down and in. I get to the right mental state and launch myself through the spiritual ether. I pick up speed furiously. After a nondescript amount of time, I screech to a stop. Just as I anticipated, the five gray blobs are there in the grayer nothingness. They're rather predictable, after all.

"Melanie Slate, we asked you not to return," a gray blob monotonously greets.

"I agreed to that before I knew you planned to take my daughter in exchange for Zane's soul," I gravel back, full to bursting with my dark-water vibe.

"Interesting," a blob says. "She's mad."

I blink rapidly. "Are you shitting me? Of course, I'm mad," I screech. "MY DAUGHTER was not up for negotiation!"

"You agreed to the exchange."

I give the blob the look it deserves. "You weren't clear. Lucky for you, *I'm* about to be clear. Release my girl, or I'm going to destroy your sanctuary."

"The exchange is done," a blob says.

"Like hell it is," I snarl back and gather a blast.

"Stop," orders the center blob. "A new exchange interests me."

I narrow my eyes at the center blob who seems to be the leader. "Details please," I demand.

"Let's unpack the situation," the lead blob says.

Unexpectedly, there's a rush of wind, and Trey appears with a skidding stop. He gasps, bending at the waist before surveying the location.

"They aren't cooperating," I inform him. "I'm getting our daughter's soul back by destroying this void."

"Kick ass," Trey replies.

There are three more subsequent wind tunnel rushes, and Zane, Adam, and Demitri appear, and look around.

"The fuck?" asks Adam, the only one of the guys who hasn't seen the memory of this place.

"Welcome to Suicide Solitary, where Zane was held after he offed himself," I say. "These are the gatekeepers." I smirk. "They aren't cooperating. I want Abigail back, and they seem to think they're in charge."

"*Seriously*, just give her back," Adam advises the blobs. "You don't want to get into it with Melanie."

"Quiet!" a blob barks.

Adam gives it a comical face scrunch while I chuckle.

"Ocean Corpse has a collection," a blob says.

"Excuse me, Ocean what?" Adam asks me, earning spurting laughter from the other guys.

"They call me Ocean Corpse," I huff. "These *enlightened* beings don't understand symbolism. Pierre called me Seashell, they view seashells as ocean creature corpses, therefore," I flourish my hands, "Ocean Corpse."

Adam cracks up.

"Let's study the collection," the lead blob says.

"Yes, yes, yes," choruses from the other blobs in quick chattering succession.

"They seem to like you boys," I chortle.

"Lucky us," Trey pensively says.

"Him, him, him," choruses excitedly.

"Oh myyyyyy," one breathes.

"Lies, lies, lies," choruses.

Trey grimaces while I give him a deadpan look.

"Learning humility is one of his life goal hurdles, much like Ocean Corpse," the lead blob says. "He serves a purpose."

"Yes, yes, yes."

I roll my eyes.

"Now for that one," the leader says.

"Which one?" I ask.

"Funny man who likes girls."

I survey Adam, Demitri, and Zane. "Well, that narrows it right down."

"Funny man is useless," the lead blob says.

"Cheater, cheater, cheater," the rest of them chatter.

"That'd likely be Adam," Trey mutters.

"Wait, wait, wait," Adam chatters back, imitating the blobs, and I giggle. "Let me hang. I want to observe your process."

"Why?" a blob asks Adam.

"Because this is hilarious."

"Funny, funny, funny," Zane, Demitri, and Adam all chatter

in quick succession, earning a deadpan chuckle from the blobs.

"You can stay," the head blob informs Adam. "*But* you serve no purpose," the blob repeats with authority.

"Story of my life." Adam shrugs. "Judge the next two." He happily waggles a hand toward Demitri and Zane.

"Big one, big one, big one," they chatter.

"Zane's up," Adam caws.

"No spark?" one asks curiously.

"Empty, pretty, pointless," another observes.

"Wow," Zane breathes in disbelief. He's used to being fawned over.

"He's one of the Nothings, Ffffffff," another blob says.

"Ffffffff," Adam repeats. "What's that?"

"That's me," a blob replies.

"It fits," Adam rudely mutters. "You're all kind of ffffffff."

I roll my eyes. "Back to the empty, pointless one."

"Hey," Zane barks.

"They said it, not me." I give Zane a look. "Rachelle and Molly are empty, pretty, and pointless, though." I Fraggle my face. "Ffffffff here makes a point."

Zane gives me the saddest look. "I lost everything tonight, Melanie. Please be nice."

"Explain," the lead blob requests.

"Your name?" Zane politely asks.

"Tttttt."

"It's a pleasure to make your acquaintance, Tttttt," Zane says without blinking an eye at the oddity. "Melanie married Trey tonight. I spent the whole night crying. Hence, losing everything."

"Tears are everything?"

Zane's eyes widen, but he politely replies without condescension, "No, Melanie is everything."

"I see. That's what we're working on," the blob informs.

"No spark, no spark, no spark," chatter the blobs.

"He *is* rather unimpressive," the lead blob expresses disdainfully, to the hilarity of Adam, Trey, and Demitri.

"Are you shitting me?" Zane blathers loudly. "I'm a millionaire, famous actor, with an eleven inch—"

"No spark, no spark, no spark," the blobs interrupt, as the guys gape at Zane.

"God DAMN! He's got all of us beat, and that ain't easy to do," Trey remarks, and I howl with laughter.

"*You* have spark," the lead blob informs placatingly to Trey.

"I was referring to . . ." Trey waves his hand. "Never mind. Continue insulting Zane. No, wait a minute." He jambs his fists on his hips and glares at me. "You never told me Zane's that impressive."

I blink rapidly at Trey. "How should I have addressed that? Hi honey, what's for dinner? By the way, Zane's got an anaconda in his sweatpants?"

"You make a point," Trey grumbles. "Did you sleep with him?"

"No, Trey. I figured it out the old-fashioned way while I rode him in a questionable film!" I snap back. "It hasn't been a point of conversation." I look to the blobs. "My apologies. Carry on."

"There's potential," the lead blob breathes ominously about Zane.

"Where is the potential stored?" Fffffffff asks.

Adam doubles over, laughing. "He keeps it in his dick like a coin purse full of glitter."

The guys all spurt laughter.

"Behave," I mutter. "I want back my daughter's soul."

Everyone tries to pull it together, succeeding for the most part.

"Potential. Look closely. He's right on the cusp," the leader says.

"Choices, choices, choices," tinkles from the blobs.

"I like him," Ffffffff decides.

"Thank you," Zane politely replies.

"Potential Glitter in the Coin Purse," Ffffffff addresses Zane, and we all lose it, howling laughter.

"You're Helicopter Hottie, Crockpot Weiner, and Potential Glitter in the Coin Purse," Demitri barely gets out.

"I always thought I was plain old Zaney until I met Melanie." Zane chuckles.

"Potential Glitter in the Coin Purse stays," the lead blob announces. "Now, for the last one." There's lingering silence that stretches on long enough that I roll my eyes.

"He doesn't know," a blob announces, sounding fascinated.

"Know what?" Demitri asks.

"What you are," the blob says, before Ttttttt silences him.

"Leave it be," Ttttttt demands. "He isn't supposed to know. He might be the one."

"She has enough of them. He could be the one," another blob cryptically says.

"Ocean Corpse, if you deal with all that comes with them, we'll release your girl's soul," the leader informs.

"I already deal with all of them," I reply. "Done."

There's much excited chattering noise.

"Be prepared Melanie. They're a lot, and a little," the leader warns.

"Yeah, yeah, I'm aware. The rest are just friends. I'm married to Trey."

Laughter peels from the blobs. Adam joins in, and Zane quickly loses his polite battle. Finally, Demitri and I can't help but cackle.

"I'm not going to screw this up!" Trey defends passionately.

The blobs laugh so thoroughly that the cacophony is unreal.

"Ohhh, that one is a funny creature." The leader sighs happily once they calm.

There's the sound of a pop, and we watch an iridescent shimmering rainbow rise and disappear.

"There she went," I say in wonder. I look to the blobs. "Thank you. I promise not to return."

"And, so it is," the leader politely replies, before a rush of wind sends me careening through nothingness.

I blink confused eyes, laying on the floor surrounded by my guys' passed-out bodies. They come to a moment after I do.

"What a rush," Demitri says.

I smile softly. "She's released."

Trey grabs my wrist and pulls me to him. He slides his hands along my sides and puts them flat on my back. He kisses me hard as he refills my energy stores. The ice and earth that's purely Trey shoots up my back, and my head spins.

He ends the kiss and says, "Thank you for avenging our child. You're everything."

"What a massive coin purse full of glittery SUCK," I expound.

Chuckles emit as the guys stand.

"I tell you what," Adam says to Trey. "You know how to throw a wedding for the ages."

"Don't start," Trey says and glares at him. "It was supposed to be special."

"It was special, all right," Adam teases back.

"We're married?" Trey asks me.

I shrug. "You requested that I try. I'm trying." My fed-up exhaustion rings through. I don't bother caring that all the guys are there as I tug the awful wedding dress over my head. It's covered in blood, dirt and regret. I scowl at it as I float it with an energy bubble. I send a spark into the bubble, and the satin monstrosity incinerates. I pop the bubble when it's ash.

"A proper ending to a monumental day," Adam sarcastically spouts.

Trey sighs. "I'm sorry about the dress."

"You should be," Zane scolds while he helps me put his T-shirt back on that Tanner left on the dresser.

"Lie down, Demitri," Zane guides. Demitri gets settled, and Zane leads me to the bed. I lie down, snuggling against Demitri's back. He exhales hard. Zane scoots under the covers before drawing them up to our chins.

"I'd like to sleep with my wife," Trey pathetically kind of whimpers.

"Very good, jackass," Adam blathers. "You learned to call her your wife."

I blink innocent eyes at Adam.

He smiles softly. "Your wife is so happy right now," he coos at Trey.

I giggle. "Zane's happy too," I tease.

Zane howls laughter. "Hush, Mighty Mouse. We have our little secrets."

"There's nothing little about that secret."

Demitri chuckles. "I'm happy also, if it helps."

"I like marriage," I tell Trey, whose mouth falls open.

Adam puts his index finger under Trey's chin, snapping his mouth closed. "Shall we snuggle in the other bed?"

I wiggle happily, before the three of us comically exhale, just to irritate Trey.

"Is it necessary for you to grind on Zane?" Trey asks, clearly pissed.

Zane props up behind me. "We've never had sex," he clarifies. A devious smile peeks through.

Trey's eyes narrow. "Then what have you had?"

"Sleepy tights," Zane innocently says.

I giggle while Zane snuggles up again.

"We've had sleepy tights also," Demitri reveals. He snaps his head over his shoulder to look quizzically at Zane. "We call it 'survival mode.'"

"I'm there for survival mode," Trey snarls.

"You *have* been," Demitri says with a hinting lilt that there are secrets. "That's true."

"Shhhhh," I whisper, and Zane and Demitri both chuckle.

Zane tap-taps my hip, and I take the memory of him thinking, '*I can't believe you played that game with Demitri!*'

I send through my tush contact, the memory of me thinking, '*I didn't. We literally just slept.*'

Zane brushes my hip discreetly with his thumb. I take the memory of him thinking, '*I need to talk to you.*'

'*Backlash shock is an ugly thing, Zane. Hang tight,*' I think before sending it as a memory.

The exhausted energy workers quickly descend into backlash comas.

Zane silently gets up before helping me shift out of the bed, I cross the room and disengage the panic locks. We make our way into the empty parlor.

"I can't handle you being married," Zane confesses.

"Then why didn't you show up to stop it?" I ask. "I had zero clue it was happening!"

"I thought you hid it from me," Zane sighs.

"WHY would I do that?" I quietly insist. "You know me! I don't hide things from you! You think I'd hide MARRIAGE to

Trey?" I toss my hands, disgusted. "I can't trust him! You think I want a husband who regularly sneaks around?"

"*You* sneak around," Zane retorts.

"I do NOT!" I hiss back. "I've attempted to be on the up and up, but you can't hold me to traditional boundaries! You think I WANT to be the girl who clings, terrified, to a few days of sanity with Pierre when I'm being hunted by a serial killer? Do you really think I want to lie on Demitri, barfing and sobbing, because I just made a trade with the suicide blobs for your soul? Do you think I *want* to get married so I can murder the biker gang that caused my miscarriage? NO, ZANE! I don't." I jab a finger into his chest. "I can't be held to normal rules because my life is a Tilt-a-Whirl covered in daggers! The good news is, all my previous indiscretions were after Trey left me each time. Somehow, none of it was cheating because he bails very conveniently."

"What do you want?" Zane asks. "If there were no insanity. Perfect world."

"I want a relationship with one man, who I can trust," I respond. "I want a life where I have no need for bodyguards, or constant fear. I want to go to school, earn the grades I know I'm smart enough to get, if I could just focus. I want to cook dinner, watch a movie, and go on a stroll through a moonlit park with a man who just held my hand in the car."

Zane swallows hard. "You want very normal things."

"To me, those things are extraordinary." My expression falls. "I don't want to be the freak who's whispered about at school because I 'burned down the theater.' I don't want to be weird, noticed, or feared. I don't want to be cheated on, pregnant at sixteen, MARRIED at sixteen, or covered in blood because I cut a man's head off."

Zane rubs his face hard. "How do we get you to that normal place?"

"We don't." My expression slides with defeat. "All I can do is accept that this is my life, and hope people stick by me through it."

I have no idea when they arrived, but Jayla, Presley, Finley, and Mama Mabel are standing by the dining room door, listening.

Zane gathers me into a hug. I melt against him for a moment before he picks me up, holding me with my feet dangling, as he crushes me to his chest. I wrap my arms around his head, knowing he needs to hide. I can't breathe as he squeezes me tight, but I let it be. He's working through a lot.

After a long moment, Zane sets me down, and says, "I'll call Demitri for updates on you."

My mouth drops open. "What?"

"I can't handle this. You just murdered bikers."

I gasp. While I know what he witnessed was a lot, I didn't think he'd abandon me for what I had to do.

Zane just shakes his head, distraught. He sets a brisk clip, passing through the dining room door. Mabel tries to stop him, but he keeps going, disappearing out of sight.

I swallow hard as Presley, Finley, Jayla, and Mabel rush to me.

"What happened?" Mabel asks.

"I married Trey. That already threw Zane off before I took down the Reapers," I reply, while I stare at nothing, in a state of shock. "I don't know how to make it without Zane," rattles from me on a stunned exhale.

Mabel looks over her shoulder at the door Zane just exited. "I had no idea Zane was really your guy. I didn't understand when I set this wedding up."

"I had to get married to avenge Abigail," I reply, emotionless and devoid.

"It's not legally binding," Mabel reminds.

"There's a step beyond legality," I reply. "Trey asked me to take this seriously, and I gave him my word." I slide traumatized eyes up to meet Mabel's. Realization that the gravity of my word was just brutally displayed with the Reapers hangs heavily in the air. My word is the backbone of my La Diabla standing, and I must adhere to the parameters of what I promise. It's a double-edged sword because the boundaries of my word are finite.

I blink stunned eyes. "Trey finally trapped me."

— —

So . . . How did it go? Well . . .

We woke to horrible news. Warlock died of backlash trauma in his sleep. Healing me was too much, and he drained himself to a cataclysmic point. We didn't know, and we weren't thinking. Rocco or I should have refilled his tanks. His death weighs on my conscience. It explained why I needed to gather his healing memories. That was a hint I should have pondered, but selfishly, I gave in to my own need to shut down after the Reaper smackdown. I've learned from it, but the cost of Warlock's life is a heavy one to pay. Adam chalked it up to karma balancing the scales. I disagree. I think my karma was seriously harmed by not saving Warlock.

I started the events coordinator position with Mabel. I've loved everything about my new job, and my first paycheck was staggering. I told Mama that I was excited because I'll be able to save enough in two years to pay my own way through college, but she informed me that I'm getting the same full ride to CSUN that she's giving to Trey. Looks like our futures really are set.

I took a chance and hired Victoria as my assistant. She's actually good at the job. She turned her attitude problem around and has seamlessly fallen into step with Trey and me. We'll see how long this cooperation lasts.

I was able to pull off the show, and it was . . . well . . . it's a show about a bunch of people pretending to be singing and dancing cats while wearing unitards. We did our best. The Hellhounds, Reapers, and Mama Mabel's entire staff came to see the show. I made it through with no issues, despite Dr. Fontaine's concern that it was too early for that level of physical activity.

I still mourn the loss of my daughter and am haunted by what we went through. I wake in a cold sweat and have night terrors. Without Demitri to help me sleep, I've come to dread the sun going down. True to his word, Demitri has been distant. I only see him in dance class now that the show is over. It's horrific. He's polite but stays away from me. It truly forced me to focus on Trey.

Zane's completely ghosted me. I've heard nothing from him, or the Surfrider guys. I ran into Cindy at a grocery store in Tarzana, of all places. She hugged me tight but said little. I've held my desperate need to see Zane in check. I refuse to be the pathetic stalker of a famous actor. With distance, I feel like I don't even know him anymore. His public persona has taken precedence in my mind. He's him, and I'm me, you know? We're still listed at the Alice Agency as partners, but I've had zero auditions or calls. Who knows what's going to happen with that at this point.

After school, on the one-month anniversary of our handfasting, I walk into the room Trey and I share at Mama Mabel's. I rush to prep the room, getting the right CD in our player, curling my hair, and putting on a dangerously suggestive dress. A quick survey in the mirror, and I look exactly right. Trey loves daring women, and we need to reconnect.

One month in, and we're at the reconnecting point. Not good, Melanie.
A deep breath, and I light candles.

I check the clock, and furrow my brow. Trey's late, but maybe he just got held up. An hour into puttering, and I finally opt to call. His cell phone goes to voicemail, and my heart races. I glance at the wedding ring box, wrapped in red paper and sitting on my nightstand with a black bow.

I exit my room, traversing to the parlor. Tanner looks up from a magazine he's reading.

"Va-va-voom. Damn, Mel," he compliments. "You look smoking."

"Any clue where Trey is?" I bashfully ask.

Tanner's brow furrows. "Late again?"

I nod and Tanner calls Trey. Apparently, he picks up, because Tanner says, "Hey, you headed home?" He listens, and his face quickly scrunches. "Did you have plans with Melanie?" Tanner rubs his forehead with his thumb as he hangs up. He smiles softly at me, but it holds veiled tension. "He's on his way."

"He forgot, huh?"

Tanner nods. "I'm sorry, Melanie. I'll talk to him."

I swallow hard. "My life is imploding, Tanner. I can feel it."

Special thanks to the incredible team of models that keep pulling through for me over and over. Thank you to Deidre Michelle for her endless ability to find the right people to depict these characters. Thank you to Anna Hall, Kyle Fager, and Stephen Knezovich for making this series magic. Thank you to Bear and Carol for their endless conceptual support.

MELISSA VELASCO is a true explorer of the arts. With a well-rounded background as a choreographer, professor, dance teacher, stage manager, author, and Crystal Grid teacher, she thrives in creation. At her core, she believes that the arts save lives and provide a route for passion and connection. The artistic ride makes life a whole lot brighter.

With a quick wit, often edgy mouth, and loud laugh, Melissa exuberantly embraces life. To find balance from the mental cacophony in her head, she enjoys expansive views in her mountain home. Her ideal day involves a mug of hot tea, music playing, and a whole day to write. Her greatest loves are her three children and husband. The four pillars of her ultimate happiness include her family, friends, dance, and laughter.

This upheaval can't go on. With her home built on unstable ground, change for Melanie is inevitable. She knows her options, but are steel blue eyes, a sense of humor, and the body of a Greek statue enough?

Lifetimes in the making, Melanie has earned Demitri. But if there's one thing she's learned, it's that nothing is ever as easy as it seems. The Universe is in charge, after all, and she's a cruel mother.